LU[...]

A Spir[...]

At the top of the page was one word – 'Ludwig' –
composed in the same fine aristocratic writing. Underneath in the same hand but in smaller letters were the
translated words: 'a letter written from his childhood
friend to Andreas Wawruch, the physician who
attended L's last illness'. That was all. The German
script seemed to glimmer, to swell and shrink as I
stared at it, the way a dark secret pulls at you when
you come upon it – a secret you don't want to know
but from which you cannot turn away no matter how
you try. Mirabehn had asked me, 'Do you *know*
Beethoven?' I had not understood her question. But it
seemed I was about to know him – maybe far better
than anyone would ever want to.

As I began to read, I had the sense that I was
breaching the fine membrane I had been clinging to –
the film that had been separating the two worlds in
which I had been living. I knew I was about to leave
behind every certainty of day-to-day life. I seemed to
be stepping through a mirror into the strange reversed
universe that lies behind every silvery surface. I was
certain of only one thing: there could be no turning
back.

Leslie Kenton, the daughter of Stan Kenton the jazz
musician and Violet Peters, a painter, was born in
California. After leaving Stanford University she
travelled around Europe and settled in Britain, where
she has lived ever since. She is well-known as a television broadcaster, writer and teacher of health, and
for fourteen years was an editor at *Harper's & Queen*.
Her non-fiction books include *Raw Energy*, *Ultrahealth*
and *Ageless Ageing*.

Ludwig is her first novel.

Leslie Kenton

LUDWIG

A Spiritual Thriller

Mandarin

A Mandarin Paperback
LUDWIG

First published in Great Britain in 1993
by William Heinemann Ltd
This edition published 1994
by Mandarin Paperbacks
an imprint of Reed Consumer Books Ltd
Michelin House, 81 Fulham Road, London sw3 6rb
and Auckland, Melbourne, Singapore and Toronto

Reprinted 1994 (three times)

A CIP catalogue record for this title
is available from the British Library

ISBN 0 7493 1578 4

Typeset by Deltatype Ltd, Ellesmere Port, Cheshire
Printed and bound in Great Britain by
BPCC Paperbacks Ltd
Member of BPCC Ltd

for Andrew
who gave me back my life

and Anthony
who died protecting it

Contents

Prelude
adagio maestro

First Movement
INNOCENCE
vivace ma non troppo

Second Movement
BLOOD
largo – allegro – furioso – prestissimo

vii

CONTENTS

Third Movement
GRACE
arioso dolente

Coda
morendo

PRELUDE

adagio maestro

What follows is beyond reason – a true tale of time and death. The manuscript passed into my hands only eighteen months ago. It was given me as a gift – if gift it can be called – by Michael, a man whose courage dazzled me – a man I could not help but love.

When first I read these pages I had never heard of the Illuminati. I knew nothing of secret societies and secret agendas which bind ordinary men and women in economic strait-jackets, convince us of our impotence then feed off our energies and lay waste our planet. Now, say some, I know too much. For too often death awaits those like Michael who dare to live their truth. Yet what other life is worth the living?

For two hundred years the tale this manuscript tells has drawn the lives of six people into a dance of fire from which there was no escape. I am now the seventh . . . God willing, the last. As such I feel compelled to make public what little we know – or think we know – about Ludwig. My motive is simple: I hope, even for a brief space in time, to crystallise the dance's movement, and thus exorcise its power – lest I too become consumed. This is no mean task when you are caught in a saraband where death weaves her web around the thighs of time as time tortures her in the sweet rhythms of his lust.

Whether or not I shall succeed I do not know. What has begun to

3

frighten me is this: in recent weeks I have found myself beyond caring. There is one thing I wish to state clearly before I begin: I did not seek to dance this dance. I did not choose to pass on this tale. Who would? Yet, like Michael, Wawruch, and the rest, I became trapped in its music. So it would seem did Ludwig.

First Movement

INNOCENCE

vivace ma non troppo

BAGATELLE

> The divine is not human; it is something quite
> different. And it is not noble or sublime or
> spiritualized, as one likes to believe. It is alien and
> repellent and sometimes it is madness. It is
> malignant and dangerous and fatal.
>
> Pär Lagerkvist *The Sibyl*

I hate Vienna. It is bourgeois, materialistic and dirty.
Besides, the people are dull beyond belief, and gooey cakes
make me sick. But the year I met Mirabehn, the powers of
destiny – in which I had no belief at all – conspired to put me
there twice. I made the first trip in April. Easter was early
that year and I was sick to death of the grey of London and
with women; with one woman in particular – Fiona. She was
a thin strawberry blonde with a turned-up nose, a list of
rights and wrongs a mile long and a pathological hankering
to get married. She also had a lot of virtues – like loyalty,
common sense and kindness. Sometimes I remember them.
Then I feel sad. Fiona was smart, too, but she made one big
mistake: she picked the wrong man.

I'm not the marrying kind. Don't get me wrong; I tried it
once. I liked the comfort – the feel of a woman's rump
against my belly, the home-cooked meals, the fresh sheets
and all the rest, but like too many things in my life it didn't
work out. So I told myself I had a big thing about freedom.
Force me to choose between comfort and freedom, I used to
say, and I'm out the door – especially when you have to

listen to a lot of nonsense about 'how-to-do-it-better'. My self-congratulatory patter went something like that, but I had long before stopped believing it. I still believe that women fill their heads with too much garbage from magazine articles, though. I know. I write them. Well, not really. I am, or was, a reporter turned medical writer for a London paper. That was when I found I could no longer stomach the politics involved in telling a tale straight. Not a bad medical reporter either. That is what gave me the excuse, when Fiona turned the pressure on, to leave for Vienna.

I went there at the editor's request to cover a conference on stress. He called me into his office one morning and told me that since 'our readers are *high flyers* they need as much help as they can get to stay afloat on the rough seas of commerce'. An editor's love for mixing metaphors is surpassed only by his glee in telling you at length what *his* readers need. I knew the truth: his doctor had recently diagnosed a peptic ulcer. He hoped, by sending me on this junket, that I would return with some little titbit that would make his life easier. It had to be something like that or he would never have coughed up the money for the airfare. He was not the most generous of men.

I got involved in journalism after resigning from the Special Forces of US Army Intelligence. During my years in SF in Burma, Cambodia, Vietnam, and Central America, I played some pretty nasty war games and learned a lot more than anybody would ever want to know about how ends can be made to justify means. For twenty years I had been a fighter, a killer, a dreamer, a Green Beret officer working behind the veil of covert operations – a man who believed in what he did to defend America from enemies and who notched up sixty-two valour citations for himself before chronic nausea forced him out for ever. 'Hero' they called me. Some hero. Real heroes don't walk away when the house of cards they believe in collapses around their ears. I did.

My switch from political reporting to medicine had taken place five years before, because of an editorial challenging the legality of interest on the US debt which I had written for an American newspaper in Paris. It was called 'The Politics of Greed'. It was never printed. It turned out to be an important article, though – a real milestone in my career. It marked the end of my time as a serious journalist. After years slogging my guts out trying to get somebody to listen to the truth – how the US government was concealing the existence of POWs held in Cambodia ten years after Vietnam, or the fact that the biggest buyer of heroin from Burma's drug baron General Khun Sa was the head of a US Congressional committee – I had had a bellyful. I was sick of fighting the system – any system.

So I learned how to read long-winded reports on double-blind studies in the treatment of diabetes, vowed to keep my head down and my nose clean and started churning out 'specials' with exciting titles like 'Cancer – How Not To Become a Victim' complete with colour drawings that would do Walt Disney proud. I swallowed my anger. I told myself I was a tough guy. But the silent worm of dissolution had already begun munching at my entrails.

For a while things were easier, although even medical writing turned out to have its down side. Everybody you meet wants inside information about how to do this or that – get rid of dowager's hump, cure a tennis elbow, slow down ageing, lower cholesterol – you name it. My editor was no different. The conference was on stress, it was stress he suffered from, so stress was what the whole world needed to know about. I was the man lucky enough to tell them.

That April I had been feeling rough, what with the

worm's munching and Fiona's little hysterical outbursts, not to mention a recent bout of overwork and a little too much malt whisky – I loved malt whisky almost as much as I loved freedom. I stopped in to see an old friend – a Harley Street doctor – to pick up something I hoped would help me sleep better. This gentleman dressed in a morning suit, spoke so softly you had to strain to make out his words and hated prescription drugs as much as he hated London, in which, it must be said, he had lived quite happily for some twenty-two years. He also had more integrity than anybody I had ever met. On hearing that I was going to Vienna, he asked me if I would do him a favour, a 'service of kindness', I think he called it. He wanted me to carry two homeopathic remedies to a friend, a sick old woman who lived just outside the city. I could hardly refuse since for many years my doctor friend had looked after me – from patching up the works after a skiing accident to teaching me how to hold down my blood pressure – without ever letting me pay him a penny. I didn't just owe him *a* favour, I owed him a *hundred* favours. I was glad of the chance to repay even one.

Vienna was exactly as I remembered it. That spring a glitzy American ice-cream was being advertised everywhere and the inevitable Benettons had opened. Both blended perfectly into the homogenised body of the city – a town that offers nothing unique, nothing special, nothing to challenge the bland middle-class stamp of acceptability which has come to be the hallmark of the Western world. In Vienna you are all right so long as you are wearing your Gucci shoes. The conference turned out to be particularly dull – a lightly concealed attempt to sell a pricey new mind-altering psychiatric drug to doctors who had long since ceased questioning their morals. Most of the delegates seemed to be more worried about holding on to their dignity – as epitomised by the half-moon spectacles they wore – than they were about stress or anything else. But maybe that is, as the British say, 'unkind'. I knew that I was often unkind. In the next few days I was to find out just *how* unkind.

After three days of pretending to look intelligent while I slept through lectures in the day, sat in bed watching pornographic films on the hotel video system at night and gulped down masses of croquette potatoes with slabs of veal, I was feeling more and more like a bear with a sore head. Fiona didn't help. She rang three or four times. Only once did she find me. Once was enough. Did I still love her? Did I realise I had forgotten to cancel dinner with her parents before I left London? When was I coming back? Did I want her to water the plants in my flat? Her voice was gentle. It had a pleading quality that would have melted the heart of a snake. But every word she spoke seemed to make me even more irritable. No, more than irritable – it had me looking for any excuse I could find to keep her away from me. When I heard her voice my body would feel all wrong, like one of those composite mythical beasts with an elephant's trunk, a bird's wings and a lion's paws – as if none of my parts fitted together. The conversation did nothing to improve things. I answered each question as politely as I could – not an easy task for an American even if he has been brainwashed into the appearance of having good manners by having lived in Britain for five years. Then I hung up, promising I would ring her in a couple of days. I never kept my promise.

Instead I rang room service, ordered a bottle of their best Russian vodka with a bucket of ice – you have to demand a bucket or you get one measly cube floating around in a glass of warm water. I drank half of it. The animals' parts blurred into one another as my limbs and head and torso settled comfortably into the sea of alcohol. I took a shower, shaved for the second time that day and splashed heavy smelling stuff on smarting skin. I stared into the bathroom mirror but didn't like what I saw. I sucked in the gut and brushed away the fear that a double chin might be developing. Then I promised myself I would start pumping iron again when I got back to London. I put on a clean shirt and descended into the plastic bowels of a hotel dining room in which everything was beige – the fabric on the walls, the table-cloths, even the face of the *maître d'*, which looked as though it might crack every time a hint of a smile came over it. I tried to cultivate an appetite for beige croquettes and beige veal again and wondered if he could accommodate my beige mood by serving me some of the day-old beige beetroot that lay in military Germanic slices on the salad bar.

I was alone. So was the woman at the small table in the far corner. I had noticed her in the conference hall several times before. Once I had even overheard her talking enthusiastically to one of the delegates during a coffee break. She was short, dark-haired and German; she handled public relations for the drug company that had sponsored the conference. Her body was ripe – like the flesh of a peach that should have been eaten three days before. Beneath her tailored blue suit I could see that it had gone soft around the middle. She looked up as I entered the room and gave me a bland professional smile. The vodka, the worm which had grown ravenous after Fiona's phone call, and the boredom of spending yet another beige evening alone drew me like a magnet towards her table. The rest was easy.

I introduced myself, wondered if she was as bored with gooey Austrian food as I was, and asked if I could join her. She put away the paperback novel she had been reading, removed her handsome hornrimmed glasses, gave me a guarded smile and invited me to sit down. I ordered a bottle of Merlot '84; we downed it quickly and called for a second. She was just finishing off a thin beef soup swimming with miniature dumplings. With what I hoped was devastating wit I told her amusing stories about everything from George Bush to Kenyan crocodiles. She laughed too much and ate too much. I laughed too little and drank too much. Several hours and six brandies later, not much to my surprise, she ended up in my bed.

The darkened room was shot through with bands of red and blue light from the window. With her back to me she took off her jacket, her silk shirt and then her skirt. She folded them and stacked them on the chair the way a good secretary tidies her desk before leaving the office. The darkness combined with shafts of neon light from the window made her body shimmer. I noticed it resembled the belly of a wet fish then hated myself for the cruelty of the metaphor. She had the palest flesh I have ever seen, pale and sad like something hung in a cupboard too long – even paler than Fiona's. I remembered the telephone call, shuddered, then quickly shut down all memory, blanking out everything that had gone before – all promises, all loyalty, all hopes.

I sat in bed while the cool air from the open window played upon my naked chest and I watched her. I knew she wouldn't like that, but I didn't care. When she turned round, her arms were folded across her chest. She wore silk lace underwear – the absurdly expensive kind you see in fashion magazines on long sleek bodies. Her bra and panties were the stuff of which dreams are made. On her flesh they took on a black humour that turns dream into travesty. She doesn't like her body, I remarked. No wonder. It was as lumpy as a mass of unkneaded dough.

She came closer to me, lifted the sheet and slipped into bed. I reached out to touch her. Her back tightened like a trapped animal. By now the silent worm had eaten all the way through my stomach and gone to work on my bowels. I felt nothing but coldness as I watched myself watching myself watching her. Her body – soft on the outside, brittle as thin glass from within – pleaded for kindness. It seemed no longer the body of a woman but that of a creature at the mercy of something infinitely bigger and more powerful; like one of those trembling small dogs with big black eyes that cries out for you to kick it.

For a while the worm ceased to munch and the cold watcher of the watcher slipped beneath the waves of human kindness. With frightening sobriety I knew I had made a terrible mistake. I didn't want this. I didn't want to eavesdrop on this poor woman's silk dreams or her pale sadness. What the hell was I doing? I should never have brought her to my bed. I despised myself for having done it. Taking her small head in my hands, I kissed her forehead, ashamed that I had created a scenario in which I now not only wanted no part but had no idea how to get out of. I tried to atone for my sin with kindness. I put my arm beneath her head and was about to let her sleep off the heavy dinner in the crook of my arm when somehow every intention slipped away from me.

My fumbling attempt at gentleness had evidently washed away her sense of threat. Her body let go, went soft. She pushed her nose against my neck, opened her mouth and moaned. The smell of her breath took hold of me. Wine, wild weeds and unbaked bread flooded my senses, incinerating my brain. Her white flesh, so foul before, turned viscous, and became infinitely sweet. I could feel myself being drawn down into it, down, down until the shape of her body dissolved and lost all form. She, it, whatever had hold of me, was asking me, calling me, to dive deep into the waters of lust, inviting me to quench the cold fire that possessed me. I covered her mouth with mine, devouring it, pressing the full weight of my body against it. I wanted nothing – only to draw the smell of her breath deep into my flesh, to let her odours fill the empty spaces in my guts, all the while pleading that this dark fragrance would burn away the grime that lay inside me like rotting meat. I don't think I even knew it was a woman I held.

Of the rest I remember little. My hands grasped pale flesh as the paws of an animal tear away the warm viscera of its prey to fill its belly. A power lay in them which was not my own. The power of anger? Of desperation? The power of taking and holding, of having, of giving up, of giving over. I do not know. Images flickered across my mind one after another – a dark woman's face, the curve of a mouth, not *her* mouth but that of a young girl with contorted limbs; my fingers tightened their grip on breasts already swollen by too much touch.

She cried out. I could not bear the sound. I crushed my hand against her mouth, twisting her neck. My head pounded. Ignoring all that is human, I sought relief from some terrible rage that rose higher and higher within me. Towards whom? For what? I did not know. Neither do I know how long it lasted. A minute perhaps, or five or twenty. Then suddenly and without warning, the fury of movement and sound gave way to a void of silence. Not even her breath could be heard – only the passing of a lone taxi in the street, and the tinsel sounds of a brass band on a hotel radio in the next room.

A cold metallic nausea tightened in my throat. I could not swallow. I looked down at her body. It did not move. It was as frozen as anything I have ever seen – like a log washed up on the shore, immobile, heavy, cold. Her open eyes saw nothing. I spoke to her, she didn't answer. My God, had I killed her? Terrified, I put my ear as close as I could to her nostrils from which in quiet rhythm her breath came and went. I covered her body. Beneath the thick, feathery duvet it looked infinitely small now and more precious than anything I had ever seen. Tears welled up in my eyes. My throat grew thick, I found I could not swallow. Slowly, automatically, I made my way to the bathroom.

The face staring back at me from the mirror was as immobile as the body on the bed. I splashed it with cold water. It didn't change. I took a shower, put on an old pair of corduroy trousers, pulled a sweater over my head and went back into the room. She lay on her side now, her eyes closed, apparently asleep. I scribbled a note on the little pad beside the telephone. 'I'm so sorry,' it said. 'I'm sorry.' How absurd. Yet it was all I could think of to say.

I had to get out. Taking the key I left the room, ran down the hall and, ignoring the elevator, went down the stairs. I took them three at time, then went out into the street. I walked on and on, not knowing where I was or where I was going. Hours later, as the sky turned light and the first proper men in dark suits began to people the street, I hailed a taxi and went back to see if I could make amends. When I unlocked the door to the room she was gone. So was the note, and the bed had been smoothed over with perfect secretarial skill. I picked up the phone to dial and then I put it down again. What was I going to say? I sat staring out the window for what could have been half an hour. Then I rang room service, ordered strong coffee and drank the whole pot. I took another shower. Wide awake despite the booze and the sleepless night, I knew I had not a hope in hell of getting through another day in the conference hall. So I climbed into a small car – rented at the editor's expense – and headed for the country to make my delivery.

The peasant's cottage to which I drove that sunny spring day was about an hour outside Vienna. A small house set high in fields at the edge of the Vienna woods, it was in every way ordinary except that it had been immaculately kept. I arrived at half-past ten. A stack of logs stood against the side of a cottage so perfectly ordered it reminded me of a Disney cartoon. About the woman I had come to see, my friend the doctor had told me a little: her name was Madeleine Slade. She was over ninety and, he had said, the daughter of a British admiral. She had lived and worked in India as Gandhi's closest helper and disciple for almost twenty-five years. I knocked on the rough-sawn door. It was answered by an Indian servant with a name so long and improbable I could never remember it. He was a timid, slight man from northern India who, the lady later informed me, had been looking after her for more than thirty years. He opened the door and, putting his two hands together in the Indian fashion, bowed. Feeling like the oaf in a child's fairy tale, I mimicked his movement. He turned and ushered me into a room awash with sunlight and peppered in bright khadi prints – the cover on the sofa, the cushions on the floor beside it, a white red and sepia sari draped above the window as a pelmet. The back of my head felt as though it had been caught in a dragon's jaws.

The spring light pouring through the window gave the room a luminosity that was almost blinding. For several moments it prevented me from seeing the features of the figure who sat propped up on a day bed with her back to the window. As my eyes adjusted, I was able to make out an old woman. Tall and pale, with handsome features, she was obviously in a weakened state. Her movements were slow and restricted. I moved to her side, held out my hand, introduced myself and said, 'Miss Slade, I am a friend of Doctor G., who sends you greetings from London. He asked me to bring you two remedies which he hopes will make you more comfortable and help your breathing.'

I slipped the small brown package into her hands. They were long and slender with tapered fingers. She had the most perfectly oval nails I had ever seen. She gave me a gentle lopsided smile and in a husky voice said, 'Thank you, my dear. Do sit down. But I am not Miss Slade, at least not any more. My name is Mirabehn. It was Bapu who gave me that name when I arrived in India. He said, "You shall be my daughter." Then he renamed me *Mirabehn*. It means "Sister Mira" and it *is* my name. When you call me any other I don't know who you are talking to.'

I opened my mouth to apologise but she continued.

'What a pleasure it is to have a visitor all the way from home. It is kind of Philip to send me the homeopathics. He knows I won't take all these nasty drugs they keep offering me. The doctors in Vienna are awfully tedious. They don't seem to know a thing but they all use frightfully long words to cover up their foolishness. I am only sorry to have given you the trouble of coming all this way.'

Still dazed by the murky memories of my debauched night, and affected by the vibrant eyes of this old woman, who spoke and moved with stunning grace despite her weakness, I was beginning to feel like an overstuffed dodo in the middle of an elegant drawing room. I fumbled for a chair three sizes too small and tried to arrange myself with some kind of decorum. There was something about the simplicity of the room that made me feel unbearably brash. Flooded with sunlight, it evoked an atmosphere of stillness verging on joy. And the old lady's face seemed strangely familiar, as though I had seen her before – on a train perhaps, in some old photograph, or in my imagination.

I remembered other things my friend the doctor had recounted concerning Mirabehn – the dreaded name 'Miss Slade' I was careful never to mention again: that she had led a life of devotion and self-sacrifice which had taken her from the sheltered parlours of Edwardian England to the furthest corners of the sub-continent, that she had frequently faced criticism for her eccentric ways of dressing and living, that she had learned to weave and spin as well as any peasant, that she had used her upper middle-class skills for communication to deliver messages from Gandhi to the British authorities during the political drama of the fall of the Raj. My doctor friend had also told me that a few months before a cavalcade of cars with CD plates had woven their way out of Vienna to present this lady with an award called the Padma Vibhushan, India's second-highest civilian medal of honour as an acknowledgement of the services she had performed for India during the almost forty years in which she lived and worked there.

The sound of a crow broke the silence. I was brought back to the room.

'It is really no trouble at all,' I said. 'In fact, you've done me a big favour. You've given me an excuse to get out of Vienna. If I weren't here with you I'd be sitting in a smoke-filled room, listening to pompous scientists drone on endlessly about things that are of no interest to anybody about a lot of stuff I suspect not even they themselves understand.' This made her laugh.

'It sounds like dinner party conversation,' she said. 'How I have always loathed it. I sympathise.'

Her skin was so fine that the clear morning light seemed to shine right through it. Her eyes were the clearest and brightest I have ever seen – so pure and icy they seemed almost inhuman, her face a map of sun-made wrinkles. When she laughed it became the face of a child, and in her smile was just a touch of the wickedness that makes lively children irresistible. I laughed too. Immediately all of my awkwardness disappeared. So, I remarked to my amazement, had the throbbing headache. Nothing remained but the beauty of a cloudless sky, a field of blue hills I could see through the window and the white stillness of the brilliant room – a room in which, with every moment that passed, my senses were becoming more and more acute. Mirabehn asked about my doctor friend, then rang for tea. The servant returned almost immediately carrying a pot of the strong, sweet, spicy stuff the Indians call *chi*. It was delicious. We talked. I asked about her health. I learned that she had been suffering from a heart condition, that she was now on her fifth pacemaker and that, until the beginning of the year when her condition had begun to deteriorate, she had always spent most of her time outdoors.

'I love to walk,' she told me. 'It comes from my years in India. There work makes you strong. Here it is different; too much is done for you. It makes one weak. Ah, but wait until summer. Then I will be bolting through the woods again.'

The sunlight played on the swirling dust in the air. My sleepless night and the sweet spiciness of the tea had made me slightly giddy. I closed my eyes. I could see her tall lean figure dressed in the same simple khadi dress she now wore, her neck wrapped in a tie-dyed homespun scarf, striding through the local woods. Seeing her on her solitary walks, her bourgeois Austrian neighbours must have wondered what a lady of her stature was doing dressed in such strange clothing. Again my reverie was broken by her voice.

'In recent weeks I've lost a bit of strength,' she said. 'But He has always been kind to me in providing everything I need. I doubt that now, when I am most in need of Him, He will fail me.'

I thought for a moment that she meant the Indian servant and turned my head to look for him. Then it dawned on me that she meant God.

It happens every time. Just when I begin to feel good, something raises its ugly head to screw it all up. I don't like god-talk. I heard a lot of it as a kid – even talked a lot myself – until I figured out that God is something invented by people too weak to deal with what Kierkegaard called 'fear and trembling, the sickness unto death' – that infinite abyss at the brink of which each of us stands when we tell ourselves the truth about the agony of the human condition and the aloneness it implies. Why create a god – the proverbial old man with white hair – just to make what is an awful bitch seem a little more bearable? On the other hand, why not? Except of course that, like hot showers, it doesn't work. While I respected the old lady's point of view – or at least pretended to myself that I did – I couldn't help congratulating myself that *I* at least didn't need to invent fairy tales to prop up my own sense of meaninglessness.

I changed the subject. 'I gather you were recently given an award by the Indian government for your services.'

'Yes,' she replied. She then began to speak of her affection for the Indian people, and of their prime minister Indira Gandhi –who, she was quick to remind me, was no relation to her beloved Bapu – yet a woman whom she had known since childhood.

'She has been so generous to me – instructing the Indian Embassy in Vienna to provide for all my needs. Such kindness, and so much of it wasted. For, you see, I need so little,' she said, gesturing with a long hand around the simple room. Then in a halting voice – probably the result of her shortness of breath – she began to speak about her life with Gandhi.

'His room was far simpler than mine,' she said. 'There were no decorations anywhere. Only a small desk, a white cushion and a few mats on the floor. He didn't need anything. He never wanted to be encumbered by the paraphernalia of life. All of us carry around so much that we don't need.'

She stopped speaking. I saw a shadow cross her face – a shadow whose darkness was so great that in the midst of all that light it made me shudder. She paused, turning with effort towards the window for almost a minute as though she were expecting someone. Then she brought her gaze back to me and went on with her rambling.

She told me how at Gandhi's ashram near Ahmadabad in the cotton-producing country of north-west India she had learned to card and to spin, how she would awaken at four o'clock every morning for prayers at the riverbank among her 200 companions, how she had learned Hindustani only with great difficulty and how she had frequently worked with a Chinese member of the community to clean the latrines.

'Bapu was not a mystical man,' she said. 'His spirituality was expressed entirely through practical actions – through his life and his ideals for human society. And he was very highly sexed, very sensitive. He felt the need to sublimate his sex very deeply.'

Again her focus shifted abruptly. Then she spoke openly, with humour and even a quiet longing about death. 'Death holds no fear for me,' she said. She was certain that she would live again, that we would *all* live again. 'He may seem wicked from a distance, but Death is an old friend to all of us. How can one fear a friend?' After a moment she continued, 'I've had three lives, you know, my dear. The first was with Beethoven, the second with Gandhi-ji, and now the third one again with Beethoven.' She paused again while the gaze of those shrewd and brilliant eyes burnt through me like dry ice. 'In a way I suppose they are all the same,' she said. 'You know, the poet Varnhagen in the early nineteenth century said of Beethoven: "Would that I could express how uplifted and earnest the man looked, as if kissed by a God, when he plays divine variations on the piano-forte."' Leaning closer she added, 'Those who have never come in close contact with a great spirit of rare quality may find such words difficult to understand. But for one like myself, who passed many years in intimate association with Bapu, there is nothing strange about them. You know such spirits often radiate a *something* which, though invisible, is very real. I say "often" because that radiance varies, depending on whether the spirit within is stirred to outward glow, or withdrawn to inward shade.' I shifted in my seat, which seemed to be getting smaller by the moment.

What the hell was she on about? I started to pick my nails, trying to figure out which was worse, the religious ramblings of this bright-eyed old woman or the murky memories of the night just passed. I was given no time to decide.

'It is no accident that you have come here,' she said. 'I knew someone would be sent. I didn't know who or in what guise, but I knew you were coming.'

I hate allusions to phenomena such as *déjà vu*, precognition and all the rest. I had, until now, enjoyed listening to Mirabehn's recollections, but I had no desire to hear any more about her mystical beliefs and religious leanings, I just wanted to clear off. Before I had a chance to say so, she went on.

'You may well object. You may say that Beethoven and Gandhi were totally different in appearance and outward temperament, and this is true. But their similarity belongs to a higher region of being.' She paused and again looked uncomfortably deep into my eyes. I was about to get up and leave when out of nowhere this batty old woman asked, 'Do you *know* Beethoven?'

Her question seemed so ridiculous it stopped me in my tracks. Now it was my turn to laugh. For the way she had asked it sounded as though she were wanting me to tell her if Beethoven had only been an *acquaintance* of mine, or if I really *knew* him as one might know a brother or a friend.

'I know his music a bit,' I said, 'and I like it very much. But I know almost nothing about his life.'

'Good,' was Mirabehn's answer. 'That is probably as it should be.' She sighed. 'You see I am different from you. I began my life with him. And if these awful Viennese doctors have their way, I may soon end it that way.' She paused again, sitting perfectly still with her hands folded in her lap. A stern look washed over her face. She asked, 'Did you ever *dream* him?'

I was taken aback by her question. Almost ten years before I had indeed dreamed about Beethoven, or rather about his music. It was a dream which, because of its unusual quality, I had never quite forgotten.

'Yes,' I replied as lightly as I could manage, while my mind raced looking for an explanation. It came up with the probability that everybody has dreamed of Beethoven at one time or another. The thought brought me great comfort. 'As a matter of fact, I did once. Why do you ask?'

My new-found sense of comfort didn't last long. For out of nowhere, in a strangely androgynous voice – the voice of a prophet or of a sibyl – this wrinkled old woman proceeded to recite with impossible accuracy the content of my near-forgotten dream.

'Let me see if I can get it right,' she said. 'You were walking in a garden – a garden in a Persian painting perhaps – full of flowers and trees in luminous colours. Beethoven's music was playing; at least you thought it was Beethoven, although it was nothing of his you had ever heard before. In the midst of the garden was a large pond. It was very dark and still as though its water had not moved for many years. The music grew stronger, wilder, louder. As it reached a crescendo you realised that the air around you had become transfigured. The colours of the trees and flowers were completely burnt out by a dazzling white light. Then a serpent's tail . . . no, I am wrong, was it the hand of God? . . . came down from heaven.' She paused and then said

24

softly as though to herself, 'But then perhaps they are the same.'

I listened to her words. I was stunned by their accuracy. She could not possibly have known such things. I had told no one of the dream, which had taken place many years before. What can you say about such a dream, anyway? I felt my pulse quickening. The headache had returned. The androgynous voice droned on.

'His index finger touched the water, sending circle after circle rippling outwards. You were frightened. The light, the power and the beauty were too much to bear. You shut your eyes and covered your ears with your hands. We all do that, my dear,' she added, leaning close to my face. 'Only most of us, myself included, hide from the *darkness* – not the *light*.'

She raised her left hand to her head, arranging a rebellious piece of white hair that had fallen over her brow again. She glanced towards the window. It was almost as if she were expecting someone and she wanted full warning of their arrival. Then she looked back at me. I realised I was staring at her helplessly. Her face softened. I noticed her eyes had begun to water. She seemed for reasons I could in no way comprehend to be filled with sympathy for me. Again she brushed back the disobedient hank of hair which was totally unwilling, despite her grace and the determination, to stay where she put it. Then she continued.

'Once the climax passed, once the colours returned to normal, you opened your eyes and took your hands away from your ears. Then you awakened. Have I got it right? Have I forgotten anything?'

I thought back to the dream. It had come at a time in my life when I was working 'lobster shift' writing headlines at the *New York Post* and trying to forget. I had a girlfriend whom I would ring at 3 a.m. to read her my masterpieces. 'Hi, Harriet, what do you think of this? "Dog Bites Man in

East Harlem."' She was seldom amused. I hated New York then, hated the lies Nixon had told, hated the fact that though we had lost 58,000 men and women to hostile fire in a war nobody wanted to fight in the first place, I knew we had also lost another 75,000 to drugs. I hated the things I knew, too – like the way the CIA had circumnavigated Congress's refusal to supply money by financing their covert field operations through cookie mornings and garage sales of drugs from the Golden Triangle. Most of all I hated cowardice and my inability to do anything whatsoever about any of it. I knew that I was stuck – impotent – against the powers that be. They were too big, too deadly. There were four of us – two generals, a colonel and myself – who knew what was going on. The colonel, a man I loved like a brother, and one of the generals tried to break the CIA cocaine story through CBS on *60 Minutes*. They got nowhere – nothing but a polite letter saying they were sorry but they had already planned the programmes for the season. Within six months all three were dead – erased and forgotten. That left only me with my broken dreams and my cynicism.

The dream had seemed like a vague promise that things would get better – that maybe somehow outside intervention – the hand of God, maybe: how I hated the hypocrisy of the word – would bring a power to change things, to make life clean again. It didn't. Before long I left for Paris. There I worked as a foreign correspondent for three years before coming to England. To Mirabehn I said nothing.

'Don't worry,' she said, reaching out and taking one of my hands in hers. It was cool and the palm was smooth as a baby's. Mine had grown hot and sticky. 'The next time such beauty comes, 'she said, 'you *will* be able to bear it. I promise.' Again her focus shifted. The voice lost all its androgyny. 'You have brought me an important package today,' she said. 'Now I have something to give you.'

Relieved by her change of tone I could feel myself shifting back into the leaden numbness of the present. I tried to engage my mouth. 'No, please, you've nothing to thank me for,' I said. 'It is a pleasure for me, an honour . . . really.'

Amidst my feeble protests, and not without difficulty, Mirabehn lifted her body from the day bed and walked across the small room to a bookshelf on which lay a package. Wrapped in cloth in the manner in which Buddhists and Hindus often wrap their holy books, it was tied with heavy brown string. The package was old and badly faded by sunlight. Several shades darker at the edges than in the centre, it looked as though it might once have been the colour of blood. The twine with which it had been tied was worn and frayed.

'This is not a gift,' Mirabehn said to me, placing the package in my hands. 'At least not in any ordinary sense.'

The package held a strange fascination for me yet I did not want to touch it. When I took it from the old woman my body registered danger. It was a feeling I knew well from days and nights in the bush – an unmistakable *smell* that warns you – a smell you get to know and trust when your life depends on it. The way a sixth sense warns you when a snake is present long before you see it, or guides you through a minefield without getting your head blown off. My body recoiled. Yet the mere fact that I did touch it somehow made the parcel impossible to put down. I sat there as stupid as a great beast trapped in manacles of its own making.

Returning to her bed, quite deliberately she added, 'It is a grave, possibly a dangerous, responsibility. Let no one know that you have it in your possession.' Then, like a bird of prey sensing some shift in the wind that threatened its survival, Mirabehn stiffened and looked towards the window again before turning back quickly to face me.

I hated her every word. I only wanted out. 'But what am I to *do* with it?' I whined like a child on the verge of tears.

'Please read it,' was her reply. 'It is, I'm afraid, only part of the whole. The rest we may speak of later, that is if . . .' Her voice dropped to nothing as the servant entered. She smiled and made some request of him, I believe in Hindi. It resulted in his leaving the house, on an errand. Then she turned back to me and continued in low tones to speak words which had no meaning.

'I do not think that any of us choose our destiny,' she said. 'We come to this earth knowing little about who we are or why we are here. Then sometimes, if we are very fortunate, or very *unfortunate*, we find ourselves caught up in something. It can be an idea – that is what makes great scientists, philosophers and engineers. It can be – as it is with those poor creatures who end up in institutions or who surrender their minds to drugs to make their lives bearable – a fear, a compulsion, a passion. It can be a surrender to beings of dazzling brilliance and power, who proceed unbeknown to you to feed off your very life-blood. These drainers of blood are far more than figments of an overactive imagination, you know,' she said, watching me closely. 'You see, in worlds both seen and unseen each and every creature has its place and its purpose. In Bapu's case he found himself caught up in a love for human freedom and dignity – a love for which he gave his life and for which he died. In mine it was an obsession – an obsession with Beethoven. It took hold of me when I was a young girl. It led me to Gandhi, forced me to give up all connections with home and family and finally brought me back to Vienna again and to try to put his life into words.'

'*His* life?'

'Ludwig's. But I fear I have failed. You see, in an odd way, it was his music that led me to Bapu. I shall perhaps tell you of that one day. And so it was to Ludwig's country, here in Vienna that I came when I returned to the West.'

'Vienna? Why?' I asked, in an attempt to regain some ground on which my earthly feet could once again be firmly planted.

'What?' she replied absentmindedly. 'My dear, that does not matter now. There is so little time.' She laughed. Then, as if to herself, she muttered, 'Funny, that is what his *first* chronicler wrote.' Then to me again she said, 'What matters is this: these fears, these passions, these obsessions are double-edged. They can either lead us towards truth – in which case we are obliged as Bapu was to give up everything, but he was a *very* great soul – or they can lead us by twists and turns so deep into a forest of illusion that we never find our way out of it. Either way they hold great power. After all, Hitler too had his passions. That is why throughout history certain things have needed to remain carefully guarded secrets – secrets after which the weak and less virtuous lust while the honourable and the innocent pray only to be left in peace.' Again her shrewd, sparkling eyes scanned me. 'There are far too many of us who have been touched by destiny but who discover too late that we would rather live in the light alone because we cannot face the darkness,' she continued, 'that, I know now, was *my* great mistake. I wanted to paint everything with brilliance, and to ignore the shadows or at best to behave as if they were but playthings – trying never to have to treat them seriously. I know it all now, but what can I do? My time is almost finished.'

I could take no more of this. Much as I felt sorry for this beautiful old woman and her regrets – regrets about which I hadn't a clue – I became aware that I had now become more uncomfortable in that room than I have ever been anywhere in my life. I wanted one thing only: to return to the drone of the speakers in the lecture hall.

'Mirabehn, I'm sorry. I don't know what you're talking about. I have to go. Is there anything I can do for you before I leave?' I rose, extending my right hand. My thighs felt barely strong enough to support my body. I looked down at the package in my left hand. The faded red cloth in which it was bound seemed to have a floral pattern of some kind all over it, almost like strawberries yet with yellow flowers instead of white. No, they were not strawberries. Then I remembered the Duchesnia plant – it grows on waste ground in Asia – the deadly *false* strawberry which you must never eat for survival. 'It will kill you as soon as look at you,' the colonel used to say. I shuddered. But when I looked again the pattern no longer seemed to be there – the cloth was only faded red. *Get rid of it.* I placed the manuscript quite deliberately on the edge of her bed. I wanted so little part of it that I was not even the slightest bit curious about what it contained.

But she knew. She grabbed my hand, taking hold of it as though she would never let it go.

'You *must* take it,' she said, her keen eyes glistening. 'I can no longer risk its being here. There have already been signs, as there were with Wawruch. The destruction of human freedom is imminent and time is running out. There is no one I can trust with it.'

I found myself weakening.

'Take it back with you to London. Read it. There is much to be done. Then come back. Come back, my dear, before it is too late.'

Like a rabbit cornered by an animal a hundred times its size I smiled limply, picked up the package and tucked it under my arm. I thanked Mirabehn for the tea and the chat, told her how much I had enjoyed meeting her and promised I would be in touch soon – all as though nothing unusual had happened. She looked back at me in silence, her face

flooded with infinite tenderness, but she said no more. From
that day forward I found myself drawn deeper and deeper
into a vortex from which there was no escape.

MODULATION

> Never mind. . . . One day, quite suddenly, when
> you're not expecting it, I'll take a hammer from the
> folds of my dark cloak and crack your little skull
> like an egg-shell. Crack it will go, the egg-shell; out
> they will stream, the blood, the brains. One day,
> one day. . . . One day the fierce wolf that walks by
> my side will spring on you and rip your abomin-
> able guts out. One day, one day. . . .
>
> Jean Rhys *Good Morning, Midnight*

Two days later I boarded the plane for London with a
migraine the like of which I had never known, thanks to too
much Viennese coffee and my anger over the strange parcel
under my arm. I had not yet opened it. In some way it
seemed like Pandora's box –something best left well alone.
Yet I guarded it as carefully as Mirabehn had implored me
to do; I told no one about it and I kept it on my person at all
times. It began to take on the quality of a talisman. I had
developed the absurd notion that it would bring me
protection – from what I was not sure – so long as I kept it
with me and kept it sealed. When first I noticed myself
developing these notions, so completely foreign to my
nature, I viewed it all with a detached curiosity, as though I
were watching someone else. I was at the same time aware of
another part of me which took comfort in the idea that if only
I could ignore the parcel's existence altogether, and forget

the strange meeting with Mirabehn, both would conveniently vanish from consciousness.

Of the German woman there is little more to tell. We were in the same conference hall several times after that night, yet she chose to ignore me altogether as though nothing had passed between us. Only once did I see her looking at me, when I glanced up from my notes. For an instant our eyes met. To my utter disbelief I detected a note of wistful longing in her face. Then she turned away. Whether or not such an unlikely feeling was really there after my piggish blundering and obscene brutality I shall never know. So I put the impression down to the wild musings of the indomitable male ego, gave thanks that some degree of normality had returned to my life, conveniently blamed my actions on alcohol and let it go at that. In any case this made things easier, since I felt sickened by what I had done and I was relieved that I did not have to face admonishment from *her* over my behaviour as well.

The trip back to London was uneventful except for two unrelated happenings. On the plane I decided to listen to piped music through earphones in the hope that it would help the migraine. After wading through '60s' Revival', 'Comic Capers' complete with canned laughter, and 'Broadway Shows', I settled for 'The Classics' only to find that some overly enthusiastic conductor with a French accent had chosen to survey the music of Beethoven. It was very much like one of those *Reader's Digest* potted versions of 'the best Classic themes with none of the *unimportant* passages to worry about'. I closed my eyes. Overlapping layers of sound filled my skull. Instead of following one another in succession as they were intended to do, themes and melodies seemed to jostle for position in my head. One would begin while the previous one was still forcing its own path through. Then another would enter, pushing the previous two aside like children vying for attention. They were accompanied by images of statues in stone and bronze – Greek gods, busts of unknown men and one or two of women together with heads of Beethoven – some tortured, others radiant with laughter or sullen or angry. They wafted through my visual field in an angular chaotic manner while the sheets of sound wove similar patterns of conflict within my head.

The second incident occurred when I arrived at Heathrow. There was a long delay in immigration because of a bomb scare in the baggage claim area. Passengers with EC passports had been allowed through while the rest of us – the *aliens* – had to stand in line for more than an hour as officious men in uniform darted about making sure the hall was safe to enter. It was early evening. The terminal was full, hot and sticky. Tempers were fragile all around. I found myself crushed between a hefty Scandinavian woman carrying endless expensive shopping bags and a tall lean man with angular features, dressed all in black. We had been stationary in the line for at least twenty minutes, captives within the chromium rails that filter human beings through small openings like animals herded towards the slaughter, before I noticed him. He had pale, pitted skin and was of indiscriminate age with a long face. He was, from the point of view not only of taste but also of temperature, very overdressed.

Having spent a good part of my life one way or another in stuffy airports standing in line, I have developed a knack for ignoring people, even when they are eight inches away. He was different. His presence was annoying, like the friend's cat who, even though you are a cat-hater, insists on rubbing its body against your chair. I first noticed that, unlike the rest of us, each of whom carried some kind of bag or bags, this man carried nothing. Nor, despite the heat and the jostling, did he show the slightest sign of perturbation.

34

I had successfully avoided involving myself in conversation with the Swedish woman who stood in front of me, despite her efforts to attract my attention. I leaned against the rail and turned my back on her. That is when our eyes met – his and mine. Mine were bloodshot. His were thin – maybe the thinnest eyes I have ever seen, hidden behind glasses so thick that when you looked at him from any direction except straight on, the lenses distorted what you saw so radically that the whole side of his cheek appeared to be missing. He smiled at me with a cold familiarity totally inappropriate to our circumstances. Then, in a heavy accent that sounded vaguely East European, and referring to Mirabehn's parcel which was tucked tightly beneath my left arm, he spoke.

'An old book?'

'My laundry.'

'Ah. Have you come far?'

'Too far.'

'Myself as well.'

For two minutes he said nothing, then he spoke again.

'We know you have the book.'

I figured I could not have heard him right. I did not reply.

'I collect books – *illuminated* books.'

'Oh, yeah.'

'Perhaps you have seen some?'

'No.'

'You do not read, then?'

'Nope, nothing but paperbacks.'

'Yes. Yes, of course. That is as it should be,' he said, 'I too only deal with *familiar* sources. It is always wise not to tamper with something whose origins one does not know.'

I decided I didn't like him any more than I liked being where I was just that moment or carrying this scruffy package under my sweaty arm. I gave him one of my toughest stares. He didn't flinch.

'Maybe you are a music lover, then?'

'Yeah. Heavy metal.'

'Ah. I myself prefer the nineteenth century. Perhaps you know Beethoven?'

I could feel heat rising at the back of my neck – for me a sure sign of danger. Ignore it and I end up putting my fist through a wall. I looked around. There was no wall available. Chit-chat with the big Swede was starting to look better and better. I deliberately turned my back on him just in time to see one of the shiny designer bags slip through ruby-nailed fingers. I rescued the package from the terrazzo floor, handed it back to her and was accosted by giggles and fluttery eyelashes. I did not look behind me again until fifteen minutes later, when I finally approached the barrier that promised freedom from the cattle corridor. When I did turn to take one more look at my irritating companion there was no trace of him. So surprised was I by his disappearance that, after carefully following the line of grumpy passengers as far back as I could see, I was forced to speak to the fat kid in the day-glo shorts who was now standing just behind me.

'What happened to the weird guy in the black coat?'

'What black coat?' he said as he bolted past me and deposited himself at the only free immigration desk.

I arrived back at my basement flat just before midnight to find that the walls in the bathroom had sprouted a new species of mushroom. But this time, instead of being repelled by the vaguely decaying smell as usual, the damp seemed to comfort me – almost to lull my senses into a feeling of safety which reinforced the notion that nothing really had changed, nothing would change and that – imperfect as it was – my life could go on as it always had.

I unpacked my few belongings, tucked my beaten-up

black bag in the cupboard and turned around to find the dark red package glaring at me from the table where I had tossed it. With deliberation and a clear sense of purpose, I opened the bottom drawer of my battered old desk, threw it in and shut it tight, locking it. Then I went through the mail. There were several overdue bills, a handwritten note from Fiona on smelly pink paper inviting me to spend the weekend at her parents' house, an elaborately engraved invitation from a self-important manufacturer of surgical prostheses announcing the launch of new colostomy equipment which, so the accompanying press release informed me, had been 'tested at three of the world's most prestigious universities and found to be a breakthrough in post-surgery care', and a letter from my ex-wife in Vermont explaining in perfectly reasonable yet highly improbable terms why she needed more money to pay school bills. I cursed myself for the hundredth time for trying to support an American ex-wife and two kids on a lousy British salary and considered the possibility of returning to the land of plenty. Then, rejecting it out of hand, I stuffed the mail, rubbish and all, into the space between the fridge and the wall and went to bed.

I slept heavily. At three I awakened, having dreamed of more heads and statues – magnificent creations they were – and of sound. The dream surprised me, first because I rarely dream, second because it was a kaleidoscopic replay of what had happened on the aeroplane and third because it was one of those dreams where your dream images get all jumbled up with the here and now. My room with its familiar smell of wool and damp seemed to have become a mausoleum in which all of these figures, who may once have had life, resided in bronze silence immersed in a medium of layered sound. I could not go back to sleep. I did not want to sleep. Yet I found myself powerfully drawn into the world of the night. I began to have wild fantasies about wandering in the streets. I tried to read, but quit. At 5.30, after a couple of hours of arguing with myself about how I should get to sleep, I got up, went to the kitchen and against my better judgement – for the migraine had only just begun to lift – made a huge cup of very strong coffee.

I was at work by 7.30 – me and the cleaner. Her cigarette smoke filled the air of the city room. I waded through the pile of paper that had accumulated during my week's absence in a detached way. Although it was comforting to be sitting once again in the familiar world of desks and telephones, newsprint and computer terminals – the world which had been my only reality for almost ten years – I noticed that now, since Vienna, it had become two-dimensional, like a moment in time captured on celluloid. It could be looked at, studied, even lived – but only in limited ways. Yet it no longer had any substance or meaning for me – no energy, no power. This familiar and comfortable world I had created for myself as a cushion against the brutal rage that had taken up residence when I left SF had started to crumble. Without warning my whole life was turning cardboard, empty and dull.

I picked up the telephone and began to dial. Then, remembering that no one I knew would have opened his eyes at that time of the morning, I put it down again and started to work on my story – the *non-story* I needed to contrive out of the junket. I wrote easily, mechanically, looking for just the right authoritative punch that would, I hoped, give the subs a chance to turn it into something jazzy designed to sell more newspapers. To my surprise the writing, which should have been difficult and demanding, was incredibly easy. It was as though everything had been put on automatic. I was only along for the ride. Meanwhile my head was still filled with statues and I noticed that my left ear had developed a kind of buzz, which I put down to the aftermath of the migraine.

I left the office at 3 p.m. and walked up Fleet Street towards Aldwych. London was beginning to fill with tourists – Japanese battery hens with cameras hanging down their breasts – the same thick glasses and the same thick smiles, Americans with their drip-dry trousers and their pot bellies, Germans with their bad manners. I turned a corner and headed north up a narrow side street that led into a small square. There I came upon a trio of birds in the middle of the street. Huge and black, they appeared to be crows or ravens. They were grouped around some kind of food. As I got closer I could make out a large piece of flesh – an animal perhaps or the remains of butcher's offal. I imagined with repulsive clarity how one of them had carried it through the air in its beak from Smithfield to drop it here on the cobblestones. The square was curiously deserted for that time of day – no cars, no people, not a sound except the bickering of scavengers as they gorged themselves on flesh. It was only later when I recalled the scene that I registered the strangeness of it. While it was happening it all seemed perfectly normal. I stood for a while staring at these birds with the same detached curiosity I felt about the dream, as though they were objects with which I had no immediate connection, yet which radiated a patent sense of another reality – a world as different from the steamy jungles and secret briefings of my past as it was from the cardboard city room in which I had spent the last decade. This new world was the most awful I could imagine. For in it I knew none of the rules and I felt completely powerless to act.

Through Bloomsbury into Camden and on to Regent's Park Road I walked, but after my encounter with the birds I didn't notice much around me. When I descended the stairs to my flat it was with a sense that I had been mysteriously transported there not altogether under my own volition. I went in, opened the refrigerator to find a jar of black olives with white scum floating on the top and a loaf of bread that had been there since before I went away. I threw the olives out and told myself I should have bought food, but I couldn't be bothered to go out again. I made myself another cup of coffee, carried it into the living room and turned on the television.

The news: cheerful people mechanically altering their tone to suit the story. Sitting behind a plastic desk complete with phoney picture of Big Ben as a backdrop, a small blonde woman who looked and sounded as though her mouth was full of porridge told us that Brazil had announced it was refusing to pay the interest on its debt and that there was to be a special meeting of wise men in New York to discuss what could be done about this grievous problem. Her colleague, a black man with a snow-white British accent, reported that some university study group or other had calculated that Britain's unemployment in *real* figures – no doubt after discounting cosmetic training schemes designed to prevent the prime minister committing political suicide – had now risen nationwide to almost 15 per cent. His voice was accompanied by a photograph of a girl who looked about twelve sleeping beneath a cardboard box under Waterloo Bridge. He droned on: 'and now for cricket. . .'. I remembered reading a few weeks earlier that in the States new current affairs programmes not only announce the news, they sometimes even re-enact events – a murder, an earthquake, a group of impassioned mothers trying to keep their town nuclear-free. It won't be long until such drama comes to Britain too, I mused. 'Violence? Pain? Joy? You saw it all on ITN.' I switched off the set and began to pace about the room.

The phone rang. It would be Fiona. I didn't answer it. I

noticed how dark and dusty the room had grown while I was gone. Maybe I should have let Fiona come in and fuss about while I was away – the female touch and all that. I noticed how frayed and worn the sofa had become.

I sat down at my desk intending to deal with the pile of bills that had accumulated in my absence. I could not. Instead, with a movement that could have been automatic I opened the bottom drawer and took out the package. The phone rang again. I dropped the package back into the drawer and turned the key. The phone rang seven times. Persistent woman. I crossed the room and picked up the receiver.

'Hello.'

'Darling, you're home, how wonderful! I thought you wouldn't be back until tomorrow.'

'Hi, Fiona.'

'Well?'

'Well, what?'

'How was the conference?'

'OK.'

'I missed you, darling.'

'Yeah. I missed you, too,' I lied. I could feel guilt raise its ugly head.

'Meet anybody interesting?'

'Nope, but I saw a lot of old movies on TV. The best were German. I didn't understand a word.'

'Oh, darling. You're teasing me again.'

'When have I ever teased you?'

'Darling, I'm sorry about being such a bore on the phone the other night. I don't blame you a bit for not ringing back. I just wanted you to know it was OK. I was beastly. Can you ever forgive me?'

'Fiona, there is nothing to forgive. I'm not the easiest man in the world to live with. I really am sorry I forgot dinner with your parents.'

'Not to worry. Mummy was *so* sweet about it. She even defended you to me when I started to moan. To tell you the truth, I think Daddy was relieved. But they're dying to meet you. They've invited us to the country for the weekend.'

I said nothing.

'Darling, I really have missed you. Can I come over now?'

'No . . . no, don't do that.'

'But darling it's been a *week*.' She punched the word with that cloying cosy quality upper middle-class Englishwomen use when they speak of 'pressies' and shopping at 'M&S'. I cringed.

'Look, Fiona. I'd love to see you. But I've got a pile of stuff on my desk, a story to file by morning, and a hangover from Viennese coffee that kept me awake most of the night. Let's wait till the weekend.'

'Then you'll come?'

'I'll come.'

'Oh, darling, I'm so glad. We won't have to spend a lot of time with them, truly we won't. Daddy's busy with two new dogs he's training. The house is big and they keep to themselves a lot. We can go for long walks, and sleep late, and . . .'

'OK, Fiona. Now look, I have to get back to work.'

'Of course, darling. You'll let me know if there is anything I can do to help, won't you?'

I promised I would; I lied. She promised she'd pick me up at midday on Friday. I slept little that night, drank more coffee – I discovered it tasted even better laced with malt whisky – and for the second day in a row ended up in my office at an hour so early any self-respecting newspaperman would kill to keep his friends at El Vino's from finding out. That afternoon the phone on my desk rang. It was the editor's secretary, asking if I would pop in to see him. I figured he wanted a few minutes' consultation about the ulcer. When I walked through the door the old man was standing behind his glass desk, looking like a hawk who had not fed for a very long time and whose nervous system is beginning to suffer. Maybe the ulcer had got worse.

'Sit down.'

I sat.

'How did Vienna go?'

'Good. Have you read my copy?'

'Yes. Fine. It's fine. Look. We've always had a good relationship, Mike, haven't we?'

I nodded.

'And I have always been fair to you, have I not?'

'You have.'

'You know we appreciate the work you do for us.'

'Yeah. I guess that's why I'm still here.'

'Good.'

He paused, turned his back to me and stared out the window. Then he started again.

'You know, running a newspaper is a delicate proposition,' he said, shuffling papers from one corner of his desk to another. 'I am a pragmatist,' he went on. 'I reckon either you make things work within the possibilities of the pressures you live with or you quit, become a drop-out and grow potatoes in Wales.'

I said nothing.

'I am no drop-out,' he continued, pausing to take out a big, red, snuff kerchief. He rubbed his nose, sniffed and then stuffed it back into his pocket.

'The trouble is,' he continued, 'you end up trying to please everybody. You try to get the news out in a way that sells papers, doesn't offend the powers that be who pay all the bills and still lets you sleep at night.'

'Yeah. I know. I wouldn't want your job.'

'Look, Mike, sometimes in balancing all the pressures it is

necessary to make a few practical compromises for the sake of keeping things on an even keel. It is not anything that I like having to do, you understand. But I'm a realist. You don't get something for nothing.'

I did not know what he was talking about and I was becoming more and more sure I didn't want to know.

'OK,' I said.

'Look. Let me be blunt: I don't know what you are involved in and I don't want to know. Your politics is your business, in fact I thought you had left all that behind. So is your personal life. I am delighted when your work or the work of any other feature writer on the staff comes to the attention of the people who matter. But I don't like getting a phone call with veiled threats in which your name is mentioned. It makes me uneasy and I hate feeling uneasy. Do you understand?'

'Veiled threats about what?' I tightened my jaw and tried to sound reasonable.

'The call came through on my private line, Mike. Only a handful of people have the number. The voice was American. It spoke in a slow Southern drawl. "I bring you a little message from those in the know," it said. "Who is this?" I demanded. "This is Mercury," the voice replied. "Surely an educated man like yourself remembers Mercury . . . messenger of the gods?" "What do you want?" I said. "How did you get this number?" "We want you to tell your medical reporter to keep his nose out of people and places that have nothing to do with him," it replied, "otherwise he just might wake up one morning soon to find he doesn't have a nose. Oh yes. And one other thing – you, sir, could find yourself without a job." Then, Mike, just to let me know it was no practical joke he told me a few things I thought – I hoped – had been forgotten long ago.' The editor paused, scrutinising my face, obviously wanting me to respond. I didn't.

44

'Now *you* tell *me* what's going on, Mike,' he said, almost pleading. I still said nothing. 'No, don't tell me. Forget it. I don't want to know. Just hear this: if you want to continue working here, and that is *certainly* my wish, let me make that clear, then you had better clean up your act.'

The back of my neck began to burn. I felt as though somebody had spilt boiling water down my collar.

'I don't know what the hell you're talking about,' I said.

'OK. Let's play it your way,' he said, his eyes avoiding mine. 'I've said my piece.'

I had no idea what he was on about but it was all beginning to sound an awful lot like something I had heard before – the veiled threats, bullying insinuations. Nausea rose up from my belly and began to burn my throat. I knew only that if I stuck around long enough to find out both of us would be sorry. I got up. It had been more than five years since I had even written about anything political – ten years since I'd been involved in CIA-controlled black operations in Central America. I had always kept my mouth shut. Didn't he know that? Did he not know why I spent my time writing the kind of drivel that tells people about the latest cure for arthritic knees instead of hard-hitting editorials on who *really* invaded Nicaragua and why? Didn't he know that issuing his hidden warnings to a hot-tempered, pig-headed American like me was like ploughing through a minefield? Was he crazy, I asked myself, or just plain stupid? I noticed that my hands had turned to ice although sweat poured down my forehead in sheets.

He crossed over to a table where today's proofs were waiting for his approval, picked up a page, glanced at it as though he hadn't seen it, put it down and turned to face me again. This time it was eye to eye.

'My wife tells me there is a doctor in north London who claims to have some new hormone that takes fat off women while they eat chocolate,' he said. 'Do you know anything about it?'

'Nope.'

'See what you can find out. By the way, if you feel you'd like a couple of weeks off, take them. You deserve a break.'

So ended the interview. None of it made sense. It was like one of those infuriating riddles that kids ask over and over again: 'What did the doctor say to the man who thought he was a pack of cards?' I hate riddles. Threats I like even less. I knew I had to get out of his office before I broke something.

I stopped at my desk only long enough to pull my jacket off the back of my chair. I didn't even bother to clear the screen of my computer. Take a couple of weeks off, he'd said. Damned right I would. I deserved it. I shot through the swing doors that let into the street, hitting them so hard they knocked over an old bike propped against the railing outside. Then I headed home. When I got there I found myself plunged into a nightmare world. These are words I write with full consciousness of what they mean.

COUNTERPOINT

In a dark time, the eye begins to see.

Theodore Roethke *In a Dark Time*

I have an indelible memory. Hear a telephone number once and it sticks in my brain for ever. It is more of a curse than a blessing since nothing gets wiped out – not even the smell of napalm and burning flesh or the whimper of a starving dog in a steaming jungle. Yet of the days that followed I remember little. I paid the bills, wrote my ex-wife, bought food and moped about the flat in the same automatic mode in which I had written the Vienna stress copy. Through all of it I had the same unreal feeling I had first experienced in the city room the morning after my return – as though everything in my brain had been switched. What was real before seemed unreal now – the realm of imagination had begun to assume gigantic proportions. I began to lose track of time. I would go to the refrigerator to get something to eat, open it and then realise that I had just eaten. The buzzing in my left ear which had at first been intermittent on my return from Vienna now became continuous. The migraine did not clear. For days it hovered at the base of my

47

skull, ready to shoot fingers of pain up over the top of my head at the slightest provocation: drilling in the street above, an extra cup of coffee, the Indian man in the shop at the corner who, instead of ringing up my order, kept on arguing with his mother-in-law.

I watched television. Or rather I spent hours sitting in the front room with the television on. Whether or not I actually registered what was happening I do not know. Except for a weird film on late one night – a detective story set in LA in the year 2019. It seemed to be acting out in visual terms the inner world in which I had found myself living. I sat on my shabby sofa drinking Newcastle Brown Ale while a beat-up young detective pursued a group of androids who had jumped a shuttle off-planet and then returned to earth in search of human identity and a longer life. Watching it was like one of those experiences when, having drunk a great deal in some dusty bar in the middle of the night, you find yourself leaning on the piano while a heavy-jowled blonde with a raspy voice sings torch songs – sure that every word she utters is meant for you alone.

In the film, the neurasthenic cop drags himself from one encounter to another in pursuit of these *replicants*, each of whom he duly *retires* with a gun so huge it would make a gangster drool with envy. Throughout the whole film a chemical drizzle falls on the overcrowded streets of the city while human beings – I *guess* they were human beings – go about their abstracted business in a grey polluted world. So consistent was the film's oppressive atmosphere that after an hour in front of the box I began to experience sickeningly sweet olfactory flashbacks: the smell of opium smoked in hidden rooms beneath wet Asian streets. I had also developed a heavy sinking in my solar plexus, as though I had swallowed too many rocks.

A cold intellectual named Tyrel, the maker of these

facsimile human beings, at one point in the film announces with pride, 'At the Tyrel Corporation, commerce is our goal. "More human than human" is our motto.' Meanwhile the replicants, pursued like rabid animals by this detective with his massive gun, become more and more frantic in their bid to stay alive. To this end, and at every opportunity, they perpetrate violence both on Tyrel, their creator, and on Deckert, their pursuer. At one point one of the females grabs Deckert's head between her thighs like a piece of wood in a vice and begins rhythmically to crush it. I watched in fascination. Each thrust echoed through my own body. I became both violator and violated. . . *more real than real*. . . . My head pounded. I began to tremble.

I switched off the set and poured myself another drink, this time changing to malt whisky. I tried to read but couldn't. I felt I was being pursued by something, although I could see how ridiculous a notion this was. After all, I reasoned, what had happened to me? Not much. I had had a run-in with my boss that I didn't understand but – what the hell – the worst that could come of it was that I took a few weeks off and then went back to work again. I began to pace the floor. I poured another whisky and revelled in the dry burning in my throat as I drank it. I told myself I should eat something, but then decided that the whisky was so relaxing I didn't want to water down its effect with food. Besides, I needed sleep. Tonight, I figured, plenty of whisky might just help me get it.

I had slept little since my return. I would drift off without much trouble, then, after an hour or two, surface so wide awake it could have been noon, only to check the clock and find that it was still 2 a.m. There was often a pressure in my chest and shoulders. Just about everything I ate made me sick – everything, that is, except whisky. I poured one more glass. Then lying down fully clothed on a bed still unmade from the day before – for the first time in several days – I fell into a deep sleep as unfamiliar string quartets echoed through my head.

How long I slept I do not know. I was awakened by the spray of water. A strong wind had blown open the french windows to the garden, allowing the storm outside to penetrate the bedroom. I got up, my head hot and reeling with whisky, my hands cold as ice. I staggered across the room and secured the doors. Then I headed for the bathroom. I filled a basin with cold water, removed my shirt and started to splash. My movements were uncoordinated. I got as much water on the back wall as I did on myself. But it felt good – the cold, the friendly look of old bottles on the shelf at the side of the mirror, the buzz of strip lighting. I covered my face with a towel and rested my forehead against the front of the basin. Such peace. I raised my head to look in the mirror. It was then that I registered for the first time that something was going on over which I had no control.

My face is ordinary; a more ordinary face you couldn't imagine. I look like a cross between a bank teller and – thanks to my size – one of those busts of a big Roman legionnaire past his prime. The face that greeted me in the mirror bore no resemblance to what I expected. Its head was massive, the hair thick and splayed out all over, giving it the look of an ancient mangy lion. A few strands of this grey mane fell over the forehead, covering the left eye. Square in shape, the face appeared to be pitted, with sunken cheeks, a heavy nose and thin lips pressed tightly together. The eyes were small and beady. I raised one hand to my flesh in an attempt to dispel the illusion, which I told myself must have come from too little sleep and too much whisky. To my horror, the hand reflected in the glass was not my hand but the hand of a much smaller, squatter man – short-fingered and practical but with long nails. The hallucination lasted for no more than ten or fifteen seconds before I closed my eyes again and began to splash madly in the hope that cold water would snap me out of it. It didn't work. When I looked again the heavy face was glaring at me in an accusing, sneering way, mocking me as though it were saying, 'Splash if you like, you fool, but you will never get away from me.'

With the same reflex action an animal takes to defend its cave, I struck out at the mirror. My fist hit it with such force the blow shook the wall. The glass shattered into a hundred pieces, shredding my right hand so badly that blood spattered all over the bathroom walls and left my body quivering uncontrollably. That's the bad news. The good news was this: the ruse worked. Although the blow came near to crippling my hand and destroyed half the bathroom, it also restored my sanity. When next I looked into the shattered glass in front of me, the strange face had gone. There instead – reflected back at me as if from a great distance – were fragments of myself.

FRAGMENTATION

Tell us, doctors of philosophy, what are the needs
of a man. At least a man needs to be . . . notafraid
nothungry notcold not without love.

John Dos Passos *The Big Money*

Fiona arrived true to form – at noon on Friday to the minute
– looking like a waif in wool. By then I had slept for three
hours, made two phone calls to cancel appointments for the
following week, packed a small bag with shaving kit and
underwear and, using safety pins, chewing gum, coffee
spiked with whisky, and every other temporary measure I
could think of, I stuck the fragments of myself together well
enough, I hoped, to give some semblance of a human being.
I stashed my overnight bag by the entrance, ready to go.
When the buzzer rang, I opened the door and stepped out. I
didn't want the woman inside. I didn't know why and I
didn't care. I gave her a quick hug and, locking the door
behind me, I bolted up the wrought-iron steps as fast as I
could and still avoid the inevitable question, 'What's
wrong?'

It worked. During the drive through the endless suburbs
of London – the blandest town in the world with its Boots
the Chemists and W. H. Smith on every high street all
looking exactly alike – Fiona only twice commented that I
looked 'a bit under the weather' and asked if I had had
enough sleep. Only once did I get stuck with having to

explain anything. It was about the bandage wrapped round my right hand.

'Darling, what have you done?'

'It's just a scratch.'

'A scratch? It looks horrendous.'

'I nicked myself shaving.'

'Oh, my love. You wear a bandage like that on a shaving cut?'

'Yeah. Americans go for sympathy.'

She laughed, reached over with her right hand and touched my cheek. Her fingers smelt like a spring garden, a mixture of wet leaves and lilies. Terrific. It was like coming upon a fresh flower while wandering in a charnel ground. For a moment it made me forget the sleepless nights, the sickness in my belly, the ringing in my ears. All I wanted was to go on smelling this smell and to listen to somebody speak about things simple and ordinary. Fiona was just the person to oblige. I didn't even have to ask. She talked about her parents, she told me about the greenhouse she wanted to buy. She asked if I would help her put it together. Then she told me how much she had missed me, how happy she was that I would be meeting her parents, and how I 'mustn't mind' if her father talked my arm and leg off. Clear, like high dominant chords struck on a finely tuned piano, her voice danced on. The words were spiced with laughter and with anticipation about what we would do together tomorrow. I didn't tell her about what had happened at the newspaper. How could I? I hardly knew myself. Besides, I was glad that this trip which I had been dreading was turning out to be an unexpected relief. I found myself grateful for her presence. It meant I didn't have to think about the weird physical symptoms or the manuscript that lay in the bottom of a locked drawer whispering *coward*.

An hour and a half later we pulled into a narrow

overgrown drive leading to a large Georgian house badly in need of a coat of paint. Fiona's mother, a tall, lean woman with parchment skin, light blue eyes and the widest mouth I have ever seen, greeted us at the door, even before we had a chance to knock. Sylvia. She was followed by a Yorkshire terrier with a bark that would make a Great Dane turn over in its grave. She reached out to shake hands, saw the bandaged fist – which by now was throbbing badly – pulled her hand back, kissed her daughter on the cheek and asked if we would like tea, all in one breath. By the time she had taken the second breath we had been whisked upstairs and shown to our rooms. They were separate but adjoining. Mine was big, complete with chintz curtains, wide plank flooring in polished oak and a chain-and-rung aluminium ladder lying in an incongruous heap beneath the huge window. Seeing my surprise, Sylvia informed me that it was to be thrown out of the window in case of fire.

She left us alone to unpack. I lay down on the bed. That was a mistake. Fiona came to lie next to me. First she chided me about having left my shoes on. Then she noticed that the bandage covering my hand had turned red, and started to make a fuss.

'Darling, your hand. Look at it.'

'It's nothing.'

'Nonsense. Let me see.'

She started to unwrap the bandage. It came away in her hand to reveal a mess of lymph and blood just beneath its surface.

'Good God, Michael, what have you done to yourself?'

I could feel myself helplessly trapped again somewhere between the two worlds in which I had been living since Vienna, since Mirabehn's weird package had come into my possession. I longed to tell someone, especially Fiona, what had been going on. At the same time I knew it was the last thing on earth I could do. I didn't answer. I didn't need to. The hand, by now a swollen mass of dark blood, bruises and misery, told its own tale.

'Michael, what's happened to you?'

'Nothing's happened to me.'

'One doesn't reduce one's fist to pulp shaving.'

'I do.'

'Michael, are you in some kind of trouble?'

'Nope.'

'Michael.' Her voice was beginning to sound desperate. 'Look if you need help, tell me. Did something happen in Vienna? Have you been in a fight?'

'I broke a mirror shaving. It was an accident. I fell against the wall in the bathroom this morning. It is a bit of a mess, that's all.'

'Were you drinking?'

'Maybe a bit.'

'A bit?'

'Yeah, a bit.'

'Michael, nobody does that kind of damage by falling against a mirror.'

I could feel the hairs at the back of my neck rising to attention.

'Fiona, I don't want to talk about it.'

'You don't want to talk about it! God, Michael. You never want to talk about anything. There is always some stupid mystery in your life, isn't there? Something I can't know. God, I get so sick of it.'

She had been lying on her stomach examining the offensive hand. Now she suddenly pulled herself up on to her knees and leapt away from the bed, thrusting my fist downwards. It retaliated by turning the fresh white lace beneath it an oozy pink. I took a handkerchief from my pocket and wrapped it up. Too late. The damage had been done.

55

'Oh God, Michael. Look what we've done. I hate this. I don't want to fight. Not now. What are we going to tell Mummy and Daddy?'

'Fiona, I don't give a damn what you tell anyone. Just get me something to wrap round this thing before I slather your whole precious room in blood.'

She left the room. I lay on the bed like a dumb animal which has wandered too far from its natural habitat – lost and diminished, its paws covered with a muck too heavy to shake off. I could feel a slow and heavy throbbing in the offending hand. Sickness gnawed at my belly. I did my best to remember if I had eaten anything that could have upset me. I couldn't remember when I last ate anything at all. Fiona returned carrying a first-aid kit that looked like it must have come from a mail-order catalogue labelled 'For the woman who has everything'. She ministered to the oozing blob with a patience that would have shamed Florence Nightingale. Fiona was in her element. Five minutes later the throbbing hand had been wrapped up as pretty as a Harrods Christmas box, its ugliness well hidden beneath a shroud of pure white gauze.

'There now, my love.'

'Thanks, Fiona. Look, I'm sorry, I just don't want to talk about it.'

'Not to worry, dearest. I understand.' She stroked my forehead. I hated myself for liking it so much.

'I told Mummy you had injured yourself trying to clear a drain. I just don't want them to worry. Oh, Michael. I so want them to like you and I know you'll like them, if only you give them half a chance.'

I kissed her on the mouth and she giggled, pretending that I was pursuing her against her will. The game did not amuse me. She pretended not to notice.

'Let's go down. Mummy has made tea,' she said. 'Then would you like a walk?'

We drank the tea in silence. Then we took the walk. It led down a farm track, around an old neglected garden surrounded by stone walls so tall it looked like a fortress – 'The winds tend to be awfully high' – then through a wood which smelled of leaf mould. We ended up at the side of a swampy lake where a decrepit rowing boat lay tied to a rotting pier. The pain in my stomach had deepened. The conversation didn't fare much better. We met a local farmer, someone Fiona knew well. She asked my permission to 'pop in at his house and pick up something for dinner'. I gave it, grateful to be left alone.

The afternoon was cool. A brilliant spring sunlight gave the landscape a crystalline look. In such circumstances the English countryside becomes far too perfect a place for fleshy, cumbersome human beings. The pain in my gut was beginning to rage and the ringing in my ear had started to sound like a cross between a sick computer and a nineteenth-century fire alarm. I crouched at the side of the water; thousands of fronds in sugar-green were secretly readying themselves to open. I reached down and broke one off, then felt guilty for having done it. I looked out over the lake. Light blazed on the water. I wanted simply to let it all in, to let it wash me clear of the past few days. I closed my eyes and took a deep breath. Visions of black birds devouring carrion in a square near Lincoln's Inn Fields flashed across my brain. I heard the voice of an old woman and saw her magnificent long tapered fingers. 'You *must* take it.'

When we got back to the house Daddy showed up, complete with two springer spaniels. He was carrying a pigeon with a damaged foot. After introductions, during which Sylvia clucked her compassion for the bird, then carried it to the kitchen while Fiona went off to retrieve the unforgettable first-aid kit, George and I were left alone to do men's things in a room panelled in dark wood and heavy with the smell of leather and tobacco. In the first five minutes it became obvious to both of us that the only thing we had in common was the need for a drink. We had one. Then another. By the time we got to the bottom of the third, we had become great pals. Wisely the women stayed away. My stomach was starting to feel better. Even the hand had stopped throbbing.

George told me all about his pigeon racing, a hobby which with each sip of Cragganmore sounded more and more fascinating. I congratulated myself in the cliché language one always finds so reassuring after a few drinks that I was now out of the woods. Just when I was about to learn from George how unjust the rules are for pigeon owners who live several miles from official measuring stations, dinner was announced. He gave me a conspiratorial smile and refilled our glasses before we left the study.

Things were looking up. Especially Fiona. She came in wearing a little peach silk number that slid over her soft breasts in a way that made me forgive every complaint I ever had against her. Her long hair was pulled up off her white neck and held precariously in place with a big pin. I ached to pull it out. We sat down to supper in a small room overlooking the garden. Obviously not the dining room, it was ideal for the warm grain-based intimacy we were all beginning to feel. The salmon was served with a rich Australian red wine which, in my generosity of spirit, I decided showed a remarkable degree of imagination. I praised my hosts liberally for their good taste. Fiona's eyes sparkled. So did the conversation. It touched on all the subjects about which any cultured person has a well-formed opinion – those covered in the pages of last week's *Sunday Times*. Then, about the time we were getting ready to consume the fruit salad and I was looking forward to the port, all hell broke loose.

The fading light had turned the garden a golden pink. Sylvia had just reprimanded Fiona's father for telling the same story three times in the space of an hour and Fiona had excused herself to make some strong coffee. My American camaraderie was beginning to wear thin. My body had begun to feel uncomfortable again, as though the clothes I was wearing were all the wrong size. I needed to stretch my legs, so I said something I hoped sounded suitably full of admiration about their house, got up from my chair and – being careful to walk with a deportment I hoped would give witness to my sobriety – went over to the window, pretending to admire the garden. That was when I saw him. Or thought I saw him: a lean figure that looked too much like the man behind me in the immigration line for comfort. It was only in my vision for a few seconds – the time it would take for somebody to cross over the tractor path on the right that led towards the walled garden where we had walked earlier. He was dressed in an ill-fitting black coat, as out of place in the gentle evening light of a spring evening in the country as I would have been caught wearing full combat gear in Fiona's parents' drawing room. He moved with a smoothness that made me shudder, stepped over a stile and – just before entering the woods – turned to look directly at me then smiled.

A sound like the referee's bell rang. Anger and fear, those ancient opponents, leapt off their stools somewhere in my head and charged to the centre of the ring ready to tear each other limb from limb inside my body. My brain began to burn. I remarked with detached curiosity that it was surprising to find the smells of a Central American jungle in this small room. Then I realised that somehow I had become involved in a game that did not amuse me. Not when the bastards have trained you as a killer. After all, it serves their purposes. They just program it all in. Nobody tells you how to get rid of it later. But, what the hell, that's *your* problem, not theirs. You figure you can drop out – just walk away from it all. Then year after year you find yourself pounding pavements, your thoughts caressing images of destruction. Or deadly and unsuspected like a timed explosive, you stand leaning against a Georgian window at dusk while somebody makes the coffee.

'Shall we go into the drawing room?'

Sylvia's voice was thin and distant. But I heard it. A bridge back. My eyes glazed with fear, I turned away from the window. The table was still there – all covered in white linen and crumpled napkins, flakes of French bread and wineglasses half empty. At that moment it seemed to me nothing could be more beautiful. I cleared my throat, crossed the room and managed to simulate a smile. Then I reached out with a hand that shook. I only wanted to touch the linen with my fingers to feel its starchy whiteness, to celebrate the way in which a small drop of wine had marked its purity. This tiny spot became for me a symbol of human intervention in the world of things, of the imperfection that makes life possible. George wrongly assumed I needed more wine. Taking my glass in woozy fingers – in an attempt to keep up with his thirsty guest, he had drunk more than he intended – he filled it. This simple social gesture of generosity brought tears to my eyes. I coughed and wiped a hand across them. Then I lied, saying something about how the country air always gives me hay fever. Fiona came in smiling.

'Coffee is ready – real Italian coffee. Michael, come on.'

I left the freshly poured glass of wine on the table. She took my hand with the gesture a good nanny uses towards a favourite child who has done something naughty and led me down the hall into a long, sparsely furnished room where the welcome fragrance of coffee mingled with an odour of dust.

Except for two small sofas on which we sat next to the fire, all the chairs were covered with white sheets. Its large windows were hung with half-shredded brocade curtains that must have been two hundred years old. Night had come, turning the room dark. But a fire blazed and dark wood tables polished by the generations of ordinary people who had used them – to lay books on, to drink tea from, to hold candles – made the room a welcome place. Sylvia poured coffee.

'I hope you will forgive the state of the room, Michael,' she said. 'We seldom use it when we're alone. It's too big for the two of us. But we thought you might like to see it.'

'It is magnificent,' I said.

'The curtains are original,' Sylvia went on. 'Last year we got a quote for replacing them – £15,000 – it was out of the question. So we decided to keep them just as they are. The trouble is, we don't dare clean them in case they turn to powder.'

'Sylvia, they're *perfect* just as they are. It's one of the most beautiful rooms I have ever seen. Don't ever clean them,' I said.

'How very kind of you to say so, Michael.' She poured another cup of coffee. George, sitting propped against a big cushion at the edge of the fire, closed his eyes and began to wheeze. Sylvia looked at him, raised her lean shoulders and let them fall again. Then she placed the cup and saucer on the table in front of him and rose to her feet.

'Do you like music?' she asked.

'Mummy, I think–' broke in Fiona.

'I find it heaven,' sang Sylvia, 'Such bliss listening to Bach while one is reading, don't you think?' She walked to the corner of the room furthest away from us, picked up a record, read the label, evidently with some difficulty for the light where she stood was poor, and put it down again.

'I used to play, you know,' she said. 'At one time I was considered quite an accomplished pianist.'

George snorted, shaking off his stupor long enough to open his eyes. He looked straight ahead, like the dormouse in *Alice in Wonderland*, apparently without seeing anything, then he closed them again. His chin sank to his chest and he began to snore. Like a shark rising to the bait, his content, relaxed sounds triggered a lightly concealed fury in Sylvia. Her voice grew thin.

'Each composer has his own special quality, don't you think? she said. 'Fiona is very fond of Chopin, aren't you dear?' Fiona, if she intended to answer, was given no opportunity to do so. 'I myself prefer Handel,' said Sylvia. 'He is so clean and ordered. Let's see.'

She opened a cabinet and shuffled through its contents with the kind of irritation a conscientious housewife betrays when looking for a rag to mop up something spilt on her kitchen floor.

'The romantics are such a bore, always moaning on about something. So bombastic.' She pulled out what appeared to be a well-worn album, drew a record from it and put it into the machine. George snored on.

'Damn,' she said. 'George.' No reply. 'George.' Still nothing. '*George*.' Sylvia's voice spiralled each time she repeated her husband's name, becoming ever more thin and shrill.

George blinked, pulled the collar of his open shirt up on both sides as though desperate to cover his collapsing neck and replied, 'Yes, my dear.'

'George, come and do something about this. I never could manage these mechanical gadgets. I've just no patience . . . no patience.'

George rose from his sofa, unfurling his soft body the way a sweater unfolds when you take it from its place on the shelf, and moved to his wife's side. Sylvia relinquished the irritating machine, and returned to refill my cup. A chime sounded somewhere in a distant part of the house. I wondered what time it was.

Moments later Beethoven's music gushed from a speaker somewhere across the large room. The Sixth, the Seventh? I couldn't be sure. Sylvia jumped. While fiddling with the dials on the machine she had evidently turned up the volume without knowing it.

'George,' she snapped. 'Turn that thing down.' Then to me, 'Beethoven's Seventh. Along with the Pastoral, it is the only symphony of his I can *bear* to listen to. The rest are all so pompous. Don't you think?'

George readjusted the volume in keeping with propriety. But instead of returning to our little group he remained near the speaker, evidently so that he could hear better.

I didn't answer. The four of us sat in silence for several minutes while the first movement played itself through. From the very first note, the mellowness of the whisky and the comfort of the beautiful room in which we sat had started to fade. They were replaced by mounting pressure. At first I could not locate where it came from. It was as though a heavy cloud had begun to twist round my body, creating discomfort against my skin, or as though all my perceptions were being filtered through some unfamiliar reality – another time or place or another set of genes – certainly not my own. The cloud swirled around me, enfolding me deeper and deeper within it, until eventually I could not even hear clearly what was being played. The room now seemed to be filled not with air but with something thicker and heavier, something that made us all go silent. Fiona touched my shoulder, smiling like a child who needs reassurance. She could not have been more than two feet from me, yet when I looked at her it was as though I were seeing her face down the wrong end of a powerful telescope.

63

It seemed to me as though everything that had gone before during this day and evening had been a lie, and that by allowing myself to sit on their sofa, to drink their coffee, I was continuing to perpetrate that lie.

Sylvia picked up her needlepoint. Moving closer to the light at the far end of the sofa, she began to sew. The first movement ended. There was a momentary pause before the second began. Then disembodied notes and chords coming at me from the end of an ancient corridor swelled into a dark fabric of sound whose warp of intense joy became entangled with a woof of unbearable sorrow.

Still at the other end of the room, and by now carried away by what he was hearing, George leaned over and began to increase the volume the way a greedy man pours more and more hot fudge syrup on his ice cream all the while hoping that mother will not notice. Sylvia sat with her sewing, lost in abstraction, seemingly unaware of what was going on. The music grew louder and louder. Whether it was George's self-indulgent adjustments or my own imagination I could not be sure. But by now every sense of relaxation or comfort had disappeared from my body as the music wound its path through my flesh. The sounds seemed to open a door to another universe – one that had nothing to do with this beautiful old room, with Sylvia's needlepoint, George's hot fudge sauce or Fiona's shining eyes. This music pulled at my guts – not in any figurative sense but literally as though drawing the muscles in my middle outward, making me tremble in my bowels, filling my viscera with terror and fascination. Still it seemed to grow louder.

That smell. It was back again – the steaming jungle – a promise of life too rich, too demanding, a dripping maw into which I could feel myself being sucked. Like the un-harnessed power of the rainforest, I felt I was being drawn down, down into a strange fecundity which dissolves everything so that you don't know who you are or what you might do. That's what they want – the programmers, those who train to kill. Dissolve it all. Let everything become fluid so there is no form, no shape, nothing you can define or know or hold on to. Then they move in. It is the road to madness which each of us spends his life avoiding. No wonder it is so easy for them to turn men into whatever mechanical beings they wish. I remembered the *replicants* in the science fiction detective film. One had sat across from his interrogator while he was asked questions designed to elicit an emotional response and therefore to reveal whether he was human or an android. 'You are walking in a desert,' says the interrogator. 'There is a tortoise lying on its back. It is completely helpless. Only you can save it from being baked by the sun. But you're not helping. Why is that?' The confusion of the android. He doesn't understand. He sits like a helpless insect while his torturer tears wings from his body. All he wants is to live. That is all any of us want. So he pulls the trigger of a gun so powerful it blows a hole through the chest of his interrogator and sends his body crashing through the wall behind him.

The music continued to swell. The textures of the room had come alive. I noticed that the hairs on the carpet beneath my feet had taken on momentous proportions, their size so distorted that they appeared to be a forest. With the toe of my shoe I played curiously with these trees the way a giant might. Then I took a sip of coffee. Maybe that would clear my head. Black and bitter –infinitely beautiful – too beautiful to bear. I set the cup down and rubbed my fingers against the tapestry covering the arm of the sofa. I found to my horror that I could feel each separate thread. It was as though a veil had been lifted. What lay behind it I had no idea. Quickly I withdrew my hand but it made no difference. Everything in the room had taken on the same living, breathing quality. Meanwhile the warp and woof of the music penetrated deeper and deeper into my body. This tapestry of sound had touched some sleeping power within me – an unknown, unpredictable and completely ungovernable force of nature. Each successive phrase eked it further out from my core. What the power was or what it might do I did not know but I was conscious of a rising pressure from within thrusting outwards. I had to move. I could not bear to sit for another moment in that room. I rose, stumbled and knocked over the coffee table, showering Sylvia with hot black fluid. She screeched and leapt to her feet. I grabbed her shoulders in my two hands and shook her.

'Shut up,' I growled. 'Just shut up.' I could not stand the sound of her voice. She had to stop no matter what I had to do to make her.

'Michael!' screamed Fiona.

I pushed against Sylvia's chest. She went down hard against the sofa and was silent. I rushed across the room to where George stood and, taking hold of the speaker from which the music came, raised it up in both hands then brought it down again against the floor. It made a strange squeaking sound. Then silence.

'Michael, my God, what are you doing?' Fiona got up and ran towards me.

'Get out of my way, Fiona.' She paid no attention. 'Get out of my way – now.' She stopped dead, her hands hanging loose at the sides of her limp body. I headed for the door. When I got there, like a destroyer pausing to survey the extent of his devastation, I turned.

The room was silent – another moment in time captured on celluloid – no more breathing furniture, no over-rich tapestry, no forests for carpets and the three people who remained in it stood as still and silent as the furnishings.

'God forgive me,' I said. Then I opened the door, ran up the stairs to my room, and without even stopping to think about the absurdity of what I was doing, threw the aluminium ladder out of the window and climbed down into the black of the night.

DISSOLUTION

> The two worlds, the divine and the human . . . are
> actually one. The realm of the gods is a forgotten
> dimension of the world we know.

Joseph Campbell *The Hero With A Thousand Faces*

I ended up hitch-hiking back to London. It took three truck
drivers, a do-good missionary who picked me up in
Richmond and was sure he had my soul saved by Hammer-
smith, and a two hour walk from Shepherd's Bush to get
back to the flat. By then it was 4 a.m. My body showed no
signs of fatigue. Nor had I thought about what had passed
only hours before in Fiona's parents' house. There was only
one thing that obsessed me: unlocking the drawer and
opening Mirabehn's parcel. This I did within two minutes
of entering the flat. My hands trembled as I turned the key
and slowly pulled out the package. So intense was the
silence of that early morning and so heightened were my
senses of touch and smell as I began to untie the ragged
string and to open the faded red cloth, that it seemed as
though the contents of this package, whatever it was, had
become a living, breathing thing.

The parcel contained two yellowed manuscripts. The first
had been written by a delicate hand in German and then –
probably much later – painstakingly translated into English
between each line by someone, presumably Mirabehn,
whose writing was small, aristocratic and meticulous. The

second was in German alone, written entirely in a heavy black Gothic script. It had a wild erratic quality as though it had been recorded by someone who was ill or under terrible strain. It would have given trouble to anyone not familiar with an eighteenth- or nineteenth-century hand. I looked closely at it and found that, owing to my limited familiarity with the German language – my only reading had been confined to wrestling with scientific papers in medical libraries – I was completely unable to decipher its meaning. I set it aside. Then, sitting slumped over the desk, I began to read the English translation. It seemed to be a letter written in the middle of the last century.

At the top of the page was one word – 'Ludwig' – composed in the same fine aristocratic writing. Underneath in the same hand but in smaller letters were the translated words: 'a letter written from his childhood friend to Andreas Wawruch, the physician who attended L's last illness'. That was all. The German script seemed to glimmer, to swell and shrink as I stared at it, the way a dark secret pulls at you when you come upon it – a secret you don't want to know but from which you cannot turn away no matter how you try. Mirabehn had asked me, 'Do you *know* Beethoven?' I had not understood her question. But it seemed I was about to know him – maybe far better than anyone would ever want to.

As I began to read, I had the sense that I was breaching the fine membrane I had been clinging to – the film that had been separating the two worlds in which I had been living. I knew I was about to leave behind every certainty of day-to-day life. I seemed to be stepping through a mirror into the strange reversed universe that lies behind every silvery surface. I was certain of only one thing: there could be no turning back.

Koblenz
19 May, 1842

Dear Dr Wawruch,

Your letter arrived a week ago. It has alarmed me greatly. Nay, I must go further. It has made me question every belief I hold about the nature of man's integrity. Are we not each of us separate beings bounded by a skin of self which separates us from our outside world? Or have I as a physician all these years simply been living under the illusion that this is so?

I know little of you, Dr Wawruch. Steffen von Breuning wrote to me of you and your work fifteen years ago, before Beethoven's death, praising the care which you gave to our dear friend those last four months of his life. At that time I also received three letters from yourself requesting information about his illness and his life. I must ask your forgiveness for never having acknowledged their receipt. Yours was, at the time, not a demand I found easy to fulfil. You requested that I share with you not only the outer details of Ludwig's life of which I have personal knowledge, which in any case are now publicly available in *Biographische Notizen über Ludwig van Beethoven* – the book Ferdinand Ries and myself published some five years hence, but also my most intimate reflections of my late friend – what I knew of his dreams, his longings and the diaries of his youth. Such information, Dr Wawruch, he left in my care in deep trust and privacy almost forty years ago. They were, until now, something I never intended to share with anyone. Even Eleonore, my dearest wife and sister to Steffen von Breuning, has been made privy to little apart from that which she herself knows as a result of her having been present, and of course she has *never* seen the diaries.

Perhaps my reticence will be more understandable if I tell

you that I am a private man, Dr Wawruch, wholly moderate, one might say even somewhat old-fashioned in my ways. I value order and am of a temper which I hope is both healthy and humane. I have attempted to be a good husband to my wife – a fine woman of kindness and breeding. I have also attempted to make a worthy contribution to my profession. I do not relish the thought that the order which I have so painstakingly established in my life might be threatened by the irrational, and the inexplicable. In the months before his death I had also heard of you from Louis himself, for that is the name by which I called him from the time of our youth in Bonn, by letter once or twice. His missals were full of rancour and rage over your inability to heal him. Judging from the suffering and mental aberrations he experienced during those final months, which you so fully described in your recent letter, it is little wonder that my dear friend wrote so scathingly about your ministrations. Dr Wawruch, you must not blame yourself. Take heart in the knowledge that Ludwig hated all physicians for their impotence – all bar myself. But then perhaps I was able to remain his friend only because I never had occasion to treat him.

Your request for information about my friend's previous existence and your description of occurences surrounding Ludwig's presence in your own life both before and after his death – had I received them even half a year ago, Dr Wawruch, I would have refused to respond to what you have written to me in the belief that it was the product of a deranged mind, so fantastic are the events you describe. I can no longer do so. This is the reason: in recent months I too have been witness to similar experiences. I have without apparent cause suffered physical and psychic symptoms which, especially after hearing your own report, have shaken my certainty about the nature of reality to its very core. More troubling still, I too received a visit from a man dressed in black whose physical appearance was virtually the same as he whom you describe in your letter.

This occurred on a Tuesday evening three months ago. I particularly recall that it was a Tuesday because on Tuesdays I am always late home. Not long after my last student left the dissection chamber, I was busy preparing notes for a lecture to be given the following day when I looked up from my desk to find this tall gentleman standing before me. His face was long and his eyes narrow. The cryptic message which he delivered still chills my bones.

'Silence is the essence of safety,' he said. 'What is past is past. Let whatever secret knowledge you have accrued of your deceased friend be forgotten.'

'I beg your pardon, sir,' I replied, assuming him to be a visitor to the university who had wandered into the wrong room in search of one of my colleagues. 'I think there must be some mistake. Whom do you seek?'

'There are no mistakes,' was his reply, 'unless it is *you* who choose to make them, Professor Wegeler.'

I dislike riddles, Dr Wawruch. Nor do I relish being addressed by name by a man of sinister mien who makes no attempt to explain his presence. I rose from my desk to remove my spectacles. For no more than an instant did I turn my back on him while searching for their case. Yet when again I turned back he had disappeared.

Soon after that evening I began to have dreams of Ludwig – but not Ludwig as I had known him. The face was older, more square. The head was heavier, yet gaunt. His hair, which had once been so wonderfully dark, was now wiry, long and dirty grey. This Ludwig looked like an old bull or lion. In my dreams he kept imploring me to tell the truth. The wild eyes were those of a tortured animal caught in a snare yet unable to extricate its paw. What 'truth' it was he demanded that I tell I do not know. Neither, Dr Wawruch, have I any notion of what Ludwig looked like before he died for we had not met for almost thirty years.

Around the same time I also began to experience inexplicable symptoms, much like your own – disturbances of vision, alterations in my physical body, cramp, migraine headaches. Then, eight or nine weeks ago, like clockwork at the stroke of three each morning I began to be visited by a spirit which claimed to be Ludwig himself. It pleaded with me, begged me and filled me with fear, demanding that I tell the truth. The first few evenings during which this occurred I must tell you, Dr Wawruch, I doubted my sanity. I knew I could speak of it to no one, not even to my beloved wife. It was after a week of this that the illnesses began – the most appalling stomach and bowel trouble I have ever experienced. I began to bleed profusely in much the way you describe that Ludwig bled fifteen years ago. None of my doctors' skills could stem the tide of these symptoms. It was almost as though whatever had hold of me was ruthlessly insisting that I accept the experience and acknowledge the visitation. Dr Wawruch, I tell you truly I feared I was going to die. I have yet to recover from the enervating anaemia which ensued. It was only when in my irrationality I came to accept that there was some inexplicable 'truth' in these hauntings that my condition began to subside. Does this of which I speak make any sense?

I sit here reading the strange words before me. Make sense? None of it makes sense. No more sense than anything that has happened to me since Mirabehn's damnable package came into my hands. The talk of dreams, the description of Ludwig's head, Wegeler's disturbances in vision. What does it have to do with what's happening to me? There has to be a logical explanation to this. I must keep a cool head. Damn it, I'm going to find it.

However one tries to explain what was happening I had, spontaneously, and without my acquiescence or understanding, become entangled in a web of phenomenological energies difficult and threatening to my work and my life. After three weeks of such torture I was forced to request leave from the university in an attempt to gather the threads of my psychic and physical well-being lest I become permanently deranged. My respite, by the grace of God, was successful in restoring equilibrium. So much so that until I received your letter last Thursday I had assumed that the matter, like some strange aberration of nature, was finished once and for all.

I do not know what any of this means. I must be quite frank with you, Dr Wawruch, I do not *care* to know what it means. Therefore I ask that after reading this record you destroy it or at least destroy all evidence that might enable anyone to trace its origins. I simply cannot risk the safety of my wife Eleonore, who loved Ludwig as I did. This request made, and I presume accepted, I will now try to put together a few memories of my dear friend's youth which, for reasons which will become clear, did not appear in our biography of him. I will also, as you have requested, try to inform you of possible social and political connections which Ludwig once had and which may or may not be relevant. Finally I will attempt to convey to you what little I know about his previous illnesses, most of which information, alas, was gathered second hand.

Let us begin with the illness.

I am much taken with your hypothesis. I find the notion that there may be within the human organism an entire system designed and dedicated to the protection of self and the integrity of the human body quite fascinating. I too have read the work of Herbart. But what you have suggested takes scientific conjecture about human consciousness considerably further. I am also in sympathy with the notion that a man's intention or will may influence physical well-being for good or ill. Yet the record of Ludwig's illness, which you have so thoroughly and generously shared with me, I find very troubling indeed. Whatever its meaning, and I am certainly not qualified to say, a crack in the vase of consciousness is real whether caused by a fall, an earthquake or an acid bath. And any crack presents one with three questions: If it is real then what was its cause? What helped to maintain the crack afterwards? And – perhaps most important of all in view of what has taken place not only to Ludwig himself but to you and me, as well as, may God forbid, to others – what does the crack have to teach us about other vases?

The shifts in mood during his last illness about which you have written were present from our earliest days together. None the less they always took me by surprise. Despite my not inconsiderable skill at rational analysis, I could never unravel the mystery of what provoked them. I found it impossible even to chart their occurrences with any accuracy. This, I suspect, was for two reasons: first because their coming and going was so unexpected that it was impossible to find resonance for them in what I knew to be true of the rest of life, second because I think at times all of us are guilty of concealing from ourselves that which, because we cannot explain it, makes us feel decidedly uncomfortable. However, there was probably something else operating as well. I frequently sensed that Ludwig himself was made desperately uncomfortable by his unexpected shifts. He tended to behave either as if they had not happened or as though he had no recollection of them, especially when he had suddenly flown into a rage and abused someone. Then he would be overtaken by a remorse so deep he would either apologise profusely to whomever he had offended or avoid meeting them completely for weeks, months or even years afterwards. I confess, Dr Wawruch, that in many ways I failed in my duty as a friend to him. His personality was robust, yet I fear I frequently avoided speaking to him about these *shifts* for fear of angering or alienating him. I much regret such cowardice. I must tell you truthfully that I have never been a courageous man.

In my early recollections of his life there is much to lend weight to your hypothesis. Haydn, who was Ludwig's tutor, used to say of him that he was a man of many heads, many hearts and many souls. As well as the *shifts*, Ludwig had moods which were, by and large, inexplicable. At times it was simply hopeless to try to reason with him. And his memory, as you have suggested, was oft-times poor. On one occasion in Vienna I went with him to the house of a bootmaker in the Bräunerstrasse – a man renowned for the splendid leather shoes he crafted. The shop was small and poorly lit, but tidy as a sewing box. Each piece of leather, each tiny buttonhook had been carefully placed in its proper position. The bootmaker was showing Ludwig pairs of boots in various lengths. Ludwig would pick them up and smell the leather, then lay them down again. He seemed little interested. His eyes, I noticed, were shining in a manner altogether unnatural. This strange glazed look would come over Ludwig from time to time, usually without warning. When it did, he would often begin to quote words he had read or heard. That morning, I believe, it was some notion gleaned from Mirabeau. He was speaking about 'brothers of the higher grade'.

'We must change things, Wegeler,' Ludwig said. 'We must free them.'

'Who?' I asked.

'Why, the slaves, the peasants,' he replied. 'We must end the servitude of men to the soil. And banish all the customs and privileges that lower humanity – the nobility of the natural man.'

He spoke with fervour and at great volume. The boot-maker looked on, wondering, I suspect, why his small shop had been chosen as the stage for such histrionics.

'Would you perhaps prefer shorter boots, Herr Beethoven?' he ventured.

Ludwig ignored the question.

'The Corvées, *this unjust and unpaid day's labour each vassal owes his feudal lord*, Wegeler, under the condition of an equable equivalent, all the corporations, all the maîtrises *they will all be finished once and for all*. . . . You know what I mean. Don't stand there looking so puzzled!'

The bootmaker, concerned that unless some decision could be extracted he would lose his sale, thrust forward yet another pair of boots and said: 'I do believe, Herr Beethoven, that black would be all the better for you. May I suggest. . . .'

'We must get rid of the burdens imposed on industry and commerce by customs,' Ludwig rattled on. 'We must banish excise duties and taxes. We must procure a universal toleration for all religious opinion. It is the revolution, Wegeler, the revolution. Now, when man's courage is most urgently needed, we must *act* if we are to bring a new enlightened order to all Europe.'

Then turning to the bootmaker, a tiny man, whose brow was crumpled in confusion, he said: 'Yes, these, these. These are fine. Do these for me. How much?'

The bootmaker scribbled a figure on a small sheet of paper and handed it to Ludwig.

'Above all we must procure universal toleration for all religious opinions,' said Ludwig. 'Do you not agree? We must tear away the arms of superstition. We must favour liberty of the press. Yes, that, above all.'

76

Crumpling the scrap of paper and slipping it into the pocket of his greatcoat without examining it Ludwig turned to the little man, looked right through him and said, 'Send these to my apartment by Friday. By Friday, you hear?' He turned away swiftly and, slamming the door behind him, left the shop.

The next morning I was breakfasting with him – he was, by the way, an excellent coffee maker – when a messenger arrived carrying the highly polished new boots. Seated in the adjacent room, I could hear a serious argument taking place. I stepped into the entrance hall to find that Ludwig had the youth by the scruff of the neck and was about to throw him down the stairs.

'Don't try to pawn your wares off on me, I'll have none of them,' he said.

I moved quickly to prevent injury.

'But these are the boots you ordered yesterday, Louis, don't you remember?' I said.

He turned towards me, his eyes taking on an uncomprehending look.

'Did I? Oh well then, of course. How could I forget.'

So he gave the young man several coins in payment for his harshness and apologised profusely, offering him a cup of coffee. The messenger, quite terrified by now, declined, and was politely shown to the door. Ludwig was frequently apologising for his behaviour.

First and foremost, I was Ludwig's friend. Many were the years we spent together. I loved him as a younger brother. It was in 1782 that we became 'officially' acquainted. He was then twelve years old and already a composer. I was seventeen. Thereafter we remained in very close contact. Then in September 1787 I travelled to Vienna to complete my medical studies and was absent from Bonn for two years. On my return in October 1789 again we became cordial friends until he departed for Vienna towards the end of 1792. I followed him in October of 1794, where, happily reunited, we passed hardly a week without meeting. I finally returned to Bonn in 1796. After that we never met again, although we kept in touch by letter. Neither of us was a meticulous correspondent, Dr Wawruch, since each was intent upon making his mark in the world and that requires a great deal of one's time and effort. I did, however, have access not only to those messages he himself sent me by post but also to letters he had written to some of our other friends in Bonn, so an unbroken chain of communication between us was by no means necessary to maintain our affectionate relations.

I speak of our first meeting in 1782 as 'official' because in many ways it may also be important for you to know about the peculiar 'meeting' which took place long before. Through no fault of my own, fate ensured that I knew Ludwig in some of the most intimate details of his life long before he knew me. I have often in the intervening years wondered why I was singled out for such knowledge. It is something I would far rather not have been given.

Have you ever been an eavesdropper, Dr Wawruch? This is, I suspect, a question which I need not ask of someone of your character and disposition. But you see, sometimes one cannot help but eavesdrop. The practice is a dangerous one. Once you become privy to events to which, by every rule of propriety, you have no right, you are put in a most peculiar position. You know things which you do not wish to know yet this knowing is indelibly etched on to the substance of your being so that – no matter how you wish you could go back and excise the memory of having entered the secret, forbidden world of another – you cannot erase what has been written in time.

As a youth I would on occasion visit the house of a friend,

Rudolph Windeck, whose father was burgomaster. His house faced on to a courtyard at the other side of which lay the apartment in which Ludwig, then a mere six or seven years old, lived with his father, his mother and two younger brothers. The chamber in which I slept in Rudolph's house was small, just large enough to accommodate a narrow bed and tiny table on which Rudolph's mother always placed a delicate bouquet of flowers. The little room was an unusual wedge shape. Having been added as an afterthought just at the edge of the courtyard, it had been constructed aslant to fit within narrow confines. It had but one tiny window, so high that one could not, in normal circumstances, look out of it. I found, however, that when I climbed upon the mattress and then further up on to the heavy wooden bedstead I could just peer through.

Because of the strange angle the room made with the courtyard, and because it was at the top of the house, my window-gazing yielded an unimpeded view of a first-floor room of the Beethoven house adjacent – a chamber in which a clavier stood. It was dark, bare-floored and sparsely furnished with ugly pieces of this and that, a room arranged by someone of no aesthetic awareness and meagre means.

One winter night I was awakened by a most awful din. It must have been past midnight for the lamps had long been extinguished. At first I was frightened. Quickly my reason overtook me and, wrapping the coverlet snugly about my body, I climbed sleepily on to the bedstead, opened the shutters and peered from the window to see what was taking place.

I looked down into the room across the courtyard and was surprised to find a boy considerably smaller and younger than myself being dragged across the floor by a rather portly man who seemed to have hold of him by the ear. The child was whimpering and whining. The man deposited him with considerable force on a high stool before the musical instrument and shouted, 'I told you to play, and play you shall when I command it.'

The child was trembling either with fear or cold. He raised his hands to the keys and began to play Bach's 'Prelude in C'. When he came to the end of the fourth or fifth stanza his small fingers slipped from the keyboard, creating discord. The man, whom by now I was beginning to suspect had drunk more of some heady wine than he could comfortably hold, did not let this pass without notice. He raised a huge hand and cuffed the child across the ear, knocking him with one blow to a far corner of the room. The boy stopped his whimpering, raised a hand to the offended ear, and looked up.

'Move', ordered the man. 'I say, move.'

Until that moment I had not realised that someone else was also in the room – a tall lean man dressed all in black in a somewhat theatrical manner. He seemed to exert a powerful influence over Beethoven's father, who would look towards him time and again for approval. The man's face was hideous – pale as parchment, long and lean – and his eyes – I shall never forget those eyes – they were the thinnest eyes I had ever seen.

'the thinnest eyes I had ever seen' . . . I read the words yet want to deny that I have read them. I go back and read them again. Wegeler's description of the man comes far too close to the weird character who stood behind me in the line at the airport, the phantom man I saw through Fiona's parents' window, even Wegeler's own dark visitor at the university. A flush of heat passes over my head. I get up to open the window. I need a drink.

Now he emerged from the shadows, laid a hand on the shoulder of the first man, and said something to him. I could not make out what. The older man then lifted his own hand to cover that of his friend in a gesture which at once expressed weariness, resignation and affection. By now the boy had picked himself up from the floor and was moving toward the instrument. I could see his face clearly since it was caught in the light of the lamp. Round it was, with a heavy jaw, a trait of Ludwig's that one could make out even at that tender age, – a face absolutely immobile. The jaw was set hard. Although the cheeks were covered with tears it betrayed not the least expression of emotion. The child sat down once again and resumed his piece, playing steadily, firmly and without mistake as would a mechanical music box. Then the man, whom I assumed to be the boy's father, crossed the room until he was standing behind the child and laid both hands on the boy's shoulders. The child gave no acknowledgement of his touch. He simply continued to play, absolutely without fault.

By now I had grown not a little cold, standing as I was on tiptoe leaning out of the tiny window in the hopes of seeing and hearing better. I shivered, pulled the coverlet around my body and, bending my knees, sank back into bed. Within seconds I found myself enveloped by sleep. I began to dream. The dreams were filled with Johannes Bach's glorious music played by unseen hands. On the morrow when I reported all of this to my hostess over bread and cheese she merely nodded.

'Yes, yes, it is so. This is not the first time, dear Franz. They are strange, the Beethovens, hardly a family at all in many ways. Have another slice of cheese before you go.'

I did not see Ludwig again until the day of our 'official' meeting five years later. Well, that is not quite true. I did three or four times catch sight of him darting here or there about the streets of our town. He never walked. He scurried like a defiant dog, slightly cowed but with a posture that told the world it had best leave him alone lest it get bitten. I, with my shameful nocturnal memory, was only too willing to do so. I had no desire to make further acquaintance of this child, five years my junior. There was nothing I could do for him. Also I was very taken up with Latin and Greek and with my natural science collections for I was determined to gain marks that would enable me to better myself. I am not proud of this fact, Dr Wawruch. I confess that many have been the ways in which I have set aside the duties of true friendship in favour of nurturing self-interest and establishing my career: not without certain rewards, it must be said. For does not the world look after those who bow down to the gods of practicality, reason and skill?

I have been fortunate to have received a certain amount of recognition for these efforts even from an early age. At the age of twenty-nine I was appointed Rector Magnificus of the University of Bonn. Like so many things in life, the honour turned out to be both a blessing and a curse. As Rector of the University it was I who was obliged to sign the decree of the Academic Senate designed to curtail the spread of hospital fever by forbidding our students to attend Napoleon's soldiers captured at Landrecies, Quesnoi and Condé who were then in the process of being transported to Vienna. Supplies earmarked for prisoners were meant to be brought to them by various clergymen. But the Moniteur who supervised the occupation did not take lightly to the decree. Ten or twelve days after it was issued he branded me, without so much as a hearing, a 'rabid enemy of the Republic'. From then on even the most circumspect behaviour on my part could not redress the harm for which I had been blamed. Ah, Dr Wawruch, those were evil times! The people's representative in Bonn gave orders that he was to be addressed with the familiar 'Du' form. It seemed that *la queue de Robespierre* was little less dangerous than had been his head. At that moment, I decided it was advisable to save my own. I recognised that I could not pursue my university career in the midst of such political turmoil so I uprooted and settled in Koblenz, where I have lived and practised medicine ever since.

Since my earliest childhood, Dr Wawruch, I have loved order. Life has not been easy for me in these times of unrest. One still hears talk of revolution, of man's freedom, of equality and fraternity, but what fraternity can there be when soldiers are marauding through the streets destroying every mark of culture and beauty?

I smile at Wegeler's words, wondering what the poor old man would make of terrorist bombs all over London, pregnant women raped at the side of highways, little old ladies mugged for their pensions, and secret police running drugs into government airfields. He didn't know he had it so good.

When Ludwig and I were young, Bonn was a much gentler town – a town made rich by its traditions, and beautiful by its position on the western bank of the holy Rhine. Scores of green-gardened inns dotted our streets. Outside the city were walls that have stood since medieval times topped by the bastion *Alter Zoll* where customs officials extracted their tolls. As children we often paraded the banks calling out to ships as they sailed by or watching horses draw heavily laden barges from faraway places.

We had a wonderful market-place – a triangle in the midst of the town on one side of which stood the handsome city hall. There as children we played hide-and-seek amongst the carts. I used to love the noise and the smells of the animals and the way in which the streets ran with water after a heavy rainfall. Of course, not all was beautiful. The poorer people of our town were forced to endure unpaved streets and shabbily built houses which could not survive five winters. An intolerable stench, even to our young noses, was created by people performing their daily functions in the streets and throwing offal from their windows to feed the chickens and pigs that wandered about in the muck. Across our sacred river lay the Seven Mountains, a collection of craggy hills where I used to wander, knapsack over my shoulder, collecting scientific specimens – beetles, birds' eggs, rocks and flowers. It was there one day – a day that began in brilliant sunlight – that Ludwig and I first came face to face.

Carrying with me a good supply of food – some cheeses and bread, two apples and a flagon of sweet wine – I was pacing back and forth in the fields and copses looking for butterflies. Alone and eagerly anticipating hours of sunlight, I relished the smell of summer grasses and solitude. I seated myself at midday on the moss beside a little stream opposite the Oelberg and had begun sorting through my specimens, naming them with the aid of my guide book, when I was seized by a sudden passion to climb the craggy peak. From the top, I reasoned, I was sure to have a panoramic view of the surrounding countryside. Quickly I packed up my belongings and began winding my way towards the foot of the mountain. Then I noticed that the atmosphere had begun to change. The wind had come round to the west. The brilliant sun, my companion for the morning, was rapidly becoming submerged in heavy clouds. Soon the blue of the sky turned an opaque mass of dead grey. The only possibility of protection from the rain which was on its way lay in my quickly mounting the peak of the Oelberg and sheltering myself in some cave or rock cranny there. I began to climb rapidly. I could feel my heart pounding in my chest. Within ten minutes the first big drops had started to fall. Climbing as fast as my lungs allowed towards an opening in the side of the rock, I darted into it like a small animal seeking shelter. It took me several moments to catch my breath. When finally I looked out from my little refuge I congratulated myself on how fortunate I had been in choosing it —first because it was an ideal protection from the sheets of water then spilling from the heavens and also because from this little hollow in the side of the great mountain I could gaze out over a vast expanse of country and marvel at the billowing darkness of the storm which just now covered my beloved land. I crouched down, content within my shelter, and made myself comfortable to sit out the storm, the noise of which had now become deafening.

Soon I noticed that something else was making noise as well, but in the midst of the rain and the thunder I could not make out what. It seemed to be coming from an outcrop of rock about twenty feet below me which looked, from where I crouched, like a flat table. They were bellowing noises like the sounds from a young bull and they came in intermittent bursts.

Curiosity overcame my distaste for the storm. Leaving my knapsack in the little shelter, I crept out and down the embankment until I could peer over the top of the outcrop. There beneath me, no more than five or six feet away, stood a boy who could not have been more than twelve, waving his arms ecstatically in the air and shouting commands to the heavens as though he were conducting the storm which raged about us.

A clash of thunder.

'Bravo, bravissimo, now an adagio maestoso.'

More rain and sheets of water. The sky lit up with lightning.

'Prestissimo furioso – yes yes!'

Still he continued his wild gesticulations. I could not see

his face for his back was to me and I stood behind and somewhat above him. He appeared to be short and thickset with masses of dark black hair and broad shoulders. He was dressed in what looked as if it had been highly respectable clothing – a brown coat with a standing collar, a peruke which once no doubt hung down his neck but now flew out behind him like a flag, some dirty yellow breeches, coloured stockings and low-cut shoes. Every piece of clothing was wet, nay, not just wet but streaming with water. Yet he appeared to be completely oblivious of it all as he continued to conduct the heavens in their fury.

Tempted at first to laugh at the spectacle, I was quickly overcome by a sense of shame at having unwittingly intruded into this boy's private world. The rain had begun to abate so I retreated carefully, making every effort not to disturb even one piece of scree that might betray my presence. He continued with his gesticulating, tossing his arms and hands about as though the whole of the sky, the whole of the earth, were under his direction. As the storm diminished so did the violence of his gestures and the grandiose bellowing of his voice in rhythm with the movements of his hands, until finally his body gave a convulsive jerk. He shuddered, perhaps at last aware of the wetness of his clothes, and turned his head to look behind.

Having had an indication that he was about to perform such a gesture, like a turtle I pulled my head quickly back into my hovel and waited. I thought it best in the circumstances to allow *him* to discover *me* rather than I him in order to spare him any embarrassment that might result from the realisation that someone had witnessed his unusual behaviour. I waited perhaps two minutes in silence and then emerged from my little cave, cleared my throat a couple of times and stretched, hoping that my noises would call his attention and that he would think I was trying to shake off any stiffness from a body which had been tucked out of harm's way for the duration of the storm. The ruse worked. I could see from the corner of my eye that he had spotted me. I continued for a moment to stretch before turning my head and looking deliberately downward in his direction. His gaze met mine. It was one part suspicion and two parts curiosity – rather like a mountain cat who, having sized up the enemy and concluded that his strength is superior to it, begins to examine what stands before him and asks if it is a friend or food.

I recognised him at once. This was the same young boy I had unwittingly spied on years before. Now I was intruding on his secret world for a second time. The eyes were dark and small, the head was large with a square nose. It was now set upon a massive neck. The hair was thick, black and wiry. His skin was much rougher than that of most boys of twelve and the complexion was as dark as a gypsy. I waved and shouted out in what I hoped would be a hearty voice that betrayed no secret knowledge. Then I moved towards the youth to shake his hand.

He wiped his face with the back of a very wet sleeve.

'Good day,' I said. 'What a storm, eh? Thunder so loud a man can't hear himself think.'

'Yes, sir. Very wet.'

'Did you just arrive? I was lucky to take shelter as it began.'

'I . . . that is no, I have stood a bit in the rain myself. I don't mind the water.'

'A braver man than I. I was about to take some food – good for warming one's body after such a soaking. Won't you join me? Would you like some bread and cheese?'

Silence.

'I do believe I brought more than I can ever hope to eat myself,' I said.

He turned away, turned back again, looked down at his

feet, then laughed with a boldness that would cause anyone to laugh with him.

'I would, very much. I am hungry as a bear.'

'Then perhaps it won't be wasted.' I reached for his hand. 'Franz Wegeler, student of science and lover of dry caves.'

'Ludwig van Beethoven, wet musician. Happy to make your acquaintance.'

'What road did you take to get here?'

'None at all. I prefer striking out on my own. First I climbed the Ennert then I went higher and higher over rocks and through the trees. Where are we anyway?'

'We are upon the sterile peak of the Oelberg.'

'To the Oelberg then, in all its glory.'

We sat atop the flat rock which had earlier hidden some of his wild gesticulations from my view. I spread out my offerings and we munched away at black bread and cheese, sharing sweet wine direct from the bottle.

'Do you come here often?' I said.

'Whenever I can sneak away. Not often enough. I should spend every afternoon here if I could manage it. In such vastness one has space for almost anything.'

'I myself like to hunt insects and gather flower specimens. Tomorrow should be a fine day for mushrooms after this downpour. Are you in school in the town, then?'

'Oh no. I am finished with all that. I am assistant court organist now – a student of composition with Herr Neefe. I expect soon to be made cembalist. Then I will conduct the whole orchestra myself from the keyboard.'

'Ah. You must be very clever. And have you composed anything of your own?'

'I am doing so now – a set of variations on a march by Dressler but I am uncertain how it will be received.'

'I should like very much to hear what you have written. May I?'

'Oh no, not yet . . . when it is complete you may come and listen, though.'

We spent the afternoon wandering the hills together. They had begun to steam as a hot sun lifted water from their grasses. At first he spoke little, regularly eyeing me as though he were either slightly myopic or I were someone wanting to steal his watch. I spoke a great deal, judging this would make him feel more at ease. Slowly his suspicion thawed and his own words began to pour forth in torrents. He talked of Nature and her power, of his grandfather whose name he had been given and who had been, he said, the most revered Kapellmeister in Bonn, of his love of black bread and his loathing of the neighbour's chickens, of Christian Gottlob Neefe, whom he said was a man with a passion for books, of the discomfort of the shoes which he had to wear in order to reach the pedals of the church organ. I remarked that my new friend had an air of awkwardness about him. He was rather like a big dog who keeps falling over its own feet: one moment he was leaping up at you or bounding about, the next he would be lost in dreams or skulking as though he had been scolded. By late afternoon as we crossed back over our Holy River, we had already agreed to meet in the same place the following Sunday. Then we parted.

We did meet the next Sunday, and the following one. The weather was good that summer. So good that we suffered no more violent tempests. By the end of August, Ludwig and I had become fast friends despite the differences in our age. So we remained, meeting as often as we could. My new friend turned out to be a good friend – true to his word. When Ludwig made a promise he would keep it. Yet he was frequently unpredictable in his behaviour. Sometimes he would appear confident, almost brazen in his bearing. At others he would seem quite timid or vague – immersed in contemplation. Ludwig dreamed a lot. Occasionally he would speak of his ambitions. But he would make me swear not to reveal a word of what had been said to another living soul. He spoke frequently of his grandfather who, although he had died when Ludwig was only three, was a hero to him. He seldom mentioned his father. When he spoke of his mother, Maria Magdalena, it was always quietly with a kind of reverence in his voice.

Maria Magdalena was a quiet woman, thin and slightly bent. She always seemed preoccupied. He once told me proudly how on a trip up the river to Flanders as a young boy she had held him in her lap most of the way, chafing his legs to warm them. Ludwig's mother brought seven children into the world. Only three lived beyond infancy. I recall that I never heard her laugh. Yet she was clever. She gave good converse and replied aptly, politely and modestly to high and low. For this, if nothing else, she was respected and she was certainly no mouse. Occasionally a hot temper would flare up. She knew well how to give and take in a manner that is becoming to a woman of honest thought. Life cannot have been easy between having to wrestle with her husband's drinking debts and the deaths of children. She appeared to bear her burden stoically – even, one might say, to play the role of the long-suffering, righteous wife with quiet aplomb. Yet despite the cloak of virtue she wore as a token of her transcendence of life's tribulations, Maria Magdalena's children were frequently neglected. In his early years Ludwig's face was often unwashed and his body dressed in torn and ill-fitting clothes. His mother never hid her disappointment with life and marriage. I once heard her say to a neighbour, 'One should weep when a girl is brought into the world, for marriage is a chain of sorrows. If you take my good advice, remain single, and then you will have the most tranquil, most beautiful, most pleasurable life. What is marriage? A little joy, and then a chain of sorrows.'

Lest I paint too sombre a picture of my friend's youth, Dr Wawruch, I must tell you that not all was sorrow in the Beethoven household. Every year at the feast of St Mary Magdalene – Maria Magdalena's birthday and name day – she was made to retire early. Music stands were fetched from the Tucksaal and placed in the two sitting rooms overlooking the street. A canopy, embellished with flowers, leaves and laurel, was put up in the room in which Grandfather Ludwig's portrait hung so that by ten o'clock all was in readiness. Silence would be broken by the tuning up of instruments; Frau Beethoven would be awakened, requested to dress, and then led to a beautifully draped chair beneath the canopy. Then an outburst of music lasting well into the night would rouse the neighbours. Even the most drowsy were soon caught in the infectious gaiety. When the music was finished a table would be spread and, after food and drink, the merry company would fall to dancing, albeit in stockinged feet to lessen the noise.

It was I myself who brought Ludwig into the Breuning family, my dear wife's family – perhaps the finest family in all of Bonn. This I did on the pretext that Eleonore and her brothers needed piano lessons – Christophe, born in 1773, who was three years younger than Ludwig, Steffen, born in 1774, Lorenz born in 1777 and Eleonore whom we called Lorchen. The Breuning house which stood on the Munster-platz in the centre of our town was a meeting place for Bonn's most illustrious citizens – musicians, writers, artists, philosophers and political leaders. Frau Helene von Breuning was the widow of a court chancellor who had been killed in our great fire – a fine woman who could take a ragamuffin like Ludwig and bestow upon him within a few months the appearance of education and breeding. I recall the day Ludwig met them all as though it were yesterday. He and I had been wandering in the hills that afternoon. I had not told him where I was taking him for I knew his shyness well enough by then to suspect that had he known he was to be introduced to new people – especially a *grand* family – he would have turned tail and left me standing on my own before the gate to their garden.

When we arrived, the Breunings were sitting in the shade of the great apple tree in the garden. It was half-past five on a summer's evening. The Holy Rhine which passed close by their house was flowing green and smooth and the children were noisily debating whether or not to swim after dinner. The sun's chains, half hidden all amongst the leaves, cast a dappled light upon the table which Frau Breuning had spread in shimmering white damask. It was laden with half-eaten cold viands and bottles and plates. A servant had just appeared bearing a giant tureen of soup – it is a Rhenish custom to finish the meal with special soups, Dr Wawruch – when Ludwig and I opened the garden gate. Frau von Breuning rose immediately and came to us, taking Ludwig by the hand and inviting us to join them. Christophe and Steffen hurried in to fetch more chairs.

I introduced Ludwig, who was then fourteen or fifteen, to each of the family in turn. He appeared excessively shy. Yet when addressed that afternoon he answered with just as excessive a boldness as though he feared his voice could not be heard unless he raised it. Once he had settled himself Frau Breuning turned to Eleonore and demanded, 'Have you brought the herbs, Lorchen?'

'Yes, Mama,' she answered, shaking her apron vigorously. A pile of finely chopped golden plants tumbled on to the table.

'I hope you will find our soup to your taste,' she said turning to Ludwig. 'I think you may approve of it once it is finished.'

'Oh yes, I am sure, madam, I will,' was his reply. I noticed that his face had reddened. He cleared his throat.

Mother Breuning dropped several lumps of sugar into the great pot, covered them with Lorchen's mixture, added some fresh woodruff leaves to it and completed the procedure, making a third layer of slivered oranges. Over this she poured the contents of several of her special bottles. The resulting aromatic blend she ladled into glasses, which were handed all about the table. While these preparations were being carried out, I was heartily engaged in eating what was set in front of me. Ludwig had refused all offers of food, excusing himself on the grounds of little appetite. When she placed the highly scented glass in his hand, however, it was as though some magic had been worked upon him. He sniffed it as a dog might sniff a tree, took a sip and then drank the entire cup –piping hot though it was – at one go. Then he looked up, smiled the broadest smile I had ever seen, threw his head back and began to roar with laughter. 'It is excellent, madam, excellent,' he said, his tiny eyes gleaming. 'What is it called?'

'Why, Maitrank,' she replied. 'I am pleased that you like it, Ludwig. I think the woodruff and the orange impart a special flavour to the wine, don't you? Do have some more.' Again she filled his glass to the brim.

It was emptied immediately, and once more refilled without a word. Within minutes this awkward stranger lost his shyness. Helene Breuning's splendid Maitrank and her gentle ways had made another conquest. Already Ludwig had become a friend of the family. So he was to remain for more than ten years until he left our Bonn to go to Vienna never to return. During those years he spent long hours with them taking meals, passing pleasant afternoons and evenings in their company and even spending the occasional night in the Breuning home. There he learned about books, the names of which he had never heard before – there was no reading in the Beethoven home. He met gentlemen and young ladies of all thoughts and inclinations and of course he taught music to the four Breuning children.

Frau von Breuning had a very special way with Ludwig. She could, in the most gracious manner, correct his behaviour without his taking offence. She also knew when to leave him alone. If Ludwig behaved belligerently or strangely, as he often did, she would simply smile and say: 'He has his *raptus* again.'

You have questioned me about Ludwig's political leanings and connections, Dr Wawruch, and ask what bearings these may have had on his mental and physical condition. Of these matters I feel myself unable to speak objectively. I myself did not care for some of the men with whom Ludwig associated in his youth. Of his companions in Vienna later on I know little. He never wrote to me of them and as you know we never met again after I had completed my medical studies. In his early life, however, there was one man in particular with whom Ludwig had a close association whom perhaps you should know more about. Although he helped my young friend greatly in developing his musical talents and furthering his career, I did not care for this gentleman. He appeared to me to have a strangely unsettling effect on Ludwig. This was court organist Christian Gottlob Neefe to whom I have already alluded. Neefe was an excellent clavierist and pianist with a passion for the works of Emanuel Bach. He had come to Bonn a few years before in the company of a theatrical group, the Grossmann-Hellmuth Society for whom he served as musical director. About eighteen months later he entered the Elector's service as assistant to Court Organist van den Eeden. On van den Eeden's death, Neefe became his replacement.

Neefe was a heretic at our Catholic Court, being a

Calvinist as well as a Freemason like myself. Twelve or thirteen when he met Neefe, Ludwig was able rapidly to develop his musical skills under his tutelage. This was all to his advantage. But Neefe had what were to my mind radical, not to say politically questionable, ideas. They turned Ludwig's young head, filling it with foolish notions. Neefe was also a member of the secret society of Bavarian Illuminati which in 1785 had been officially outlawed, although it emerged two years later in even greater secrecy in the form of a 'reading society'. I did not like Neefe despite his cheerful air and his hard-working musical craftsmanship. Nor did I care for the things of which he spoke with his Illuminist friends – wild plans for the controlled destruction of governments, philosophies and religions, strategies for polarising human masses into opposing camps and ideologies, means of organising revolution which they claimed had overthrown the French monarchy and caused the colonial wars in America.

I have devoted myself, Dr Wawruch, to the goals and visions of Freemasonry. I have always desired in my actions and in my words to influence the affairs of men for the better. In such principles Freemasonry provides a training wherein we who have been initiated can strive to perfect ourselves and work together for the betterment of humanity. The same, alas, cannot be said of Illuminism.

The Illuminati, I fear, were created not by the great white brotherhood as they would have one believe, but by brothers of shadow working secretly behind the scenes to instigate political domination and spread their influence throughout Europe. Neefe was the leader of the Illuminati in our Bonn. At first when he spoke to Ludwig of his ideals of universal liberty, brotherhood and the spiritual progress of civilisation, I too believed he was echoing the sentiments of Freemasonry. Later I discovered otherwise.

It was the winter of 1790, I remember it well. Ludwig and I had been away from each other for two years whilst I was in Vienna studying medicine and I had not long before returned to Bonn. That same year an edict had been issued against secret societies. In France there had been much confusion following the storming of the Bastille several months earlier. (Mirabeau had been elected to head the National Assembly in Paris, yet it was whispered everywhere that he had also become secret adviser to Louis XVI.)

One night, after performing an arduous operation upon a woman in childbirth – in which I barely saved her life – I stopped at the Zehrgarten in the hope that a glass or two of wine would induce a propensity for sleep. In this tavern-cum-bookshop owned by Anna Maria Koch, Ludwig and I had frequently passed long winter evenings in conversation with friends. That evening I found him sitting with a group of men, only two of whom I knew: Neefe and Count Ferdinand Waldstein.

A man of aristocratic Austrian blood, Waldstein was familiarly known as the chameleon. He had a passion for disguising himself and for imitating accents: later he was to become involved in questionable financial matters which in time were to render him completely impoverished. The Count had not long before arrived in Bonn at the invitation of the Elector to be made a Knight of the Teutonic Order. Ludwig and I had made his acquaintance at the house of the Breunings, whom he visited frequently. Although Waldstein always appeared to help Ludwig – having a piano delivered to the Beethoven house when the family was at its poorest, and later financing his trip to Vienna and introducing him to the aristocracy there – I never liked him. He was a decent pianist who fancied himself a composer. Yet instead of composing himself he commissioned Ludwig to write a ballet which he passed off as his own. I also never trusted him.

I found Waldstein, Ludwig and the other men huddled close together around a circular table on which a single candle burned in a glass cover. Seated as they were with heads bowed they gave the impression of conspirators, shifting through secret matters and speaking in low tones. Neefe, I noticed, was dressed strangely. He wore a brocade frock coat – very formal attire for the setting. When I entered the tavern Ludwig showed no sign of recognising me, so immersed was he in the discussion. I saw that his eyes were shining in that unearthly mode I had come by then to know.

I chose not to interrupt the gathering but to sit quietly on my own at a table nearby and I settled near the glowing fire in the hopes that it would remove some of the chill from my arms and legs. That winter had been a heavy one, and as I had not long qualified, I found myself shaken by the knowledge that only the slightest delay in acting or the tiniest miscalculation of my scalpel an hour before could have resulted in the death of both mother and child. On this occasion at least their lives had been spared. I shook the frozen rain from my hair and opened up a journal I had been carrying, intending to make the best of what light there was to read. So unsettling was the conversation I overheard from the table behind me, however, that I hardly read a word.

The men addressed each other not by their proper names but using strange classical aliases: 'Varo', 'Casca', 'Aurelius', 'Cato'. Frequently, they also mentioned another, whom they called 'Spartacus' – someone whom they appeared to consider a leader or mentor. I learned later that this Spartacus was a pseudonym for Adam Weishaupt, founder of a secret sect to which Neefe belonged. They were attempting to solicit Ludwig in the performance of a duty on their behalf – seemingly to write a cantata on the death of the Emperor Joseph who had passed away only a fortnight since.

'His was an extraordinary accomplishment.' I heard Neefe, whom they called 'Aurelius', say.

'Indeed,' broke in Waldstein – whom they referred to as 'Cato' – 'was it not Emperor Joseph who chose Maximilian Franz, his brother, to be our Archbishop Elector? Was it not our Joseph who legalised Freemasonry and abolished Catholic schools? His actions show he is worthy of the title 'Bringer of Light', Ludwig. Joseph's death is a sad day in the history of our cause, a day which must be remembered. Its remembrance, dear Ludwig, lies in your hands. Only you can write the music that will transmit the power of his visions – *our* visions.'

Ludwig responded with unusual modesty: 'But I am unskilled in composition. I am uncertain I could as yet compose music worthy to honour an emperor. I would like to take the task upon myself Herr Neefe – Aurelius, I should say – but I have had so little practice in such matters. How can I be sure the Muse will not fail me?'

'That she will not,' replied Neefe. 'Your talent is of the finest. It is time you took up such a task. Spartacus has willed it so and he is a man of vision – vision great enough to rule the stars themselves should he so choose.'

I watched as Ludwig seemed to grow visibly taller.

A sudden silence followed, then phrases uttered in tones so low I was unable to make them out. Though I did not hear these words, Dr Wawruch, I must tell you I sensed a quality in their speaking which imparted yet a deeper chill to my body – a chill which even the richly blazing fire could not dispel.

'Music has power, Ludwig,' I heard the voice of a man they called Varo say, 'power to weave the web that traps the man's soul – power therefore to save him from himself.'

'From himself?' said Ludwig.

'Ah yes,' whined Waldstein, with what sounded to me like a mock sadness. 'Rousseau wrote the truth: the common man has lost his innocence and abused the purity of his nature. He cannot be allowed the freedom of making his own decisions – although he must of course be made to *believe* that he is doing so.'

'Hence the revolution,' added Neefe.

'What revolution?' asked Ludwig.

'It matters not,' said a second man, who spoke slowly in a heavy Eastern accent. 'Any revolution will do, so long as the words one uses to describe it–'

'So long as the music one plays fires men's passions,' Waldstein interrupted, 'and induces them to follow where we want them to go.'

'I don't understand you, Waldstein,' said Ludwig. 'Why need we deceive a man to bring him benefit?'

'Let me explain,' said the man with the Eastern accent. 'The necessity of those of us with vision guiding those without has come about as a result of Man's sad loss of innocence Rousseau so eloquently laments in his *Contrat social.* . . . How does he phrase it? "Man is born free, and everywhere he is in chains."'

'Rousseau wrote the truth,' said Varo. 'Man has fallen from his innate liberty and abused the purity of his nature, he has become subordinate. That is why he lives in bondage. This – and only this – is the fall of original sin. We must help men regain their state of liberty and divest themselves of the trappings laid upon them by civilisation. That is the crux of our great task. We must destroy the monarchy and re-establish freedom. Joseph in his secret loyalties began this process. Now we must continue it.'

'So we must,' echoed Waldstein.

I saw Ludwig nod, in agreement.

'We must fire his enthusiasm for the courses of action that are right for him,' said Neefe, 'inspire his imagination through high-sounding words and majestic music – music that speaks of new visions, of brotherhood, music that you write, Ludwig. Spartacus himself has chosen you for the task. He has also decreed that in time you shall be trained to sit at the core of the inner circle – a locus which shapes the future of the world.'

Ludwig took a sip of his wine and nodded. 'I shall write your music,' he said. 'I will give you a cantata on the death of Joseph which can be played to the glory of man's freedom. What form does the training for the inner circle take?'

'It is gradual,' answered the Eastern voice. 'Spartacus has learned much from the Jesuits and although he despises their views and despises the ends to which they fashion their skills, he has taught us to imitate their training method skilfully. There are circles within circles.' The man paused, took paper from his inside pocket and began to draw upon it with what appeared to be a small piece of charcoal. I noticed that his hands were unnaturally small and covered with hair – altogether ugly. He continued, 'There are circles within circles, Ludwig. At each level you penetrate more deeply the secrets of the universe and gain greater power to sway the minds and hearts of men.'

When he finished speaking there was silence for some time. Finally, Ludwig asked another question but in a tone so greatly subdued I could not make out his words. At this moment Frau Koch appeared at my table with a glass of wine, some cheese and bread.

Then I heard Neefe speak again: '. . . such training shows the profound subtlety of Spartacus. He has taught us to speak sometimes in one way and sometimes in another so that our real purpose remains impenetrable to inferiors. To some must we profess disapproval of revolutions and proffer peaceful methods for the attainment of world persuasion. While to others. . . .'

'The common man,' broke in Waldstein, 'unaware as he is of his latent nobility, has neither the intelligence nor the imagination to be received into an inner circle. So naturally deception must play a part in the accomplishment of our noble cause. We therefore apply ourselves to the art of counterfeit.'

'So do we choose to work in the dark and wrap ourselves in mystery, concealing even the very existence of the Order – always covering our trail with the name of another society. . . .'

Again there was silence. I took a sip of wine and waited, uncertain of what to do. When I had first entered the tavern I would have been glad for Ludwig to look up and greet me. Now, so troubled had I become by the words I had overheard and the company he was keeping, I desired only to slip away without notice.

Waldstein spoke again: 'You see, Ludwig, we use for the good of men those methods which others in their ignorance have used for evil. We choose only the finest talents. Only the bravest and noblest of spirits are made privy to our inner secrets. For only men of gift and vision have the power and the wisdom to guide the rest until such time as even they, the lesser men, become infused with the spirit of freedom. You are such a man, Ludwig. It is, as Spartacus says, a question of helping us to breathe the spirit of freedom . . . *illuminating* those who have not yet attained the wisdom to embrace it by personal choice. Music is of great importance to that end. . . . Your music.'

'I am honoured to be given such a task,' said Ludwig solemnly. 'I will do my best to prove worthy of it.'

'Your music will become a carrier of light not only to men who know the power of true freedom but to those who slumber still,' said Neefe. 'It must radiate to each man whose mind has become confused with false religion and political exploitation the spirit of true humanity and freedom. Like a herb or potion which acts upon the body, music can infuse the spirit with our vision in each man who hears it, setting hundreds of thousands, nay, millions, of souls on fire. Your music can be used to ripen minds and persuasions to embrace orders and visions necessary to bring about a new world order.'

I had by this time finished my wine. I could swallow none of the bread and cheese for I had not the stomach for it. I rose and left without Ludwig ever having known that I had come. I carried in my bowels a leaden weight which had nothing to do with bread and cheese, and a profound uncertainty about Ludwig's future.

Words overheard by Wegeler in a dark tavern two hundred years ago – they sound uncomfortably familiar. They come too close to words spoken to me – by me – at other times and places yet always within a murky secrecy – words I don't want to remember. Yet they come flooding back: special groups – inner circles – secret agendas: 'You see, Mike, it's like this, subversive networks create the linchpins of every successful insurgency. Just where they come from or what their political leanings are is of minor importance. Since many dissidents are Marxist-trained we will focus on the communist infrastructure much admired by would-be revolutionaries. . . . It is of course essential that each operative be familiar with the immediate revolutionary situation before we move into action. Ignorance of local religious customs or political sensitivities can result in unnecessary security problems and ineffectual action. . . .' I know too much about secret organisations where ends justify the means – where even the operatives don't know what they are being used to do.

Ludwig spent many a night with Neefe and Neefe's friends discussing such matters in taverns and secret meeting places. I had noticed that he would appear particularly unruly after one of these discussions. He would be filled with the peculiar theories of history which Neefe and his friends propounded – such notions as the cycles of five movements from *Verwirrung* –the supposedly chaotic period, through *Unordnung*, the balance time, on to *Grummet* during which all human institutions were to be dispersed and dissolved. He would also become overexcited, his ruddy pitted skin glowing red for hours afterwards and his eyes displaying all the signs of fever. Several times I ventured to suggest to Ludwig what rubbish these men talked and to advise him that he should not allow them influence over him. But he would have none of it. At last, in respect for his privacy and his opinions, I ceased to speak with him on the subject. He in turn uttered no further word to me of their strange fancies. But there was gossip about Ludwig's associations at Court even in his youth and I was always fearful that his headstrong nature and outspoken ideas would cost him his employment by the Elector, which he so needed to support his family.

It is strange, Dr Wawruch, but people always liked to gossip about Ludwig – even when he was a child. During our early years together, although he spoke to few people and none knew him well, not even, I fear, I myself, although I did not realise this at the time, some of our citizens praised him to the heavens. Others dismissed his precocity as nothing more than a fiction invented by an ambitious father wishing to enhance his own fading reputation as a court singer.

In regard to what you have called his 'fugues of consciousness', even as a youth Ludwig was given to such peculiar alteration of moods and changes in physiology as you have described in your letters. They were always impossible to fathom. He was also unnaturally forgetful. One morning when I arrived to fetch him (we had planned to walk to the convent of Heisterbach), in answer to my knock I was greeted by a parchment face which showed no signs of recognition.

'Good morning Ludwig, are you ready?' I said.

'Ready?'

'You have not forgotten our meeting, have you?'

'What?'

'The meeting – the brother sacristan is waiting for us at Heisterbach. The abbot has given his permission for you to play the organ. There will no doubt be cold viands and a bottle of Mezenberger waiting for us when we arrive. Come on.'

Ludwig shrugged, lifted a ragged brown scarf off the hook in the entrance way and without saying a word descended the steps to accompany me.

'Are you unwell?' I asked him. 'Do you not want a coat? The autumn air is cold and I have none to lend you.'

'I desire nothing but to be left alone,' was his reply. 'I care nothing for the cold – yours or anyone else's. What difference does it make? A man's destiny is just so. What he is, he is. Nothing can change that. I shall not die of the cold. Don't speak to me as if I were a child. You are not that much older than I. One day you and all the rest shall know it well enough.'

We walked on in silence, crossing the river and making our way over the hills. Still pale, despite the exertions of our journey, Ludwig pulled his collar high and wrapped his scarf well up under a sullen chin. Valleys gently revealed themselves as the eastern landscape shone forth in a rare glow of late autumn sunlight. In the valleys between the mountains, clouds, like overstuffed feather beds, settled down for the night. When at last we approached the peaceful vale at the foot of the Strom which was our destination, I was relieved to see the stately buildings of Heisterbach in front of us. After a sombre, silent walk with this strangely inhuman creature, its sight reassured me that the world of civilised man still existed and that I still belonged to it.

On our right, orchards now barren of fruit gave way to meadows. At the edge of the wood to our left, large artificial fish ponds belied the abundance in this bastion of poverty, chastity and obedience. The path took us next to the high stone wall which enclosed the convent, its park and garden. At the portal we rang the bell. It was hastily answered by the porter, who drew the bolt, greeted us affably and invited us to follow him to the convent itself which stood some distance ahead. On entering the buildings we were greeted by Brother Kitchener and Brother Cellarer whose hospitality, as I predicted, left little to be desired. When we had eaten and drunk our fill, my still silent companion having devoured virtually every morsel that had been laid in front of him, the abbot and the lecturer joined us and we – that is *they* and I – carried on a conversation in Latin.

I spoke, as I recall, with what turned out to be unwelcome enthusiasm about their new ecclesiastical superior, Elector Max Franz – a man of learning whom I believed was proving himself a good friend to science, art and the university which he was about to inaugurate. Their response to my praise was not positive. None of these holy men saw any advantage to be gained from the establishment of a university. The old, highly respectable school of Cologne offered every requisite of education, they informed me. It was, they corrected me, worthy of far greater respect, having remained true to the teachings of the Holy Church and uncorrupted despite the deleterious tendencies of the new incendiary doctrines. I judged it best to take the conversation no further so I suggested that the young musician I had brought was most anxious to delight them with his ability to render sacred music glorious on the organ of their magnificent Romanesque chapel. It was agreed. Still no word passed Ludwig's lips. As we proceeded in a little group through the cloister towards the church the Abbot whispered to me in German, 'Is he not a little young to play adequately?'

'I think not, holy Father', I said. 'But of course, you must judge for yourself.'

The abbot ordered Brother Sacristan to call all the brethren into the church. When they had arrived and were seated, Ludwig took his place despite grumbles from the deposed organist who continued to issue mistrustful glances in his direction. Without hesitation, he struck a few preliminary chords on the organ, acquainting himself with its power. Then he started to play.

The music began slowly with simplicity in a halting rhythm. At first it gave me worry that my young friend would fail through his playing to affirm the praise I had lavishly poured upon him in my most learned Latin. I glanced around me. The abbot looked quizzical, the organist smug. Then the melody deepened and darkened so that the notes twisted strangely together in a rich fabric of sound that drew us into it, soft as velvet, demanding we enter body and soul into the depths of its pile. What Ludwig played that afternoon was far more than an exquisite melody embellished by delicate harmonisation. It had a kind of daemon to it – something neither angelic nor demonic, both human and divine. Years later I came upon a description by Goethe of the Daemonic Man. Although I have no personal knowledge of the phenomenon which took place that afternoon, I knew of what our great poet spoke when he wrote that from the Daemonic Man:

An incredible force pours forth, exercising an incredible power over all creatures, perhaps even over the elements. Who can say how far such an influence may not extend? It is like chance for it points to no consequence. Like providence, it indicates connection and unity. All that hems us in seems penetrable to it; it seems to dispose at will of the inevitable elements of our being, contracting time and expanding space. . . . It fashions a power which, if not opposed to the moral world order, yet intersects it in such a way that one might take one for the warp, the other for the woof.

Such was the character of the performance my young friend gave that day. While his fingers touched the keyboard, not a monk stirred on his wooden pew. Ludwig's face, previously so sullen, turned frightening in its mien, quite different to anything I had seen before. When the music finished the church lay silent with a quietude that seemed to echo resonances within the body of each man, so that none of us was willing yet to surrender to the ordinariness of what was left of the day.

I never knew what occasioned the brooding aggression and amnesia of Ludwig's mood that day. Nor could I tell you what occasioned its removal, but when we left the monastery his dark forgetfulness had completely vanished, leaving no trace. He could not have been more boisterous, light-hearted and gay. Perhaps it was his playing. He was like that: difficult to get to play but once caught up in the flow of the music and the touches of his hands – light or heavy – on the instrument, he would become lost even to himself. At times he would appear not even to know where he was or what he had been doing until the piece he was playing was over.

I recall many obvious incidents such as this one, but more

subtle alterations in his personality took place frequently as well. As you have described in your letter, sometimes within a two-hour period Ludwig's demeanour would seem inexplicably to change – not only in attitudes or sentiment but, as you yourself report, even in *appearance* and in the sound of his voice. In one mode his small deep-set eyes would shrink even further and the timbre of his voice would grow tight and shrill. In another they would glaze over, and in yet another their pupils would dilate giving him the appearance of a cat which has sustained a severe shock. What to me always seemed most surprising – indeed I have never until now articulated this perception even to myself – was the way in which even the shape and movements of his body would become greatly altered so that Ludwig would appear fatter or taller, weaker or stronger. I fully realise that this sounds absurd and yet as a scientist it is as objective a description as I can manage of the phenomenon I witnessed frequently in those years we spent together.

Oft-times it seemed as though several streams of life, each quite separate from the others, flowed concurrently through Ludwig, yet at any particular moment only one or two would manifest themselves in his outward behaviour. After one particularly severe incident where he had behaved in a highly abusive way to my wife Eleonore and in which she was severely wounded by his apparent lack of regard for her, I remember thinking, as it says in the Bible, 'His left hand doesn't know what his right hand is doing.' This rent between the two people most dear to me in the world took place but a few weeks before Ludwig's final departure from Bonn. It may well have been occasioned by a misunderstanding over his affection for Lorchen, who had presented Ludwig with one of those little shadow profiles of her, so fashionable at the time, cut from black paper. Ludwig was, and I believe always remained, deeply fond of Eleonore.

The breach was not healed until more than a year later as a result of a long apologetic letter he sent to her. But she, like I, never saw him again in the flesh.

The remorse Ludwig always felt after having provoked an argument or offended any of his acquaintances cut deep into his heart. Yet he would frequently discourse at length on extenuating circumstances which he insisted had provoked his behaviour as though, not being able genuinely to forgive himself, he sought refuge in what he insisted was 'beyond his control'. Ludwig was also obsessed with the notion of self-improvement, always hoping and believing that he would become more wise, more kind, more loving, more reasonable and often making such promises to his friends.

'The next time you see me,' he would say, 'you will find me quite a different person.'

It was all so unnecessary. Those of us who loved him were all too willing to accept him as he was, regardless of his moods. It was *he* who could never accept them.

All through his life Ludwig hated giving lessons. He used to say to me: 'I am not a teacher. I don't know how to tell anyone what I do. I but do it. Even I myself do not know how.'

Is any of this relevant to your enquiry, Dr Wawruch? It all seems so useless to your task of making sense of the strange night events you describe yourself as having witnessed at his bedside in the weeks that preceded Ludwig's death.

What night events? What did Wawruch ask Wegeler to tell him about Ludwig and why did Mirabehn insist on stuffing this scruffy manuscript into my hand? I just want to be rid of it. I don't even want my questions answered. Of both things I am sure and yet like a rabbit hypnotised by the silent gaze of a serpent I am caught up in something I cannot fathom. I read on . . . and on . . . and on. . . .

Let me now tell you about our life together in Vienna. Whenever Ludwig performed he was quiet, noble and masterful. He relished the appreciative response of his audience but he hated being asked to play. When first we were in Vienna his hatred for performing had become particularly severe. If urged to play in the drawing room of an aristocratic house, he would frequently turn his back on his host and storm out, leaving coat and hat to be sent for the next day. In an attempt to get round this intense reticence to perform I would attempt a ruse: I would ensure there were too few chairs in the drawing room to accommodate all the guests. Ludwig and I would arrive only after the others had already been seated. He would in this way be forced to sit before the piano since that was the only empty chair to be found. If all present had been advised to make no mention of his playing, sometimes after an hour or so of desultory conversation Ludwig would half turn to the keyboard and begin to toy with the keys. Still it was imperative that we took no notice. Then, after a few minutes he would start some kind of variation on a theme, soon to become so caught up in it that when it was finished and applause flooded the room he would be genuinely surprised, having been largely unaware of what he had been doing. Once applause had warmed his heart he could be prevailed upon to repeat again and again the most remarkable figures on the piano, oft-times bringing his listeners to the point of tears with his constant shifts between *piano* and *forte* and his remarkable ability to encompass emotion in his playing. Ludwig relished this power above all else. He would lift his audience to the heights of expectation again and again, postponing the resolution of a series of arpeggios. Then he would laugh out loud, contemptuous of his ability to make them weep.

'It is all such nonsense,' he would say.

Of his own emotions and what bearing they may have had

on his final illness it is difficult to speak. Ludwig was always as much a collection of contradictions in what he felt as he was in his behaviour. Few thoughts or events could bring tears to his eyes. When at the age of seventeen he returned to Bonn after his first brief and abortive visit to Vienna, to nurse a mother rapidly drowning in consumption, I could tell he was horribly distressed by the condition in which he found her. Yet the tiny dry cough, the reddened cheeks, the limp wrists, were all registered by him in silence. He set about issuing orders to his brothers, his father, the physician, the servant. Then he would sit motionless for long hours beside his mother's bed, taking her withering hand in his, his face betraying not the least flicker of emotion. When she coughed or requested water he saw to her needs with an immediacy that belied his intense concern although in his countenance no hint of sympathy could be read. When at last she succumbed to the disease that had gripped her in its jaws, although Ludwig was heartbroken, not a tear did he shed.

Within a week of burying her he himself fell victim to attacks of asthma, which restricted his breathing and necessitated care by the physician's helper who, in an effort to bring relief, would spread long hot strips of wet cloth along his spine every hour and massage his back with the expensive Neapolitan olive oil sent by Frau von Breuning. If at the time Ludwig had had any idea of its cost, he would have returned it to the fine lady with an expression of independent pride that would have prevented her from ever sending another bottle. Above all else, my friend abhorred being patronised.

In truth, Ludwig hated excessive shows of emotion from anyone – himself or another. Yet there were two circumstances which I noticed continually moved him. The first was any occasion in which someone whom he felt to be in his care – a brother, a friend, a young lady he admired – was perceived to be an object of criticism or derision. Then he would rise to their defence with a ferocity that was oft-times inappropriate. The second was when he had been transported by an idea of beauty, as often as not the beauty of Nature, or fellowship or the creative power of men. Then he visibly trembled with feeling. Both circumstances had the power to wrest tears from him. His voice would grow thick and his beady eyes would mist over. However, I never saw him shed a tear over the death of anyone. Of the intimate details of most of his relationships with women, about which you have asked, I can say nothing, Dr Wawruch. He was most secretive about his passions.

Of Ludwig's later relationships with women I also know little. I do know he was frequently disappointed in love. He was, you must remember, Dr Wawruch, not of the same station as those women in whose social world he moved by grace of his music, and they never let him forget it. I fear he became for the fine ladies of Vienna an idol, a curiosity one might say, with which they loved to play. And Ludwig was not someone who allowed himself to be toyed with.

He was, of course, forever falling in and out of love, constantly caught up in one liaison or another from which, I fear, he did not always escape unscathed. I mention this only in the context of your medical enquiries, which I shall deal with in a moment. I know that Dr Andreas Bertolini who knew Ludwig well as a friend and treated him for a period of over ten years did prescribe a salve of mercury – as well you know a substance commonly used to treat syphilis, although often used for other ailments. It was not without a sense of physician's honour that some years after Ludwig's death, Bertolini, believing himself to be at the point of his own demise from cholera and too feeble it was said to examine his large collection of letters and notes from

Ludwig, ordered them all to be burnt. Bertolini wrote to me, for we corresponded frequently in an attempt to allay Ludwig's anxieties over his physical condition and then later on scientific matters. 'I burnt them all, Wegeler. A few, I fear, were not of the nature to be risked in careless hands.' Strong as a horse, Bertolini did not die as he had feared. He made a remarkable recovery. But the papers are now lost to us for ever.

Ludwig had a certain fascination with women of darkness, Dr Wawruch. I do not mean ladies of dark skin although there was a period in Vienna, I am told, in which dark-skinned women of the lower order carried curious interest for gentlemen. I speak of a different kind of darkness. Ludwig simply could not turn away from the lure of soft female flesh. He loved passionately, and hated just as passionately. Particularly when, for any reason whatsoever, he believed himself to have been betrayed. Although he adored women he was also terrified of them – particularly of *immoral* women. He made many frantic attempts to exercise control over the behaviour of his brothers Nikolaus Johann and Caspar Carl, lest they fall into the hands of such women – women he believed to be immoral.

One woman in particular did Ludwig fear and loathe – his sister-in-law Johanna, the wife of Caspar Carl. He hated Johanna with a passion bordering on madness. She was, he wrote in several letters, 'the epitome of evil sensuality'. 'Queen of the Night', he called her. Aware of her moral laxity he did his best to prevent her son, his nephew Karl – whom Ludwig adopted on the death of the boy's father – from seeing his mother again, unfortunately without success. Of Johanna I shall speak further in a moment yet I fear it is not a pretty tale. For she was by every estimation a most wicked and depraved woman. Ludwig himself created much confusion about what really happened between them.

The strands of the Johanna story are therefore tightly bound and I am by no means skilled enough to unravel them all.

It has always saddened me, Dr Wawruch, to know that Ludwig's brothers were of so little help to him in his suffering and his need. His relationships with them alternated between effusive fraternal affection and intense rivalry, even culminating in physical violence. Both brothers followed Ludwig to Vienna. Caspar Carl, Ludwig's favourite, arrived in 1794. After trying his hand at teaching music he became a bank cashier. This he remained until his death. For a time Caspar Carl also acted, not altogether honestly or successfully, as unpaid secretary and business agent to Ludwig. The other brother, Johann, with whom you are acquainted, followed Caspar Carl to Vienna in 1795 to become an apothecary. Ten or twelve years later he bought his own shop in Linz and proceeded to gather much gold from war profiteering during the French occupation.

Ludwig took far too great an interest in the way both brothers conducted their lives. He was continually interfering with their affairs and made no secret of his dislike for their wives. Caspar Carl's marriage to Johanna led to a long estrangement between them. Ludwig took little pleasure in Johann's choice of wife, Therese, a woman once Johann's housekeeper with whom he became intimate. Ludwig even tried to take out a court injunction against her to send her out of town and prevent the marriage. But it was Johanna who was to become the *bête noire* of his existence and whom I fear may in the end have played no small part in Ludwig's eventual destruction.

My knowledge of Johanna has come to me mostly through Ludwig's own letters. In them he described at times most shocking scenes. At others he made quite terrifying allegations about this woman. I also know of her through the letters of another man, Anton Schindler, who for a time acted as Ludwig's unpaid amanuensis and for a period corresponded with me about Ludwig and his life for reasons which I could not altogether comprehend.

The daughter of a paper-hanger, Johanna's reputation was never of the highest order. She had married Ludwig's brother when five months' pregnant with a son. She was possessed by kleptomaniac tendencies, her father having taught her as a child that the only way she could have money from him was for her to steal it without his knowledge. Caspar Carl had even once, I learned from Schindler, charged and sentenced Johanna to a month's house arrest for embezzling his money. Despite his dislike for his sister-in-law, during one particularly difficult period of Ludwig's life he was forced to spend several weeks in their home. It was 1809 or 1810, during Napoleon's attack on Vienna. I received a letter from Ludwig describing an event which had taken place a fortnight before in the home of his brother, Caspar Carl, and Johanna.

The bombardment of Vienna had been agony for Ludwig. The cacophony of guns going off drove him mad with pain as his hearing diminished rapidly day by day. For a day or two he hid himself in the cellar of the building in which he lived in the centre of the town. Then, forced to seek further refuge from the explosions, late one night he arrived on Caspar Carl's doorstep to ask if he could pass a few nights with them until it was over. To bring himself to make such a request was, I am sure, a difficult decision. It meant giving up his independence and staying for a time in the house of a brother for whom he had contradictory feelings and the wife whom he knew to be an unprincipled harridan.

The house was small but Caspar Carl offered Ludwig a small study just below the room he and Johanna shared. On the second night in the house Ludwig was awakened by the sound of screaming and shouting in the room above. This was followed by the sound of the outside door slammed with all of someone's might. Rising from the day bed on which he had been sleeping, Ludwig staggered to the window. Almost full, the moon cast a shimmering veil of white over the garden and the woods beyond which belied the hour – just gone three.

Ludwig watched in silence as, head down, the figure of Johanna shot beneath the window. She was draped in a billowy shift fashioned from linen so fine the light of the moon passed clear through it. Her hair unbridled and her feet bare, the figure darted across an expanse of whitened earth. Then, half hidden in the shadow of an old oak, she turned her back upon the house, fell on to to her knees in a heap and began to sway forward and backward and to tear her hair like someone possessed.

No sound had come from the room above, at least none that Ludwig could perceive. But from this woman in the garden a hollow keening now rose and fell in jagged ridges. This continued for perhaps two minutes, to be followed by what Ludwig described as 'unholy animal noises'. 'It was', he wrote,' as though this woman in her grief or rage could by her will summon wild familiars from the earth to plead her cause.'

'Then her whole body took on a dark luminosity,' Ludwig wrote, 'as though every wild malignancy called forth from deepest recesses had risen to the earth's surface to keep her company. Wegeler, I have never witnessed anything of the like before. It was terrifying, hideous yet still I could not turn away.' He stood still, his heavy forehead pressed against the glass, every nerve, every vein, every fibre stretched in tension and he watched like a man himself possessed. Many minutes later the woman rose and turned back towards the house.

Ludwig could see in the moonlight that her face had been smeared with earth, some of which, melted by her tears, flowed down to mar the whiteness of her breast. The woman, he said, stood still for only a moment. Then she began to move again – slowly to twist and sway as though entranced, entwining her hands in snake-like hair then raising them above her head in honour of some ancient rhythm only she could hear. Still blinded by the moon, Ludwig remained silently in attendance. As suddenly as it had begun, her movement ended, her face raised to the window at which he stood. Ludwig knew he had been seen yet still he could not turn away. It was then the horror began.

This woman, this Johanna, knowing her indecent behaviour to have been discovered, showed not modesty enough to bow her head. 'She stood,' wrote Ludwig, 'stark still gazing up at me, as brutal as a man, whilst I remained transfixed. Then lifting her shift above her head she ripped it from her body, giving no thought to her nakedness. She smiled the smile of a whore or of an ancient crone and, caring nothing for her appearance, with great purpose strutted past the window.' Before he had time to register what was happening she had climbed the steps, re-entered the house and flung open the door to the room in which he stood. He turned to find her spread across the doorway in the posture of some fairy queen – her body shimmering with the strange unearthly light it had carried with it from the garden.

Until that moment Ludwig had heard nothing from the brother in the room above. He was therefore surprised that within moments of Johanna's entry Caspar Carl descended in full dress, boots and all. Saying not a word, he grasped his wife's right wrist and tore her from the doorway, forcing her naked body to the floor. She shrieked and tried to raise herself, grasping a small table in the entrance way to lift her body. It was not until the knife struck that Ludwig saw it. Caspar Carl had been carrying it in his right hand, grasped in perfect readiness for use. Without hesitation he brought it down upon his wife's hand, pinning it to the table through the centre. Suspended like a piece of meat from the hook of a butcher's shop Johanna began to weep, silently now. All the shrieking was finished, as though the demonic power had deserted her crumpled body.

'My God what have you done!' Ludwig shouted at Caspar Carl, now standing limply next to the naked body of his wife. She gazed up at Ludwig with repentant eyes and pleaded, 'Please, Ludwig, please, keep your voice low, we must not wake the child.'

Johanna – the terrible female. As I write these words I remember a drawing I saw many years ago of the Indian goddess Kali who represents the terror side of the Shakti principle. She was shown wearing a necklace of human skulls and a girdle of human teeth. Between the huge fangs which protrude from her mouth hangs a long pendulous tongue dripping gore. Ludwig, for whatever reason, seemed to see Johanna like Kali – this goddess to whom human entrails are a special delicacy. The goddess who in one hand holds a human head and with the other wields a bloodstained sword with which she has severed it. The name Kali, as I recall, means 'black'. Kali, like Ludwig's Johanna, is blackness personified – ruler of all the dark elements of nature. No wonder he calls her 'Queen of the Night'.

You can see what kind of a woman Ludwig was having to cope with, Dr Wawruch. It is little wonder that when Caspar Carl died he insisted upon taking over the guardianship of his nephew Karl. This decision, made out of love for the child, then nine years old as I recall, may ultimately have cost Ludwig his life, for the boy, I fear, bore the same bad blood as his mother. In fact, a good deal of what I learned about the wicked Johanna and the quite inhuman consequences of Ludwig having to cope with her over the years did not come from Ludwig himself. For many years Ludwig ceased to mention Johanna in his letters. It came instead from Ludwig's unpaid amanuensis – Anton Schindler – the same Anton Schindler who has now written a biography of Ludwig. I have not myself read Schindler's book nor do I intend to. This letter to you, Dr Wawruch, will be the last thing I ever write or read about my friend. There comes a time when enough has been said and the dead must be left to the dead.

Ludwig had first written to me of this Schindler in 1815 or 1816, not long after they met. He was at that time much taken by Schindler's political ideas. However, it was not until as late as 1822 that Herr Schindler, a lawyer by training and a musician by choice, took up his position as private secretary to Ludwig.

At first Ludwig was full of praise for Herr Schindler's devotion to him. Schindler, he said, was most efficient in everything, from running errands and handling his correspondence to hiring and firing servants and renting apartments.

Herr Schindler, for reasons I never fully comprehended, took up the habit of writing letters to me about Ludwig. They began as notes added to those Ludwig had dictated himself. Before long, however, Ludwig's offerings dwindled and Schindler's notes grew until in time it was Schindler's words and none other I received. I never met Schindler but I am certain he is a peculiar animal. He never seemed to know the difference between the important and the incidental. He would take the same meticulous care over the way a particular letter of script was formed as he did over the purport of an important piece of information. He was also possessed by insatiable curiosity. Like a mole, blind yet bearing huge claws, he always seemed to be burrowing deeper and deeper – insistent upon knowing everything. Left alone in Ludwig's study Schindler probably delighted in reading every piece of paper on his desk.

The letters he wrote were full of gossip. At first this was of some interest to me for Ludwig himself had been at best an erratic correspondent and I was frequently having to rely on hearsay to know what Ludwig was doing in Vienna. Schindler – the mole –supplied me with all I could ever want to know. But in time his letters became an unpleasant nuisance – missals conceived in a rodent's brain and with a rodent's cunning. What I found most irritating was the way Schindler was continually trying to wheedle out of me as much information as he could about Ludwig, about the Breuning family, even about myself – to what end I have no idea. I concluded that he must be one of those small-minded men who insinuate themselves into people's private lives by collecting hearsay and gossip the way a rat forages with its long nose to gather grain for winter, believing that whatever is available may one day prove useful. I also think that, like many rather insignificant men, Schindler, himself a violinist, liked to bask in the glory of Ludwig's fame – even perhaps to feed off his vitality. Eventually I realised that this obsequious creature looked upon Ludwig as a possession over which he attempted continually to exercise proprietorial rights. So I stopped answering Schindler's letters. Yet it was not for many months that he finally ceased to write them.

Then all at once, soon after the premiere of Ludwig's magnificent Symphony in D Minor – his final symphony, alas – I received a letter from my friend in which Herr

Schindler was mentioned with what I can only describe as a strange mixture of fury and fear. Last evening I made a long search for this letter through my papers but sadly could not locate it. I shall have to rely on my memory in an attempt to describe its contents.

In the letter Ludwig, previously so full of praise for his private secretary, used such words as 'I have never on God's earth seen a worse wretch', describing the gentleman as his 'appendix'. He went on to say that he intended to sever all relations with Schindler. This I believe he did until a little while before his death, when the two of them were for a time reconciled. Given Ludwig's tendency to violent reversals of attitude and behaviour, such a dramatic change was not altogether surprising. What I did find curious, however, were certain phrases Ludwig used in the letter which gave indication he had something to fear from this man Schindler – particularly in relation to his Symphony in D Minor. I by no means remember them accurately but they included references to certain dangers Ludwig perceived or feared which he described as 'usurping the power of music for despicable ends', 'trapping men's minds through mathematical chains' and 'the esoteric prerogatives of melodic minor scales' and such other phrases which made no sense to me, I assumed at the time because I am not myself in the least musical. What also concerned me about the letter were certain anxieties Ludwig expressed about his own person. He told me that he was experiencing difficulty with his breathing. At times, he said, this had led him to fear – how did he phrase it – that 'my spirit was being pulled out from my body'. He questioned me about how to prevent such an occurrence. I, who have no experience in such matters yet sensed the urgency of his trepidation, wrote by return post suggesting that whenever such a breathlessness overcame him he sit quietly and repeat the words, 'God help me . . .

God help me . . . God help me . . .' again and again until the spell passed.

Several years later as you know, Dr Wawruch, Schindler returned. I hope you will not judge me too harshly when I say that rodents can be hard to exterminate. Rodent or not, it was through Schindler's letters that I learned much of the story of Ludwig's struggle with Johanna and the nephew. It too was not a pretty tale. Ludwig was in his forties at the time of Caspar Carl's death. He had already established himself as the greatest living composer in Vienna – in all of Europe – yet his life was not a happy one. His dreams of marriage had more than once turned to ashes. He had grown eccentric in his habits: not the easiest man to live with nor perhaps the best companion for a nine-year-old child, especially a boy with Johanna's bad blood in his veins. Anxious about the consequences of leaving the lad in the care of such a mother as Johanna, Ludwig went to court to secure full guardianship for himself – for in his will Caspar Carl had indicated only that he wished Ludwig to *share* the guardianship of young Karl with Johanna. At first Ludwig's plea was granted. He was given an injunction which forbade Johanna to see her son without his consent. This, I feel sure, he did entirely for the boy's own good. Yet Ludwig became quite fanatical and, I believe, acted unwisely by refusing the mother any access whatsoever to her son. This forced the child to meet his mother in secret.

Ludwig's hatred of Johanna would flare up in his letters to me and then quieten for a while as though some temporary reparation of their relationship had been made. In one letter he wrote, 'Wegeler, you would not believe what has been happening here. Last evening at the Artists' Ball until three in the morning, the Queen of the Night exposed not only her mental but her *physical* nakedness. It was whispered she would sell herself for twenty gulden.' In another he told me Johanna had been involved in a liaison with another man during his brother's mortal illness. Later I learned that Johanna had borne a daughter out of wedlock – a girl who no doubt had the same propensities as her mother. Bad blood, I have frequently observed, tends to be passed down from the female side of a family. It takes several generations for its effects to be diluted.

As I say, with obsessive single-mindedness Ludwig tried to take on full responsibility for the boy's life – a task for which he was singularly ill prepared, having lived as a bachelor all his life and possessing no notion of what constitutes sound paternal behaviour. For years Ludwig moved Karl from one school to another, fretted over the boy's conduct and morality and worried about his physical health. I frequently received scribbled notes from Ludwig with absurdly simple questions regarding the child. 'Is it necessary, Wegeler,' he would write, 'to put on a pair of underpants immediately after a bath in the cold weather?' and, 'Where do lice come from, is it healthy to have lice?' or, 'Karl has five corns on each foot, please advise on what should be done to eliminate them. Do they encourage the development of chilblains? Wegeler, please write in haste, Vienna doctors are not to be trusted and I must find out what action is to be taken. . . . Yours, L.'

Ludwig was always overprotective of the child and often unpredictable in the way he treated him. One moment he would fawn on him with the excessive affections of a fearful mother. The next he would turn cold. 'I adamantly refused to take his hand, Wegeler,' he wrote. 'When he expressed sorrow for his actions I did not let him near me. I am well aware that he must be made to suffer the demons which possess him – demons the source of which one knows full well – which cannot be exorcised.' As Karl grew towards manhood Ludwig was continually cross-questioning him about his activities while Karl, shuffled about from one place to another, forbidden to see his mother and constantly admonished by his uncle for his minor faults, became increasingly erratic in his behaviour and disturbed in his demeanour. He was expelled for misconduct from a boarding-school at Modling run by a priest named Father Frölich.

Around that time, I believe it was 1818 if my memory serves me correctly, Schindler wrote to say Johanna had tried again through the court to recover her right to her son. With evidence given by servants about Ludwig's irrational behaviour and from the priest, Frölich, who testified that Ludwig encouraged the boy's disrespect for his mother, rewarding any signs of hatred – real or pretended – towards her, the court ruled that the boy had been tossed about too much and awarded custody to Johanna under nominal supervision of the State Procurator. The decision devastated Ludwig, whose entire personal life had become centred upon Karl. He quickly countered with an appeal claiming that the evidence given by Father Fröhlich had been invalid since he was 'a drunkard and a libertine'. Ludwig even went so far as to suggest to the court that the priest had fallen under the destructive power of Johanna's sexual wiles – an accusation which, the rodent assured me in his letters, was soundly based on fact. Ludwig approached the court again, putting forward the names of two men of impeccable character, Karl Peters and Prince Lobkowitz, to become Karl's joint legal guardians together with himself. In the spring of 1820 the courts reversed their decision and once again granted Ludwig's right to the boy.

As a result of his preoccupation with his newly found 'son' – for that is how he had always referred to Karl – and of all the strife which came out of it, Ludwig's musical output decreased to practically nothing for five years, although it did begin to improve with the final decision of the court granting him guardianship. Meanwhile his letters became replete with obsessive domestic concerns about the price of food in the market, about how much one is expected to feed a servant and with worries about money and whether or not he would be able to provide for the nephew. During this period too his dealings with publishers, I learned from Steffen von Breuning, became dishonest. He would promise the same composition to more than one publisher and receive money from each. But when the final decision of the court was made in his favour, my friend began to work again with renewed vigour.

Then to my utmost surprise, quite inexplicably, Ludwig's attitude towards the wicked Johanna altered radically. He wrote me that the Queen of the Night had become ill and he was determined to assist her as she was unable to pay for her medicines. The following year, while busy composing the choral finale of his last symphony, he wrote: 'Wegeler, I have arranged for Karl's mother to draw a good pension so long as I am alive and should I become more comfortably well-off in the future and be able to provide her from my income a sum large enough to ameliorate her circumstances I shall certainly do so. After all, one must show compassion. Why should I not wish her all possible happiness – she cannot be held responsible for her heated blood.' It is not surprising, however, that his tolerance towards Johanna did not last.

Ludwig seemed to have no awareness of the fact that Karl, whom he worked so hard to protect, had by now grown to manhood. Instead of releasing his hold on the nephew, he became even more obsessive in his attempt to look after and protect Karl, interfering in every area of the young man's life. To this end he even solicited Schindler and other friends to spy on Karl's activities, to find out how much he drank, if he gambled, if he played billiards. Ludwig would also set Schindler on Karl's trail with a directive to steer the nephew away from areas of the city frequented by prostitutes.

During this period Ludwig's letters – if letters they could be called for they were more like hastily scribbled messages, sometimes even written on the back of music copy paper – became increasingly full of anger and fear. 'Wegeler, what can I do to prevent the horrific things from happening to Karl? How do I prevent him from visiting dark women? Is it his blood? For I am sure that is what he is doing. I berate him, I forbid him, I warn him of the dangers, I have him followed, yet still I fear he is enjoying himself of an evening in company which is not desirable. I have written to Schlemmer with whom he is boarding and demanded that he prevent Karl from leaving his house at night under any pretext whatever without written permission from me, yet I fear Schlemmer may not heed my plea. What, Wegeler, is a father to do to protect his son? Please write immediately, L.'

Ludwig's own health continued to be eroded as the quarrels between uncle and nephew continued, becoming increasingly bitter sometimes, according to both Schindler and Ludwig, even ending in physical violence. Ludwig wanted Karl to take a university degree and to settle himself into a secure career. Karl wanted to join the army – a desire which was anathema to Ludwig. Schindler wrote that Karl had begun seeing his mother again in secret and even intimated that he feared Karl might have been participating in a forbidden liaison with her himself. The conflicts between nephew and uncle reached a climax in 1826 just before Karl was to sit his university examination. It was a day after Ludwig had written to Schlemmer asking him to restrain Karl from his evening sorties. Schlemmer apparently was not discreet enough to conceal the uncle's letter from the nephew.

Schindler described to me what took place. Karl arrived one morning at the house in Baden which Ludwig had rented for the summer. Schindler and Ludwig were together in 'The Master's' workroom. Ludwig was weak in body. He had been ill for a fortnight, fighting against severe stomach pain which all of Dr Braunhofer's admonitions against coffee, spices and wine had been unable to alleviate. He was also deeply involved in a creative battle, trying to harness a lunging base line of arpeggios in the last movement of his new symphony.

They heard a violent banging on the outside door. Schindler rose to answer it. There stood Karl, his hair in wild disarray. In his right hand he held a pistol, in his left he gripped a crumpled piece of paper – his uncle's letter to Schlemmer. The nephew said nothing. He barged in, ignoring Schindler's presence by knocking into him with such a blow that he was thrown back against the wall, upsetting a pile of manuscripts. Karl stormed into the room where Ludwig was working, throwing open the door with a force that caused the plaster to crumble. The amanuensis picked himself up and followed close behind the nephew, fearful that Karl was intending to kill the Master.

'Uncle, I will have no more interference from you,' said Karl. 'My life is my own. I am no longer a child for you to play with. What I do is no business of yours. How dare you write to Herr Schlemmer and ask him to restrain my movements?' The volume of his voice rose with every sentence. So close did Karl come to Ludwig's face as he spat out the final words that Ludwig visibly recoiled as one might when faced with a venomous snake. Karl thrust the crumpled letter to Schlemmer into his uncle's face, then grabbed the back of Ludwig's head and pushed it into the paper the way a trainer might do to a dog that had urinated in a forbidden place.

127

Ludwig had been seated in front of his piano. He pulled his shoulders back, tilted his head to one side and glared into the eyes of his nephew. Neither moved for several seconds. Then, all at once, overcoming his physical weakness and bodily pain, Ludwig rose like a great bear, in a movement so slow yet so inexorable that Schindler told me it made his bowels tremble. Ludwig grabbed Karl by the shoulders and tossed him back across the room in one fell gesture, evincing an inhuman strength that belied his frail condition. Karl fell stunned to the wooden floor. He lay there for a few seconds then, drawing himself to his feet, advanced on his uncle again. Ludwig held one arm against the nephew's chest to prevent his coming closer.

'I will not be spied on any longer,' hissed Karl.

'You stupid, fat, overgrown infant,' growled Ludwig. 'Don't you know I hover over you to protect you? To guard you from the scum of the earth who would drag you down?'

'Nothing drags me down but you, uncle. I am sick of your pretensions to my welfare. I will not support imprisonment any longer. You care not a fig for me, you have never cared for me. You want only to torture me.'

'Torture you? I have given you everything I have,' shouted Ludwig, grabbing the nephew by the collar before he could step back, and shaking him like a pile of rags. Again Schindler was awed by the power in Ludwig's body. Ludwig had no difficulty handling this muscular young man who was several inches taller and thirty years younger than himself.

The gun fell to the floor in the scuffle. Karl knelt to retrieve it but Ludwig was too quick for him. He kicked it violently to one side. It went off as though the trigger had been pulled, skidding across the wooden floor to land against the wall across the room, out of reach of them both.

'Given me everything you have?' whined Karl. 'My dear,

sweet uncle – do you not know just how impoverished you are? You old fool. You have nothing to give – nothing. You never did have. You want only to steal my life since you have none of your own.'

'As God is my witness I want nothing from you!' shrieked Ludwig, 'except to get away from you and your whore of a mother and from every obligation your wretched father threw at me when he died.' Ludwig stood in the centre of the room flailing his arms about.

'Very well, I am leaving, uncle,' said Karl in a low voice. Slowly the young man walked over to where the gun was lying, knelt, and picked it up.

'Good,' said Ludwig. 'Leave, you ungrateful little bastard. Leave me in peace so that I never have to look upon your ugly, deceitful face again.'

'Goodbye, uncle,' said Karl moving towards the door.

Ludwig's arms dropped to his sides. He stood still as death. All the strength in his body seemed to drain away making him look, in Schindler's words, 'like a deflated sack'. Then, as if awakening from a long sleep, Ludwig reached out a hand toward Karl who had crossed the threshold into the hall.

'Do not leave, my son,' he said, softly, in a voice altogether different from any Schindler had heard before. Ludwig moved swiftly through the door of his workroom into the hall, grasped Karl's shoulder to halt him in his tracks, and in the same soft voice said, 'I embrace you.' He wrapped both his arms around the nephew's shoulders and chest from behind, pulling him backwards towards himself, then he rested his head against the young man's back. 'I embrace you, my son. Be my good, diligent, noble son, and I will be your faithful father . . . my Karl . . . my Karl. . . .' Ludwig's eyes filled with tears.

Schindler watched as Karl's body stiffened then shrank

beneath the embrace of his uncle. 'He looked like a creature,' wrote Schindler, 'trapped too long in a snare, whose will had dissipated.' The nephew stood helpless in the uncle's embrace, the gun still hanging from his hand, his head bowed. Then, without warning, he turned and with slow deliberation wrenched Ludwig's arms away from his body and lowered his uncle on to a small love-seat set against the wall.

'Uncle, I cannot bear any more,' Karl said in a low voice. 'I cannot bear it, do you not understand? . . . I cannot live any more with this torture.'

Ludwig stared into the nephew's eyes with a complete lack of comprehension. A shudder passed over Karl's body, then, gun in hand, he turned to Schindler and said, 'Look after him, Schindler. My time is finished,' and walked through the outer door, pulling it to quietly behind him.

The rest I learned from Ludwig himself. It seems that the day before Karl had made a trip to the pawnbroker and pledged his watch in return for money, with which he had purchased the gun. When he left the small house in Baden it was at half-past ten on a Sunday morning. He wasted no time climbing the mountain to the ruins of Rauhenstein in the lovely Helenenthal which the two of them – Ludwig and Karl – loved greatly. There he discharged the pistol in the direction of his left temple. The bullet ripped flesh and shattered bone but did not penetrate the skull. Later that day a peasant worker discovered Karl's crumpled body amongst the ruins and carried him, presumably at his request, to the house of his mother in the city.

Johanna sent word to Ludwig immediately, telling him what Karl had done and asking Ludwig to send a surgeon who could conceal the attempted suicide – a serious crime in Vienna – from the police. But the surgeon was too long in coming and so another had to be summoned. Thus were

Ludwig's hopes of being the perfect father and providing all good things for his 'son' shattered for ever. With them went his pride and, I believe, Dr Wawruch, what remained of his health as well.

Karl was taken into protective custody at a hospital while the magistrate investigated the reasons behind his actions. Under Austrian law the nephew was obliged to enter a religious house where the monks could keep an eye on him and give him religious instructions 'to cure him of his folly'. Ludwig used all his influence to secure Karl's release on the understanding that he would take the nephew to the country to give him time to recover himself. Karl had begged and begged his uncle to allow him to leave university and take up a commission in the army. But Ludwig had always refused. Now he relented. Through the influence of Steffen von Breuning Ludwig was able to secure a cadetship for the nephew. So in October of 1826 uncle and nephew left Vienna for his brother Johann's estate in Gneixendorf to give the head wounds time to heal before taking up his commission. It was there that Ludwig completed his late quartets and there, it would seem, that the final seeds of his physical dissolution were sown and the final illness which you, Dr Wawruch, were forced to live through, developed.

Ludwig was a solitary man who had two very strong tendencies, both of which, I feel sure, influenced the development of his illnesses. The first was to hold on to whatever came within his sphere of interest or control — whether it be a friendship, an intellectual idea, or even the waste materials from a rancid food which he would have been far better expectorating; vomiting did not come easily to him. He once confided in me that he would do anything to avoid it as the action frightened him, he said, and taxed his strength. The second was, despite constant expressions of general worry and his physical condition, never to speak of what specifically ailed him until the suffering had become so intense that it could not be ignored. In both cases this constraint mounting from his will to internalise his experience would grow to a point at which whatever had been hidden would issue forth violently. Then a torrent of disease symptoms would make a volcanic appearance or an outpouring of hypochondriacal fear and the *idée fixe* that he was ill without cause and that no one could help him would develop. I have always believed – alas, without any scientific reason – that much of Ludwig's illnesses grew to exaggerated magnitude because of this tendency to hold within his heart all things which caused him distress or pain as well as every product of toxicity and tension. Such was his predisposition.

As I write these words, Dr Wawruch, I am made aware that one of the reasons I have so willingly discarded the dozens of letters I received from Ludwig about his medical treatments and illnesses, which now I deeply regret being unable to share with you, is simply this: for one who loved him to read missals so full of anxiety and confusion is a painful task. It requires a strong stomach – something which, despite my good intentions and my medical training, I fear I have never possessed. Over the years I would receive Ludwig's letters and respond to them with friendship yet in a cool professional way. Perhaps this offered my friend the reassurance he needed. I don't know. I do know I have been guilty of cowardice. It is a guilt that arises from only half hearing a cry of pain issue from someone to whom one feels one should have been more open. This is for me an uncomfortable consideration, Dr Wawruch, even after all these years – one which on its own I fear could provide ample justification for my recent hauntings.

Apart from the odd chill which resulted from exposure to weather, usually either the wet or the cold, the first of

Ludwig's illnesses of which I was aware were his continual asthmatic attacks. They began as I have mentioned in the wake of severe melancholia at the time of his mother's death. They may well have been the result of the serous and mucous profluvia to which he was prone – or of the prolonged and weighty persuasion of sentiment both for his mother's loss and from his attempts to take up the reins of the family. In any case he was at that time possessed of a dark fear that the consumption which had claimed her had also been bequeathed to him through her blood. For several years afterwards, during which he was applying his will energetically to gathering money enough to care for his younger brothers, he lived in the shadow of such fear.

Then, in 1797 or 1798, Ludwig suffered a terrible typhus. I have often wondered if this typhus was not an insidious bridge to his loss of hearing, although he himself seemed unaware of any difficulty with his ears for a year or two afterwards. The fever had been produced by a thorough chilling which resulted from his having sat down to work immediately after taking a long walk during which he had been caught in the rain. After the typhus he was to contract both bronchitis and rheums off and on for the rest of his life. If not directly causative of the deterioration of his hearing, they surely exacerbated its progress. I myself knew nothing of the insidious deafness until I received a letter from him in the summer of 1801 pleading with me to tell no one of his disability and asking if I would correspond with his current physician about the prognosis. Ludwig never believed that any doctor told him the truth. In that letter he also spoke of an intention to visit us. Alas he did not come that next spring as planned, although I greatly urged him to do so.

Ludwig consulted Johann Peter Frank, Pater Weiss and others whose names I no longer recall about his loss of hearing. They disagreed as to its cause. Some said *neuritis acustica* or labyrinthitis while others favoured *otitis media*. The onset of the deafness I believe was around 1796 although the first humming, ringing and buzzing Ludwig confided to me did not appear until somewhat later in 1798 or 1799. It all began as a partial loss in his ability to distinguish high frequencies and by sudden loud noises causing him discomfort. But I believe for the first few years those with whom he conversed and worked remained largely unaware of his condition. Ludwig wrote to me several times later asking for medical advice and requesting my thoughts on various doctors whom he had consulted not only about his deafness but about his innumerable other difficulties.

Truly, Dr Wawruch, my friend's body was like a battlefield on which the forces of life and death raged continually. I gave him my opinion of Schmidt – of whom Ludwig had grown quite fond and to whom he even dedicated a piano trio. His next queries concerned whether or not I thought Mesmerism might hold an answer for him. He told me he had visited a priest in Stefanskirche who was known to have effected the most miraculous cures. Alas, despite his good cheer and his defiant will, it was not to be. The hearing continued to deteriorate and he went on being plagued with the same agonising internal symptoms year after year. He was never again to escape them.

During his later years in Vienna he experienced several fevers with Katarrhe, a septic foot, rheumatic attacks, colic, typhus and rheumatic fever. Around the age of fifty Ludwig again wrote to me to say he had been in bed for several weeks with gout and earaches, to which he was prone during the winter months. A year or so later, as I recall, he experienced severe eye inflammation which lasted many months. Then during the year that preceded his death I remember him writing to say that as a result of his spitting blood, constant belching, fever and inflammation of the bowel, his physician at the time – Braunhofer, I believe – had forbidden him wine, spirits, spices and coffee. He had also been taking Brown's treatment of purgation for a stoppage of the bowel, with disastrous results. What folly! Brown's horrific theories have by now, I am certain, disposed of more people in Europe than the ravages of Napoleon's armies.

The illnesses in Ludwig's later years were aggravated by the agonising worry and trouble brought down upon him by his wretched nephew Karl, who seems to have done everything within his power to undermine his uncle's strength and to destroy his belief in life. Johanna too, I feel sure, had a great deal to answer for in the development of his final illness: I gather she frequently brought her lovers into the house and I am told spent many nights away from home even during her husband's last illness. Dr Wawruch, is there anything quite as destructive, quite as vicious, quite as hideous as a dark woman in a man's life? Johanna I have it on good authority was . . . is . . . a woman who has neither respect for reason nor any sense whatsoever of propriety. Such women, like madmen who have rejected every moral rule, seem to amass a power of evil against which man in his honest simplicity is rendered impotent. Ludwig no doubt felt himself to be swamped in the sea of the dark forces which she embodied. I know that the years after his brother's death during which Ludwig was forced to fight unpleasant legal battles with this woman – sometimes not knowing from one week to the next if he was to lose the nephew whom he so devotedly looked after despite the boy's ingratitude and dishonesties – extracted a heavy toll from his mind and body. It seemed only to grow worse and worse as time passed. The year of the wretched nephew's attempted suicide Steffen wrote these horrible words to me: 'Our friend Ludwig suddenly looks and acts like a shabby old peasant.'

You have asked about Ludwig's consumption of alcohol. I can assure you that it was, at least while I knew him, not excessive. Nor did Steffen von Breuning ever convey to me the slightest hint that it had become so during his later years in Vienna. Ludwig was a temperate man. Except when one of his wild moods overtook him. Then quite literally anything could happen. I am afraid it is not my place to speak with authority about whether or not my friend ever suffered *Lues venerea* or any form of cachexia either in the genitals or throughout the whole body. In any case Ludwig never reported to me any such condition. Such things are perhaps best left unspoken between friends. I personally do not credit that even if a *Lustseuche* had been present it could have played a major part in the development of his deafness.

There is, I now recall, an incident about which Ludwig wrote to me that may be of interest to you, Dr Wawruch, I only wish I had the letter to send to you but I have searched all my papers and cannot locate it. He told me of a choleric attack at or near the time of the first onset of deafness. He had become furious, he said, over the behaviour of a refractory musician and thrown himself on the floor in a rage, beating his fists against the boards as actors sometimes do. When he got up he could no longer hear properly in his left ear. Whether or not this story has substance in truth I do not know. Certainly Ludwig believed it but my friend at times had a tendency to imagine one thing and another so I cannot be sure. As a physician I find it doubtful that such an event could precipitate deafness.

I do not know if this information is in any way relevant to your enquiry but I offer what I remember of the incident in the hopes than you, Dr Wawruch, can make more sense of it that I have been able to do, but this brings me to the end of what I feel I can profitably tell you about Ludwig's illnesses and personal dispositions. I enclose a copy of his early journal – the only one of which I am aware. He left it in my keeping when I departed from Vienna in 1798. He was, I think, concerned it might be lost with his many changes of address: he was so restless that he seldom remained in the same apartment more than a few months.

It is in the spirit of a need for truth and sanctity that I have committed to paper what memories remain of early meetings with my friend, and in the hope that in some way they may shed light on your enquiry. I, in turn, have two demands to make of you. First I ask that you destroy this record once you have read it and that in no circumstances do you communicate its contents to any other person. I want nothing more to do with the dark phenomena of which you write. These recent 'fugues' appear to have cleared from my own life some three or four weeks ago as spontaneously as they first appeared. God willing, in completing this record to you I shall have finally heard the last of them. This brings me to my second request: I ask that you respect my concern for protection as much as is humanly possible both for myself and for my dear wife, Lorchen. I therefore ask as a gentleman and an honourable man that you do not attempt to communicate with me further. This request I make in the name of all that is holy. May it, despite all else, remain so.

There is one matter further, Dr Wawruch. I had on beginning this missal intended not to mention it. It is such that I myself do not wish to recall the event in detail. However – briefly – in the interest of science and with a certain, if I may be so bold as to say, *compassion* for you in your current state, allow me to describe the incident. Many weeks ago in the midst of the hideous bodily occurrences which had gripped me, similar to your own, I spent the night in a hunting lodge which belongs to a friend of my wife. By a series of unforeseen events, including an un-expectedly severe snowstorm for the season, I found myself alone in the large house. That evening, as I recall, I had been experiencing the ringing in the ears which you say has accompanied many of your own strange symptoms. Fearing by now that I might quite literally be going mad, and well aware of the necessity for sleep after almost a week of lying silently awake in my bed while drowning in a sea of unnameable fears and shifting bodily symptoms, I prepared a sleeping draught for myself and went to bed.

I slept. Yet my head was filled with wild dreams of music played by unseen hands. I awakened before dawn to find the bed drenched in sweat. I arose, abandoning my attempts at restful sleep, wrapped myself in a heavy dressing gown and, sitting before the washstand on which stood a rustic mirror and several candles which I lit, I began to shave. To my horror, on glancing in the mirror I discovered that the face peering back at me was not my own but his – that of Ludwig – looking not as I had known him in his youth but as he must have appeared much later, near to his death. Only for an instant did I behold the image before leaping to my feet. I screamed, lashing out with arms and legs, and overturned the table, smashing the mirror into a thousand pieces. For the next hour, until dawn brought the blessing of a magnificent white sunlight through the window, I remained shamefully huddled in a corner of my bed trembling like a child.

That is all that I can tell you. I know no more. In conclusion may I say once again that I continue to be deeply troubled by the atmospheres and events which you tell me have taken hold in your life and which by some stroke of fate seem also to have entered my own in recent months. I pray that you will find some explanation for what has been occurring to you, even more that you too will eventually find rest.

With good wishes for your research and in the hope that

you too will soon be spared any further anguish over this matter.

I remain your most respectful servant,
Franz Gerhard Wegeler

SCHERZO

'You have probably not heard of macrobes.'

'Microbes?' said Mark in bewilderment. 'But of course –'

'I did not say microbes, I said macrobes. The formation of the word explains itself. Below the level of animal life we have long known that there are microscopic organisms. Their actual results on human life, in respect of health and disease, have, of course, made up a large part of history: the secret cause was not known till we invented the microscope. . . I have now to inform you that there are similar organisms above the level of animal life. . . I mean that it is more permanent, disposes of more energy, and has greater intelligence.'

C. S. Lewis *That Hideous Strength*

As I laid down the papers I had been reading I noticed that my hand was shaking. This manuscript – Wegeler's letter – whatever it was – had cut right through me. It demanded I pay attention to it. Too many of the events of which Wegeler spoke paralleled events in my own life since Mirabehn placed the package into my hands – the physical symptoms, the hauntings, the appearance of men dressed in black. I had to make something of it all but I didn't know what. I found myself moving in the world of the unseen for the first time in my life, a world I not only did not believe existed but in which I had no training, knew no rules. They taught you about how to use silent assassination weapons powered by compressed air that deliver undetectable *fléchettes* into the enemy but they didn't teach you a damned thing about the powers of the unseen world. That I would have to learn for myself. The names Wawruch, von Breuning, Neefe and the rest meant nothing to me. About secret meetings I knew too much, as I did about the arrogance of elitists. I had been an elitist. About Beethoven himself I knew virtually nothing – only that he'd written incredible music, music which, when I first heard it, had taken my breath away – and that he was deaf.

I got angry. I told myself I had had enough of mystery and games – that I had let my imagination run away with me and been carried away by a lot of nonsense – hearing music in the night and smashing up perfectly good mirrors – simply because some old woman insisted I take a package from her and told me it was a 'grave responsibility'.

I got up from the table and stretched my legs. Light had begun to filter through the window. I wanted to go out, go to work, get away, 'snap out of it'. But there was nowhere to go. Besides, the manuscript fascinated me. What was this letter about? Was it real or phoney? Then greed raised its ugly head. It might be an excellent opportunity to make some money for myself, I reasoned – to do something besides write endless newspaper articles about the latest cure for colitis. What the hell. After all, I had been trained as an army intelligence officer. It was my job to be able to take what is known and put it together with new facts in order to project what was going to happen. This was a perfect opportunity to use my skills. Besides, I had nothing to lose. The editor had for stupid reasons of his own given me two or three weeks off. I would take them, and more – I would spin them out into six or eight weeks – all the time any good journalist needs to research Beethoven's life a bit and knock together a tidy little book about it all. I figured if this stuff about Ludwig had hold of me, then I would do my damnedest to make it profitable. I went to the kitchen and made a huge cup of the strongest, blackest coffee I could muster.

Then I caught a glimpse of myself, the way you do when you walk through a door and unexpectedly come face to face with a full-length mirror, but this time it was a look at my insides. Instead of a spreading waistline and sagging flesh, I saw for the first time just how far I had come from my beginnings – just how distorted my values had become. Values? What values? Yet it was not always like this. I remembered a time when I believed in something – when I believed in just about everything.

I was born in Kansas in the middle of one of those wheat fields that goes on as far as the eye can see in every direction – dead flat and glittering gold. It sings to you and the song is always the same: 'everything is possible,' it says, 'just choose your direction and follow it.' I chose mine early. I was absolutely sure what I wanted and I was pretty certain I would have it too. But I found it tough going to have to wait so long. I would trudge down the dirt path that led from my uncle's farmhouse to the road where the yellow school bus picked me up each morning, lost in my own world – a world filled with heroes who fought for freedom and banished tyranny, men of honour who were part of a long grey line – and right in the middle of them was me, dressed in the uniform of the United States Army.

Both my parents were dead. My mother died giving birth to a brother when I was four. He survived her by only six weeks. Aunt Emma said she had done everything she could to save him but 'The Lord called on your brother, Michael, and we had to let him go. He probably knew your mama would be lonely without him.' I remember my mother – well, not really, but I remember her smell: it was warm like

fresh churned butter and soft as down. After she died my
aunt and uncle – thirty years her senior – looked after me.
That was how I came to grow up on their farm.

The memories of my father smell different. When I think
of him I remember leather and the odour of saddle soap
which he rubbed into his boots – to keep them from
cracking, he used to say. I did not see much of my father. It
was wartime and he was a Lieutenant-Colonel in the United
States Marines. He was in Guam when my mother died.
Uncle Rob wrote him a letter giving him the news. I don't
remember that. I do remember the letter he wrote back,
though. It had a paragraph in it which my Aunt Emma read
to me over and over again during the years I grew up on
their farm, 'Mike,' it said, 'the Lord giveth and the Lord
taketh away. We cannot understand the will of the Lord.
Mama is with him now and you must stay with Aunt Emma
and Uncle Rob to look after them – for they are bound to
miss your mama something awful. I want you to help out
with the chores and say your prayers just like your mama
taught you. Soon you will be a big boy, then you can go to
school and learn all the wonderful things that will help you
grow up big – and strong – and smart too. You got to be
smart, Mike, but most of all you got to be true to yourself.
Love, Dad.' I only saw him once after that. Then we got the
telegram from the War Department saying he would not be
coming home. I spent the rest of my childhood on my uncle's
farm. I don't even know that I missed my parents much for
my aunt and uncle were good to me and I knew my father
had died in the most honourable way a man could die:
fighting for his country – fighting for what he knew to be
right.

I loved the farm. I loved the freedom and the space of
America. Years later I saw the painting *American Gothic* and
identified with the people in it – the man with the pitchfork

and his wife – staunchly independent and, like my father, willing to fight for what they believe in. The wheat fields in that painting were my wheat fields – the fields I loved to go into when the wheat was high, to burrow great passages all through them. I had to be careful though, because if my uncle found out what I had done he would be very angry. He said it spoilt the harvest. So I had to find ways of crawling through the wheat to make my tunnels without crushing it so they could not be detected from the outside. I loved the secretness of it, I always loved secrets.

My parents left me a little money. Since I was an only child it turned out to be just enough to send me away to school. When I was ten I started to clip ads for military academies from Aunt Emma's copy of the *Ladies' Home Journal* and to listen to John Philip Sousa marches on my uncle's Victrola. Both made my flesh ripple. Every night as I lay in bed I imagined myself dressed in a fine uniform learning to shoot a gun as well as my daddy had done. Finally they gave in and let me go to a small military school in Iowa. I loved it – the discipline, the sense of purpose – even the school emblem which depicted the eagle of honour subduing the serpent of tyranny. I fell for it all hook line and sinker. And when taps were played each evening at sunset the sound of the trumpets made my eyes glisten. I knew I was going to defend my country against all aggressors – to fight for freedom and banish tyranny.

I worked hard, and apart from a couple of incidents – like the time I got put in detention for letting loose a greased pig in the dorm – I did well. They wanted me to go to West Point. But when the appointment came I hesitated. I had seen another ad which was to change the course of my life. Crumpled and frayed, it had been stuck up on the bulletin board just outside the school mess. Nobody knew where it came from or who had stuck it up. It had a drawing of twelve men dressed in battle fatigues and berets, their chests layered in ammunition. They were carrying the biggest rifles I had ever seen. 'The Special Forces Green Berets,' it said, 'the toughest troopers in the world.'

Who were the Green Berets? I asked everybody I could think of, but nobody could even tell me if they existed. Nobody that is except Mac. Mac was a retired sergeant major who came in twice a week to train those of us who wanted it in aikido, the Japanese martial art. An ex-army featherweight boxer he stood no more than five feet six but he had a voice like a foghorn. When Mac's voice was in gear the whole world trembled. 'Green Berets? Yeah, I know about the Green Berets,' he said, 'what do you want to know?'

'I want to know everything,' I said.

'Everything?' he said, smiling broadly.

'Yes. Who are they? Where do they come from?'

'OK,' he said. 'But you better sit down. It may take a while.'

We sat on the edge of the bleachers overlooking a training field. I was like a six-year-old listening to some wonderful tale unfold.

'The Green Berets are members of the Special Forces, Mike,' he said. 'They go back to the old OSS.'

'The OSS?'

'Secret Services.'

'Go on,' I said, doing my best to appear as casual as possible.

'The SF have something in common with other units born out of the Second World War – the Commandos in Canada, for instance, the SAS in Britain. But the SF is tougher and far more secret. It was originally part of the psychological warfare centre at Fort Riley, Kansas. The Green Berets are the real elite, Mike. The Commandos and the SAS, the

Rangers and the Marines —they all go in for a time. The Special Forces go in and stay in until they get the job done, no matter what it costs.' Mac looked at me, studying my face. I wondered what he was looking for.

'Go on, Mac,' I said.

'SF was the brain-child of Aaron Bank, a colonel and OSS operator who knew as a result of his Korean war experience that a guerrilla warfare team was needed to offer behind-enemy-line assistance.'

'What do the SF *do*, Mac?'

'What do they do? They do everything. They use five basic operational skills, Mike. Every SF officer is an expert in at least two, but highly proficient in the others.'

'Which skills?'

'Well, there's demolitions/engineering, communications, light and heavy weapons including enemy weapons, medicine, and operations/intelligence. The Green Berets are warriors, Mike. They work behind the scenes – so far behind that most soldiers think they are only a legend. They know how to use every weapon available – including all enemy weapons and weapons so secret that generals in the regular army, navy and marines don't know they exist.'

'Why did nobody I asked know about the SF?' I said.

'No one knew about them because the work they do cannot be known. The Green Berets turn their back on public recognition —decorations are often given in private. They would rather be honoured in secret for what they've done, knowing that they are the best in the world. Make no mistake, though, these guys have brains as well as brawn. They usually speak several languages and are skilled at winning over the hearts and minds of people. They're often involved in revolutionary activities in different countries. Most of all I guess they're skilled at doing the impossible, and they love it.'

By this time I was pretty certain West Point was not for me. 'I guess that makes them kind of special,' I said.

'You bet they're special, Mike – special because they have to make up their own guidelines, their own rules and regulations. Every man in the SF has to think for himself. His mind can't be rigid. His thinking can't be limited by the ordinary ideas of what can or can't be done. Every situation that he finds himself in is new and without precedent. Every situation demands he use everything he has – his brain, his body, his skills, his independence, his faith, the whole kit and caboodle – to come through.'

'And *do* they come through?'

'A lot of them get killed, and the ones that do get killed you never even hear about.'

'Yeah,' I said with stars in my eyes, 'but if you die, it is an honourable death. My father always said, "If your cause is truly just then sooner or later you win." How do you know all this, Mac?'

'I know about the Green Berets because I used to train them.'

'Here?'

'No, not here. At Fort Bragg in North Carolina.'

'And what about the berets – the hats themselves?' I asked.

'The berets are what SF operatives wear. The hats are totally unofficial but they set them apart from the regular military. They're not very well liked for it, either. There's always some colonel or general in the army or the navy who hates unconventional warfare and is trying to get rid of the berets, but that's what they choose to wear and there's not a helluva lot anyone can do about it.'

No longer able to contain my enthusiasm I leapt to my feet, 'Mac, how do I join?'

He laughed. 'You don't. You have to be selected. Only three out of a hundred men get through.'

'OK then, how do I get selected?' I asked impatiently. 'What do I need to do next?'

'Next, Mike, you graduate. Then you join the army. Then you get in touch with me.'

I had a tough time getting through the regular army into SF. I got court-martialled three times in basic training for various forms of insubordination and I had to do everything I could think of to get out of being sent to OCS – Officers Candidate School. I made a deal with my recruiting officer that if I failed even one qualification he could throw me into the infantry. If only a handful of hundreds of men made final selection, I was going to make damned sure I'd be one of them. More than anything in the world I wanted to earn the right to sew the SF patch on my shoulder that would for ever show the world that I had served in combat – I wanted it so bad I could taste it.

Mac was true to his word. In April 1962 I received orders to report to the special warfare school at Fort Bragg. There was only one thing that worried me – I was terrified of heights. It was just my luck that the first skill they made me learn brought me face to face with my own fear. Jump school was the most agonising three weeks of my life.

We spent a couple of weeks preparing for our first jump with the help of a whole load of complicated devices that were supposed to simulate the real thing. I was busy congratulating myself on how well I had handled it all when the moment of truth arrived: my first jump from a prop plane at 1,200 feet. 'Get ready!' I heard the jump master cry. My stomach felt like a force 12 was blowing through it. 'Hook up!' I hooked my static line to the cable running the length of the fuselage roof. 'Approach the door,' the voice barked. I figured the best way of not chickening out would be to keep my eyes closed all the way down. 'Jump!' it shouted. I couldn't believe this was happening to me. With both eyes firmly shut I leapt into space. A few seconds later my parachute opened and pulled my body harness up so hard between my legs I thought I had been damaged for life. With my eyes still closed I gave thanks that the canopy had opened and was even beginning to feel a bit self-satisfied. I opened my eyes and looked up. But instead of a beautiful pattern of rigging lines from my shoulders to the chute, there was a mass of knotted tangles all twisted up in a bunch behind my head. I panicked. What was I going to do? How could I untangle them? No one told me about this. I didn't know it then but I was only experiencing a common hiccup called twists caused by a bad jump from the aircraft. The normal process of falling sorts it out – but not until you are spun round like a top. I hit the ground like a dead weight. The next few jumps went better, although I continued to keep my eyes closed most of the time and hoped like hell that nobody would notice.

Then came the crunch. It all revolved around our preparation for HALO-SCUBA infiltration – a technique used to drop infiltrators near enemy shores. Jumping from a plane at 20,000 feet or more – high enough so no one on the ground can see you –you are trained to free-fall, moving across the horizon as well as straight down. Then at about 1,200 feet you open your chute. When you hit the water you just keep going down, disengaging from your parachute and, using your scuba apparatus, continue infiltration. To prepare for HALO-SCUBA we had been doing water-jump practice. We had already been taught various techniques that would be useful in simulations such as how to disengage the chute just before landing. So I assumed that the next dive from an aircraft was to be into water. It was night when we went up. By this time I had overcome my fear of heights just enough to be able to peer downwards after leaping from the plane. As I did so I saw a sleek, silvery surface – a lake –

so I headed straight for its centre and began going through all we had learned about water landings, striking the big steel release to my parachute harness so that it was only held in place by my hand. All the way down I mentally reviewed the procedures, reminding myself that since I had no breathing apparatus I needed to let go of my parachute just before hitting the water. But my hand slipped so I let go a second or more before contact. It was not until I hit that I realised the enormity of my mistake. What I had thought was water was ground mist. It was the worst landing I have ever had in my life. I felt as though every part of me was ripped to pieces.

The demands made on all of us were tremendous. A few men broke legs, one died from exposure during operations in the wilderness and several cracked under the mental strain they put us under. That was all part of the SF selection programme. We also had to undergo intensive psychological testing and top security clearance. We learned to use every known kind of domestic and foreign weapon well enough that we could fire and field strip it blindfold. We learned how to defend ourselves against an assailant with a knife, a pistol and a blunt instrument. We learned to use crossbows, longbows and the garrotte. We picked up just about everything there was to know about demolition – from how to measure the tensile strength of suspension bridges and calculate what charge is needed to destroy them, to the mathematics of fuse burning rates. We also learned to build bridges out of virtually nothing. And we learned to survive in the wilderness and to move about for days on end with no food, without being seen by troops sent out to find us.

SF taught me everything I knew: to shoot, rig bombs, pick safes, bug buildings, build self-destruct devices, talk in Spanish, Portuguese, French and Swahili. We learned communications, medicine, engineering and operation skills. We learned to infiltrate and sabotage nuclear power stations. I loved every minute of it. The training demanded that I use my body, which was growing stronger by the day, and my wits. It gave me the chance to do things that were outside the rules of ordinary society. For the first time I found myself able to express my rebelliousness. In the SF I had found my mistress – a mistress so exciting that no matter how much you gave her there was always more you could give – a mistress who demanded that every thought you had be original, insisted that everything you did erased all your past concepts of what was possible. She taught me that every challenge was new, that every success brought more power, and that every victory is a victory over yourself. She also gave me the chance to live in the hard-headed and independent way I had always dreamed of living and not only get paid for it but even pick up a decoration or two doing things which in civilian life I'd get thrown in jail for. I ate it up – all of it. My father had won a hero's decoration when he died and my grandfather had been a champion marksman – a member of the US Army Pistol Team. When finally I took the oath of secrecy and service to defend the United States it made the tiny hairs stand out on the back of my neck, and moved me to tears.

After I completed my training at Fort Bragg I stuck around for a while as a trainer myself. I also got married. Why, I am not sure. Probably because the girl was there and she thought it was a pretty good idea. I finally came to the point where I got itchy. I had been trained in just about everything that you could train a soldier in and more and there was only one thing left to do – go into combat. When Vietnam came along I was dying to go. I saw it as a testing ground. I believed I was being sent there to protect the world from communism. There, as a commander of an American guerrilla force destined to carry the war as deep into the communist heartland as it could go, I had my real training.

I learned for real that there are no rule-books you could go by and no one to tell you what to do. My mistress had given me a field to work in that was just like the fields of wheat I used to burrow through as a kid – where anything is possible, where you make the rules as you go along. Like the wheat fields, everything was brand new and open ended. I thrived on the bonds of trust that grew up between myself and the men and the way you have to use all your power, your physical strength, your daring, your wits, if you are to succeed. I loved the games too – learning how to keep people away by intimidating them to whatever degree was necessary and how to camouflage the nature of black operations. Most of all I loved the sweet smell of life lived with men who have to cut passages through charnel grounds just to survive. There is always a wonderful sense of defying the odds – a feeling that no matter what happens you can never be defeated.

I also loved the thrill of knowing that anywhere just around the corner death could be waiting. In Vietnam I was shot at many times and hit twice. I held men in my arms who gave their life's blood, their life's breath for their country. My motto became 'Don't tell me what can't be done, while you're explaining why, I'll go ahead and do it.' In SF you don't know how but you survive, you are just too busy looking forward to look back. I guess it is that which keeps you alive. You know somehow *if your cause is truly just*. . . . There were those damned words again. Now, years later, I wanted to smile at the irony of them but somehow I couldn't manage it.

I finished my coffee then poured another cup and stood staring out the kitchen window and thought about how small my life had become – as small as a basement yard with a garbage can sitting in the middle of it. That was when I still believed in just causes. That was before everything started to fall apart – before I learned that it is not soldiers that mostly die in war, it is the non-combatants, the children, the women. It was before I began to be aware of how we were being used – all of us – not to protect freedom and fight tyranny, not even to defend the rights of our country but as hammers and screwdrivers in the hands of men for whom war is a profitable business, men who exploit the military in the same way the men in the tavern had used high-falutin' words to exploit Ludwig's music – all for their own ends.

After the war, as a member of 'Task Force Condor' in 1975, I took part in black operations carried out in Latin America designed to protect US interests in the Panama Canal zone, at least that's what we were told they were supposed to be doing. But it was there that I became certain that the cause we were involved in was anything but just – there that I began to get sickness in my guts that I couldn't shake off. I was part of a team that ran missions out of Colombia along the Darien Highlands into Panama City. Over eighteen months we built and maintained navigation installations from Bogotá to Panama City via Turbó on the Urabá Gulf next to Panama's northern San Blas territory. They were built to provide all-weather NAPE – Nap of the Earth – night navigation aid for contract aircraft flying under 500 feet, well below the radar mask, from Colombia to Albrook army airfield, a US base. Once they got going there were thirty flights a month – all of which had to be kept secret from the Panamanian Canal Zone and Colombian authorities. After all, these guys were not on the payroll – the CIA's payroll. That was just before I quit. I couldn't figure out why we were doing what we were doing. Maybe I was just dumb. Or why the hell the CIA was in cahoots with the syndicate and Mossad, Israel's deadly secret police, and all three were using US air bases to shift cocaine. All I needed was an explanation. Instead, they only told me to *erase and forget* everything I knew.

That was when I realised I knew too much. About everything. I knew that a complex secret organisation exists within the structure of the US government dedicated not to fighting tyranny, protecting freedom, but to the ultimate dissolution of the United States as established under the Constitution – I had been aware for some time that the CIA was funding covert operations which had nothing to do with the good of America. I knew that POWs from the Vietnam war had been left to die in the hands of the enemy because to demand their freedom would be to expose the illegal activities of high-level government officials, who were nothing more than 'patriots for profit' – arms sales, drug deals and money laundering. I knew that American hostages had been used as fodder for bartering in illegal arms deals, and that corruption penetrated deep into the highest levels of the American government. Most of all I knew that this government which was supposed to be 'of the people by the people and for the people' had become all too willing to justify any means for its own ends – ends that in no way benefited the American people.

Until then SF had been everything to me – a mistress so seductive she destroyed a perfectly good marriage, chewing up the lives of two great kids. The clean raw connections with the men, the power we had to operate beyond the rules, my rejection of convention – she had given them all to me. I had been young, an idealist, a dreamer – Tom Sawyer. I probably watched too many John Wayne movies growing up. For me the Green Berets had always stood for freedom, the substance I valued most in the world. No longer. My mistress had been perverted, damaged, made sleazy and ugly. I felt she had betrayed me. I had given her everything and she turned out to be a whore. That was something I couldn't live with. Like every man betrayed I had two choices – either kill or leave. I got out.

I was lucky. While in Colombia in the spring of '76 I picked up an unusual bug which infests your liver, turns you a deadly yellow for several months and makes it impossible for you to do anything but lie around and watch TV until the thing works its way out of your system. They shipped me back to Johns Hopkins hospital in Baltimore, where I lay for endless weeks and was pampered like a war hero before receiving – at my request and to the total disbelief of the men in my troop – an honourable discharge.

My marriage had ended two years before. I had no skills – apart from those of use to criminals – except a half-assed ability to string a few words together well enough to sell myself as a journalist. That is what I did, thanks to a pushy nature and an assistant editor on the Baltimore *Sun* – who when he learned I had been an SF officer hoped we would spend long hours together in dark bars while I told him drunken tales of what it's like to be an 'American Samurai'.

I didn't. I didn't talk to anybody. Like Wegeler I wanted to forget, only in my case it was to forget how dirty my hands had become working behind the veil of covert operations in support of the activities of a secret government. I knew too much about what was going on to let me pull the wool over my own eyes any more. But I didn't have the guts to do anything about it. After all, I told myself, what could I do? I would be like a gnat trying to fight an elephant. I was a little guy – speak up and you get a bullet through your head. I knew how easy that was. I had carried out assassinations myself. It was not death I feared though – death would have been a relief, is infinitely preferable to betrayal. It was death without meaning. Letting them kill me would have put the final seal on a life without purpose. I knew I had to stay alive to do anything at all. Maybe, I told myself, what I had not been able to accomplish with a gun and garrotte I could do with words. After all, didn't someone say – how did it go – the pen is mightier than the sword.

After eighteen months at the Baltimore *Sun* during which I served my 'apprenticeship' – which meant keeping my nose down and taking on the pretensions of being a reporter – I moved to the *New York Post*. There I worked 'lobster shift' and kept fit by going to the gym on my way home each morning while the rest of the world was on its way to work. There too I developed the veneer of the disillusioned tough guy. I don't suppose it fooled anyone, least of all myself.

Free now of my war games, I swallowed hard to keep from throwing up at all the filth I knew and opened my eyes for the first time in my life to look around. I became intrigued by just how little real information ever reaches the American people. I became fascinated by a society which each day gets drunk on talk-shows and worries about Liz Taylor's latest romance then continues to reassure itself that it needs to take action to protect itself from a 'Soviet Threat'. All around me I saw people who believed that all darkness lay outside of themselves, people for whom there was always a scapegoat – the blacks or the hippies or the Puerto Ricans. Yet these people were *my* people. This was *my* country – a country whose wilderness gave me chills, whose generosity of spirit brought tears to my eyes. The country I had forsaken.

I swallowed my anger and I chose to leave. I realised I could no longer bear to be in America. Somebody offered me a job working as a foreign correspondent in Paris. I jumped at the chance to go. I stayed in Paris for three years. There, thanks to my background in languages, I wrote freelance for a couple of French papers as well as covering my regular beat. I had some idea that I might be able to get the truth through to people using words. That turned out to be another self-deception.

The one thing I always hated in SF was paperwork. Commanding officers always gave me a lot of stick about this. I never bothered to prepare reports properly on the missions I carried out, it was all too boring. There was a certain irony in my becoming a journalist. What I didn't see until now, however –and I was pretty sure reading Mirabehn's manuscript had made me conscious of it – was that after leaving SF, instead of using words as instruments of truth as I intended, too often I had used them to build a wall between myself and my ability to take action. Now, suddenly I saw that for ten years I had been hiding behind them. I saw too how far I had come from the optimist, the dreamer, the pig-headed and independent idealist that I had once been. Where I was going now, I had no idea. But one thing was for sure, I was sick of hiding. Whatever these hauntings were about I was going to get to the bottom of them. The one thing that Mirabehn and all her words had done was break open my protection against the ugly truth that I was living.

I felt a strange excitement – as though for the first time in a very long while I had a purpose. Immediately I did two things. I sat down and wrote a letter to Mirabehn telling her that I had read the Wegeler letter and that I was going to get the other manuscript translated. I told her I was fascinated by what I had read and asked her if I could come to see her again as soon as possible. Then I went for help to get the second manuscript translated.

In the flat above mine lived a young man named Charles Progoff. Charles was busily engaged in producing a highly specialised, very academic and as far as I could see totally unreadable newsletter about politics and economics in Soviet-allied countries. I knew that he read German fluently and that, since his newsletter had only a very small circulation mostly among American academics with equally obscure curiosity, he was always short of money. As soon as it was suitably late in the morning to pay him a visit, I climbed the stairs and knocked at his door in the hope that I could get him to do a bit of moonlighting. At first he didn't understand what I was getting at. In his absent-minded way he assured me that he really wasn't interested in nineteenth-century German history as his newsletter dealt only with current affairs. However, after a lengthy discussion during which a fee of £5 an hour was mentioned, he agreed to tackle the job.

When I got back to my flat there was a message on my answerphone from Fiona. Was I all right? I pulled the plug on the phone and closed my eyes, which were stinging now from lack of sleep. Visions of the previous night's events floated behind them. I felt bad about Fiona – very bad. Something told me there was no way of putting things right. But cowards take a long time to die. I sat down at my desk again and wrote a note to her saying that I suddenly had to go abroad on assignment, that I would be gone for six weeks or more, that I was sorry for ruining her weekend and that I hoped my business trip would help me to sort out my head. I promised I would get in touch when I returned. Then I shuffled through a pile of postcards in the drawer, chose a card from the National Gallery of Antonello da Messina's *Saint Jerome in his Study* which seemed restrained enough and wrote a hasty but sincere note asking Fiona's parents' forgiveness for the ugly scene I'd created. I also rang John Lewis and ordered a new stereo to be sent to them. As I slipped the card into an envelope I was struck by the unintentional irony of my sending this particular postcard in the light of my plan to spend the next six to eight weeks with my head buried in books and papers.

I began to weave a perfect web of lies and deceit, one that would buy me the time I needed to get to grips with this Beethoven thing and make sense of it. The editor in his ham-fisted way had handed me a gift of two weeks away from work but I would need to play for more time. That meant I had to get sick – not *really* sick of course, but I needed to develop some fictitious condition for which I could continue to receive medical certificates, an excuse for, say, two months – more, if necessary. I knew only two things: I had to find out what was going on with all this manuscript stuff – the hauntings, the threats, the secrets and the power – and I had to stop running from myself. What I didn't know then was how inexorably bound together the two would be.

LUDWIG'S THEME

I can see in your face that you're under god's curse
and that what you say is true. It's plain that you're
not free, that you're bound to him and that he
doesn't mean to let you go. He is your destiny.
Your soul is filled with him; through his curse you
live a life with god. You hate him, you mock and
revile him. But judging by your indignant words
you care for nothing in the world but him, and are
filled with him alone. With what you call your
hatred of him. But this very red-hot hatred of god
is perhaps your experience of the divine.

'Perhaps one day he will bless you instead of
cursing you. I don't know. Perhaps one day you
will let him lean his head against your house.
Perhaps you won't. I know nothing about that.
But whatever you may do, your fate will be forever
bound up with god, your soul forever filled with
god.'

Pär Lagerkvist *The Sibyl*

Within the space of ten days I was doing nothing day and
night but reading, making notes and listening to
Beethoven's music. I have always been a lone wolf. I don't
go to dinner parties – a man who gets off on his own
company. But never had I become so reclusive. I would
awaken in the mornings after two or three hours' sleep,
drink several cups of strong Italian coffee and settle down to
read whatever books or papers I had been able to borrow or
steal from the library.

During the first three weeks I hardly left my flat except when I needed to get a book, buy food or visit my chain-smoking GP for a sick note. The ailment I had chosen for myself was simple: acute pain in the lower back – the most obscure and impossible to verify complaint in the world. With each day I became more consumed by my researches – work for which intelligence operations had well prepared me, work carried out in silence and in secret.

I found that a great mass of documentary material on Beethoven had been left at his death. It consisted of manuscript scores of both published and unpublished works, sketchbooks and leaves from sketchbooks. Ludwig's own library included many books in which he had scribbled comments in the margins or underlined passages; he also left behind a collection of 400 notebooks known as the 'conversation books', which contained records of uncensored personal exchanges between himself and his friends during the last decade of his life. A few revealing documents were found hidden among his personal effects after his death. They included the *Heiligenstadt Testament* which he wrote in October 1802 at a time when he was contemplating suicide. In it he makes a declaration to resist this self-destructive impulse and affirms his commitment to art as the only salvation from despair. It was in Beethoven's *Tagebuch* or diary that I found Ludwig at his most self-questioning. Written between 1812 and 1818 it too was discovered at his death, although now only copies of the original remain, as were a few letters written by him to an unknown woman whom he called 'My Immortal Beloved' on 6 and 7 July – the year remains uncertain. During his life the composer had kept them hidden in the secret drawer of a desk.

I discovered from my researches that – provided of course it was not a fraud – this letter which Mirabehn had translated had been written by a certain Gerhard Wegeler, a physician and boyhood friend of the composer in Bonn. Wegeler was born in Bonn in 1765. That made him five years older than Ludwig. He died in Koblenz in 1848 – four years after the date of the Wegeler manuscript. I read immediately the book which Wegeler himself wrote. It did not contradict what was in the manuscript but it was far less personal. It contained no references either to the incident with the bootmaker or to the scene witnessed through the back window.

Then I went through book after book on Beethoven – biographies, letters, stories. But instead of leading me closer to a clear sense of who he was they seemed only to draw me further and further into a world of speculation and illusion. I began to feel I had entered one of those magic theatres where every light focused on the subject only further distorts the way it looks. And the irony behind all this is that before his death Ludwig expressed to his closest friends a passionate wish that after his death the truth be told about his life with no holds barred. He feared that the facts might be deliberately twisted or concealed.

As it turned out, Ludwig's concern in anticipating the way in which truth and fact surrounding his life would be altered or suppressed after his death turned out to have been no idle worry. One of his so-called friends, Anton Schindler – the same man who had corresponded with Wegeler – went so far as to destroy 264 out of the 400 existing conversation books. Why he did this is something no one has ever been able to find out. The other 136 he sold to the Royal Library in Berlin. There they remained until the 1950s. Then on 14 September 1951 even those remaining papers disappeared from the former Prussian State Library. So did one of the library's senior curators, Dr Joachim Kruger-Reibow. Both vanished without trace.

To my surprise I found that despite the great volume of Beethoven materials available in libraries throughout the world, one event after another has served either to distort or destroy evidence about the composer and his life – papers lost or stolen, records deliberately falsified to conceal the truth, whatever it may have been. The whole thing reminded me of the way we used to alter official reports in SF or see that they had been conveniently destroyed. But why? What possible information could they have contained that would have rendered them 'dangerous' to anyone?

Ludwig's estate was not sold off until some eight months after he died. His apartment was left virtually unguarded. It was plundered by 'friends' who made off with many of his effects. Quite apart from losses in factual material which resulted from this kind of thing, a lot of evidence about the events in his life and about his personality also appears to have been suppressed, lost or distorted. Even bodily tissue – part of one ear – taken from Ludwig's corpse for medical study at the Pathological Museum of Vienna mysteriously vanished and was never found.

Working day and night, I read character portraits and biographies one after the other which varied so much in their description of both the physical and psychological characteristics of Beethoven that I sometimes wondered if they had all been written about the same man. In the first twenty years following Ludwig's death several biographies appeared in Germany, only a few of which were translated into English. It was not until 1866 that the work which is still considered to be the authoritative biography appeared: *Thayer's Life of Beethoven*, an exhaustively detailed tome written by an American librarian from Harvard University named Alexander Thayer. A meticulous scholar, Thayer had been put off by the inconsistencies of Schindler's biography and decided that a definitive study of the

composer was needed. Thayer spent twenty years of his life
eking out a living while researching the book. His motto
was: 'An ounce of historical accuracy is worth a pound of
rhetorical flourish.'

Thayer's biography, published serially in German in
three volumes in 1866, 1872 and 1879 and later in English, is
scrupulously objective. But I found there was even a
mysterious ending to the Thayer story: although Thayer
lived until 1897 and his passion for researching Beethoven's
life and for completing his work on it in no way diminished
during the last fifteen years of his life, the volumes he
completed during his lifetime only covered the composer's
life until 1817. Thayer developed such severe migraines
each time he attempted to work further on Beethoven's
biography that he could not continue, although during this
period he was able to publish two scholarly books on other
subjects. I knew about the migraines only too well myself.

Everywhere I turned I came across evidence that I was
not the only one who had been drawn into the web of
Beethoven's life and music either during his lifetime or after
his death, not the only person who had been inexplicably
altered by it – unfortunately not always for the better, either.
As Thayer's own experience attested, the more intent any
person seems to have been to discover and reveal the truth
about Ludwig's life, the more detrimental did these alterations become. It all seemed too bizarre to be true yet
somewhere inside I knew it was.

As my research continued I grew dimly aware of new
changes taking place in myself. My reading and note-taking
by now completely filled my life. I was losing weight. I could
not sleep. The ringing in my ears continued, as did visual
disturbances. Intense pains came and went here and there in
my body without obvious cause. But I chose to ignore all of
these things and to give myself over to the task I had chosen.

By the end of the third week I had begun to organise the facts I had unearthed about Beethoven and to record them, working long hours in front of a word processor.

With complete detachment I realized that what I had originally called 'my research' had by now developed into an obsession. The more I read, the more notes I made, the less anything else mattered. Food held less and less interest with each day that passed. I did not watch television, listen to the radio or read newspapers. Letters which came through the door were examined quickly for a Vienna postmark. When it was lacking, they were tossed into a drawer where they remained unopened. At first when the telephone rang I would answer it and go through the charade of pretending I was recuperating from a back accident. Before long I stopped bothering. I figured that whoever wanted me could write instead. After all, they would know that my 'illness' made it painfully difficult for me even to move to answer the phone. Before long it stopped ringing altogether. The only person I made any attempt to contact was Charles. Every few days I would climb the stairs, knock on his door and ask how the translation was going. At first he responded to my enquiries absent-mindedly and told me not to worry, that he was getting on with it. After my fourth or fifth query he showed signs of irritation so I decided to leave him alone – to wait. I read and reread the Wegeler letter. I became more and more fascinated by what lay within. It was as though I had become caught up in the world he wrote about and, although I did not understand it, it had become absolutely real and compelling to me – more real than my own world, more real than the world of SF. Often I would awaken in the middle of the night with Mirabehn's words echoing in my brain: *This is not a gift – at least not in any ordinary sense. It is a grave, possibly a dangerous, responsibility.*

Mirabehn also became the subject of investigation. I found a book, her autobiography, in the London Library. Called *The Spirit's Pilgrimage*, it not only told about her life with Gandhi, it described her own all-encompassing obsession with Beethoven, which led her to forsake the conventional world of post-Victorian Britain and to begin a long spiritual journey – a journey which took her deep into the political and spiritual struggles of modern India. An upper-middle-class Englishwoman, the daughter of an admiral in the Royal Navy, Mirabehn – then known as Madeleine Slade – was born in 1892. During her teenage years she developed her passion for Beethoven's music and a fascination with his life. She even arranged concerts of his music in England when, after the First World War, German and Austrian music was boycotted because of anti-German feeling. In her early twenties someone told Mirabehn about a French writer by the name of Romain Rolland who had written an epic novel called *Jean Christophe* in ten volumes. It was said to be a fictional marriage of Beethoven and Wagner. She knew that Rolland had also produced a biographical sketch of the composer. He was later to write a scholarly seven-volume study (never finished) about Beethoven's creativity – *Beethoven: Les Grand Epoques Créatrices*. The books were available only in French and Mirabehn was desperate to read them but her school-grade French made this impossible. She decided to learn the language, hoping that one day she would meet Rolland and spend time with him talking about her beloved Beethoven. To these ends – much to the horror of her conventional family to whom a young lady let loose abroad seemed a dangerous proposition – she travelled to Paris alone to study.

A year later with many thousands of foreign words under her belt, she tracked down Rolland, who was living at Villeneuve on the Swiss-French border. She wrote him a letter in her finest French, requesting that they meet. To her unexpected delight the ageing writer invited her to tea. There they discussed Beethoven, music, spirituality and her overriding ambition to write a biography of Ludwig. In the course of their conversations – their first meeting turned into many when the vibrant young Englishwoman and the ageing French writer found how much they had in common – Rolland advised her that, although her literary ambitions were admirable, she would be better off pursuing a more practical career. He then asked: 'Do you know Gandhi?'

'Gandhi? Why no, Monsieur, should I know the name?'

'Indeed you should, my dear. For he is the spirit of freedom – a very fine young Indian about whom I am currently writing. You must go and see him.'

All this took place in 1923. On Rolland's suggestion the determined Miss Slade wasted little time in writing to Gandhi, the address supplied by Rolland himself, asking if she could come to India to be of service in his work. The answer was quick in coming: 'No'.

Gandhi told her she would only be a burden if she left Europe to come to a country of which she had no knowledge and with no practical skills – either she should give up the idea, he said, or learn to weave, to have something to offer in the way of service.

It took Mirabehn just over a year to perfect the art of weaving to a high level of competence. Again she petitioned Gandhi, sending him samples of her newly developed skill and asking once more if she could join him. He agreed. Six weeks later, after a long and dusty journey over land and sea, she arrived in Delhi to take her place beside him – a place which she never left until his death in 1948. Afterwards Mirabehn remained in India, continuing the work until 1954 when she travelled back to Europe to settle in the small wooded cottage near Vienna where we had met. She had come there with her original ambition in mind: to write a biography of Ludwig. (I was to discover later that Mirabehn wrote two, or rather a longer and a shorter version, neither of which has ever been published.)

To my surprise I found no reference in Mirabehn's autobiography to the manuscripts now in my possession so I still had no idea when they came into Mirabehn's hands. Judging by the way in which they were wrapped they had spent many years in India before being carried back to Europe. I began to speculate that Rolland himself had sent them to his young friend before his death. This further fed my passion to find out as much as I could not only about the dead French writer whose obsession with Ludwig paralleled Mirabehn's own, but about anyone else who had, like the two of them – like myself – become obsessed with the composer and his music and – of course most important of all – about Ludwig himself.

This forced me out of my hovel. I would leave the flat and scurry across London like an overgrown cockroach unwilling to be exposed to the light lest something crush me in my search for more information. Combing the dust-filled shelves of the London Library and sitting for endless hours in the stuffy reading room of the British Museum, I delved back in time, searching through everything I could get my hands on that had been written about Ludwig. I discovered that not only since his death but even during his lifetime a whole industry in myth-making had grown up to distort whatever truth had ever existed. By one author Ludwig is seen as the temperamental peasant with aristocratic pretensions, by another as a reclusive Titan, by a third as the archetypal hero who triumphs over adversity. Schumann called Beethoven 'a never-ceasing moral force'. Two German psychoanalysts named Sterba, who wrote an elaborate analysis of Beethoven's erratic relationships with his nephew, insist that he was a psychotic consumed by unalloyed 'blind', 'bitter', 'relentless', hatred for his sister-in-law Johanna. Everywhere I turned for information I found that Beethoven had become a screen on which is projected the political and religious fantasies as well as the hopes and dreams of those who write about him.

In the early 1970s during the Civil Rights movement in the United States Beethoven was made a symbol of racial power expressed through the popular slogan, 'Beethoven was black'. To the hero of Stanley Kubrick's film *Clockwork Orange* his music was a catalyst for maniacal violence. This theme of violence, I discovered, occurs again and again around Ludwig – sometimes with weird twists and consequences. I discovered, for instance that in 1903, at the age of twenty-three, a Jewish writer called Otto Weininger (1880–1903) also became obsessed with him. Weininger wrote what was at the time considered an electrifying book called *Sex and Character*, which when published became an instant bestseller. But its success did not exorcise the Ludwig demons that haunted the author. In 1903 Weininger rented a room in Schwarzspanierhaus where Ludwig died and shot himself through the heart, leaving two suicide notes. The inscription on Weininger's grave reads: 'This stone marks the resting place of a young man whose spirit found no rest in this world. When he had delivered the message of his soul, he could no longer remain among the living. He betook himself to the place of death of one of the greatest of all men, the Schwarzspanierhaus in Vienna. There he destroyed his mortal body.'

I found that many people in the past 200 years have believed that Beethoven's music carries with it an uncanny power which can be used for many purposes. His music has been called on to communicate whatever messages its purveyors were attempting to convey – even to symbolise totally conflicting values and intentions. During the Second World War British short-wave broadcasts were signalled by the opening four notes of his Fifth Symphony – three dots and a dash standing for the letter V, victory, in Morse code. Hitler made use of the same music for different propagandistic purposes. The Führer's violent contempt for Austria, his own birthplace, led him to repudiate Vienna's claim to Beethoven by vigorously and continually pointing out that Ludwig had been born in the Rhineland. In the Soviet Union Ludwig's scores became symbols of class struggle and the triumph of the proletariat. The fourth movement of his Ninth Symphony, which the Soviets called the 'anthem to human freedom', was frequently performed in front of the Supreme Soviet at Stalin's insistence. Lenin himself once intimated to Gorky that he found Beethoven's Appassionata 'formidable, super-human music'. In the People's Republic of China, the party publication *Jenmin Jih Pao* condemned all music written by the 'German capitalist musician Beethoven' – especially his Sonata for Piano and Horn in F Major op. 17 – maintaining that it epitomised the 'filthy nature of the bourgeoisie'.

Writers too have been fascinated with the dangerous power carried by Ludwig's music. For example, in Tolstoy's 1889 novella *The Kreutzer Sonata*, the husband Vasa fears he has been cuckolded as a result of the lust-inspiring nature of a Beethoven composition. The Kreutzer Sonata so ignites Vasa's insanity that he mortally wounds an innocent wife. 'Is it right to play that first presto in a drawing room to ladies in low dresses?' he says. 'To play that presto, then to applaud it and immediately afterward to eat ice creams and discuss the latest scandal? Such pieces as this are only to be executed in rare and solemn circumstances of life. . . . It is meant to be played and then to be followed by the feats for which it nerves you. . . . Upon me, at least, this piece produced a terrible effect; it seemed as if new feelings were revealed to me, new possibilities unfolded to my gaze of which I had never dreamed before.'

When I delved further into Rolland's connection with Ludwig, which I was curious about because of his friendship with Mirabehn, I found that he had written his highly acclaimed lyrical biography of the composer in 1903 to celebrate the notion of joy through suffering. It captured the hearts of turn-of-the-century readers oppressed by what Rolland called 'undignified materialism'. In the preface to the book he calls on the French people to emulate Beethoven's example – 'to throw open the windows and breathe the breath of heroes' and by doing so 'to conquer all adversity'.

Aware of the strange symptoms that continued to plague my body, I was not reassured to discover that throughout the many years during which Rolland wrestled with and wrote about his beloved hero, he, like Thayer, suffered the same kinds of symptoms, one after another – from migraine and stomach upset to mysterious and severe nervous disorders including a ringing in the ears and distortions of vision. They not only left him exhausted but also distorted his reason. In researching Rolland's life I also discovered that a close friend of his, the French sculptor Antoine Bourdelle who was Rodin's principal apprentice and whose own vast array of colossal sculpture many critics believe to surpass Rodin's own, had similarly become obsessed with Beethoven. I made a mental note to ask Mirabehn about Bourdelle.

Meanwhile my own strange life continued. Once a week on Monday mornings at 8.20 I would leave my flat in Camden Town and walk quarter of a mile to my GP's surgery – three dismal rooms last painted twenty years ago in two-tone gloss paint (brown from the picture rail down and cream above) now turned a darkish flaking tan. I worked out that if I arrived there before 8.30 I could minimise the time spent in this dreary crowded room waiting to see the great man – which meant less time away from Ludwig.

With each week that passed I hated going into the world more and more and felt greater relief each time I returned to my familiar hovel. I would deposit the prescription in the kitchen drawer, slip the sick note into a stamped envelope, and stick it in the slit of the door for the postman to pick up the next morning. I slept less and less. I began not even to take the trouble to change my clothes, living day after day in an old pair of soft black trousers and a holey black sweater. When I became drowsy I would drift off sitting in a chair or lie down on the bed fully clothed then crash into oblivion from which I would emerge a few hours later to drink some more coffee and return to my work. I began to lose track of time. After the third or fourth week I showed up one morning at the doctor's surgery to find the door locked. It was, I discovered, a Sunday not Monday as I had thought. I shrugged. Why bother to keep up this charade any more? I cared for nothing but my research – nothing that is except some news of Mirabehn.

Next morning it came: a postcard written in the meticulous hand which by now I had come to know so well – the hand that had translated this manuscript which now consumed my life. But it was not what I expected. It read: 'I have been visited by two men in black. They know about the manuscripts. Be careful, Michael. There are more papers but they are not in my possession, and I think there was a child. Does the name Bourdelle mean anything to you? I fear that your life may be in danger. Please do not try to contact me again. I do not wish to implicate you further. I pray to God that you will one day forgive me for having involved you in all this. God bless you. M.'

EIGHTH HARMONIC

They held up a stone
I said, 'Stone.'
Smiling they said, 'Stone.'

They showed me a tree.
I said, 'Tree.'
Smiling they said, 'Tree.'

They shed a man's blood.
I said, 'Blood.'
Smiling they said, 'Paint.'

They shed a man's blood.
I said, 'Blood.'
Smiling they said, 'Paint.'

Dannie Absen *Way Out In The Centre* (adapted
from the Hebrew of Amir Gilboa)

Most groups also preach world-federalist politics,
and centralization of world control is needed as
part of a certain takeover attempt by forces who
once ruled and wish to rule again. Other of their
human allies – who have vast resources – are busy
in necessary secret political work and in researching ways to make control more complete, involving
both occult knowledge and electronics.

Anthony Roberts *The Dark Gods*

Mirabehn's postcard lay in my hand like a chunk of lead.
Just when everything seemed to be coming under control –

just when I had created for myself some order – some idea of what I was going to do with all this Beethoven stuff – just when I had found a way of making things *ordinary* – the ground beneath me collapsed leaving me floating in a viscous mass of uncertainty. By now several weeks had passed. I could not be sure; for with each day I had become less and less interested in anything but my research. The conversation with Mirabehn that took place the day we met kept playing over and over in my brain. Why had she given me this manuscript? I thought back to the meeting with my editor and to the meeting with the tall man in black at the airport and the encounter through the window at Fiona's parents' house. From my SF days I was familiar with secret agents and all their paraphernalia – but this guy was ridiculous, absurd, like some pastiche from a B-movie. 'Two men in black', Mirabehn had written. It all began to smell like some ugly joke. Why should anyone care about two nineteenth-century manuscripts about a dead composer anyway? These are questions I asked frequently, a glass of whisky at hand to dull their sting. I found no answers.

I became aware that beneath the fascination with my research I harboured a lot of anger towards Mirabehn – the anger of a man whose life has been turned upside down by some chance event and who tries to place the blame for it all squarely on somebody else's shoulders. I thought back to that simple, beautiful room in which the two of us had sat – a room so full of light and colour that it had lifted away my tearing head pain and, for a time, made me almost drunk with joy. And now? Now despite my beaver-like research and the almost obsessively ordered written narrative on Ludwig's biographical material I knew each time I stopped to think about it that each day my life sank deeper into darkness and confusion. These are no idle metaphors. My flat no longer bore any resemblance to how it had been only weeks before. There were masses of papers and books stacked everywhere, empty whisky glasses lying about and the occasional plate of half-eaten food on chairs, the bookcases, the floor. So severe had the physical disorder surrounding me become that at one moment two or three days before I had searched for an hour for a particular photocopy of an article from a medical journal on Ludwig's deafness. Unable to find it, I flew into a rage, overturned the dining table and spilled another twenty books and piles of paper on to the already cluttered floor. I cursed Mirabehn out loud. She was the one who had caused all this. Then I cursed myself for being so out of control.

It felt as though I was becoming consumed by darkness. I was less and less able to bear light. It was not so much that it hurt my eyes as that it overwhelmed my mind. Living like a hibernating animal, I had even begun to look like one. One morning I noticed in an abstract way that every blind and curtain in the flat had been pulled tight to cut out the light for days on end. I would switch on an Anglepoise lamp on my desk or a tiny reading light at the side of my bed – just enough light to be able to make out the words on the page. Otherwise I lived in darkness and drank more whisky – a darkness which, like the black oblivion into which I plunged each time sleep overcame me, seemed to comfort me. I did not care if I ever saw the sunlight again. The outside world no longer existed. I only wanted to be left alone. I was.

I told myself that I had no fear. Yet somewhere beneath a thin veneer of macho cool there lay a well of terror such as I had never known. I watched myself clutching at anything to keep myself from tumbling in. My only firm connection to the reality I had known before became my ever more frantic attempt to put together all the information I could gather about Ludwig, Mirabehn and the rest.

I read and wrote in desperation. I was aware of all this, but could do nothing to change it.

I needed to know everything about the world that Ludwig had grown up in. The more I read the more it came alive to me. I would feel a trembling in my belly when I came across Neefe's name, knowing Wegeler's dislike of him. I also had to know about the society in which Neefe was a driving force – its *Lokaloberer* –and which numbered a great many of the men with whom Beethoven grew up. I was unable to find many references. The Illuminati I found held a wild fascination for me. I could find no record of whether or not Beethoven himself belonged to this society, yet throughout his youth and manhood he appears to have been surrounded by men who did.

Wegeler's description of Neefe and his influence on Beethoven made me keen to learn more about him. I wondered if Neefe was in some way 'moved aside' by the powers that be to make way for the young Ludwig whose talent and personality may have seemed more useful to their purposes. I knew about people being 'moved aside', I had seen it happen over and over again to men in the SF. Yet I found no grounds for this idea in anything I read. It surprised me to find how few references there were to women in the literature on Ludwig. It was almost as though someone had done his best to erase the traces.

The more I read about Ludwig's music the more obsessed I became with listening to it. I felt I needed to *know* what he felt when he wrote each piece in order to enter into the worlds he lived in when he worked. I began to listen at all hours of the day and night, fearing as I did so that this might be the road to madness. After days and sleepless nights of Ludwig through my headphones the tension in my body became so extreme that at times I felt as though I would break apart. Yet still I continued, all the while asking myself where all of this energy that spurred me on was coming from and how I was able to go on and on without sleep.

I was alone, yet in this aloneness I was living with Ludwig as if he were in my presence. I would close my eyes and see his heavy head bent over a kitchen table wrestling with papers on which were scribbled notes about the price of fish and the cost of laundry. He seemed like a dog with a rag in its mouth. He would not let go. He trusted no one. Sometimes I saw him as a young man, his peasant body dressed awkwardly in city clothes, expecting to become part of an aristocracy to whom he was only an amusement – like some pop star everybody wanted a piece of. He must have been like a trained bear in their dining rooms and they put him through his paces. The image filled me with rage. I wondered if Ludwig himself knew how much he had been used.

As I leafed through book after book on Ludwig's life and letters I could not avoid the sense that he had been forever doing everything he could to take control of his life – to create for himself some kind of comfort, some place he belonged. Yet it seemed that whatever he built was torn away, before it could be of use to him, and he was continually forced back on his own emptiness. Then I asked myself if it was Ludwig or myself I was seeing. I finally realised the two had become so interlocked that it was impossible to tell.

One day I came across a photograph of Schindler taken late in the nineteenth century. He was a pompous self-glorifying man with the face of a pock-marked bloodhound; the kind of man you would weed out of unconventional warfare training before it even began. He was standing with his hand beneath his coat, like Napoleon. In his other hand he held a pair of suede gloves. His eyes looked dead. Although hidden behind glasses, they had a fishlike quality like someone drugged or possessed. He gives me the creeps. No wonder Ludwig called him his appendix.

The more I read about Vienna in Ludwig's time the more sure I became that Ludwig hated the place. I suspected he only stayed there because it was the centre of music in the world. No wonder he took every opportunity to leave the city and spend time in the country he loved. I couldn't help but wonder if he ever walked where Mirabehn had walked, where I had walked. The more I read about Schindler and his destruction of the letters and conversation books the more certain I became that he – perhaps with others – had been behind some kind of cover-up. But what they were trying to conceal, I was not sure. That Ludwig had relationships with women? That he was part of some secret group? I needed to know, yet the records which could have told me all seemed to have been destroyed.

Everything I learned about Johanna, Ludwig's hated sister-in-law, beguiled me – so much so that I would find her appearing in my dreams. At first she was no more than a shadow, a beautiful woman who passes momentarily before your eyes when watching a film but whom you have no chance to get a clear picture of; – like a siren who sings a song but the moment you turn your head to see her, vanishes in the mist. Then her presence began to linger. I would awaken sometimes knowing that I had been in Johanna's presence. The knowledge would fill me with fear as though I were being drawn down, down into a place of infinite sweetness, a place that could consume me.

One night she appeared quite clearly. It was in a dream in which I was wandering the streets of Vienna – Ludwig's Vienna. I had passed before a large building, which seemed to be the town hall. It was decked with ribbons of gold and green and red to mark a celebration of some kind, maybe Christmas. The air was cold and I was alone, looking everywhere for Ludwig. A woman –Johanna – stepped out from behind a huge wrought-iron gate in front of the building and took my hand. She was dressed strangely in a gown of the same colours in which the building had been decorated. It was cut low, revealing small, soft breasts. Her shoulders were almost naked. The green bodice of the gown had an altogether different look and texture to any of the other materials: it was luminous like the scales of a fish, vibrant, dazzling in the way it reflected light. I felt myself drawn to it almost against my will, the way once twenty years before I had been drawn into a rainforest, mesmerised by the fecundity of the green life that lay within, wanting to enter deeper and deeper into its mysteries no matter what dangers it held. I reached out to touch the luminous green of her dress, but when I did so my hand passed right through the bodice. It was like walking through a mirror into a different world. Then I awakened. Is Johanna really the evil principle she is made out to be? If she is she must border on the demonic. If not, then somebody – probably Ludwig himself – has a big stake in seeing her this way. I decided to ask Mirabehn.

The deeper I delved into Ludwig's letters, diaries and biographical reports, the longer I listened to his tapes, the more curious a notion about him began to pursue me: that practically everything he wrote echoed two opposing forces within him – one which was absolutely determined to take control of the elements of his life and music and bend them to his will, the other a power which prevented him from being able to do that in every possible way. It was a force so overwhelming that Ludwig's every sense of structure, of values, of relationships and all certainty was continually dissolved by it. Each time a wave of this dissolution breaks over him, whether it comes in the form of a loss of revenue as a result of the devaluation of currency, a disappointment in love or lack of acceptance of a piece of music from his public, Ludwig is left again without an anchor, adrift in a sea of uncertainty, the single state which I feel sure he found most difficult to bear, the state in which I find myself more and more deeply submerged day after day.

Through all of this I knew that my body, my world, had been invaded – by Ludwig I was certain, but perhaps by others as well. I was filled with fear. It was nothing like the fear I would feel in battle, that is a fear that is manageable, containable, because you know where you are going, you know what you have to do and you just hope to hell that luck is on your side and you get on with it. This fear was different – amorphous – it seemed to permeate my whole existence and the more fearful I became the more rational grew my narrative about Ludwig's life. I hurled myself into the writing of it with a diligence that I had never shown before, hoping that doing so would ward off a growing sense of terror about what might happen when it was finished.

Finally I completed my narrative about Ludwig. By now I had devoured and digested more than a dozen of the most authoritative books on him I could find and nibbled at scores more, as well as examining papers, letters, reports and records. I found many facts – although they often contradicted each other – yet few answers to questions like who or what was Ludwig, and what was going on beneath the surface of his life. I figured it must have been pretty hot stuff or Schindler would not have destroyed so much evidence to conceal it and nothing I found helped to explain Wegeler's symptoms, hauntings and hallucinations, or why they echoed my own so perfectly.

Although the strange fear persisted, while I was absorbed in putting down in words the facts of Ludwig's life I experienced a few brief but welcome respites from the physical symptoms. The continuous ringing in my ears eased off for a while: a glass of good whisky could blur the edges enough to drown it out. The headaches and the nausea were also less in evidence. But the moment my narrative came to an end they returned in full force. I was faced with the naked fact that all my delving, all my training as an information officer, had taken me not one step closer to being free of this oppressive and all-consuming obsession with Ludwig – a man I had never known, would never know, and, whenever for a brief moment I found myself capable of rational thought, was pretty sure I never wanted to know. In short, I was nowhere. I had been away from the newspaper for more than six weeks by now. I continued to make my weekly journey to the chain-smoking doctor and to hang about hoping Charles would arrive with his translation of the second manuscript. But he didn't, and the symptoms were back. I had no choice but to delve deeper.

Not everything I needed for my research could be borrowed or stolen. Every few days I was forced to leave the darkness of my underground hovel and travel across Bloomsbury to the reading room of the British Museum where more materials were available. It was the only library whose security system had defeated my criminal skills. There, while filtering through material on the second day, I came upon some handwritten notes in the back of a French book on Beethoven written by Romain Rolland and published in 1903. The notes were in English. They had been inscribed on yellowed paper carefully cut to the exact size of the book's pages and fastened just inside the back cover with the kind of translucent paper tape librarians used years ago to repair torn leaves. They were written in a hand so small and meticulous that this, combined with the age of the paper, which by now had begun to disintegrate, made them very difficult to read. What was even more curious was that at first glance they appeared to have nothing to do with the book itself, at least in so far as I could tell. They were entitled 'A Brief Chronology of Illuminated History'. I began to read:

> It would appear that Ludwig van Beethoven was himself at one time a member of the organization known loosely as the Illuminati whose secret mission its members claimed to be the restoration to man of his original liberty and equality lost after the Fall. The Order of the Illuminati, ostensibly founded by Adam Weishaupt in 1777, abjured organized religion and political systems and espoused a doctrine of Brotherhood epitomized in the final movement of Beethoven's Ninth Symphony. It would appear, however, that the history of the Order of the Illuminati stretches back to pre-history. At each juncture it includes the appearance of certain figures . . .'

I could not make out the words that came next. But there followed a long list of chronological events which started with 30,000 BC when 'Graud, the first Illuminatus, governs mystical Atlantis' and ended with the date 1910 which read something like, ' Secret meeting of politicians and bankers at Jekyl Island in Georgia bringing the Federal Reserve Act into being.' The words sent a hollow echo through my whole body. I knew nothing about 'Graud the first Illuminatus' – if he ever existed, but I knew a hell of a lot about Jekyl Island. It was the beginning of the establishment of a consortium of economic power in the United States which still rules – a secret government of which the majority of the American people to this day still have no knowledge. It was a giant step towards the control of man by a few greedy people who didn't give a damn about human freedom or even human life.

The Jekyl Island meeting had been organised by Nelson Aldrich, a senator who ran the National Monetary Commission set up by Congress after the 1907 money panic. Aldrich, a mouthpiece for international bankers on Capitol Hill, met secretly with Paul Warburg and representatives of the Morgan and Rockefeller interests, converging at Morgan's hunting club on Jekyl Island, off the coast of Georgia. There they formulated a plan for an American central bank which was later to develop into the Federal Reserve.

Following Jekyl Island, Aldrich proposed a bill to Congress to bring the new power bank into being. But the fact that he was to be in bed with the banking establishment in both the US and Europe shadowed his proposal in suspicion, so it did not pass. A couple of years later, though, a new bill under a different name did. It was pushed through Congress on 23 December 1913 in the dead of night and made law. It established the Federal Reserve System, to which was then given control over interest rates and the power to regulate the national money supply. The Fed had been hawked to the American public as a great idea, with the claim that its creation would stabilise the economy and prevent runs on bank and economic crashes – none of which, of course, turned out to be true.

Meanwhile a world banking system was being set up, a super-state controlled by international bankers and industrialists acting together to enslave the world. In effect the Fed has usurped the government.

Few people in the United States even now know that the Federal Reserve Bank is no more *federal* than Fred Smith's Federal Express – that it is privately owned and subject to no control by either the President or Congress – that it makes its own policies and that private banks within the system itself select two-thirds of the directors of Federal

Reserve Bank while the Fed's own board chooses the rest. Never in its history has it had to undergo any substantial audit from an independent source. A cartel of international banks – men who would be kings – still regulates the levels of currency which the US treasury mints and these Federal Reserve notes, which are called money, are in reality only *loaned* to the United States, yet American wage earners pay interest on the loan every time they pay their income tax.

Once the Fed existed, the bankers who were behind it could loan the United States colossal sums of money and wrest repayment for the loans. There was only one thing missing – a good reason. In 1914 they had one – they *made* one: the war in Europe. America took the bait quickly and got into it. Then men like me and all the other poor bastards who believe they are defending freedom against tyranny, got in on the act and made a fortune for the financiers. The American public still doesn't know that the $3 trillion national debt which is shoved down their throats as an excuse for poverty and lack of social responsibility is capable of being wiped clean legally. The act that brought the Federal Reserve into being contains a clause that makes it easy for Congress by simple vote to nationalise the Federal Reserve Bank. It only has to do that and the US is out of debt completely. You can't be in debt to yourself. ENOUGH.

It was painful for me to go over all this again – to be forced to remember all I had tried so hard to forget, what nobody else wanted to know. It was easier, more comfortable, to worry about Liz Taylor's latest beau and watch soap operas on TV. I was sick to the teeth of secret governments and secret societies – of the arrogance of men for whom ends justify means. I had spent too much of my life being used by them, being one of them. The contempt they hold for life – human, animal, plant life – the life of the earth itself – was most sickening of all. I realised I had locked all this away like an abscess somewhere inside, where it had been festering all these years while I told myself everything was OK, that I could *erase and forget* what I knew. That is, until Ludwig. Now that abscess had been lanced by some crazy notes stuck inside an old book. I could feel the anger again and I hated it. A deadly anger at men with cold hearts whose greed cripples their brothers and lays waste the planet; anger at myself for my impotence and my cowardice. Wegeler's words echoed in my brain: *I much regret such cowardice. I must tell you truthfully that I have never been a courageous man.*

I turned back to the book, trying to make sense of the strange collection of dates and events recorded in it. I wondered what on earth whoever wrote them thought they had to do with Beethoven and his Ninth Symphony, but it was closing time in the British Museum. So I shut the book and went home intending to return the next day and finish them off.

As well as my reading, note-taking and ever-increasing whisky drinking, there was one other thing that had occupied me during those haunted weeks: Ludwig's music. I had first heard it at the San Francisco Opera House when I was thirteen. Sir Thomas Beecham it was, conducting the Fifth Symphony. The simplicity, power and the depth of this first encounter so stunned me that from that day forward I had decided that, no matter how bleak life became, no matter how empty or without sense, if something as rich and real as those sounds existed in the world, then it was probably worth sticking around. After that I gave little thought to Ludwig's music until my mid-twenties, when I dreamed the dream which Mirabehn had inexplicably related back to me. It was then that I had begun to buy tapes of his various works in a random, desultory way. I would listen once or twice to each and then toss it in a drawer. It was not that I had not liked what I heard. I liked much of it – from the Seventh Symphony and *Fidelio* to the Moonlight Sonata and the Grosse Fugue – but, with the exception of the Sixth Symphony, the Moonlight Sonata and a few other pieces, I found listening to his music made me decidedly uncomfortable. It often seemed to demand something from me which I was unable or unwilling to give. That was why I always insisted that I preferred Mozart, with his comforting transcendence and his dazzling but disembodied clarity. Ever since Mirabehn's manuscript had come into my hands, all this had changed. I dug out every Beethoven record and tape I had ever bought and set about listening to them over and over through earphones, while I read, while I wrote, even while I slept, setting the cassette player I used for my newspaper interviews in the 'auto-reverse' mode and letting it run hour after hour.

I listened indiscriminately. As the days went by, my every thought, every concern for people or places or things became replaced by Ludwig's sounds. They flowed through my head. Often they made my body tremble. They were sounds which drew me deeper and deeper into isolation. Each was different. Each acted like a bridge to some singular and often peculiar universe in which Ludwig had lived. What continually amazed me was how many different universes there seem to have been yet how frequently echoes of a universe created in one of Ludwig's works would come through in another he had composed at a different time and place. The *Eroica* and the C Minor Symphony, for instance, though distinct in form and content they seemed to come from the same root sense of life. They took me into the same universe. Others created worlds of their own as different in their landscapes as Annapurna is from the Sahara. I listened to the *Pathétique*. The fervent rhythmic twists of its first movement would tighten my nerves and sinews to the point of physical pain each time I heard it. It seemed to pose questions which neither the adagio that follows nor the final rondo ever answers. The 'Hammerklavier' with its furious titanic leaps shouted at me about an excruciating, irresolvable, heroic, internal battle, then hinted at transcendent resolutions which never came, before finally giving way to the grim fire of a fugue where violence seems to annihilate even the form itself. It left me naked – like a creature caught upon on a mountain while the north wind rages. The C Minor Symphony with its complex and elusive scherzo hinted at borderline states of consciousness like those I had found myself drawn deeper and deeper into since my trip to Vienna. I listened frequently to the Ninth Symphony. I became convinced that Ludwig had cheated himself and his listeners by turning back from the unearthly heights of his magnificent adagio to the warm world of humanitarian ideals – by evoking optimism and rejoicing in the final chorale instead of wrestling with the longing for ultimate sublimity which he postulates in the previous movements but found himself without the courage to pursue. I lived them all as if they were taking place within my body. As I grew familiar with each piece it became like a friend: someone whose habits you know well, yet who frequently surprises you with his behaviour. Of them all, one alone haunted me most. It would sound over and over in my brain even when I sat in silence: the 'Hammerklavier' sonata. Its universe seemed like the world I was living in: a world of cold harmonies, a world where human life in all its joys and sorrows – marriage, friends, love – does not exist, a world where there is but bleak courage and a will to live, yet where you can only live alone, without God and without hope. Its crisp and savage scherzo knows no lightness, no humour. Then comes the slow movement telling of a hypnotic woe so cold and bleak it lies beyond what any living creature can endure, only to be followed by the largo where man's same furious will to live is stripped naked of all hope and reduced to nothing –save the final refusal of total obliteration. Such sounds, such energies, such universes became my only companions as one lightless week turned into another.

When I got home from the British Museum that evening, my curiosity inflamed by the notes I had found in the back of the Rolland book, I lay down on the bed to sift through a pile of papers I had photocopied the day before – when the damned machine was working – but not yet read. I began to read bits and pieces of it. Most of it looked nothing more than a lot of anti-communist or anti-Zionist disinformation. I put it down again. Then I noticed some clippings from the stuff I had found in the library of the British Museum. I had torn it out and filed under the heading 'Conspiracy?' I picked out a few paragraphs from the collection and began to read:

The name 'Illuminati' means bearers of light. The particular light in question does not appear to be the holy light of pure Spirit but rather the blinding light of Lucifer. In 1775 a cabal of international financiers elected Adam Weishaupt [*there was that name again*] to reorganize the protocol of Luciferic canons into a plan for a new world order. This plan by a conspiratorial clique is skilfully designed in time to bring about systematic destruction of every religion, state and philosophy and to polarize human beings world wide into warring camps and ideologies. Once divided it should be a simple matter – via economic manipulation – to bring about wars and revolutions and to completely undermine every sense of each individual's power and self-worth until, in time, the whole social order will be dissolved in cataclysms and humanity reduced to ruins and thus easily manipulated by the elect.

Next I found two pompous-assed letters from an American general named Albert Pike which I had photocopied in the British Museum. I remembered Pike from the history books. He and his auxiliary troops had carried out a lot of military atrocities against the American Indians in the 1830s and 1840s. One letter was addressed to 'The Grand Masters of the Palladian Council', whoever they were, dated 15 August 1871. I read it. '. . . After the Third World War we shall unleash the Nihilists and Atheists, and we shall provoke a formidable social cataclysm which in all its horror will show clearly to the nations the effect of absolute atheism, origin of savagery and of the most bloody turmoil. Then everywhere, the citizens, obliged to defend themselves against the world minority of revolutionaries, will extermi- nate those destroyers of civilization, and the multitude, disillusioned with Christianity, whose deistic spirits will be from that moment without compass, anxious for an ideal, but without knowing where to render its adoration, will receive the pure doctrine of Lucifer, brought finally out in the public view, a manifestation that will result from the general reactionary movement which will follow the destruction of Christianity and atheism, *both* conquered and exterminated at the same time.'

Pike's words read like a perfectly accurate prediction of what is happening in the world right now. There was more, but it was pretty ugly and by this time I had had enough. Exhausted, I fell asleep, the papers still lying on my chest. I awakened a couple of hours later to find a terrible chill had hit my body. It was so cold I could have been floating naked on an iceberg. My head hurt – such a sharp pain that it felt as though it had been jammed into a vice which was being screwed down tighter and tighter against my temples. I noticed that a strange odour had invaded the room, a bit like an egg sandwich left out too long on a lunch counter. I closed my eyes. Tiny blue lights swirled through my brain, blinking like the flashing lights of a police car. I felt dizzy and the area above my eyes seemed to swell and get puffy as the pain in my head grew worse. I opened my eyes again and was horrified to find myself floating some three feet above my bed. It was terrifying to find that I could look down upon my own body. A prickly feeling rose in the back of my spine and I noticed that my eyes had started to water. Then I heard a faint voice. I stopped breathing to listen. Again the same sound. Yet somehow it was not really *audible*. It seemed to arise out of the darkness of the room itself. By holding very still I found I could just make out the words:

'Your curiosity has taken you far enough. It is time to desist delving into unspoken things. If you disobey we will make an appearance.'

I replied in words although my mouth made no movement and my lips never opened: 'What do you want? Who are you?'

As if in response to my questions, the room, already black, grew infinitely darker – as dark as if, in a cave buried deep in the earth, all the lights have been shut off. Yet to my amazement I could still see. I made out a shadowy figure standing in the centre of the room dressed like a clergyman in black clothes. He wore a hat which obscured his face completely and his feet hovered a foot or so off the floor. By now my eyes had adjusted to the darkness and I felt as though I had come under the power of someone or something. The figure spoke.

'You have taken it upon yourself to investigate connections between light and dark. That is an honourable thing to

190

do but it is also very dangerous – more dangerous than you with your limited imagination can know. Let drawers remain locked and secrets die with those who gave them birth.'

That is all I remember. When I awoke several hours later it seemed like a dream – all except for an inexplicable scorch mark on the carpet in the shape of a crescent moon just where the dark figure had hovered.

It was just what I needed to send me racing back to the reading room of the British Museum. I wanted to be there when it opened, to examine at length the handwritten addendum to Rolland's book and to find out if these scribblings could shed light not only on Ludwig and hidden agendas but – which seemed a lot more urgent – on what was happening to me. But my sleep had been unusually long and heavy, so long that I had not awakened until noon. Since this was the day on which I had to make my weekly visit to the doctor I did not arrive at the British Museum until late afternoon. I requested that the book be brought again from the stacks. True to form, it took the librarian more than two hours to retrieve it.

I opened the book eagerly. The chronology turned out to be even more curious than I had first thought. It consisted of a list of dates and events, sometimes with questions written at the side of each. I went to make a photocopy of it but the machine was not working. So I jotted down a few notes at random:

30,000 BC First Illuminatus GRAUD descends to rule Atlantis – one of the 'great ones' who drink from human life energy.

1,500 BC Estimated date of destruction of Thera believed to be the source of Atlantian legends. Mood quadrants first recorded in China.

AD 1119 Knights Templar founded in Palestine. (cf. Andromeda connection).

AD 1167 Cathari council held near Toulouse.

Then more recently:

AD 1717 Grand Lodge of London founded by Desaguliers. Beginning of modern Freemasonry. Voltaire is imprisoned in the Bastille.

AD 1761 Emperor of China suppresses secret societies. St Germain goes to Russia after founding chemical plant in Holland and disappearing with 100,000 guilders. Evidence of his links with Dark Gods emerge.

AD 1776 Illuminati founded 1 May by Weishaupt. [The same Weishaupt, I was sure, whom Wegeler speaks of and whom the men in the tavern called Spartacus] Xenu, one of the 'great ones' from Markab, descends to take over Weishaupt's body. American Declaration of Independence written by Jefferson following an alleged meeting with man in black.

The list seemed endless – a conglomeration of information about scientific, political or historical events intermixed with religious, esoteric, extraterrestrial and alchemical references. Who had written it and why? I could make no sense of it. I turned over the page. There I found more jottings, but this time they seemed to be passages that had been clipped from some old Bible interspersed with comments from the person who had copied them down:

Did the 'hungry ones – eaters of souls' – feed on

Weishaupt and the Illuminati? Blood. Ectoplasm. Possible cause of Rolland's illnesses? There are elaborate rules for blood rituals in Illuminati initiation. Yahweh masks his butchery in sacredness.

> . . . And he shall lay his hand upon the head of his offering and kill it at the door of the tent of meeting; and Aaron's sons the priests shall throw the blood against the altar round about . . . he shall offer the fat covering the entrails and all the fat that is on the entrails, and the two kidneys with the fat that is on them at the loins . . . shall burn it on the altar upon the burnt offering, which is upon the wood on the fire; it is an offering by fire, a pleasing odour to the Lord. (Leviticus 3: 2–5)

If this was all some kind of joke it no longer amused me – and what in hell did it have to do with Ludwig? With me? I turned back the page and found a strange drawing. I decided to copy it. But by now the reading room was closing again. The man in the uniform told me I would have to come back at opening time the next day then assured me the photocopier would be repaired by morning. I took the book to the desk to ask that it be put aside for me for the night so there would be no delay in the morning. A tall lean man with a large nose reached out to take it from me. He looked as though he had been living behind the stacks for a century or more although he could not have been over forty. Despite the late hour he did not seem to be busy. I decided to ask him if he had any idea where the notes had come from.

'Let me see, sir. . . . Mmmm. They do appear rather ancient, don't they?' he said.

Then turning to the final page he examined what appeared to be three initials in the lower right-hand corner of the paper.

'Yes, how curious,' he said. 'Yes, I do believe it might be.'

'Might be what?' I snapped back, annoyed at his collected manner.

'What?' he said, looking up as though surprised to find me standing there. 'Oh yes,' he went on. 'Look here. If you examine the page closely it would appear that the initials E.M. have been written in the same hand, and the date 1913. Would you not say so?'

He passed the book back to me. I looked carefully. The date seemed pretty clear. I was not so sure about the initials. It could have been a B or an E so far as I was concerned but I figured my young friend was right about the M. It was one of those Ms that looks like the way kids draw birds, starting at the lower left hand corner and going in a fine curve upwards, then down up and down again all in one swoop.

'What does it mean?' I asked.

'I am not sure,' was his reply. 'There was, I believe, a librarian at the Westminster named Elizabeth Masterson or Masterlin around the time of the First World War who had quite a reputation for this kind of thing. You know, annotating and cross-referencing books. They called her "The Scribe" ' he said, looking towards me with an air of conspiratorial disapproval that anyone should ever mark a precious book.

I wondered secretly what he might think of somebody who not only marked his books but stole them from public libraries, but I scowled my fiercest scowl and replied hypocritically: 'What a shocking thing to do!'

He smiled agreeably, able to admit me into his inner circle now that we had so much in common. He leaned forward then and in an exaggerated whisper added: 'She became a bit daft, I gather . . . believed she was being followed by a man dressed in black or some such nonsense. She had rather a nasty end.'

'A nasty end?' I said, opening my eyes wide in the hope that my interest would encourage him to say more.

'Yes,' he said. 'Fell in front of a train.' He smiled in open approval, probably hoping that a similar end would come to anyone who marked his precious books.

I was dying for him to say more. My heart had begun to pound at the mention of yet another man dressed in black. He chose to remain silent. I asked him if he would keep the book for me until morning so it would not take another two hours to retrieve it. He agreed. I left feeling like a small animal being stalked by a very large cat which it could only just smell but had no sense of when or how it might pounce.

That night I worked until four then slept fitfully until the doorbell rang. I dragged myself from the bed, and clumsily hacking a path through the piles of books and papers on the living-room floor, stepped over them to open the door. It was raining. I found Charles standing outside like a dazed, half-drowned rat. In one hand he held a scruffily typed manuscript, in the other a bill for several hundred pounds. Looking expectantly into his distracted eyes I asked:

'What did you think of the manuscript, Charles?' Having read the first manuscript I expected some extreme reaction from him to this one. Totally misunderstanding my question he replied, 'Oh not too bad although some of those pages are in frightful condition – watermarked tissue paper smeared with God knows what.'

I brushed my hair back off my forehead. Noticing that it had grown far too long after many weeks of no attention, I made a mental note to get it cut, *later*. I apologised for having given him such a difficult task.

'Funny about the MIB,' he said. I did not reply. He went on, 'If that manuscript had been written in this century, I would swear the author had had a close encounter.'

I knew that Charles' 'hobby' was reading science fiction. I have never had much patience with flying saucer freaks and all the UFO nonsense. In fact I had always dismissed the whole thing as utter nonsense. That was until I picked up a book in an airport bookstall called *Above Top Secret* by somebody named Timothy Good. I'd bought the book because I noticed that the foreword to it – in which Good's research and handling of the material was liberally praised – had been written by Lord Hill-Norton, Admiral of the British Fleet at one time and Chief of Defence Staff. Hill-Norton was a man I had once met at a reception and for whom I had the highest respect. I read the book on one of my many long-distance plane rides. In it I came across a well-documented reference to Barry Goldwater's having been denied access to a particular facility at Wright-Patterson airforce base in the US. According to the book, reports had reached Goldwater that a master computer centre at the base contained a great deal of hidden data supporting the existence of UFOs. There were even said to be alien aircraft and deceased alien bodies taken from UFOs at the base. Goldwater, former chairman of the Senate Intelligence Committee, visited the base in the hope of receiving permission from General Curtis LeMay to examine evidence for the existence of UFOs, but was, according to Good, refused entrance.

During my years as an intelligence officer, I spent a lot of my time one way or another taking VIPs into classified areas whenever they requested it. I knew there was no way a politician of the stature of Goldwater would have been denied access to this area – I think it was called the Blue Room – at Wright-Patterson unless somebody was trying to conceal something pretty big. All this went through my mind as I stood there in the doorway watching Charles get wetter and wetter.

I had no idea what Charles was on about since I hadn't yet read the manuscript, which he still grasped in his wet fist. I did know that Charles, like a lot of his UFO-freak friends, firmly believed that 'good-guy' visitors from outer space were going to come and save all us muddled humans from the mess we had got ourselves into and the niavety of such an idea irritated the hell out of me.

'Goddammit Charles, what are you talking about?' I snapped.

He shrugged, said 'Not to worry,' took his money and went back upstairs – the work paid for and forgotten.

My heart beat heavily in my chest, so eager was I to read what he had brought me. But I knew that if I didn't get to the British Museum reading room when it opened I would have to stand in line to photocopy the notes in the Rolland book and I couldn't put that off any longer. So I unlocked the bottom drawer of the desk where its predecessor lay, placed the wet pile of papers inside and locked it up again, slipping the key into my pocket. I headed for the door congratulating myself on what a great idea it is to sleep in your clothes so you don't have to bother to get dressed in the morning.

I was the third person through the door to the British Museum. I went to the desk to ask for the book. A soft-fleshed, grey-haired man in his late fifties handed it to me. When I got to the photocopier and opened it I found that although the book was intact – exactly the same as it had been last night – the handwritten pages had been removed. I hurried back to the desk.

'What happened to the handwritten notes that were in the back of this book?' I asked.

'I beg your pardon, sir?'

'The notes, the handwritten notes that had been stuck inside the back cover here.' I shoved the book under his fat yellow nose, pointing out the traces of tape still left inside.

'I'm sorry, sir. I have no idea what you are talking about.'

'There were notes – lots of them – written on piles of thin yellow paper by some librarian, some woman from Westminster a long time ago. Where are they?'

'I am sorry, sir. It is not our practice to keep handwritten notes in any of our books. I am afraid you must be mistaken.'

'Listen, you. Don't preach to me about your practices. The young man here last night told me all about it. That's why I came back this morning – to photocopy the notes.'

I could hear my voice getting louder and louder. I felt a hand on my shoulder and turned to find an elderly man in a guard's uniform standing behind me. I could easily have flattened him. But his eyes had that moist look a dog's get when asking for approval. So, I slammed the book down on the desk, looked once around the room now filling up with readers, each one of whom was doing his typically British best not to notice what was going on, and ran for the door. I had to get back to the flat before the manuscript too disappeared.

Second Movement

BLOOD
largo – allegro – furioso – prestissimo

MERCURY

> The great separation was here... a peculiar, special feeling of utter lonelines... it cannot be compared to any feeling of loneliness we all experience sometimes in our lives. All seems dark and lifeless. There is no purpose anywhere or in anything. No God to pray to. No hope. Nothing at all.
>
> Irena Tweedie *The Chasm of Fire*

From the hand of Andreas Wawruch: Vienna, 1842

Lies are dangerous. Yet we destroy the truth and in its place build papier mâché images which challenge no idols and create no fear. So will it be with Beethoven. Schindler has burnt 300 of his conversation books and forged a score of letters. Wegeler is gone, von Breuning dead. As for Karl and Johanna, they will carry his secrets to the grave. So should I. For I am a physician and by every rule of honour sworn to silence. Yet I can remain silent no longer. Death sits upon my shoulder. Although it is too late for me to know the whole story, if I can but evade his dark shadow a few days more I will do my best to record what I do know. It must be done. For these are evil times – times peopled by men who wrap corruption in pious cloaks. I know Ludwig will never let me rest until I do. Last night he came again.

I was sure sleep never touched me. Yet there he stood as real as life in boots and nightshirt in the centre of that filthy chamber where he died. His legs were spread. His hands were on his hips. That huge head covered with wiry grey hair was thrown back and he was laughing. Bathed in a strange grey light, I could see every detail of that room I had come to know so well: the pianoforte was piled high with unfinished sketches for compositions that would never be written – on the floor the same ruby stain of wine spilt and then forgotten. The long rent in the curtain half covering the window was still there too. When death calls there is no time for repair.

Suddenly the laughter ceased. His eyes grew dark and sunken. His limbs and body shrank to those of a starving child. Its dirty hands gripped my trouser leg as it cried out: 'Hear me, hear me, hear me.'

I shuddered, closed my eyes and pulled away. When next I looked the child had gone. In its place stood a terrifying beast –half-bull half-man with massive arms and shoulders all covered in hair. Staring at me, its eyes filled with tears. Then it turned and began to beat its head against the door. Oozing blood flowed down the wall to flood the floor. I turned to run but my feet stuck fast to this insistent darkness.

These dreams began three months hence. Since then I have become not fit to live with. Every structure of my existence has been ripped away. My dearest wife is gone. My home has been destroyed, and my health. Even the records of Ludwig's life which I so carefully guarded for fifteen years have been burnt. Only a few remain. Yellow now and curled at the edges, they lie silently on the counterpane before me. The lily is here too, now brown with death – the one that fell from Ludwig's coffin – the one I slipped beneath my coat hoping no one would notice. I reach out to touch them, wishing they could tell the tale for me. Let me begin with Ludwig's death and with the autopsy report. For that after all was when it all ended and where it all began.

I pick up *Der Sammler*'s summary of the funeral:

> Vienna, 1827   On 26 March at 5.45 the composer
> Ludwig van Beethoven died in Vienna. Three days
> later the funeral took place. It was the most elaborate
> function of its kind ever witnessed in the city. The
> scene was imposing. The coffin, with its richly
> embroidered pall, the clergy, the distinguished men
> who were giving the last escort to their colleague, and
> the multitude round about – all this made a
> stupendous picture.

The public reports were so different from the private world
in which we knew him. That was always true with Ludwig.
But nothing was more private than Dr Wagner's summary
of the dissection of Ludwig's mortal remains. It reached me
the evening of the day following his death. Pathologists
waste little time.

The Pathological Museum, Vienna   28 March 1827

Herr Professor Wawruch,

You will no doubt have cause to peruse the autopsy report
on Herr van Beethoven which I completed this morning. As
you yourself witnessed the operation, I will not repeat my
findings in minute detail. I am, however, as you suggested,
most amenable in the name of science, to a confidential
exchange of information about the deceased. Indeed I must
admit to having found the task of examining the corpse most
fascinating.

My interest in the project is of course purely scientific. I
have the misfortune of having been born devoid of musical

gift, nay, worse – without even so much as a musical ear. To put it bluntly Herr Professor, I have a greater interest in an *os petrosum* than an ostinato. However, in the course of my daily work, and with the possible exception of one or two quite exceptional forensic explorations, I have come across no case quite like this one.

As you know I found the corpse excessively emaciated – especially about the limbs and face. The head and hands were sown over with black petechiae of great variety and profuseness. Had I not known better I should have wondered if I were dissecting an Ethiopian instead of a Viennese. His abdominal cavity was unusually dropsied, stretched and distended. When punctured, four litre measures of greyish-brown turbid fluid were effused. His vital organs, with the exception of the heart, were severely distorted. The liver appeared shrunk to half its proper volume, of a leathery consistency and greenish blue in colour. It was beset with knots the size of a bean on its tuberculated surface as well as in its substance. The spleen was more than double its proper size, dark in colour and rigid, and I found the pancreas just as hard and firm, its excretory duct being as wide as a goose quill. Stomach and bowels, as one would expect in such an illness, were greatly distended with air. Both kidneys were invested by cellular membrane an inch thick, infiltrated with a brown turbid fluid. Their tissue was pale red and opened out. Every one of their calices was occupied by a calcareous concretion of a wart-like shape as large as a split pea.

Quite apart from your description of the case and what you might call the patient's 'psychic aberrations', I find it difficult to imagine how this gentleman could possibly have sustained four months of painful physical degeneration before succumbing to the silence of death. From the condition of the corpse I would judge that every vital function had continued only through the most Promethean effort of will. I cannot imagine why any human body so in torture would make such an effort. But then you have said yourself that he was an *unusual* man.

With respect to your enquiry about the possible pathology behind his deafness – on that I can comment little. There is always the possibility of a syphilis but the strange configuration of his skull leads me to believe it may have had other causes. As you yourself observed, the external auditory canal was covered with shining scales, particularly in the vicinity of the tympanum, which was totally concealed by them. His Eustachian tube was much thickened, its mucous lining swollen and somewhat contracted. I also discovered that the corpse's facial nerves were of unusual thickness while by contrast the auditory nerves were shrivelled and destitute of neurina. Accompanying arteries were dilated to more than the size of a crow quill and cartilaginous.

Quite apart from the overall picture of disintegration which the corpse presented, I found the exceptional thickness and density of his skull most curious. It was more what you would expect to find on an ox than a man – exhibiting a thickness throughout which amounted to half an inch. Prodigious delving with saw and scalpel revealed that the convolutions of the brain were full of water and remarkably white. They appeared very much deeper, wider and more numerous than is usual. It is little wonder, locked inside such a brutal skull.

I fear, Herr Professor, that I have little more in the way of scientific observation which may be of use to you. The autopsy revealed a picture of pathological degeneration *unequalled in any man* whom I have personally been privileged to dissect.

When I had finished my investigations the corpse was not

a pretty sight. As you know, I had to saw through the temporal bones and carry them away for detailed investigation by my colleagues. I will keep you informed on that account as I become privy to further details. I have however done my best to piece things together, so to speak, since I understand that the painter Joseph Danhauser has received permission from Herr von Breuning to make sketches and a plaster cast of the face tomorrow in the morning hours. You should warn him not to expect the impossible – there will be no silk purses from sows' ears no matter how prodigious the gentleman's talent. I gather the funeral will be a large affair. It is something in which I do not intend to participate. Industry calls me to previous obligations.

In the expectation that this will in some small way serve your enquiries.

I remain, most respectfully and humbly yours,

Dr Joseph Wagner
Assistant in the Pathological Museum

I never received the report on those temporal bones of which Wagner speaks. They disappeared mysteriously without trace – like Ludwig's conversation books and so many of his personal belongings and diaries. In death as in life we were, all of us, prevented from penetrating his mysteries. Even Steffen von Breuning, who was closest of all to Ludwig, was himself plagued by questions and uncertainty. Here is the letter Breuning wrote the day of the funeral to Ludwig's oldest childhood friend, Dr Franz Wegeler in Frankfurt:

29 March 1827 – Vienna

My dear Franz,

We buried him this afternoon. His lifeless face was framed with artificially made grey curls, his folded hands grasped a cold wax cross and a large lily. The funeral took place at three o'clock in the afternoon of this mild and beautiful spring day in Vienna. They say that 20,000 people filled the streets to say good-bye to our dearest friend. So large was the crowd that the military assistance I'd arranged from the Alser barracks could hardly contain them. People of all classes and dress crowded the square at Shottentor in front of the Schwarzspanierhaus where he died. They pressed so insistently into the large courtyard where his bier was on display that eventually we had to lock the gates for it could no longer accommodate them.

At 4.30 we set out in procession to cover the 500 feet to the church. It took us more than an hour and a half to move even that short distance through the swaying masses for it had to be done slowly in order to keep peace without resorting to violence. Eight singers of the Royal and Imperial Court Opera carried his coffin – a dark oak affair drowning in flowered wreaths. Before they lifted it to their shoulders they intoned the chorale from Weber's *William Tell*. Then we mourners formed queues, each of us with black gloves, fluttering crape and small bouquets of white lilies fastened to our sleeves. We set off carrying torches with crape ribands. Schindler and the others were holding long white ribbon ends which trailed to the ground.

When we reached the church and the blessing had been given, a sixteen-voice male choir sang the hymn 'Libera me, Domine, de Morte Aeterna' in the 'lofty style' – it would have pleased Ludwig, I am sure. Then a hearse drawn by four horses and escorted by more than 200 equipages bore his lifeless form to the gates of Währing cemetery where Master Anschütz awaited us. He delivered an incomparably beautiful funeral oration written by Grillparzer. It drew tears to my eyes:

'He was an artist,' said Anschütz, 'and who shall arise to stand beside him? He was an artist, but a man as well. A man in every sense – in the highest. Because he withdrew from the world, they called him a man-hater, and because he held aloof from sentimentality, unfeeling. Ah, one who knows himself hard of heart does not shrink! The finest points are those most easily blunted and bent or broken. An excess of sensitiveness avoids a show of feeling! He fled the world because, in the whole range of his loving nature, he found no weapon to oppose it. He withdrew from mankind after he had given them all and received nothing in return. He dwelt alone, because he found no second Self. But to his end his heart beat warm for all men, in fatherly affection for his kindred, for the world was his all and his heart's blood. . . . Thus he was, thus he died, thus he will live to the end of time.'

It was fitting and appropriate that such words be spoken and that almost a quarter of Vienna's population should turn out to witness his funeral. Even the schools were closed. Yet I could not help thinking that if Ludwig had known his death would cause such a stir, it would still not have made him the least bit less of a misanthrope nor would it have banished the heavy weight of solitude he had carried since his nephew Karl's attempted suicide. These past months have been difficult for us all.

I am sorry that you have had to hear of his death from others. I would have written before but I myself have been rather unwell recently and there has been such a diversity of arrangements to make – invitations to be printed and hundreds of copies of the funeral poem to be prepared, one of which is enclosed for your perusal. We distributed these as we lowered his coffin into the earth. The sky was just turning dark. My feeble excuse is simply that I have had not a minute to sit at my desk. I hope you will forgive me. In a way I suppose I have kept myself busy every moment to avoid thinking. Now as I allow my mind to wander, my head begins to spin and my hands are like ice. Of course his death came as no surprise to any of us. Nor did it to Ludwig himself. A few days before, as the doctor was taking leave after yet another *endless* consultation, Ludwig muttered 'Plaudit, amici, comoedia finita est,' with his familiar sarcastic humour implying that nothing could be done. Indeed nothing could.

The end came on Monday afternoon in the midst of a violent thunderstorm. He had lain in coma for two days by then. How I wish I had been with him at that moment! Schindler and I had put off making arrangements for his grave not knowing how much longer he would still hang on in that ghastly slumber. The death struggle lasted more than two days as his defiant but wasted body lay upon its little wooden bed breathing so strenuously that the rattle could be heard well into the anteroom where his sketches and unfinished manuscripts lay heavy under layers of dust. But his powerful frame and his still unweakened lungs fought like giants with approaching death. Truly I am glad you were not there, dear Franz. As a physician and his oldest friend you might well have found it too painful to bear. The spectacle terrified me – watching him lie there like a wretched animal irredeemably prey to the powers of dissolution. Far away seemed our days of boisterous youth and hearty laughter. Gazing down on his matted grey hair and the sunken cheeks, I found it hard to imagine that once long ago the three of us had spent idle sunny days dashing about the countryside playing pranks. He lay for days beyond mental and physical communication, a whitened shell of the man we so loved.

Schindler and I felt we could wait no longer. We left him at three o'clock still breathing heavily and went to choose a spot for the grave. At dusk when we returned they greeted us with: 'It's over.'

Only an acquaintance and one of his sisters-in-law were present and of course his single servant, Sali. Such are the ironies of fate. I am glad at least that I myself have lived long enough to tuck him into his final resting place.

His attending physician, Andreas Johann Wawruch, professor of special pathology and clinical medicine in the Vienna Hospital, a gentleman of whom you have no doubt heard, has looked after our dear friend with the efficiency of a good scientist. Wawruch arrived faithfully, sometimes two or three times each day, throughout the four-month period preceding Ludwig's death. I am told he even passed many nights alone with his ailing patient – all this despite Ludwig having unleashed not infrequent fury on the good doctor. Yes, even Wawruch's most careful and considered ministering was frequently met with hostile oaths. You know how L. hated doctors. You are the only physician alive whom I believe he loved and trusted and of course you were always too far away to help him.

Despite all this I think that Wawruch has come to love Ludwig as we did. Perhaps 'love' is too strong a word. For the doctor's interest in our friend and in the nature of his illness appears to have become almost an obsession. Wawruch claims that certain extraordinary and seemingly unexplainable events have taken place in recent weeks as Ludwig lay imprisoned in his cold and dreary chamber fighting for life. He has some complex theory about how Ludwig's consciousness was fragmented and how a frag-

mented consciousness both creates and heals illness —
something I'm sure you would understand but which is
quite beyond my own unscientific mind. Wawruch has
chosen to make a study of our friend in the belief that it may
carry in it a clue to preventing and healing others. He says
he professes: 'to examine the development of Ludwig's
dreadful mortal illness'.

As a result Wawruch has already begun to visit me daily
and plague me with questions about the past. Why, dear
Franz, do so many people want so much to delve into what is
dark and unholy? Are there not some things better left
unsaid — unknown — unexamined?

But I do Wawruch an injustice. His fascination with
Ludwig, I feel, goes beyond scientific enquiry, though he
would perhaps not admit this to himself. I suspect that he,
like all of us, has been drawn into the circle of L.'s life. And,
as you so well know, once that happens, there seems no
escape from either its beauty or its horror.

For myself, I am sick with loss. In some way I feel as
though my task here is finished. I have now only to
distribute his meagre belongings. Everything of course went
to his nephew Karl except a few personal papers, some of
which are either in my possession or with Schindler. They
consist of letters, manuscripts, sketchbooks, diaries and
several hundred conversation notebooks which, as you
know, in recent years Ludwig has used copiously for
communication ever since his hearing failed him.

The day after Ludwig's death, Schindler, Johann and I
met at the Schwarzspanierhaus to begin the sad task of
sorting through his belongings. We had arranged to meet at
ten in the morning. I made my way through a mist so thick I
could barely see my boots. The half a mile distance between
my home and Ludwig's apartment seem like an endless
journey. Schindler was already there when I arrived. As I

entered he was engaged in sifting through the contents of the desk in Ludwig's workroom.

'Good morning, Schindler,' I said.

'Ah, yes, Breuning,' was his response. 'I have been expecting you. I have, of course, been here for some time perusing the Master's belongings in search of those things which we must make sure do not fall in the wrong people's hands as well as memorabilia which may be useful to his biographer. Naturally this task, grievous though it is, falls upon my shoulders.'

'Yes, Schindler,' I said, 'it is good of you to take it upon yourself.'

The room echoed with emptiness. After week upon week spent in this small chamber caring for my friend, it had now, with his death, became a dull, hollow space. A scent of camphor permeated everything. Evidently as a last offering Sali, the servant, had been over every surface cleansing it.

Johann arrived a few minutes later, glaring suspiciously at Schindler and myself over the top of his spectacles.

'Good morning, Schindler,' he said. Schindler bowed formally.

'Good morning, Johann,' said I, crossing the room and taking his hand. 'These are sad times . . . I am deeply grieved by the death of your brother.'

'Yes, yes,' replied Johann, 'so are we all, Breuning. Thank you for saying so. Now, shall we get on with things?'

The three of us set about the unpleasant task of hunting down the bank shares which Ludwig had so carefully preserved as a legacy for his nephew Karl – despite the fact that he, himself, towards the end of his life, was in dire need of the gold they represented. Schindler rose from the chair on which he had been sitting. 'I have, Herr Beethoven,' he said to Johann, 'been through all of the papers and drawers in this desk. I have also searched through all the manuscripts sitting on the piano and spent some time looking through the books on the shelf thinking the Master might have chosen to conceal his financial matters in such a way. However, so far I have found nothing.'

'Did you look in the entrance hall, Schindler?' I asked. 'There is that small table. . . .'

'I shall do that now.' He darted through the door like a ferret, leaving Johann and myself staring at each other. In less than a minute he returned to report, 'Alas, there appears to be nothing but a pile of old sketchbooks and some conversation sheaves. I shall gather them together, take them home and look through them to see what may be of use to whatever biography we decide shall be written – always following the Master's wishes, of course.'

'Yes, of course,' I said to Schindler, 'as you please.' I could not get away from the sense that I stood in a sad, empty room in the presence of two people who cared little about the man who less than twenty-four hours before had lain dying in the little bed against the wall – a bed now stripped bare of the linen that had cosseted his body during those final hours. One of them seemed more intent on grasping to his bosom all that in any way appertained to Ludwig, while the other examined everything through gold-framed spectacles – suspicious, it seemed to me, that Schindler or I were concealing the extent of Ludwig's fortune. Forgive me, Wegeler, for writing as I do but I must confess some bitterness towards them both.

For an hour the three of us searched while Schindler made small clicking noises in his throat and Johann continued to peer over his opulent eye-glasses, yet not a word was spoken. We looked everywhere, even beneath piles of scrap paper in the kitchen and in a small chest which contained Ludwig's most personal items of clothing. That was most difficult of all, Wegeler. As we sifted through his shirts and shifts I could smell the fragrance of my friend. I could even tell which shirts had not been worn since the onset of his final illness, after which his smell so drastically altered.

At last even Schindler had to admit defeat. I thought perhaps we should ask Holtz, the fair-haired violincellist who was such a favourite of Ludwig, for his help. Beautiful Holtz. I remember how during those final weeks Ludwig used to sit staring at him whenever he was in the room, as if he could not drink enough of his physical beauty and his vibrant health.

'Shall I fetch Holtz?' I asked. 'Ludwig was very fond of him and I believe did share with him many secrets of his personal life.'

'That, Breuning,' said Schindler, 'I am certain is not true. Holtz would like to *pretend* it to be so but your assumption that Ludwig would have made him privy to the where-abouts of the banknotes is highly questionable.'

'Of course, Breuning, let's call Holtz,' said Johann, taking his watch out of his pocket and gazing at it. Evidently he had some essential meeting from which our task was keeping him. I left the apartment myself in search of Holtz while Johann and Schindler sat silently in that gloomy chamber glaring at each other.

Holtz was easy to find. He sat amiably involved in conversation at a nearby tavern sipping a glass of wine with friends. I brought him back with me. When we entered the room neither Schindler or Johann had moved an inch. Nor, so it appeared, had they said a word to one another. The atmosphere in the chamber had grown leaden.

'Good morning, Schindler,' said Holtz, reaching out his hand and smiling broadly.

'Quite so,' said Schindler. 'Breuning is under the impres-sion that you might know of some secret hiding place in which the Master may have tucked away his private papers.'

'Good morning, Johann,' said Holtz, not stopping to shake his hand, but moving directly to the same desk that Schindler had so thoroughly searched an hour before.

'Mmm . . .' said Holtz. 'Now, what did Ludwig tell me? Let me see, it is here, I believe.' Schindler cringed at the sound of Holtz's words. Holtz removed a long, narrow drawer from the top of the desk. 'Ah, no. I fear it is sealed shut,' he said.

'I will get a knife,' I offered, and went to the scullery, returning with a stiletto-like affair I found sticking in a mouldy piece of cheese. Holtz held the drawer in his hand whilst I prised open the bottom of it. A pile of papers tumbled into my hands. At the top of the pile we found a portrait of the Countess von Brunsvik. She was, you may remember, one of the several women whom Ludwig at one time fondly hoped to make his own yet who, like all the rest, denied him that privilege, believing that he was far her social inferior.

'There they are!' shouted Johann, 'there they are!' and sure enough, there lying beneath the portrait were the bank shares made out to Karl. Johann took them and began making calculations with a pen he found atop the desk.

'But what is this?' said Schindler, snatching the papers from my hands. In the packet too were a collection of letters, three of which – or perhaps I should say one letter in three parts – were scribbled in Ludwig's wild hand. To whom it was addressed we are not certain, but it was written to a woman – a woman whom Ludwig appears to have loved most tenderly and passionately. He calls her 'My Immortal Beloved'. So full of grief and passion and longing is this painful missal that it seems impossible he could so have loved a woman who remained unknown to any of us. I could not but wonder how much of the love belonged to the flesh and blood woman to whom these letters were addressed and how much to the longing for union with his own soul – a union I fear he was never to experience. (It moves me to remember how desperately he always longed for marriage and how capriciously it eluded him.)

It was Schindler who opened the letters first and read through them all. Then, after Holtz and I had examined them cursorily, he quickly folded them again and put them in his pocket. 'We must not let any word of this get out,' he said. Johann was still busy with his calculations. 'Why not?', asked Holtz. 'What difference could it possibly make, Schindler?'

'The difference that it makes, Herr Holtz, is something that you with your callow ways would not comprehend,' snapped Schindler. 'We must protect the Master's reputation at all costs. It will not do to have him thought to have been involved in a secret liaison with a woman, the identity of which even we ourselves do not know.'

'Oh rubbish,' said Holtz. 'What a load of nonsense, Schindler. Who cares?' In an attempt to calm them both I ventured, 'Perhaps Schindler is right, Holtz, it may be wiser for the moment not to speak of this. Ludwig's biographer can deal with them in due course as he must.'

'I have counted thoroughly the banknotes,' Johann broke in suddenly, 'and we are still 250 gulden short. What do you make of that, Breuning?'

'Well I would say then that perhaps our original estimation was in error, Johann.'

'Ah, that is a possibility,' admitted Johann. 'None the less, I shall hold on to these myself, ensuring that my nephew receives the benefits they offer in their entirety. I must excuse myself, gentlemen, I have another engagement.' With that Johann rose, bowed stiffly and – still looking at us over the top of his spectacles – left the room. Holtz, too, soon departed, on his way to meet friends before dinner.

To Schindler and myself fell the task of examining the papers that remained. One other extraordinary find occurred amidst unimportant letters of commerce and with two sketches for an unwritten sonata, a sonata which I keep reminding myself will now remain unwritten for ever! This was also a letter Ludwig had written – a kind of soul testament apparently written on 6 October 1802 from Heiligenstadt, the village surrounded by vineyards to which, you may remember, Ludwig retired in that summer in the futile hope that the country air and quiet life would help his rapidly failing hearing. It begins, 'To my brothers Caspar Carl and ——— Beethoven.' (He seems to have left out Johann's name. Probably it was one of those periods during which Ludwig refused to talk to his brother – you know how frequent they were!) I shall not attempt to copy it, dear Franz. The night is growing on and I must send this on the dawn coach if it is to reach you before the cold public announcement of the funeral. I need only to tell you that the document we discovered is filled both with despair and with that strange hope to which our friend always clung as does a small child to its ragged toy. Reading it made me realise that in the year it was written he had been on the verge of taking his own life. Yet Ludwig told no one.

Even we, his friends of almost forty years, knew so little of his mind and understood even less of his moods. Like you, I *believed* I knew him. So does Schindler, to whom he is 'the Master', the handsome Holtz whom Ludwig adored as one might a lover, and young nephew Karl, whose regiment alas was posted so far from Vienna that he did not arrive in time for his uncle's funeral. But just *whom* did we know? The angry child determined to bend the world to his will? The practical joker never at a loss for some clever, or not-so-clever, verbal pun? A deaf composer struggling to conceal his infirmity and to preserve his pride? The uncle who loved

217

his nephew so obsessively that the boy was at last forced to put a gun to his own head to break free? A devout child of God who one moment cried out to his Beloved Father in pain and the next cursed the heavens? Was he any of these things or none of them? Again and again these days I ask myself such questions.

Schindler seemed to want to guard everything else in the apartment so I have left him to it. I left him to sort through many of Ludwig's conversation books, those books that were used to write to him after his hearing had disappeared. What use they may be to anyone it baffles me even to think. Of course, the world may one day delve through his private conversations. Alas, Wegeler, that appears to be the way it is with those on whom fame has been bestowed. How long Schindler remained in Ludwig's room – probably sifting through every piece of rubbish he could find – I do not know, but I passed the Schwarzspanierhaus again late that evening and noticed the light in the window still burning.

Forgive me, dear Franz. I fear that the tension of recent weeks has begun to sear my brain and crack my reason. It is late. The candle on my desk burns low. If I do not extinguish it I shall have the smell of burning leather on my conscience. I am tired and I feel utterly impotent.

Give Lorchen, my dearest sister, a gentle kiss from her most adoring brother. I think it unwise to reveal the contents of this rather strained letter except to convey the facts to her – better from you than from some cold newssheet. She loved him too.

I have agreed to meet with Wawruch in the next few weeks and to help him with his posthumous investigation. It will do nothing to bring back our beloved friend but perhaps somehow it can help further the aims of science. I can almost hear Ludwig's mocking laughter as I write that phrase. No wonder he hated doctors so. They could do so little to help him.

May God keep you and protect you both. Your most devoted friend,

Steffen von Breuning

PHYSICK

Every lock has its key, which fits into it and opens
it. But there are strong thieves who know how to
open locks without keys. They break the lock. God
loves the thief who breaks the lock open: I mean,
the man who breaks his heart for God.

Martin Buber *The Ten Rungs of Hasidic Lore*

Until that icy December day, fifteen years ago, when I was
called to his sickbed, Ludwig was nothing but a stranger to
me. I knew his music of course. Everyone in Vienna knew
his music. Yet I especially well. For when in conflict with my
conscience over the existence of God the Father I turned my
back on the seminary to take up a career in medicine, I
began to play the violincello with a fervour only the amateur
can muster, learning every one of his quartets as soon as it
was published and practising it at every opportunity.
Although much of what Ludwig wrote was troublesome to
play and disturbing to the ear, I loved his music passionately. It was not fraudulent – or very seldom – as is so
much music. It was never written from cleverness alone,
which is what lies behind most of what today is called art.
The pieces of music, paintings and sculpture which receive
the highest praise in the salons of the wealthy are these days
nothing more than decorative flourishes pretending to have
meaning. I have always despised such 'art' and held in
contempt those who patronise it. But Ludwig's music like

any *real* work of creation was never written to a formula that followed the latest dictates of fashion. It was written from the truth that was his being. That is what gave it power. That was why I so loved it.

Ludwig himself had quite a reputation in Vienna. They say that as a young man he had been proud and well dressed. But he grew dirty, irascible and wild in later years – so much so that he had once been picked up and jailed as a beggar despite his furious insistence that he was 'Beethoven'. The police were not to be taken in by some ragged impostor. 'Absurd,' they retorted. 'Beethoven doesn't look like this.' So they tossed him into a cell for the night to cool his head.

Once or twice in the days before I was called to Ludwig's bedside, I had glimpsed his bulky figure draped in black scurrying through the streets of Vienna – a top hat placed so far back on his massive head that God alone could have kept it there. This was, however, all I knew of him until that fateful day when the golden-haired Holtz summoned me to his sickroom. I was not the first that Holtz had tried. Dr Braunhofer, who had tended the composer in the past, had already refused to come. The distance was too great, he said. Staudenheim had also been sent for and had promised to arrive but failed to do so. Even the great Vivenot was mysteriously 'unavailable'. So the task fell to me – Andreas Wawruch – the competent self-assured physician, born in Moravia, tutored in Prague, a man who, until that day, had lived an ordered and peaceful life.

I passed through the great gate and climbed the broad staircase leading to his four-room apartment in Schwarz-spanierstrasse at four in the afternoon of 5 December 1826, my boots echoing sharp cracking sounds of ice against ice at every stone step. It was a grey day in the rawest, dampest, most miserable Viennese winter I remember. I knocked. A tall servant woman with a bad limp opened the massive dark green door on the second floor and led me into an anteroom in which every surface, floor to ceiling, was covered with scribbled manuscripts and with dust. From there I followed her through open double doors into an untidy chamber where the composer lay tucked into a dishevelled bed that had been shoved against the wall opposite the windows.

He was not alone. He was rarely alone those final months. During the daylight hours Ludwig's apartment was most often full of friends and admirers, hangers-on and curiosity seekers – the genuine and the sham. Day after day, their voices echoed in that dingy room – men who spoke in whispers of everything from revolution and gold to alchemy and strategies for control.

It was just after dinner when I arrived. Holtz himself was there. So was the young Karl, Beethoven's nephew, whom the composer always referred to as 'my son'. Also present was Anton Schindler – 'defender of the right'. Once Beethoven's unpaid secretary and now, as I write, the author of a recently published posthumous biography, Schindler was a pock-marked stiff man with a rodent's face, deathly pale flesh and strange glassy eyes. He has the habit of standing as they say Napoleon did, with one hand slipped beneath his coat. There was something chilling about Schindler. Present also during my first visit was Steffen von Breuning whose own life, although I knew it not at the time, hung by a thread.

The four men stood awkwardly about the bed where the sick man lay. The room was littered with what appeared to be old clothing or rags. It seemed to be a workroom, for a pianoforte stood at one end. Adjacent to the french windows, which were then tightly closed in a vain attempt to shut out the winter, a small coal fire burned reluctantly. A battered writing desk stood opposite. The only other furniture consisted of three straight-backed chairs, none of which was then in use, a tiny bedside table on which stood a battered metal ear trumpet and a pair of spectacles, and a small French day bed on which the ailing man lay. I approached the bed but was unprepared for what greeted me.

Beethoven was smaller than I had anticipated. His short stubby fingers, renowned in younger days for their ability to make an audience weep at the keyboard, were curled like paws atop linen sheets. His feet reached nowhere near the end of the small bed. Only his head was large. Nay, more than large – huge and heavy with a damp simian brow. He also had the most startling white teeth I have ever seen. Just now they were bared in pain.

I could see that my patient was afflicted with serious symptoms. He grimaced, spat blood and frequently appeared to be suffocating. An excruciating pain in his right side made lying on his back intolerable. His body continued to twist from side to side and moan. Then, without warning, he drew himself into a ball, his right knee almost reaching his lowered forehead, and lay like an unborn child – still as death. Bending over him, I began to speak. Quickly Breuning stepped forward, handed me a pen and a notebook in which he indicated that I should write.

'Herr van Beethoven is almost completely deaf,' he said.

I took up the pen and as carefully as I could manage fashioned: 'One who greatly reveres your name will do everything possible to give you speedy relief – Prof. Wawruch.'

I held my words close to the head of the sick man who, on reading it, looked up at me with small glassy eyes and smiled. The nephew Karl then moved to my side. Taking the notebook from his uncle's hand he offered to write down whatever questions I had for my patient. I sped through my queries in an attempt to determine the nature of his illness: 'When did the sickness begin? What has been done about it? Where is the pain? Do you suffer haemorrhoids? Have you a headache? Does it hurt to pass water? When was the last opening?'

I learned that this sickness was only the latest and most severe onset of similar illnesses from which the composer had suffered for many years and that these ailments had grown much worse during the previous eighteen months. I was told that the present acute symptoms had begun when he returned from the country three days previous. He and nephew Karl had been staying at Wasserhof, his brother Johann's country house in Gneixendorf near Krems. There he had repeatedly suffered an erratic abdominal complaint which prevented the enjoyment of his food and had been intermittently plagued by biting pains in his abdomen together with a certain mental unsoundness characterised by delusions and hallucinations. The nephew whispered to me that more than once during their stay, his uncle had accused their hostess, Therese – Beethoven's sister-in-law – of trying to poison him. Evidently he had also complained of a great fear of being closed in. Thus in an anxious state of severe depression, faced with the unhappy prospect of a dismal future so long as they remained there, he had developed a sudden but passionate longing to return to Vienna.

The family carriage, for whatever reason, and there were to be many accusations on this account made later, was not available. The sister-in-law Therese had used it the day before and remained away. Instead of following a sensible course and waiting for her to return, Beethoven had insisted on leaving immediately in any form of transportation which could be secured. In the end the two of them made the journey in a most wretched vehicle – a 'milk wagon' as he later described it. Uncle and nephew had arrived in Vienna three days before soaked to the skin after having spent a cold wet night in an unheated inn on the way. It was on that night, according to Karl, that his uncle's fever began in earnest. I was greatly surprised and more than a little annoyed that any man should be left in such a state for three days without proper medical care. But at that moment there was nothing to be done but turn my medical skills towards the alleviation of his suffering.

My patient had all the classic symptoms of serious lung inflammation: elevated temperature, chest pains, precordial oppression, dyspnoea, cough and blood-tinged sputum. I first examined the nature of the sputum after which I percussed his chest and abdomen using Auenbrugger's technique to determine the condition of the lungs and bronchi. Then I began counter-treatment for inflammation at once by way of purgatives and enemas: two drachms of liquorice root and two and one half drachm of senna. I also gave instructions that he was to be given small quantities of a warm almond milk four times a day to support his strength and I described the preliminary programme of treatment on which I had decided to Steffen von Breuning, who seemed the only member of the entourage fully capable of ensuring that it would be followed. Finally I turned towards the servant, who I assumed would be dealing with my patient's physical comfort. I told her that he was to be kept in a cool room, that his body and limbs themselves were to be periodically heated by applying warm poultices on the shoulders and chest and that he was to be given clear broths, decoctions of rice and large quantities of fluid, especially cool water.

I was particularly concerned about the pneuma of the chamber. For although its air could be kept cool – indeed it would have been difficult to keep it any other way since the fire burned so parsimoniously and the winter was so bitter – its quality was musty, oppressive, unclean. I spoke firmly to the servant about the necessity for conscientiousness and insisted that the room be cleared within the hour, the floors washed thoroughly and that the sheets on my patient's bed, which at that moment would have been more suitable on the bed of an ailing animal, be exchanged immediately for fresh linen. Then I leaned over the bed. Taking Beethoven's small hand in one of mine and my pen in the other, I assured him that I would return early the next morning and that within a few days he would be up and about. In response he directed towards me the most extraordinary gaze. How can I describe it? It was one part the glance of an angry untrusting child who is not to be fooled by fairy tales, and the other the intensely hopeful longing of a terrified man whose death sentence has just been reprieved. To my surprise, despite his great weakness, his small stubby fingers gripped my hand with the force of a vice. So powerful was the hold they had on me that several minutes passed, during which he had his eyes closed and appeared to be asleep, before I could extricate myself from his grasp.

Such was the first day of our meeting – a day which, although I little dreamed it then, was to alter the rest of my life. For from the moment I came into Ludwig's presence I had unwittingly been made the victim of a rare force. Like a tidal wave emerging from the sea, it swept away all landmarks, leaving in their place a terrain for which I had no map.

SULFUR

It is abundance that seeketh union with emptiness.
It is holy begetting.
It is love's murder.
It is the saint and his betrayer.
It is the brightest light of day and the darkest night
of madness.

To look upon it, is blindness.
To know it, is sickness.
To worship it, is death.
To fear it, is wisdom.
To resist it not, is redemption.

C G Jung *VII Sermones ad Mortuos*

When I visited my patient the following day, his state had
altered little. But the morning light and the fact that I had
established a treatment plan the night before gave me the
opportunity to make a more detailed examination. His
stocky, powerful body lay in a wasted state. My first
observations of his remarkable head were confirmed by this
second encounter. It was indeed massive with prominent
parietal and temporal bones, making his forehead pronounced, wide and powerful without being particularly
high. In the daylight I could see that the shock of thick curly
grey hair which covered it was shot through with occasional
strands of black and that his face had been savagely pock-
marked with scars from an old variola.

That face was quite unlike any other I had ever encountered. In profile the top of his head appeared to bulge forward. His eyes were small, dark and glazed with fever. They receded deeply beneath the great brow, giving him the air of a beady-eyed creature. The nose was flat. It broadened out near the nostrils which were themselves uneven, the left being smaller and rather higher set than the right. This configuration, together with the mass of tangled grey hair gave him a curiously leonine quality. Although Ludwig could in no way be construed to be handsome, in better, more youthful times, when the cheeks were not so wasted, such a combination of qualities had probably given him a rugged appeal. He also had a highly defined philtrum running from just beneath the nostrils to the middle of the upper lip, a deep scar on the right side of his chin and a pronounced cleft which appeared to be not so much the consequence of a prominent bone in that part of the face as the result of an overdeveloped mentalis muscle which both lifted his chin and raised his lower lip.

Since I had little knowledge of Ludwig's previous medical history I made an attempt to question him about his manner of living, his foods and his personal habits to assist me in evaluating the course of long-term treatment that he would require.

Gleaning information about my patient's history was no easy matter. Ludwig himself was weak and frequently incoherent. The fever had affected the functioning of his eyes so that the laborious method I was forced to use of writing my questions in a book, holding them at just the right distance from his face and then deciphering whatever response came from his lips was laborious and not very effective. When after the first day or two he could speak, things were but little improved. Frequently his responses to my questions were erratic and inconsistent. Sometimes I would query him about earlier illnesses or previous attacks of colic and he would answer me clearly and concisely in a staccato voice, giving detailed information at such a rate that it was difficult for me to note it down. At such moments, despite his fragile state, his voice would grow shrill and take on a sharp, piercing quality. On other occasions he would not respond at all to my queries but would stare up at me in what appeared to be total incomprehension, or he would grab a conversation book, let loose some epithet in a heavy, gritty growl and then, despite his frailty, hurl the papers the full width of the room. There were also periods when he could speak only with great hesitancy as if he hardly knew the way to form words. Then the sound that emerged from his throat would become as soft as a young child.

During that first week, I visited Ludwig twice each day – at eight in the morning before going to the hospital and then again at five, just after dinner – to examine him, to gather more information about his background, to further assess his condition and to verify that my orders were being properly carried out. Seldom did I find him alone. Most often the room was peopled by one or more of the men whom I encountered on my first visit. Sometimes they would be joined by others who were not part of the 'inner circle'. All his visitors were men. He seemed to like the company of men. During those first weeks the only female ever present was Sali – the lanky servant, a woman with pale yellow skin and such a reluctance to smile that it bordered on the fanatical. Sali was reasonably efficient in her ministrations but she had a certain slyness to her nature. She was the kind of woman who would do the minimum necessary then pass on the blame for what remained undone to whomever or whatever could be made to bear it. Let it be said that Ludwig's room was never properly cleaned during the four-month period of his illness and his food was never as well prepared as it should have been.

The men who surrounded Ludwig in those days were an unusual group. Often when I entered the room I would have the sense that I had just interrupted some kind of secret meeting or ceremony. I was aware of how absurd a notion this was yet I could not completely erase it from my mind. They seemed to hover around him like birds in search of food. I don't by any means want to imply that Ludwig's entourage formed a homogeneous group. Far from it. I was conscious of powerful tensions between its members. Yet each man appeared in one way or another to be intimately connected with my patient. And each was in his own way useful to me in building up a sketchy picture of Ludwig's present pathology.

Steffen von Breuning, who had known Ludwig as a youth in Bonn, was the most attentive. Some four years younger than his friend, Breuning was a fine-boned, lean gentleman of good breeding, always impeccably dressed. His affection for the ailing man more than once transcended what, to my physician's eye, appeared a state of growing physical weakness in Breuning himself to which he would have been better advised to attend. He acted like a mother to Ludwig – one who in her devotion can never do enough to care for her favoured child. He would sit for an hour at a time writing stories in the conversation books for his friend, although acknowledgement was seldom given that his words were even read. He would patiently spoon soup into Ludwig's mouth, never letting the smallest drop escape. He was quick to empty a commode before unpleasant smells could contaminate the small room. Ludwig seemed to take for granted Breuning's ministrations – when he was aware of them at all – behaving much as a favourite child might, with total naturalness and unconscious acceptance of the privileges bestowed on it.

From Breuning I learned that my patient had a history of

smallpox in childhood and of typhus in early youth. It was this that had left his face heavy with pock-marks and lent his complexion a hardiness of aspect that belied the severity of the present illness. Breuning also told me about repeated attacks of asthma in Ludwig's youth which, so far as he was aware, first appeared at the time of the death of the composer's mother when he was seventeen. Together with a severe productive cough, Breuning told me, this asthma had tended to recur each winter. Ludwig suffered frequent attacks of sinusitis, he said, and of cephalalgia which I suspected may have been a direct result of them.

The connection between Ludwig's past respiratory and skin conditions and the current inflammation of the lungs was obvious. In a body already weakened by fever the focus of illness invariably becomes that part of the organism least able to resist contagion. This I was certain was what had happened in Ludwig's case and the fact that my patient was to all intents and purposes deaf, although I noticed he did from time to time rather inexplicably pick up words or phrases with surprising alacrity and that some days he would appear far deafer than others, led me to speculate that the deafness itself may have gradually appeared as a consequence of the weakening of the respiratory system. And had that been the only major system to be severely disordered, I might have contented myself with such a theory. But there were too many indications of chronic pathology in other areas of the body for me to ignore the possibility that both the current illness and the degeneration in his ears had no simple aetiology.

For instance, my patient's bowels demonstrated an uncertainty in their actions which is altogether uncommon in inflammatory illness. Ludwig ate irregularly, poorly and whatever was nearest at hand, often limiting himself to broth, coffee and fruits with a minimum of animal protein.

Early on in the history of his digestive problems, the drinking of wine eased his condition so that when he was stricken he would sometimes drink heavily. But Breuning assured me, and Schindler was quick to chime in with his agreement on this point, that this overindulgence occurred only in periodic bouts. When I asked my patient himself, one morning during which he was of a more co-operative disposition, if quantities of wine seemed to ease his belly, he informed me that in recent years, instead of bringing relief to his painful gut, alcohol seemed to exacerbate the colic and to render him excessively weakened. I also learned that for the previous five years he had often become jaundiced and been treated by Braunhofer, who restricted his intake of wine, coffee and spices and periodically sent him to Baden for balneotherapy. Ludwig told me, too, he had frequently suffered severe bouts of spontaneous bleeding from the nose, eyes and head area including conjunctival haemorrhages. In short the diagnostic picture which emerged from my observations and my questioning those first few days was one of the most strange I had ever seen. I can only describe it as one of a man who had so many desperate things wrong with him that he was like a creature progressively eaten out from within by some forces which had their own volition and showed little regard for the body they inhabited. I had never come across anything like it before.

Holtz stood apart from the other men who visited Ludwig's apartment during those last months of his life. Holtz alone brought with him a buoyant physical health, life, and a sense of playfulness and fun to which Ludwig almost always responded. He was always unpredictable and usually arrived unexpectedly. His visits delighted Ludwig.

My patient's relationship to Holtz had quite a different quality to his friendship with Breuning. Whenever Holtz was in the room, provided Ludwig was strong enough to open his eyes, his attention was focused on the young man's face. A superbly beautiful face it was too – sculpted after the manner of busts I have seen of Alexander, with a fine chiselled nose and chin, warm blue eyes and thick blond hair. Holtz looked like a Greek demi-god, someone whose head would seem most appropriate basking in full sunlight against a background of blue sky and airy clouds. An excellent violinist, active here in Vienna in the quartets of both Schuppanzigh and Bohn, Holtz was no stranger to me. We had played together several times – I on the cello and he on the violin – often Beethoven's own string quartets. Playing with Holtz had always been a joyous experience for me, for his virtuosity carried great wit. He toyed with his instrument as a young man toys with his lover, teasing it, caressing it, calling forth its life, until it surrendered the full richness of its beauty to his hands. I believe it was through Schuppanzigh that Holtz and Ludwig met when he was playing as second violinist. He then become one of Ludwig's copyists and before long his intimate friend. Like Ludwig himself, when he was strong enough to speak, Holtz was a master of the joke and pun. From the second time I saw them together, I could see that Holtz and Ludwig shared many secrets. Both adored practical jokes. Anton Halm, the well-known music tutor and pianist, also a great admirer of Beethoven, but whose piano arrangement of the Grosse Fugue had displeased the composer, had once approached Holtz on his wife's behalf. She longed for a lock of the composer's hair as a souvenir. Holtz had promised to secure one from his friend. Soon after, he returned with it in his hand. Delighted with her treasure, Frau Halm displayed it proudly at her soirées. That is, until Ludwig himself, on entering her drawing room one evening, announced that the hair which she so carefully guarded in a velvet-lined silver box, had been cut, not from his head but from the back of a goat.

233

One evening, after carrying out a particularly demanding surgery on the leg of an old man I rushed to Ludwig's bedside, feeling guilty that the hour had grown late. When I entered his room I found Holtz there, sitting on the edge of his bed. Ludwig was gazing up at him with glistening eyes. Holtz was forever touching Ludwig – hugging him or running his hands through his hair the way one does with a child. Although far younger than my patient, Holtz gave the distinct impression he was a slightly unruly older brother to Ludwig, who lay watching him with admiration. There was an easy, simple closeness between them like the intimacy between animals of the same family. They shared many private jokes and secrets, all of which seemed to bring Ludwig the most enormous sense of joy. I never saw his face light up as I did in the presence of Holtz, who usually came bearing harmless gossip that amused Ludwig enormously. When they were together everyone else in the room faded into the distance. That evening Holtz took up one of Ludwig's conversation books and smiling scribbled something in it then held it up to Ludwig's face.

'So what did he do?' replied Ludwig. Holtz took the book. Ludwig waited patiently to have the next sentence of the story revealed. Holtz held up the book again.

'They put them all in the same room?' asked Ludwig. 'How many were there?'

Holtz held up his fingers, indicating nine. Ludwig began to laugh. Again Holtz picked up the conversation book and scribbled some more. Ludwig replied, 'He turned the key and put it in his pocket?'

Holtz nodded. Ludwig smiled.

'How long were they there?' he asked. Holtz took the conversation book, scribbled some more and held it up to his face. They both laughed out loud. The laughter tired Ludwig, who laid his head down heavily on the pillow and shut his eyes. When he opened them again Holtz took from his pocket two small leather balls and began to toss them in the air with one hand while Ludwig watched. I was surprised by the skill he showed. Reaching with his other hand into his side pocket, Holtz drew out another ball and added it to the two now whirling in the air. Ludwig gazed in rapt attention. Holtz stopped his juggling and handed one of the balls to Ludwig, who held it in his hand. Calling upon all the strength he had in his wasted body, he tossed the ball a few inches into the air, attempting to catch it but failing. Holtz was quick on the mark to pick it up again.

At that moment Schindler entered the room. Noticing Holtz's presence he bowed formally. Neither Holtz nor Ludwig paid him the slightest attention. Schindler crossed the room to seat himself against the far wall. The two men, Holtz and Schindler, were like oil and water. They did not like to occupy the same space. It was not long before Holtz, leaving two of the balls in Ludwig's hands and scribbling a few instructions presumably about how to use them, ruffled him by the hair, rose and left the room.

Although Holtz's presence in the sickroom always lightened the mood I noticed that it often brought a restlessness to Ludwig's heart, giving him the air of a man longing for something he can never attain. The handsome Holtz had married a few months earlier and I believe the demands of his new life had by necessity caused him to withdraw somewhat from his older friend. Holtz could tell me little of Ludwig's former illnesses. He was a man for whom illness didn't exist, a man who loved life. In time I came to believe that it was just this love of life which so dazzled Ludwig – as though he saw Holtz as the carrier of an energy, a vitality, a wholesomeness which Ludwig himself in all the chaos and confusion in which he lived had never quite been able to touch except by association with this beautiful young man. No wonder Ludwig loved him.

Of Anton Felix Schindler, alas, I have much to say. A violinist like Holtz, Schindler became a musician only after abandoning a career in law. He was – he *is* – a man possessed by strange, chilling passions. The greatest of these is a self-appointed vocation to protect, at all costs, the public and private honour of Ludwig van Beethoven, whom he still, more that fifteen years later, refers to as 'the Master'.

Schindler, I learned, had enjoyed a chequered political background having, earlier on, taken part in many subversive activities. Like most of the men who visited Ludwig those final weeks, he was said to belong to certain secret societies whose real purposes remained obscure. Schindler had been involved with the police as a result of taking part in some student riots for which he was jailed. Ludwig had evidently heard about this encounter with the law and invited him to tell everyone about it at the Blumenstockl tavern. Schindler professed a belief that the monarchy should be destroyed and a political system allowing equal rights established in its place – a state in which each individual man had a say and there was justice for all. Yet he insisted at the same time that too many men were nothing more than cattle and needed to be led by the nose for their own good. Ludwig, Schindler had been quick to inform me, shared many of his beliefs. The second or third day, just as I was leaving Ludwig's apartment after making my morning visit, Schindler called me aside as if wishing to discuss a matter of grave importance.

'A word, Wawruch, if you would be kind enough to step into the antechamber for a moment.'

'Why yes, of course, Schindler.'

As I followed him out of Ludwig's room I noticed that Schindler had a peculiar way of perambulating over the floorboards. He scurried like an animal with a low centre of gravity almost as if he did not have to lift one foot and put it in front of another. There was something altogether objectionable about Schindler's physical presence. His skin had a lifeless quality to it as though all the blood had somehow been drained from his body. As he took me by the shoulder to draw me into a corner where we could speak in private, I shuddered despite myself, so unpleasant was the touch of his cold hand against my coat.

'Professor Wawruch,' he said, 'I wish to thank you for having come so swiftly to care for the Master.'

'Herr Schindler, there is no need for thanks. It is only my duty as a physician.'

'The Master is, as I am sure you are aware, a most unusual man, gifted as are few with – shall we say – the power of the artist.'

I listened in silence with as little understanding of what Schindler was leading up to as I had of why he had chosen to speak to me in *private*.

'I have known the Master for many years,' Schindler continued. 'I am, as you may have noted, his *closest* friend. I have always endeavoured to be loyal and to care for him in every way a friend can.'

I was becoming impatient now. I had duties to carry out at the hospital and I did not need the pompous proclamations of a stoat-like creature to detain me. I could feel irritation pricking in my neck. I bit my lip and continued to listen.

'You may find some rather, shall we say, unusual occurrences around the Master, but these artists are altogether different creatures, are they not, Professor Wawruch?'

I nodded my head and wondered how much longer this was to go on.

'He is prone, shall we say, to *moods*. I am familiar with

them after many years at his side. However, it is important not to take everything he says seriously. For like any artist who lives in, shall we say, his own world, the Master is not always aware of – how shall I put it – *reality*, perhaps.'

'Herr Schindler,' I said, 'you must forgive me but I need to return to my duties at the hospital. Was there anything specific you wanted to tell me?' I said, drawing my watch from its pocket.

'Ah yes, Herr Professor, I do not mean to delay you. It is only this: should anything unusual occur with the Master, I would be grateful if you would inform me of it. I have, as you may have discerned already, a certain intimacy with him, which enables me to interpret unusual behaviour when it occurs and, shall we say, calm the ravings of a fevered brow.' He paused to brush lint from his sleeve. 'And . . . umm . . . there is one other matter,' he continued. 'If I may speak candidly, Dr Wawruch.' He hesitated, lowering his head to look down at his feet. I remarked that the back of his collar bore a rim of oil where his hair touched upon it.

'Yes, Schindler,' I said. 'What is that?'

'It is about a woman,' he said, shuffling his feet. 'A woman who is, if I may say so, quite dangerous, Dr Wawruch. She is the mother of young Karl – little wonder he himself is such a wicked young man.'

I did not reply. Schindler looked at me with glassy, unfocused eyes.

'She *hates* the Master,' he said. 'Many years ago the Master removed the ungrateful nephew Karl from her clutches in an attempt to aid him.' Here he leaned closer to me. I could smell a strange sweetness on his breath which I could not identify – almost like the odour of fresh blood. I pulled away without thinking. Then, in a stage whisper, he told me, 'It was even rumoured that this woman – this Johanna – ended her own husband's life – by poison.'

'I should not believe in rumours, Schindler,' I said. 'In my experience they are too often the fabrications of twisted minds.'

'Yes, Herr Doctor, of course. I quite agree. In any case I fear that this woman will stop at nothing to destroy the Master. Should you need to know more I shall of course provide whatever –'

'I don't think that will be necessary, Herr Schindler,' I replied, 'and now I must –'

'Very well, Dr Wawruch,' he said, interrupting me, 'I simply wanted you to know that should there be anything whatsoever that I can do to help you heal the Master, you have only to call on me night or day. I shall be here,' he said.

'Herr Schindler, should I need any advice or information I will most certainly call upon you. As for the work that I shall be doing here, that is my affair,' I said, retrieving my hat from the table and bowing before making my exit. Schindler smiled a smile without warmth. As I passed through the great green door out on to the stone steps that would take me to the street I felt infinitely grateful to be out of his presence.

Such was my first encounter with Schindler. I wondered how anyone could have anything to do with him for very long. I wondered too what the nature of his relationship with Ludwig had been. I learned from Breuning that, not long after Ludwig and Schindler met, he became Ludwig s secret private secretary without pay. During the next fifteen years their friendship had weathered many storms, including at least one breach that was to keep them apart for several years. Submissive, righteous and superior in his manner, Schindler, even in those last months of Ludwig's life, was not infrequently the target of Ludwig's jokes. Everyone knew that Ludwig had never treated his amanuensis with the greatest of respect – often referring to him as 'my appendix', getting him to hire servants, rent apartments, deal with the police, run errands and for several years even spy on the comings and goings of his young nephew, Karl. Yet like a soldier reporting for duty or a trusty bodyguard, the loyal Schindler was present at Ludwig's bedside every morning when I arrived to care for my patient. He never gave the least indication of feeling slighted by the jokes or what little attention Ludwig paid him. Schindler told me only one thing about the development of Ludwig's illness: that there *was* no development. He insisted again and again that although his friend had 'had the odd problem here and there with his digestion in recent years, he was always hale and hearty, apart from the hearing of course . . . the fever is simply an accident of nature . . . nothing more.'

Of Karl, Ludwig's nephew, I knew little except that he had been living with the composer for more than a decade since Ludwig's brother died, that his mother, Johanna van Beethoven, the brother's widow, was said to be a woman of uncertain virtue, and that, some six months previous, Karl had been involved in a scandal in Vienna – attempting to kill himself by putting a gun to his head and pulling the trigger. The young man must surely have been in earnest, for a nick from his left ear had been removed, presumably by the bullet, as had a patch of hair on the same side which had now grown back lighter in colour and finer in texture than the hair on the rest of his head. Karl was always well dressed, polite and helpful, yet he frequently slunk around the room like a small animal kept too long in confinement – a creature whose spirit is elsewhere. He loved to talk and he took on an air of great importance as he spoke of his uncle's wishes or opinions.

From Karl on that second morning I learned more about how Ludwig's present fever had developed. He told me that in recent months his uncle's chronic digestive problems had grown much worse than before; so much so that Ludwig frequently suffered a loss of appetite followed by indigestion and unpleasant belching as well as alternating constipation and diarrhoea. Despite consulting several physicians who tried to help him, Karl said, his uncle had never been very conscientious about following medical advice. This had led him to rely more and more on spirituous beverages to stimulate his weak appetite and aid his stomach weaknesses. His uncle, he said, was particularly prone to taking strong iced punch and then making long excursions on foot which he believed improved his appetite. All of this only weakened him further, until in late September the composer felt an irresistible urge to withdraw to the country to recuperate. That, said Karl, was how the two of them went to stay with Karl's uncle and Beethoven's brother, Johann, and his wife Therese at their large estate in Gneixendorf, although I suspect it also had something to do with giving Karl himself time to heal the scars of his attempted suicide in August and probably removing him from police jurisdiction in Vienna. When I asked Karl what had happened while he and his uncle were at Johann Beethoven's estate, his eyes brightened and he began to talk in an animated way.

'It's a magnificent estate, Dr Wawruch, with vast acres of woodlands and vineyards and the most wonderful view of the Danube. We went there because it seemed to be the perfect place for him to finish a quartet he had begun. As for myself,' he said, looking down at his feet then back at me again, 'I could not take up my post with the army until the healing was complete.'

'Yes, of course Karl,' I said. 'It would have been difficult for you to stay in Vienna. People love to gossip and you certainly gave them something to gossip about,' I said, smiling. Karl looked at me to determine whether or not I was condemning his actions. Reassured by my smile, he continued, 'Yes, Dr Wawruch. I did not want to stay in the city. It was a great relief to be in the country where no one knew me for I still had the bandages wrapped around my head.'

'What was that like?'

'The bandages or the place?'

I laughed, 'The place, Karl. I have a fairly good idea about the bandages.'

'It was wonderful,' he said, 'that is, when we first arrived.' His voice raced as though he wanted to tell a story faster than he could remember it. 'At first everything went brilliantly. My uncle was given a room overlooking the valley. The country air improved his breathing.'

'And what did you do in your new surroundings?'

'Oh, I amused myself and I walked a lot. I love meeting new people. My uncle and I made daily excursions into the local villages. Sometimes we would go to fetch milk or special meat that he particularly likes. Sometimes we would sit in local taverns and drink wine. It was good fun,' said Karl smiling broadly, then suddenly looking round to see if anyone had noticed, as though he was not allowed to smile.

'That's good, Karl. Then your uncle's general health improved greatly in the country?'

'It did at first,' said Karl. 'But soon, because of his deafness I think, he began to avoid society. He would go out on his own in the morning and work on his compositions on wooded hillsides. Then, when his writing was finished for the day he would tramp about for hours even if the weather was most inhospitable.' Karl lowered his voice. 'Sometimes when he was composing he wandered through the fields humming to himself or shouting and beating time.' I smiled, but Karl's only response was an embarrassed silence.

'That must have been worrying for you,' I said.

'It was not so good,' was Karl's reply. 'One day he disturbed a team of oxen. They were terrified by his bellowing. They stampeded and damaged two vineyards, very badly. Uncle Johann was not pleased. Two or three days later Ludwig left his sketchbooks in the fields. So we had to send Kren out, the servant Therese had lent to my uncle, to look for them. He spent hours hunting for them.'

'And were they found?'

'Oh yes, in the end,' said Karl, 'but not without great difficulty for everyone. You see, uncle cannot bear the slightest criticism of his actions. He became angry at all the fuss, even though he himself had been the cause of it. Before long he grew negligent about taking food regularly and even began to ignore the necessity for wearing protective clothing. So as the autumn drew on he was often caught out, even in heavy snowfalls.'

'I see,' I said. 'And then what happened?'

'Then his feet would swell, Dr Wawruch. But he refused every offer of care. He started to take his meals in his room and to spend all the time with the old servant Kren.'

'What was he like?'

'Kren?' asked Karl. 'Oh, he was quite ugly. A bony, ragged old man with one eye that would not close properly. He smelt like a goat. I don't know how uncle ever bore him. But as for the other servants in the house, my uncle would not tolerate their presence.'

'Really?'

'Actually I think it was the cook's fault – you see, she laughed at him.'

'At Kren?'

'No, at uncle,' said Karl, smiling. 'One day she found him sitting at his work table throwing his hands about in the violent way he does, beating time with his feet and singing.

It can be very funny, Dr Wawruch, to see him when he is composing. She burst into laughter. My uncle rose from the table like a wolf defending its den, grabbed her by the back of the neck and threw her from the room. Kren was there. He tried to leave too but my uncle prevented him. He pulled him back and pressed coins into his hand and told him that he had nothing to fear. Then he demanded that from that day onwards Kren himself make up his room and see to his every need. He would have nothing to do with any of the other servants. Nor did he see Therese and Johann any more.'

'So was your uncle alone all the time?' I asked.

Karl nodded. 'He would awaken at five and work at his writing table for a couple of hours, stamping and shouting and singing so loud that everyone in the house could hear. Then at seven Kren would bring his breakfast. After that uncle would leave the house to roam about the fields and woods until half past twelve when he returned for dinner – always alone. Then he would rest until three and go out walking again until sunset.'

'Alone?'

'Always. I was the only one – except for Kren, of course – who saw him. During the day I would amuse myself visiting friends nearby, playing billiards or talking with the peasants. Then each afternoon I would come to visit my uncle. He was always glad to see me yet it was all rather difficult. You see, he often tried to prevent me from leaving,' said Karl, 'and he was forever questioning me about where I had been and who I had been with.'

'It is sometimes hard for a man who loves a child very much to accept that the child has grown into a man,' I said.

'It was the accusations I could not bear,' Karl said. 'One day he even accused me of carrying out an ... illicit relationship with my aunt, Therese ... Dr Wawruch, I assure you, there was no truth whatsoever in that accusation.'

'No, Karl, I am sure there was not. Why did you and your uncle decide to leave Gneixendorf?'

'As for me, I would have stayed for months. It was uncle who insisted that we go. One evening he became very angry. He stamped about the room; he even broke a chair. He insisted that Therese and Johann had been spying on him. The next morning he announced that we were leaving.'

'Thank you, Karl, for describing to me what occurred. It will help me with my treatment. You are good to care for your uncle as you do. It is good also to care for your own life, Karl,' I added. He looked at me, his dark eyes shining, and he smiled.

I had less opportunity to observe my patient's mannerisms or deportment those first few days than I would have liked. Ludwig moved and spoke little and was far too weak to do more than respond in the most cursory manner to my written questions. He would beg for sips of water with which to moisten a thin, cracked mouth. Yet I was struck by several unusual characteristics which he displayed. Because they were completely unfamiliar to me I only noticed them obliquely, and without full consciousness of what I was seeing – much as one remarks on the visual illusions caused by brilliant summer light cast on long roads where there appears from a distance to be a small body of water stretching across the path. As you draw closer, you find that it has disappeared completely.

There was something uncanny in the way his face appeared to change, even from one moment to the next. One morning when I arrived I found it particularly bloated and without shape; yet before I left the apartment less than half an hour later it had grown quite hard, with the shape of the jaw and brow, lips and nostrils sharply defined. His eyes too went through alterations from time to time, changes which, so far as I was able to discern, had little to do with the amount or quality of light which, at any one time, filtered into the small room. At one moment they would appear a soft grey colour tinged with brown. The next, they would have grown so large and dark that the pupil could not be distinguished from its surrounding iris. I noticed too that the strength and quality of his pulse would alter for no reason, giving quite a different picture from one day to another, even from one hour to the next. His voice, too, when he did begin to speak, went through a wide range of variation in volume and timbre. I had no frame of reference in which to place these changes so I conveniently tucked them away below the lumen of my conscious awareness and addressed the task at hand – that of breaking his fever. To this end I continued to administer body compresses four times a day, and to carry out forced openings with cool herbal waters. I also made further dietary restrictions. I would come in the morning each day, stay for an hour or more carrying out many of the procedures myself, as I did not trust the capacity of the servant to do them well herself, then leave to fulfil my duties at the hospital, returning again after dinner.

Only once during those early days did I find Ludwig alone in the room when I arrived. It was an evening on the fourth or fifth day after I had dined particularly early. When I entered the room my patient was sleeping, but, it must be said, in no sense peacefully. His brow drenched in sweat and his wiry grey hair sodden, he was tossing back and forth, muttering strange disconnected words most of which I could not fully make out:

'They betray . . . stop them . . . they speak with forked tongues. . . .'

I wrung out a cloth in cool water, laid it across his brow then leaned down to listen to his pulse.

He opened his eyes and looked up at me, 'You will help me will you not?' he said.

'I will do everything I can to help you, Herr Beethoven,' I replied.

'Good,' he said, closing his eyes. A moment later he lifted his head off the pillow, attempting to raise himself with his elbows. I put one hand underneath his shoulder. He opened his eyes again and looked at me imploringly. 'It is the light that is all wrong, you see,' he said. I nodded in the way one does with a patient in delirium. 'The light,' I repeated. 'Yes . . . umm . . . I understand.'

'Oh good,' he said. 'Then you will not let them use my music?' he asked.

'Try to rest, now my friend, ' I said, lowering him back on to the pillows. 'We can speak later.'

Suddenly his eyes glared at me with total lack of recognition. 'Who are you?' he demanded. Then he panicked. 'Where is Bertolini?' he squawked. His body had begun to tremble. 'What have you done with him? Are you one of them too . . . dear God!'

I answered him at once, keeping my voice low and calm for I perceived by his questions he was in a state of confusion. I introduced myself, told him I was the physician looking after him because Bertolini was not available. He was not to distress himself, for everything would be well.

While it is not unusual for a man in feverish condition to momentarily lose memory, what struck me as strange was the extent of his amnesia. It remained for over an hour while I tended him and gave my evening instructions to the servant. Besides his lapse of memory did not relate only to myself. When Schindler arrived at the apartment a few minutes before my leaving, Ludwig was awake yet showed no signs of recognising him. And when he crossed the room to give his usual formal bow and greeting, a procedure I had observed him carry out with religious persistence each time he arrived, something extraordinary occurred: demonstrating a physical strength which belied the fragility of his body, Ludwig rose up in his bed, raised one arm and smote Schindler across the chest with a force that sent the poor fellow staggering back halfway across the room.

I could make no sense of this behaviour – nor of Ludwig's lapses of memory and recognition nor of the uncanny alterations in his voice and face which continued to happen spontaneously or at least at the bidding of rhythms and forces of which I had no knowledge. I was aware of something else too that is hard to put into words – especially hard for a scientist who has no belief in that which cannot be measured, reproduced and evaluated by the reason. I myself often felt strange, as one does before a thunderstorm breaks – that is in the presence of powerful energies whose purposes I could not begin to understand.

Somewhat shaken by his unexpected and unwelcome greeting, Schindler, to my surprise, showed no outward signs of irritation. He looked towards me, nodded and smiled slightly as though implying that the two of us were involved in a conspiracy the intention of which was to care for an unruly child. Then he drew himself together like a man gathering his luggage about to make a trip, and backed the rest of the way across the room, lowering himself into a straight-backed chair near the hearth. Later that evening Ludwig's amnesia was also accompanied by one of his strange facial alterations, this time one which made his face seem leaner and, how shall I put it, somewhat 'otherworldly'. It persisted throughout the whole of my visit. The next morning when I returned he greeted me most civilly, enquiring about my own health. He appeared to have no recollection of what had taken place the night before.

On the sixth day Ludwig's fever reached a peak. One

moment his flesh flaked and burned with fire, the next it grew oily and he trembled with a chill which demanded the application of every blanket I could lay my hands on. Then, after half an hour, the burning would begin again. I applied cold linen compresses to his liver during the burning phase. So hot was his body that they dried completely within a quarter of an hour. But the treatment was to good effect. By midnight, the fever had burned itself out and he slept peacefully. When I arrived the next morning he was joking about the poor quality of broth which the servant had prepared for him.

'It's enough to make a greedy sow moan in envy,' he said.

I had not as yet been able either to comprehend what the underlying conditions were that had made my patient so susceptible to such a violent fever or to make any real sense of his unusual alterations in countenance, voice and manner. I knew of course that he would need time to regain his strength and would probably have to live on a stringent diet for the rest of his life, yet I could not help but be pleased with the results of my healing procedures. They had brought him to the state at which the second phase of healing could begin. I welcomed the opportunity now of calling on new skills to strengthen the underlying weaknesses in his body and of readjusting his diet and life patterns so that he could continue for many years to do his work and enjoy his life. By the end of the seventh day he felt remarkably well. He was able to raise himself and walk about the room. He read and even wrote some notes in his sketchbooks. In fact he had grown quite jolly.

When I returned in the evening I found Ludwig in excellent humour. The fever was completely gone. His face was of good mien and he was rapidly gaining strength. He was sitting up in bed and smiling. A massive ear trumpet lay in his lap. He was making sketches for an oratorio he planned to write, and issuing bad puns for Holtz's benefit in that lion voice of his which could purr soft as velvet one moment then rise to a frenzied roar the next. It was evident to everyone present that the crisis was over. This knowledge seemed to trigger a kind of intellectual frenzy in Schindler, who I noticed that evening became involved in a heated discussion about the future of both Ludwig and of mankind.

Schindler thought and spoke in grandiose terms whenever the opportunity presented itself. I wish now that I had paid closer attention to what was being said but at the time I was concerned only with keeping my patient from completely exhausting himself in a frenzy of excitement over his new-found sense of well-being. At last Ludwig appeared ready to sleep despite raised voices from the other side of the room issuing forth phrases such as 'monarchistic nationalist governments must be destroyed', 'private property, sexual laws and moral codes can never be the province of the family', and 'only religious disciplines based on reason will be acceptable'. I implored the gentlemen to silence their chattering and asked them to leave. To my surprise Schindler left too, evidently to attend one of his secret meetings, which I learned from Breuning he did frequently. I found this somewhat strange given Schindler's almost continuous presence until now. I wondered why, now that 'the Master' was so obviously better, he had not taken part in the celebrations of his return to health. I made Ludwig comfortable, left final instructions with the servant that he was not to be disturbed in the night and made ready for my departure. As I rose to leave Ludwig grabbed me by the hand and smiled the most magnificent smile. 'Thank you, Wawruch, for all you have done,' he said.

As I pulled shut the great green door to Ludwig's apartment and began to descend the staircase I took several deep breaths of cold misty air. It felt wonderful. I felt wonderful. In any serious illness there is always a time of unknowing, a time in which shoulders grow tight with effort and one goes to bed at night hoping that one's experience and medical skills will be just enough this time to pull the patient through. Now that fearful time had passed. We had won and I was grateful as I walked through the beautifully lit streets of the city. It was a gift simply to be alive on such an evening. Thus ended the seventh day, 11 December 1826, in peace and gratitude. I had not the slightest hint of the horror that was to greet me on the eighth.

DE STATICA MEDICINA

> The shadow of death and the pains and torments
> of hell are most acutely felt, and this comes from
> the sense of being abandoned by God . . . a terrible
> apprehension has come upon [the soul] that thus it
> will be forever. . . . It sees itself in the midst of the
> opposite evils, miserable imperfections, dryness
> and emptiness of the understanding, and aban-
> donment of the spirit in darkness.

St John of the Cross *The Dark Night of The Soul*

For me, God has always been a problem. Not that I do not
respect the notion of God in His goodness. I respect it well
enough. Yet I have never been able to reconcile it with all I
see around me – the pain, confusion, brutality, cruelty and
evil. Why again and again does He allow it? Why are the
innocent left to suffer?

Six weeks ago – before all the hauntings began – walking
through the streets of Vienna at dusk I watched a carriage
deliberately hit and maim a young boy. The child, a
shabbily dressed boy of eight or nine, was carrying a mangy
cat in his arms. Standing in front of the carriage door which
had not yet been shut, he was begging coins from a
gentleman who had just entered the vehicle. The man
looked at the boy, shuddered, and shouted to the driver to
drive on immediately. This he did – whipping his horse so
that the carriage took off with a great jolt. The opened door
dragged boy and cat to the cobblestones, twisting the child's

body so that his left arm, the arm nearest the coach side, caught in its back wheel. It took three full turns of the wheel to wrench the limb from its shoulder. Then blood flowed free, spurting silently with each pulse of his heart. So quickly and violently had it all happened that the boy did not even cry out until it was over. The man in the coach sped on with complete indifference to the pain he had caused and the blood he had spilt –like the indifference God shows his creatures. Only the cat remained, hungrily licking the spilt blood from the pavement. Once again Wawruch the physician knelt beside the latest victim of life's cruelty hoping to piece together a brutalised body and to forestall yet another needless death.

Some physicians, they say, become hardened to the misery they see around them – the old man screaming in agony from a malignant pain which never leaves his liver, the woman in childbirth who bears her burden stoically, the child himself born into a world that despises him. I have never been fortunate enough to be counted amongst them. The pain I witness each day in the process of carrying out my duties has never ceased to draw echoes from within. Oh no, I do not wail in supplication like the peasant women you hear on their knees in the shadows of St Stephen's. Not I. For I am an educated man – a man of reason, as it is said. I bear it in a different way – through anger and hypocrisy. That is why I, Andreas Wawruch, have always had the demeanour of the compassionate man. In truth I am a killer –just as angry as women who keen or the man whose impatience maimed the child. But it is God, not man, I have killed. In his place I built my own belief in man's nobility: belief in honour, goodness, service and loyalty; beliefs which the longer I have lived with Ludwig – Ludwig the living and Ludwig the dead – the more I have found impossible to uphold. Noble, man may have been born, yet his behaviour bespeaks selfishness and cruelty. So it was with Beethoven. As I sit here in this small room alone, fifteen years after his death, a death I was powerless to prevent, I am aware that his heavy presence bears down on everything I write.

Ludwig was not intentionally a cruel man. He was a man of noble feelings, an artist, a man who loved life as much as any I have known. I remember one morning during those last weeks when Breuning's twelve-year-old son Gerhard arrived with a bunch of snowdrops he had gathered in the wood and presented them to Ludwig. Ludwig was so moved by his gift and so touched by the beauty of the tiny flowers that he held them against his breast unable to speak for several minutes. Yet violence and cruelty seemed to follow in Ludwig's wake – a violence he had turned against himself and which in the end like a dark serpent ate away the very core of his life.

As I climbed the twisting stone staircase leading to Ludwig's apartment on that eighth morning, I could not help but be filled with a certain pride that my physician's skill had once again served me well. Having brought under control what had threatened to be a fatal illness, I knew that from now on everything would become easier – a little rehabilitation, a further change of diet, the occasional purge, and in a few weeks this man, whose work I had long admired, would be engaged in composing more music which I and others could delight in playing. Smiling quietly to myself, I approached the vast green door and knocked firmly. It was opened almost immediately.

'Good morning, Sali,' I said. 'And how then do we find the Master this morning?'

She neither smiled nor responded to my greeting. Turning her spindly body, she shuffled through the anteroom, which was still overflowing with dusty manuscripts, and unlocked the door to the chamber in which he lay. I followed.

I had expected to find him striding about the floor in his boots and nightshirt issuing orders or perhaps searching for some manuscript he had misplaced. Instead his body lay across the bed, with one swollen foot pressed against the cold floor. Linen had been strewn everywhere. On the table near his head lay his spectacles, or what had once been a pair of spectacles, for now they were twisted and broken beyond recognition. Next to them were the remains of a supper, probably prepared the night before but left uneaten, and an unemptied chamber-pot. Quickly tossing a soft rug over the lower half of his body, I ordered Sali to remove them from his presence. Then I lifted his feet on to the bed and proceeded to make him warm.

How do I begin to describe the terrifying alterations that had taken place in Ludwig since the previous night? His short stocky legs had swollen to three or four times their normal size. His face was grey, his breathing was heavy and rattling interspersed with strange vocalisations – words one could only just make out, but which had been strung together in ways that made no sense. The heavy brow was deeply furrowed, the hair matted with dried blood, and his body exuded a most unusual smell. As a physician I am no stranger to the odours of the sick – the sweet fruity breath of the diabetic, the burnt-out fragrance of the man whose heart has failed, the decaying stench of the typhoid child. But I had never come across an odour like the one which permeated the bed of this swollen figure. It was acrid and stale yet powerfully sweet too – like something overripe which lay before me rotting.

Having secured my patient in his bed, I turned in anger to confront the servant and found the room in chaos. Papers had been tossed about everywhere, a curtain torn from its rail, the carpet blotted with red stains. On the floor were patches of what appeared to be human excrement or vomit, or both, all of which lent the room a sordid, uncanny atmosphere. There was even a broken music stand which looked as though it had been twisted in the jaws of some great monster then spat out in disgust as splinters.

'What the devil has happened?' I demanded, barely able to conceal my rage.

'I don't know, sir, I heard such bad noises. In the middle of the night they was, sir. When I opened the door to see what was amiss he was standing in the middle of the room throwing papers everywhere. And cursing he was, sir, in words I never heard before,' said Sali. She looked up to see how I was responding. I had the sense that she was concealing something. Casting her eyes to the floor, she continued.

'The window it was open wide and rain was pouring in on to the carpet, sir. The candle wax it had dripped all down the front of the table. Truly, the whole place looked like a pit of demons had taken it over. "Master, are you all right?" I says. Then I tried to cross the room to close the windows. But he turned on me. "I'll have none of your damnable nonsense," he shouts. "I've been cheated enough. I hate you, you're like all the rest. I hate them with every vile dark force there is in me." It was as if I'd been the cause of his affliction. Yet truly, sir, I had done nothing to deserve such treatment. On my life, sir, nothing.' Again she looked to me for reassurance. I found my anger softening. From the heap of bedclothes came a dark moan as though whatever pain this crumpled figure had been suffering was beginning to ease. I reached across Ludwig's body and took hold of his wrist to make sure his heart was beating regularly. Then I stroked his dry brow and turned back to the servant.

'All right, Sali, it's important that you tell me everything. Go on,' I said.

'Well, sir, I don't remember exactly what happened next.

The Master's face was red and his veins all swole up at the sides of his head. So bad it was I feared they was like to burst. And you have never heard such noise. Bellowing like an animal, he was. Only once have I heard such sounds — when my brother tied a pig ready for the slaughter then plunged a knife into its breast. The Master stared at me but I don't think he even so much as knew who I was. The sound of my voice seemed to anger him something dreadful. Then he picks up a music stand and dashes it against the window. Truly was I scared half out of my wits. "Is there anything I can do, Master," I says. But he only looks me through with them strange eyes and all over again begins to moan and curse. Then with a great bellow he shouts out, "Will nobody help me?" He kept on and on saying it over and over again.'

She paused, rubbed one finger over front teeth black with decay, then continued her tale.

'A minute passed, maybe more. I hid myself behind the piano. Still he bellowed but his voice was softer now. I saw my chance. "Come Master," I says, "Calm yourself. You must get yourself back into bed now and keep warm." I was able to close the window but when I turned to help him back across the room he picks up the bottle of wine — you know, sir, the Rhenish one you gentlemen was drinking to toast his recovery — and he throws it at me. It is only by God's grace that I'm alive to tell the tale. I'm a good lady I am, sir, God's truth, but I could take no more. I ran to the fire and grabbed the poker. It was the one thing I feared he might use to cause himself harm, sir, and there was nowhere for me to turn. Then I pawed my way to the door and darted through it, pulling it to behind me. I took the key from my pocket, slipped it into the lock and turned it as quick as ever I could. But he was on to me. He raced after me towards the door. When he found that it was fast he started beating his fists against it like a madman. I sat trembling against it, I felt his every blow, I did. I feared that it would give way, and him just the other side.' She looked up, shuddered, then resumed her tale.

'For quarter of an hour I listened to his bellowing – I know because I'd heard the clock chime just when I nipped from the room and there it was again. Master had gone quiet. But I feared to unlock the door even when the pale light of morning raised her face. After maybe an hour or more, I turned the key and opened the door. The Master was lying on the floor, his nightshirt up around his belly, his head all a mess of bruises and blood. I pulled down his shift and tried to move his body. His legs had gone big and funny. I took hold of him under his arms and pulled from behind but he was so heavy that I could hardly budge him. I pushed and tugged and after quite a time I got him close enough to the bed that with one great heave I could push his chest on to it. All the while he made no sound. Then suddenly he growled like a dog. His eyes didn't open, sir, but he growled I swear he did. Well, I was at my wits' end, I was – scared and cold and all but faint with my pushing and pulling. I covered him, stoked the fire and went out. And you can be sure I locked the door behind me. I have heard only the sound of his breathing and some soft moaning since, sir. That's when your good self arrived.'

Having finished her tale, Sali placed both palms of her hands against her face and rubbed the base of them into her dark-rimmed eyes in a demonstration of earnestness and fatigue. She seemed to be telling the truth. I had a strange sense that Schindler might have had something to do with all this. I dismissed such suspicions, aware that in my over-impatience I was willing to clutch at any straw.

A violent rage, a great grief, evidently because of some sustained ingratitude or undeserved humiliation, appeared to have provoked this tremendous explosion. Its cause I knew not. My first concern was to examine the damage it had done. I turned towards the bed. My patient was bent double from the pain which now raged in his liver and intestines. His legs and feet were grossly inflated and his brow, his hands and his arms were a mass of dry blood. I had the servant bring some hot water; then I washed the blood away myself fearing to leave the task to her in her present state of agitation. By the time I had finished, his body had developed severe dropsy. Although he appeared to be conscious he would not or could not respond to any of my questions. I saw that the violent fit, whatever its cause or reason, which had taken place in the night had almost killed him. All at once he began to shake uncontrollably. He showed no signs of recognising me. It was as though I were tending a complete stranger – I was someone on whom he had never before laid eyes. I spent the whole of that day at his side, neglecting my duties at the hospital. When the admirers, the secretaries and the hangers-on arrived I told them they could remain only on condition that they maintain strictest silence and did not interfere in the slightest degree with my work. Meek as young rabbits they followed my instructions while I gave this battered swollen body all the care I knew how to bestow. By afternoon Ludwig was severely jaundiced. On examining his liver I found it full of hard nodules. It was evening before he finally spoke.

'I am thirsty,' he said.

When finally I was able to question him about the events of the previous night he appeared to remember nothing. He only complained of pain in his abdomen and greeted people perfunctorily when they came and went. In the days that followed he was to pass long hours silently staring at his hands.

That evening I gave my patient a draught – valerian,

passiflorine and opium blended with a little fruit punch and sweetened with honey. This he drank willingly. It seemed to bring him some relief. I was not sure if that was a result of the mixture or simply the promise of oblivion which it held. I had explained to him that he had undergone a severe setback in his recovery and that what was now needed to regain the lost ground was rest, and I had told him that the potion would provide that. As he took it from the chalice held to his cracked lips he seemed to savour every drop. Its cool sweetness comforted him. He let his head fall back on to the fresh linen of the pillow – I had demanded that his bed be changed twice that day so dishevelled and strange smelling had it become – and closed his eyes. His left hand reached out for mine. I held it firmly in my own, hoping that my grip would impart to this small, spent figure some sense of strength or hope.

Again he held on for several minutes before dropping back on to the bedclothes as his body surrendered to the narcotic. I experienced a peculiar sensation that we – Ludwig and I – had from that moment become bound together in a strange, not altogether holy, alliance. In that instant there remained nothing of the composer and the physician, nothing of the great man and the servant, nothing of the wounded and the healer. All personality had been washed away in the space of a moment. Suddenly none of the day-to-day rules of living could be applied. In that brief space in time there remained only the meeting of two beings and an inexplicable emptiness such meetings give birth to. I knew from a level far deeper than I had ever touched before, a level beyond knowing and beyond explanation, that inside something fundamental had shifted, been altered, been created perhaps. Meanwhile in the outside world all remained as it was: the room was peopled with the same group of men engaged in the same subdued conversation. The servant came and went again taking the tray on which sat the metal goblet from which the draught had been drained. Yet for two conspirators – Ludwig and myself – all time had ceased to be. And as his hand dropped away from mine I had the certain knowledge that a dark promise had been made, a promise to be honoured regardless of cost and irrespective of when or how. It is only now as death draws near that I begin to understand the cost at which such promises can be kept.

ALUM

And what rough beast, its hour come round at last,
Slouches towards Bethlehem to be born?

W.B. Yeats *The Second Coming*

In the course of my work as doctor I had never witnessed a reversal of such intensity. This man should by rights have been gaining strength with each passing day. Instead he had undergone a sudden, violent disintegration despite a strength of constitution unequalled in anyone I had ever met, and a powerful determination on his part to get well. The day the fever broke –that seventh day – he had spoken incessantly about a new symphony he intended to prepare for the London Philharmonic Society and had spent most of the time I was with him scribbling notes in one of his sketchbooks. Now, only two days later, so greatly had his condition deteriorated that he could barely speak. Several more days were to pass before the jaundice cleared. The dropsy which appeared after the choleric outburst never again left him. The segregation of urine lessened and his liver showed plain indication of hard nodules from that day forward.

Not long after, incidents of nocturnal choking and suffocation set in, and with them the strange night events began of which I shall speak shortly. The most urgent matter was the enormous volume of water which had collected in his abdomen. It demanded speedy relief.

I decided it was best to call in my colleague Ritter von

Staudenheim for a second opinion. Staudenheim came. He was of the same opinion as I and insisted that an urgent tapping be made. On learning this, Ludwig's deportment became more amenable. I called on our first surgeon at the General Hospital, Mag. Chir. Herr Siebert, to perform the operation. He arrived forthwith, tools in hand. To my surprise, after so many difficulties over the matter, Ludwig greeted Siebert heartily and behaved with excellent manners and acquiescence both to Siebert and to myself. He even evinced a bountiful good will of which I had seen no trace since before his relapse. When Siebert raised his knife to make the first incision, not a whimper was heard from Ludwig.

The flow of fluid which the puncture released was of such volume and intensity that we had difficulty containing it. Much spilled over on to the wooden floor. We later measured what we were able to collect. This amounted to 25 pounds in weight although the after-flow must have been at least five times as much. Ludwig's relief was immediate. He threw back his head and laughed with a power that startled both of us. 'Gentlemen, you are like Moses striking the rock with your staff and making the waters gush forth,' he said. Such was the first tapping. There were three more to come over the next few months until at last his wretched body let go of life. Although they were necessary to keep him alive, each was for him more burdensome than the last and each left him even more wasted.

Apart from meeting the day-to-day demands of caring for Ludwig's body, which was being pushed to the limits of human endurance, and often having to do so with very little co-operation from my patient whose moods and passions shifted often from hour to hour, I had nothing else to do but be there in that musty chamber with him day after day and watch what was going on. Observing both his physical and psychic condition after the tapping, I became aware of certain energies – influences – what do I call them? Certainly I am, even now, unable to describe them in medical terms. Something unnatural appeared to be at work. It was as though I was caring for a man in whom two forces were at war – the one an irrepressible hunger for life which simply would not allow him to let go, the other a chaotic power which was pulling his body to pieces from inside out.

One question plagued me with such insistence that I found myself, a man who had always slept soundly, awakening several times each night: what could have happened to Ludwig that seventh night to set off a frenzy of rage of such magnitude? What had been said? Or done? And by whom? Did Ludwig's reversal have something to do with the nephew Karl who, although he carried out whatever duty he could in tending for his uncle's needs with reasonable good will, yet seemed always on the smallest pretext to leave the apartment. Had Ludwig received some insult from publisher or patron that had wounded him to the quick? News of some event which threatened his safety? Or was this horrific relapse the result of something far more sinister? I hardly dared to let my imagination address such a possibility.

One morning two or three days after Ludwig's reversal, as I arrived I found Schindler talking in low tones to Sali. I noticed when I entered the anteroom that he had slipped her some silver. This could have been a perfectly ordinary event. He could have been sending her on an errand for food. I would not even have remarked upon it if the servant had not made a rather clumsy attempt to conceal what was taking place. I wondered if they were concealing something that could be important to Ludwig's recovery. Then I dismissed such a notion as little more than an expression of frustration with my own impotence as a doctor.

I questioned each of the men who visited Ludwig daily but to no avail. Breuning told me he himself had remained that seventh evening until half-past eight – long after the other men had departed – at which time his young son Gerhard had come to say that supper was hours overdue and that his wife was awaiting him at home. Breuning assured me that Ludwig had been in the very best of spirits when he departed. He left him rummaging through a pile of sketchbooks in search of a particular melody he wanted to use. The others were of even less help, including nephew Karl who had left the apartment at midday on the seventh day not to be seen again until late the next morning by which time most of the mess had been cleared away. Of the explosion and its possible cause, Karl claimed to have no knowledge, although he was certainly visibly shaken on being faced with his uncle in such a degenerated state that eighth morning.

From Ludwig himself I could glean nothing. The second day following the reversal he passed a couple of hours during which he was lucid enough and co-operative enough to communicate with me, but he appeared to have no recollection of that night whatever. I was forced to return to questioning the servant, who from that time forward had gone about her business with a firmness of purpose previously not evident.

Sali, could, or would, tell me little more. The Master had retired around nine o'clock after taking a cup of warm almond milk. He had complained that the supper she served him a few hours before was 'inedible', and demanded to know the name of the market trader from whom she had purchased the beef from which the bouillon had been boiled. He had asked exactly how much she had bought and what price she had paid for it. He had then told her that, since he was now better, she would have to be more frugal about expenditures, that she was to have roast meat herself no more than twice a week and that she was not, in any circumstances, to remove any food from the premises. On these matters the servant was particularly accurate in her reporting. There was one question, however, to which her reply was not straightforward,

'Did you for any length of time leave the Master that evening?'

'No, sir. That is, sir, only to go about my business as usual in other parts of the apartment,' was her reply. 'You know I could not be with him every moment and still complete the work in the kitchen.'

Looking at me soulfully as though she were a starving dog which I had deliberately kicked, Sali dropped her head forward and rubbed the palm of her bony hands against her greasy apron making it clear that there was little point in questioning her further. I resigned myself, for the moment, to not knowing and waited for an opportunity to speak privately to Schindler who I sensed might have information that could be useful to me but who, being a reserved man by nature, made more so by the presence of others, would consent to speak to me only in private. Only on musical, moral and political subjects did Schindler relish giving highly vocal opinions.

During the first weeks I attended Ludwig I had grown used to his apartment being filled with the men. They seemed almost to live there. I would come in, examine my patient, and give orders to the servant or explain to Breuning some reason for a change of treatment. The men would stand silently watching my ritual ministrations. Other days, particularly when Ludwig was at his poorest, they would converse – generally in respectful, low tones so as not to disturb the man whose room they occupied. They would frequently speak of music as most of them were competent musicians either professional or amateur. They would gossip about events taking place in the city, or about the course of the Prussian wars which had begun that year or about political changes that one or another believed were imminent.

'Herr Sedlnitzky has been busy playing the buffoon again,' said Holtz as he entered the room, tossing a copy of the *Allgemeine Musikalische Zeitung* at the foot of Ludwig's bed.

My patient was fast asleep at the time thanks to a draught I had given him to relieve the pain in his liver. Also present were Schindler, Breuning, young Karl and two other men whom I had seen in Ludwig's presence only once or twice. Holtz was referring to Metternich's censorship chief who was not the most admired of government officials at the time.

'The ass has even taken to concerning himself with what music can and cannot be played at public concerts,' he said. 'Where will it all end?'

Karl had been sitting in one of the straight-backed chairs near his uncle's bed, reading. He closed the book, got up from his chair and moved across the room to where Holtz was now leaning against a window, watching the snow fall heavily. 'But surely you do not disavow all forms of censorship, Holtz?' he asked.

'I damned well do,' replied Holtz. 'I cannot see that there is ever the slightest justification for it. We had great freedom of thought and political action in Vienna before all this talk of revolution in America and France. The disorganisation of the electorates saw to that. Now that is all finished. Now men in power are busy producing policies for life instead of letting us all get on with the living of it.'

I watched Holtz as he spoke, with a certain fascination: this stunningly handsome young man with the body of an athlete and the proclivities of a warrior. Breuning always spoke in low tones, stood quietly, was gentle in his manner and appeared highly self-contained. Holtz was his opposite. He moved with wild and graceful innocence. Everything he said was accompanied by a physical gesture of some kind. It might begin as only a hand movement, but then it would ripple throughout the whole of his body. During those last months of Ludwig's life, Holtz spent many long hours in his friend's apartment. Yet I never once remember seeing him sitting or standing still. He was forever doing something with his hands, shifting his weight from one foot to another or staring through the window like a spirited horse pulling at its tether to be set free of such confinement. In earlier days, before I met Ludwig, when Holtz and I used to make music together, I noticed that even when he played violin Holtz's whole body would move in a way that was beautiful to watch.

Breuning was seated in the chair in front of the pianoforte. He had been sifting through some papers, looking for some musical notes that Ludwig had misplaced. He was often asked by Ludwig where he had put something and sometimes would spend hours mulling through his dusty, untidy apartment in search of what was wanted. 'Come, come, Holtz,' said Breuning, 'you must not fill the young man's head with such notions. Things are no more repressive now than they were before the so-called democratic disturbances. What has truly changed? I grant you the braggart reactionaries have been marked down and removed, but the real scholar and autonomous thinker is no more persecuted in Germany now than then. I believe the new fascination with democracy is bound to bring us even greater freedom.'

'Breuning, you believe in fairy tales,' Holtz replied, raising his voice so much I feared it would waken Ludwig. 'Egalitarian democracy and all the revolutionary hotheads who shout about it are as nonsensical as our absurd Austrian police state. They talk about *liberty*, *equality* and the *rights of man* but they are as easily controlled as Metternich's mechanical toy ministers. Don't you see how fraudulent it all is, Breuning? They fabricate high-sounding phrases designed to turn men into sheep while they are led to believe they control their destinies. Then these great democratic thinkers of ours herd the flock just where they want them to go.' As he spoke Holtz was flicking layers of whitewash from the damp wall with his fingernail. 'Of course,' he went on, 'there is much to be said for Metternich's vision. We mustn't underestimate its far-reaching effects. I hear the Congress at Laibach is proposing a fine new law that will regulate how high birds may fly and how fast hares may run. . . .'

Karl laughed then turned to look at Breuning.

'What matters, Karl,' said Breuning, speaking with the gentleness of a father to his son, 'is not so much what your political leanings are as whether or not your *intentions* stem from the ideals of reason, tolerance and humanity.'

'Much as I disapprove of the repressive state of affairs in Germany,' Holtz went on. 'I do not believe that revolutionaries will change anything. Concealed within their propaganda I think you will find an iron hand in a kid glove that intends to steal a man's power and subdue his wild will. A man needs real freedom, Karl,' said Holtz, moving to just behind Karl's chair and resting a hand on his shoulder, 'freedom to control his own destiny and live his own life the way he chooses, not some ideology designed to tame him while he doesn't even know that this is what is going on.'

All this time Schindler and the other two men had remained silent. Standing near the fire – he was always cold – Schindler had the fingers of his left hand tucked into his half-buttoned waistcoat. His skin, I remarked, was the colour of a calf bled too long before slaughter. He had assumed the posture of a sombre professor waiting for the perfect moment to correct his students. That moment had evidently arrived.

'Gentlemen,' he said, tilting his head to one side slightly, 'let us be realistic. Men are not *wise* enough to be free. They must be guided for their own good. That is where the new politics comes in. After all, we are not living in the Middle Ages when flagellation, maiming, tying to the wheel, binding and the "iron maiden" were used. Democratic persuasion is the key. If those of us with real vision do not act now to establish order amongst lesser men, we will all come to live in social conditions created by fools.'

'Schindler, your bloody democracy is as big a sham as you are,' said Holtz.

'Of course democracy is a sham, Herr Holtz,' replied Schindler, drawing himself up to his full height – to let Holtz know he had been unruffled by his accusation. 'But it is a *useful* sham. Men need *something* to believe in. One allows them to believe. Then when their eyes are filled with stars, one leads them down whatever pathway is best for them.' Schindler cleared his throat before continuing. 'But take the notion of justice and equality for all seriously – leave the common man to decide for himself, and you are courting disaster.'

'I am stunned by your words, Schindler' said Breuning. 'How can you speak about democracy with the tongue of a cynic – you who profess brotherhood, co-operation and freedom? You also completely forget the will of God, dear Schindler, and his consortium the Holy Church.' Schindler stood in silence, every bit the grand professor, letting his students 'think for themselves'. 'Do you jest?' continued Breuning, 'for if so it is a poor enough joke in young Karl's presence.'

'I jest not,' said Schindler, 'I –'

'Beware of Schindler's consortia,' Holtz broke in. 'Schindler and his friends would like to control the future of life on our planet through such a consortium.'

'I would rather be part of a consortium,' said Schindler, raising his voice, 'than one of the sheep who follows, Herr Holtz.' Schindler adjusted his coat. 'As for the Church,' he said, 'well Breuning, if you think you can take refuge in the Church you are a fool. A skilled devil can do far more harm to humanity through a single Church than through all the black temples and Satanic covens combined.'

'Quite right, Schindler,' said Holtz, gesturing towards the two men who remained silent and knocking his boot against the skirting board. 'Why should you gentlemen toy with the trappings when you can use so many other emblems to touch a far greater number of people and pervert them.' Holtz crossed the room to stand face to face with Schindler. Schindler took a step backwards wary, I presume, of Holtz's strength and uncertain of his intentions. 'There is only one thing you do not take into account – you who would rule the world and crush man's soul into the bargain,' said Holtz, tapping Schindler on the breast with his fingers. 'It is the artist. The artist, Schindler, is the only man who is truly free. He can see right through the illusions you and your friends spin to entrap him. Any man who knows the truth,' continued Holtz, 'can banish your power with one snap of his fingers.' Holtz snapped his own fingers in Schindler's face with such force that Ludwig's sleeping body shuddered in spite of the deafness. Schindler moved back from Holtz as quickly as he could without betraying fear, took three steps across the room and then turned back, raising his right hand and tucking it into the breast of his coat.

'You are a fool, Holtz,' he said. 'You are like those who think they can brandish a crucifix at the Devil and force him to depart. You do the Dark One an injustice. Without so much as the blink of his eye he will snatch your crucifix from your finger, from your lily-white hand and turn it towards you laughing, "Look hard young man. It is I who chose to hang your body from a cross that you yourself invented for my sake alone though you do not know it!" ' Then, addressing Breuning, Schindler said, 'Ask not your God to rescue you, Breuning. By your crucifix we shall conquer.'

Breuning started to protest but Schindler went on, interrupting him. 'I and others – the *guardians of life* – know only too well what evil is to come in the future – evil that will make Sedlnitzky with his notions and you two with your high ideals look like a pair of babies.'

'Of what evil do you speak, Herr Schindler?' asked Karl.

'I will tell you about Schindler's evil, Karl,' said Holtz, leaning back against the wall again and crossing his arms. 'Schindler's evil will resemble an impersonal agreement – something *detached* from each individual. In the future it will appear anonymously as a kind of injustice from which men have no recourse. Men will kill as they do today yet no blood will you detect on their hands. They will be able to sit behind desks and sign orders for the murder of thousands in the name of democracy, or freedom, or preserving the purity of the race, or some such nonsense. The motivation for their deeds will not be found in passion but in sober calculations, bland notions and twisted thoughts – such is Schindler's evil.'

'Perhaps. But you must remember, Karl, even evil is put at the disposal of the *guardians* to use as we see fit in the regulation of mankind,' said Schindler. Aware that he had the full attention of his audience, he spoke slowly with a quiet flair for self-deprecation. He removed the hand from beneath the waistcoat and plucked off a piece of lint which had settled on his trousers, then he looked up.

'You paint a chilling picture, Schindler,' said Karl.

'Chilling yes, inaccurate, I think not,' replied Schindler. 'That is why now, and in the future, great leadership is essential to Germany. I don't mean the leadership of Metternich and his lackeys. These men are not leaders, they are puppets and must be treated as such. Nor do I mean Breuning's soft-bellied liberals and religious devotees or those dreamers who would attempt to convince us that all men are created equal. Real leadership, Karl, can come only from men who have been illumined – men of intelligence and discernment – men who have the strength and skill to carry forward the great vision of a new world.'

'And you, of course, are one of these visionaries,' said Holtz.

Choosing to ignore Holtz's remark, Schindler continued, 'United in their vision of brotherhood such men guide both the politicians and the masses. They will have no need to display themselves to public life. From behind the scenes, they will make the decisions and then use the powers of persuasion to carry them out – through gold, religion, politics, music – even brute force if absolutely necessary. We will use whatever lies at our disposal to bring to the masses all that is good for them. We are the real statesmen of the future.'

'Music?' said Karl. 'Why do you speak of music? What does it have to do with leading men?'

'A good deal,' said Schindler turning his head slowly in Karl's direction, 'provided of course that it is the right kind of music – music to fire men's passions for an ideal, music to channel their instincts. Used skilfully, music can become the "eighth harmonic" – a bridge between the unseen and the seen world. It is completely *neutral* in its charge. It can be employed for whatever purpose wise and clever men wish to use it. If you want the masses to follow you, you have but to make use of the mathematical patterns of the highest music to evoke their passion, to inflame them with a desire to stand up and fight for freedom and good will or whatever else you would have them fight for.'

'You preach a terrifying doctrine, Schindler,' said Breuning sharply. His fair skin had reddened and he was showing a volatility uncharacteristic of him, 'I ignore your absurd misuse of the art of music. As for the rest – how can you be certain that those who choose to offer this new leadership are themselves ethical? It seems to me that it is difficult for any statesman to be fully conscious of the consequences of his actions. A man may act with the most noble of intentions yet his actions can lead to despicable and deplorable results, if his soul is stupefied or shrouded in darkness. A leader must align himself with the Divine will. If any man makes choices out of a dark or cramped state of mind his psyche may become a doorway for destructive forces. . . .'

'Indeed it can,' replied Schindler. 'That is why *light* must be shed on the stage of human interactions by great men. The mind of a leader, his being, his judgement must be guided by a greater intelligence, a greater power, a power that knows the needs of the people and makes judgements for them which they are neither equipped nor interested in making for themselves. Such leadership transcends *human* vision and value – it is even beyond notions of good and evil. It makes use of whatever proclivities, passions and energies are necessary to do what needs to be done. It is, I am afraid, a question of *noblesse oblige* and of conscious choice on the part of all of us with real vision – a question of universal brotherhood and national melioration.'

'Conscious choice? What rubbish,' growled Holtz, having returned to and then completed his self-appointed task of removing all the loose plaster from around the windowsill.

'You have never made a conscious choice in your life. You are a pawn and you don't even know it. All of you are pawns,' he said with a sweeping gesture towards the two silent men. 'Your philosophies of oligarchic leadership and brotherhood are no better than Breuning's of liberalism and Christianity. The ideals you profess and the methods you would use only mutate and distort human life. Given time they turn men and women into travesties. If the lot of you have your way you will destroy not only the Church and the monarchy, you will even destroy the earth itself.'

'We say let be destroyed what must, Herr Holtz,' said Schindler, 'to further the higher order. That is the only conscious choice a wise man can make.'

'How naive you all are with your secret plans and your pompous phrases' said Holtz, 'and you do not even know it. A ruler has no power through politics or by creating prosperity to improve the quality of life, nor the lives of those he rules. Quality of life is not a moral or an economic issue. And it has nothing to do with the historical and political events you would like to manipulate. One thing only makes man higher than other animals: he is able to create beauty. Toying with politics and ideologies is playing the games of adolescent boys. Some say you are dangerous. I say you are pompous fools. Forget politics, Schindler. Go and play your violin.'

On hearing Holtz's words Schindler's countenance altered strangely. The controlled deportment with which his previous words had been spoken gave way to a smouldering fury most clearly detectable in his eyes which flashed in my direction. They resembled the eyes of a rat focused on an animal whose succulent flesh it is preparing to devour. Then they looked beyond me at the sleeping form of Ludwig and they softened. The glance of cold fury dissolved. In its place arose a strange and troubled look of

275

uncertainty. A shudder passed through Schindler's body. Regaining his deportment and drawing himself up to his full height, which was not – I was quick to remark – very tall, he turned back to Holtz.

'Sir,' countered Schindler, addressing Holtz with obvious distaste, 'you are mistaken. Aesthetics is the finest political tool of all. Consider the Master's music. The finale of Ludwig's Symphony in D Minor, does it not speak of brotherhood? Does it not foreshadow what is to come – an age of undreamed-of miracles whose small-minded nationalist interests have dissolved to create a new order in the world? It can be used to fire men's passions. It could even, were one inclined to employ it in such a manner, be used to fire opposing camps who sit like dog to dog within a ring then proceed to destroy one another. Whatever is necessary to control the process of man's development, to purify the strains of human life, we must do. Whatever tools – aesthetic, political, moral – we may need to carry out the task, we will use. Out of charity to mankind of course, gentlemen, out of charity and light – the highest wisdom of brotherhood.'

Schindler's voice had so risen in volume that Ludwig, who until that moment had been sleeping soundly, suddenly shook, opened his eyes and made an effort to sit up in bed. Earlier in the day, when I had left his apartment to descend the steps into a heavy blizzard after my morning visit, Ludwig's eyes had been glazed and, with the exception of myself whom he greeted with characteristic disapproval, he had shown no evidence that he recognised any of his friends. Now on awakening he looked completely different. There was a softness to his skin and a gentleness to his manner. The snow had stopped. Brief traces of rare winter sunlight filtered through an extremely dirty window. Turning his head towards the light, Ludwig saw Holtz and smiled. The men continued their discussions but so quietly now that I could not make out their words. For this I was grateful. Their intellectual banter always frustrated me while I was involved in my vain attempts to restore health to this man who lay before me. It also often interrupted Ludwig's sleep, which he needed greatly, and created agitation in him – particularly, when the word 'brotherhood' was mentioned. This particular afternoon however, I was not displeased at Ludwig's awakening for I had been waiting for his sleep to end that I might change the dressing to his wound. To my surprise he did not greet me in his usual disdainful manner.

'Good day, Herr Professor,' he said.

'Good afternoon, Ludwig. How is the pain?' I asked, gesticulating to convey my meaning.

'Hearty,' was his reply and with it his soft face broke into a charming grin, 'The pain is doing very well indeed, Wawruch. I am not so certain the patient can be said to be doing altogether as well. But that is for you to say.' He pulled back the covers of his bed to reveal the bandages with much the same flair a French chef uses to take off the covering of a rich dessert.

I removed his surgical dressings to find bandages soaked in pink fluid beneath. I did not like the look of what I saw. Despite my elaborate instructions on how dressings were to be changed, again my orders had been carelessly and wrongly carried out. This resulted in an erysipeloid infection which must not only have given him considerable pain but was also exceedingly dangerous. I bathed the area in bromine and iodine, from which my patient's body recoiled violently although he did not utter the slightest word of protest, and redressed the wound with Breuning's help. After that I determined to return yet again very late in the evening and whenever possible to change dressings myself,

WAWRUCH

and when I could not do so to call upon Breuning, regardless
of whatever strain this might put on his own failing health.

Despite changes of linen as frequent as the servant could
manage, which was by no means what I would like to have
seen, and the best care I could bring to it, over the next few
days Ludwig continued to be plagued by bed bugs. His
wounds became gangrenous and the poison never cleared
completely. I knew that only meticulous attention to
cleanliness and to keeping the sores dry prevented further
deterioration. I decided to make my morning and afternoon
visits shorter, in an attempt to avoid distractions and in the
hope of becoming as efficient in my ministrations as
possible. I would come, examine Ludwig, give whatever
medication or treatment I deemed necessary, issue orders to
Sali or Breuning concerning that which had to be done in
my absence and then depart, leaving these gentlemen to
their lengthy discussions. But the fact that I was spending
less and less time at his bedside during the day, instead of
releasing me from the increasingly heavy burden of
impotence and frustrated efforts to heal Ludwig, only
seemed to worsen matters. I found myself neglecting my
work at the hospital, postponing operations which I should
have performed with haste or passing them on to other
physicians. I started to spend hours in my study delving
deep into the medical literature for some clue that might
help me discover a key to heal this man. It was also at this
point – late January 1827 – that I began making secret visits
to his bedside: late-night visits.

At first Ludwig's friends thought my behaviour somewhat strange but I quite deliberately let slip comments
about keeping watch on his nocturnal progress in the hope
that I would be better guided towards designing effective
treatments. This sufficed to alleviate their curiosity. What
time was there for sleep, I asked myself, when there was so

much to be understood? If I was to prevent the approaching death of this man who had become not only the most difficult patient I have ever had but also the most cherished, perhaps *because* of the difficulty, it would call for all the attention I could give to the matter. What was especially strange, although I did not think so at the time, was the hidden way in which I, who had always been a particularly direct man, carried it all out. I told no one of my coming and going, not even my wife. She, I think, assumed I was leaving our bed in the middle of each night to see to an emergency at the hospital. In this way I began to live what can only be described as a secret life. If one of my kind-hearted colleagues had uttered the word *obsession* it might just have sounded a bell in my fragile mind which was day by day sinking deeper into its own world. But my ordered habits as a physician and my even-tempered manner well concealed the secret life we began to live, Ludwig and I – a life which even now fifteen years later I hardly understand. Yet from that time forward I found myself drawn deeper and deeper into Ludwig's web – so deep that in time I began to wonder if I knew where I ended and he began.

That evening I took a dusty Bible off its shelf, although I had left it undisturbed where it sat for many years. I called to mind Ludwig's words: 'It is a fearful thing Wawruch, to fall into the hands of a living God.' Having no idea for what I was searching, I opened the book at these words from Isaiah 45.7: '*I form the light, and create darkness: I make peace, and create evil: I the Lord do all these things.*'

MELANCHOLY

The awful thing is that beauty is mysterious as well
as terrible. God and the devil are fighting there
and the battlefield is the heart of man.

Fyodor Dostoevsky *The Brothers Karamazov*

Of the medical facts that emerged during the following
weeks I shall duly speak if time enough remains. Far more
pressing and mysterious were the unusual events, or moods,
that I witnessed when night after night I sat in Ludwig's
room. I began these visits, I told myself, because I did not
altogether trust the servant Sali and I believed there was no
one else in whose care I could leave my patient. My
obsession with Ludwig's case was not only because I was
failing in my ability to heal him, although that was certainly
a factor, it was something more. I simply could not stop
thinking about him, or delving into his history and his mind.
I began to arrive each night some time between eleven
o'clock at night and one in the morning to take my place at
his bedside. In the beginning I would knock and wait for the
door to be opened by Sali. Some evenings, when I arrived
early, Breuning would meet me at the door, usually on his
way home. As my night visits became regular, however, I
arranged with Sali to have the blacksmith file a new key. I
carried it on my person at all times but told no one about it. I
could thus let myself in, even if she were asleep, without
disturbing anyone. This suited the servant admirably,

giving her a sense of freedom which she had hitherto not enjoyed. She was able to sleep peacefully thereafter, all the more readily when of an evening she had consumed what remained of a bottle of wine.

At first I was present only on intermittent nights. Within three weeks, however, my night visits became so regular that I missed only three nights between January and the end of March in 1827 when Ludwig died. My possessing a key provided the servant with an opportunity to leave the apartment without fear of reproach. I wanted to be left alone with Ludwig. For when the night events began – unsettling though they were – I started to fear that they would not continue at all unless I could ensure that nothing or no one would disturb us. Secondly, so strange was the relationship that was developing between Ludwig and myself that I did not want anyone to know of it.

Often I would arrive to take my place by his bedside and find him sleeping heavily. I would then light candles on either side of the pianoforte and, taking a seat on the stool which stood before it, lean forward to read or make notes propping my papers against its top. The first three or four nights Ludwig awakened periodically. I went to his side, made sure he was as comfortable as possible, examined the condition of his dressing and offered him a drink of cool water so that he could slip back into slumber. Five or six days after my first visit a most unusual event took place. He had awakened for the third or fourth time that night in considerable discomfort over the wound in his belly which, inflamed as it was, was healing slowly. Because of the extent of his dropsy, which the tappings only partially relieved, his face, his belly and his legs were greatly engorged, giving him the look of an overripe fruit. All the hard planes in the structure of his face had become subsumed under this cushion of fluid that covered his bones. This oedema also made his movements sluggish and rolling.

He awakened at three that morning and cleared his throat as though he were about to speak. I was sitting at the pianoforte. I had evidently fallen into slumber myself for I was wakened by the sound to find my face pressed hard against the book I had been reading. I arose at once and moved to his side. He was attempting, with obvious difficulty, to sit up in bed so I quickly fluffed his pillows then lifted his body from under the arms in an attempt to make him more comfortable. His skin had the familiar swollen look. His eyes were dark and sunken. They stared straight ahead in a kind of brooding gaze as though he were drugged and completely unaware of my presence. What happened next was so far beyond anything I had ever seen before that it is almost impossible to describe. Suddenly and without warning, before my very eyes, the impossible occurred. Ludwig's posture changed. His body stiffened so that within moments he was sitting rigidly erect. Then an alien, unaccountable expression passed over his face which seemed somehow to erase it. It became — how should I describe it? — a featureless blank. I watched as the lines on his face dissolved, shifted, became barely discernible. Then they underwent a rippling transformation which completely washed away the swollen character of his countenance. The hard lines of browbone, cheek and jaw, previously hidden beneath the swelling, emerged almost as though a sculptor working from within were transforming soft terracotta beneath his fingers. Ludwig closed his eyes and winced, put his fists to his temples pressing hard and twisted them as though trying to banish unexpected pain. A mild shudder passed over his whole body. The fists dropped to his lap. He took a deep breath, let his body sink back into the pillows with an evident pleasure demonstrating a freedom from pain that I had never witnessed in him before. Then in a warm teasing voice which I had never heard before, said,

'Wawruch, should you not be at home looking after your reputation?'

I was much taken aback. This man who only two minutes before had been oblivious to my presence, racked by pain and so swollen with fluid that he was hardly able to move unaided from one side of his small bed to the other, had physically metamorphosed in front of my very eyes into someone who now sat before me in what appeared to be total comfort and considerable physical strength. It was as though someone else altogether, not the Ludwig I had seen and cared for all these weeks, were sitting before me.

'Never mind, since you are here, you can make yourself useful. Hand me that sheaf of manuscript paper,' he said with a broad gesture towards the pianoforte on which lay a huge pile of papers. 'And I had better have something to write with.'

Stunned by his order and the apparent ease with which it was issued, I moved quickly to give him what he wanted. This person bore many of the characteristics of Ludwig – the brow, the small hands, the wild grey hair – yet how vastly different he was: his posture, the strength his body displayed, a strength which as a physician I knew well was utterly impossible in the state he was in. The eyes had now completely lost their glazed quality. Even the voice was new. What, I asked myself, was happening? Was I dreaming all of this? Had the stress of recent weeks dissolved my reason, distorted my vision, destroyed my judgement? Or was Ludwig performing some kind of act and was this strange phenomenon the result of a sardonic and sinister joke on his part – a way of further undermining my reason and shaking my faith in my powers as a doctor and a man?

Then this man before me who was Ludwig and yet not Ludwig began to speak. 'Thank you, Wawruch,' he said. I stood in stunned silence staring at him as he began to scribble on the manuscript paper. He worked for a minute or two then suddenly looked up to see me staring down at him. 'Oh for goodness' sake,' he said, 'do sit down. Look, I will show you what I am doing.'

I sat on a small chair, pulling it close to his bed, and looked down at the paper on which he was working. It appeared to be the scherzo of the string quartet written in C minor. 'It is the fugue that is the stumbling block,' he said, pointing to some notes halfway down the page. 'You see, it is a set of variations, two pointedly contrasting sonata movements,' he went on, turning to look into my eyes. I nodded. 'In the first,' he explained, 'I used a truncated structure, but I am having trouble with the second. It is not adequate. It needs to be larger, more magisterial, more expansive.'

I took one of the sheaves in my hand and looked carefully at the notes but was still so stunned by what was happening I was unable to make sense of the words he spoke.

'You see, it is a question of continuity and surprise,' he said. 'I need a startling assertion, a discontinuity to propel the movement inexorably to its conclusion.' The clipped manner of his speech and the cold intellectual way in which he was looking at the music seemed altogether uncharacteristic, not to mention the fact that this man, this Ludwig, this whatever he was, showed no signs whatsoever of either pain or weakness as he spoke and scribbled.

'The sub-dominant F sharp minor is the link between the fugue and the finale but it is not enough. I need to take the challenge a step beyond,' he said. 'I believe I need to develop the C sharp minor as a kind of transcendent opposite.'

All the time he spoke, his voice was perfectly modulated, his eyes were clear and he gazed into my face as though I were not the despicable doctor whom he so hated, but an intimate friend and musician well versed in harmony and counterpoint who would understand every word. After several minutes he stopped speaking. Then Ludwig's eyes blinked several times as though he were uncertain where he was and what was happening. His whole physiognomy underwent a strange transformation, rather as one would see in a dream. His face lost its pointed quality and became rounder and softer. His shoulders slumped against the pillow. His hands and arms which had worked so intensely for the half-hour before became limp and lifeless as he let the pen fall from his hand. I gathered up the manuscript sheaves and took them away from the bed. When I returned again to look at him his appearance had altered greatly. When next words issued from his mouth, the focus of his thoughts had shifted. His voice took on a powerful resonance, deep and dark and rich. He began to speak as a prophet might.

'All things flow clear and pure from Him,' he said, looking towards me with heavy eyes for some acknowledgement that I had understood his words. I nodded. 'If afterwards I became darkened through passion for evil, I did return later after manifold exorcism to the elevated and pure source, to the Godhead and to Art.' I noticed his hands were trembling.

'I have,' he said, taking hold of my shoulder with immense difficulty as though even the slightest movement was agony, and whispering as one might to a fellow conspirator, 'no interest in business, sir. You see it is always and forever thus, dull – tedious and boring – an occupation of no value. Art is what I do because I cannot do otherwise. Are not trees bowed low by the abundance of their fruit? Do not clouds shed their burden when sated with water?' He paused for a moment gazing in complete stillness deep into my eyes, then began to speak again. 'Wawruch, you must exercise restraint,' he said. 'When tears lurk beneath your lashes let resolution hold back their first efforts to fall. . . . In thy wanderings sometimes a road will be high, sometimes low. Seldom will you walk along the true path. So let the traces of your tread remain unequal. It makes no difference, the true virtue of the power of life itself will press you forward. . . . Seek asylum in that alone.'

Thus did Ludwig speak in unfamiliar, disconnected phrases until he had exhausted some imperative from within so that after a while the words ceased. His body grew still as a statue. The trembling in his hands ceased. I sat beside him dazed by this man's strange eyes and by the deep peace which dissolved all pain from his body. I, the doctor, man of science, worshipper of reason, had become overcome by what I had witnessed. For how long the two of us sat in silence I do not know. It was as though once again we, Ludwig and I, had been sucked through a dark hole into some timeless place between worlds for many minutes, perhaps even hours. The spell was broken finally by the chime of the cathedral bells making six o'clock. I was drawn back into the ordinariness of the small room in which we sat, a room which for a time had become a great space permeated with silence so deep that I could hardly bear the noise of it.

A cold drizzle fell outside the window. It could not make up its mind whether to become snow or retain for ever its dreariness. The fire, left untended in the night, had burnt dangerously low. I reached forward to pull up the covers which had fallen away from Ludwig's chest. His body rested peacefully against the pillows. I found myself staring at folds of skin on his pitted neck. It had a beauty that is impossible to describe, like the bark of a great oak which has stood for three centuries while sun and wind and thunder bear down upon it – so permanent yet so fragile – as all life is fragile, for with the power of but one man wielding an axe it can be destroyed for ever. It was then that I noticed how small was his hand which for so long had rested on my left shoulder and then that I remarked with an all-consuming pity the myriad small red marks near his left ear left by bed bugs, which, despite all my urging for clean linen and all my herbal potions, I had been unable to eradicate. I placed my hand on the crest of his heavy brow. Ludwig smiled and shut his eyes. Within a few moments he was asleep, so peacefully that not even the hint of a snore was evident. I rose, added coal to the tiny fire and used the bellows to raise a flame. Then I moved to the window, seating myself next to the shredded curtain which still bore the marks of violence from that eighth day. There I remained until dawn.

Just after daybreak I heard the sound of a key in the latch and the shuffling footsteps of the scarecrow Sali slinking down the hall to light a morning fire in the kitchen. I waited until they had died away. Making sure that Ludwig was covered, I picked up my notes and books, pressed them beneath my overcoat to protect them from the drizzle that was still falling and, opening and closing doors as silently as I could manage, slipped out. I descended the spiral stone staircase to the street. I saw no one except a woman in a soiled red dress locked within the embrace of a very fat man standing in a doorway and a dog who crossed the cobbled street heading purposefully towards the palace kitchens in the hope of discovering some small morsel that might sustain it through winter.

PHOSPHORUS

Turning and turning in the widening gyre
The falcon cannot hear the falconer;
Things fall apart; the centre cannot hold;
Mere anarchy is loosed upon the world,
The blood-dimmed tide is loosed, and everywhere
The ceremony of innocence is drowned;
The best lack all conviction, while the worst
Are full of passionate intensity.

W.B. Yeats *The Second Coming*

The morning after the first night event when I returned to
carry out my official visit I found Ludwig in a peaceful but
weak condition. The rain had stopped. An icy winter
sunlight filtered through the curtains. When I greeted him
he turned his face towards the wall in what I perceived to be
irritation and gave no acknowledgement of what had passed
between us the previous night. Thus began the pattern of
my secret life with Ludwig. During the day he treated me at
best with indifference, ignoring my presence. At worst he
showered me with contempt, frequently hurling verbal
abuse at me. Nightly we met in our strange secret world – a
world which now, later, I hardly know how to describe. It
was as though several separate selves – not so much aspects
of Ludwig's own character but altogether different
presences – existed simultaneously within his body. A
switch would take place from one to another with little
warning. It always occurred in the same manner. His eyes

would go blank for a few seconds, his breathing would shift and grow deeper or more shallow or occasionally very rapid, but for not more than half a minute at a time, and then, as I watched in silence hardly daring to believe what was taking place, another being would seem to emerge from his body. This would happen without warning. Always it occurred without apparent consciousness on Ludwig's part.

I do not believe in demonic possession. Yet I am aware that the mind in its myriad facets throws out strange and powerful lights. What I have just described was but the first in a long line of events during the last weeks of my patient's life which dazzled my wits, dissolved every certainty I had about good and evil, and left me humbly ignorant as to an explanation. We, each of us, assume a constancy, a dependability in the human being, one might describe it as a centre to the person, which we call the I. Someone is left-handed or skilled at chess or colour blind. All such traits we associate with that particular person. We also, I have observed, believe that a set of unspoken rules limits the plasticity of a human being so that if, say, he always sneezes when near flowers this will remain so. This, Ludwig taught me during those weeks, is not the case. I came to know that some of us – perhaps most, although who would like to admit this? – undergo dramatic shifts not only as though from one persona to another but occasionally even from being left- to right-handed and from having an aversion to flowers to being able to sniff them with impunity.

With these events – the appearances of what I chose to call Ludwig's 'personae' – I was both fascinated and disturbed. Several times I wondered if Ludwig, whom I knew had a penchant for jokes and pranks, had been playing with me. 'Is this real?' I would ask myself. 'Is he acting?' But when, after the first few nights, these fugues of consciousness began to occur regularly during the hours of deepest darkness and only when we were alone, I reasoned that artifice was unlikely to be a cause of what I was witnessing. Some of the truly remarkable and most troubling aspects of the alterations I saw lay not only in the different words that issued from Ludwig's mouth or in how his behaviour would alter, but rather in certain rich, intangible changes which my medical training told me were virtually impossible to feign.

His voice would alter in timbre and accent. The patterns and rhythms of his speech would change and numerous physiological features would metamorphose – his posture, his physiognomy, the texture and dryness of his skin. The rate of his heartbeat and the quality of his pulse would change beyond all recognition. Even his hearing could alter dramatically during a fugue – so much so that, despite the deafness, we could, the two of us, carry on a reasonable conversation without my having to resort either to raising my voice or scribbling notes in the much-used conversation book. Ludwig in his normal state was decidedly right-handed: he wrote, ate and gestured with his right hand. But one night as I was witnessing yet another shift in his consciousness he asked me for a sketchbook in which he scribbled several bars of a trio for strings he was composing. Every mark that issued forth from his broken pen dipped in thick black ink was made with his left hand.

At first I had entertained the notion that there was only one persona who intruded into Ludwig to stay for periods of a few minutes to several hours. I was soon forced to revise my assessment as one by one I was brought face to face with many beings – each unique and separate from the others. When one was present Ludwig would soar above the mediocrity of intellect into distant regions of consciousness. I would sit in silent awe of the things of which he spoke – as though he had become a voice for higher levels of being –

wise, peaceful, all-encompassing in vision and purpose. Then all at once his eyes would glaze over and within the space of a few seconds he would switch into another totally different person. Always it seemed that some connection, some interaction with me was necessary for the people who inhabited Ludwig's body to remain present.

Sometimes he would become as a child, wanting to play or describing to me some ancient event as though it were taking place before his eyes, and both of us could see it, smell it, feel the textures and the qualities of that other time and place and people. 'I won't do it,' he said one night, suddenly, as I was standing at the window. I turned to find that yet another metamorphosis had taken place. His face looked strangely impish and unformed.

'I won't,' he said, 'I won't do it, no matter what you say.' I moved to his bedside, searching for a conversation book that I could write in. He became very impatient. 'Why do you not answer me?' he demanded.

I replied, 'Ludwig, I do not answer you because you cannot hear me.'

'Of course I can hear you,' said the voice – a voice which sounded very much like that of a child of perhaps seven or eight. I did not believe that this could be happening.

'You can hear me, Ludwig?'

'I am not Ludwig,' the voice said.

'But who are you?' I replied, stunned to find that he could hear my every word although I was not raising my voice.

'You may well ask,' he said. 'They call me gypsy. But I am not a gypsy. I hate them all.'

I drew a chair up beside Ludwig's bed and sat down, looking into the face of this strange childlike creature with the body of a man. 'Who are *they*, Ludwig? Who calls you gypsy?'

'They all call me gypsy but I do not listen. I do not listen to anything they say. I do not care for them. I shall care for no one. When I grow up I shall do exactly as I want and I shall listen to no one. They will be sorry that they laughed at me. I will make them tremble.'

'Who are *they*, Ludwig?' I repeated, by now getting used to the fact that this strange child-man could indeed hear my every word without difficulty.

'Why, everyone,' he said. 'They all do it. They say my skin is dark and my hair is dark and that I am not of their station. But they shall see in time. I am hungry,' he said, 'why do you not feed me?'

'What would you like, Ludwig?'

'I am not Ludwig. Do not call me by that name. Why do you insist on calling me by that name?'

'I am sorry, I did not realise. What would you like to eat?'

'I should like some sweetmeats and some honey.'

I rose and left the room to see what I could find in the kitchen, but when I returned no trace of the gypsy child was to be found. Ludwig lay with his eyes closed, asleep.

Other times he would become imperious, arrogant, even violent – shouting abuse at me or attempting with subtle cunning to provoke me into argument.

'What a fool you are, Wawruch, why do you continually snivel? You are entirely fraudulent, Herr Doctor, but of course you know this,' he said one evening. 'You hide your hatred beneath a cloak of human kindness. It does not become you. You think yourself in some way superior, Wawruch. But you have many things to learn.'

Although each of these personae appeared to be unique, occasionally the boundaries between one and another would for a time become blurred: as when one image momentarily overlaps another in a dream and you find that a certain character, without your noticing when or how, has turned into another person.

My literary researches went on. The appearances of Ludwig's ghostly selves continued – some of whom in time I came to name: the Left-Handed Scribbler whom I had met early on would often emerge when Ludwig had been asleep, sit up in bed without pain and gesticulate madly for paper and pen to sketch some new melody or harmony. His voice was shrill and when he spoke it was almost always to elaborate the reason why some or other musical figure he had used was the only possible choice. The Scribbler was arrogant in manner, imperious and had no awareness of any of the others. The second persona with which I became familiar I came to call the Gentle One. His voice was deeper than any of the others and when he was present Ludwig's eyes took on a faraway look like someone who had difficulty remembering why he was here or what he was doing. Gypsy Child was the youngest of them all. He spoke with a defiant, snapping quality. He was shy, awkward and quick to take offence if ever he said something I did not understand or did not respond to. I am unsure how many different personae I met during those long nights at Ludwig's bedside: perhaps six, perhaps a dozen.

There was one persona, however, who was quite different from all the rest. He first appeared early on one evening while I was busy tidying some papers I found on the floor beside Ludwig's bed. Ludwig's body always took on the heaviness of a bull or a bear when he arrived – infinitely dense. The voice was cold and exacting. It had a stark cruelty about it and although he spoke softly the words seemed to reverberate through the very walls of the room. I came to call him Storyteller, for not only did he appear to describe ancient events, in Ludwig's own life, as though he were witnessing them, he was the only one of the personae who seemed to have some knowledge of the existence of the others.

I had not slept for perhaps a week before the night he first appeared. Storyteller's face hardly moved when he spoke in his slow, heavy voice. He always spoke in a cryptic language, as though all politeness had been torn away from the words. Unlike the others, he seemed to need no response from me to remain present. He demanded only one thing: that I record everything he said. This I did, writing on the back of whatever sheaves of paper were at my disposal.

Note: Inscribed on 6 February 1827, 4.30 a.m.,
Schwarzspanierhaus, Vienna
'She had lived it once before. The midwife had come, the pain had come, the bed turned wet with her sweat . . . seventeen hours of hell then the thing had been born. Within hours it was dead. Would this be the same? She cared not. Let it be over. Only let it be finished.

'Blood . . . water . . . the power that splits life from body. Clouds of hell draw close. Hers is no clean, clear pain – a murky darkness of pressure and sickness – no relief – fury and desperation. This thing within, this beast, this child, this torturer – it will kill to live. It will take over her body. Kill to live – tear from life, from her, whatever it can, whatever it needs to survive.' [*He stopped speaking and turned to me with glazed eyes – eyes lost in visions of far away*]. 'Write,' he said. 'You will write.' [*I nodded in absolute obedience. The voice rolled on,*] 'Dim – dark, the thing knows nothing – it feels only heat and crushing power, it wants nothing, only to be free of the pressure on its body.

'Its birth is long and hard. It is a heavy child. The woman refuses to surrender. Each time her belly takes hold, it pulls the struggling ball upwards – ugly mountain of stretched white flesh. She shouts for help. None comes. She breathes heavily. She howls, the howling eases the pain a little. But soon the quickening is too strong. Even wild noises bring no help. Waves of pain crash over her, tearing. She hates the room, hates the sounds of men speaking in the street, hates the bed, hates the life in her belly. Why does it not die now? Why wait until it is all over to slip away?

'She lies back on the pillow, her wet hair is scattered about her face. She has not the energy to push it away. May they all be damned. Why had she let this happen to her? The man no longer pleases her. His breath stinks when he comes to her. It is forever in the same dim, disgusting animal way – wanting, needing, grabbing at breast and belly to tear out their secret treasures. She closes her eyes. His face floats before them dripping with the treacle of greed. Union with him had, except for those few weeks before they were married, been utter misery. Another quickening is coming. She can tell that it will soon take her body over. She raises the ravaged body upwards, making ready to fight. Hopeless. . . . There is nothing to fight, no way to win. It is his fault – the fault of the union. Out of that misery has come this one. She never wanted a child, never wanted anything except peace. The tightening rises up in her, again it lifts her belly turning it into a hideous mountain.

'No, this birth, this ugly spewing of tissue dead or alive . . . she will not let it happen to her. She will stop it now. It has all gone far enough. So she lies back calm now, sure of herself, holding her power. She refuses to be there, refuses to push, refuses the birth. "No," she says to the mousy-haired woman. "It is all a mistake. You can go now. It is finished. I never wanted this. Never. . . ." She draws herself to full height and tries to leave the bed. Another quickening. Worse than before. She is trapped – caught in something she cannot conquer, cannot run from, cannot bear.'

I wrote obediently, recording as much of Storyteller's words as I could, in disbelief of what I was hearing. No man witnesses birth. Birth is the realm of the wise woman. No man can know such things unless it be from some other level of knowing, some other world. The tale he told in faltering words was stark in the extreme, as stark as the language Storyteller used to tell it. I wrote what I could – words that now too are destroyed by fire. Here in all its starkness is what remains of the tale in my memory.

'The midwife, a squat woman with short fat hands that bore the smell of ancient garlic, pushed the woman down on to the mattress with the same movement a butcher uses preparing to spear a ham. Then she covered the woman's naked body with a counterpane that the woman neither needed nor wanted although icy December winds shook the windows and licked the glass with flames of ice. The midwife would brook no nonsense. She could ill afford the time. So far the birth had been too slow for her liking. She was hungry and impatient with this thin and sweaty olive-skinned woman. If things did not happen soon she would have to inform the master of the house that her fee would be raised. After all, one had to make a living. One couldn't spend sleepless nights and be paid a pittance.

'The woman cried out one last time. The midwife grabbed her by the arms and shouted in a voice so deep that it could have been a man's, "Push, woman – push – push." Clawing animal noises emerged from the woman's throat and fluids ran red and brown and white. Then the crown appears. It is black. Another quickening, another tear, another scream or two and it would all be over, the midwife knew. Then she could leave and have her tea. It would not be long now. Ragged flesh, as the gaping wound gives forth its treasure – a grey infant with a head so large and spewed forth from so much pressure that it has taken on the shape of an old monk wearing a strange round hat cut deep into the crown. Not a happy sight, she sighs. But then birth seldom is.

'She grabs the infant, a boy, and shakes it hard, hanging it upside down to clear the head of fluid. The cord pulsates. It is a full minute before the ugly thing draws its first breath, makes its first sound. And what a sound it is – more like the bellowing of a bull than the crying of any human child she has ever heard. She puts the thing to the woman's breast and makes quick to draw forth the afterbirth. Then she pulls out two lengths of cat-gut, dipped in a murky bowl of water drawn many hours before to soften the thread and proceeds against screams of protest from her patient to suture the ugly gap. She pays no attention to the sounds. It is a job that needs to be done and she will do it with all the precision of her trade. The child's mouth closes around a nipple. It begins to suck. But with such force that the mother's breath is taken. Disgusting. She has never felt anything like it – the greed, the disregard for herself, for her body. Unharnessed she knew it would suck the very life from her. It was ugly, as ugly as the man. No wonder she hated the very sight of it. The man repelled her because of his greed and his weakness but at least he was manageable – like a sloppy animal. The greed of this creature is different – relentless, single-minded, too demanding – revolting. She looks down at the back of its bloody distorted head. To think this thing so ugly, so greedy had poured forth from her body – a body once so fine and white and beautiful. Love? How did one love such a creature? Why, it was unreasonable to expect it. Her life was hard. She did not need such a burden placed upon her. She had told Johann that he would have to find help. He knew that she was delicate, fragile, not up to dealing with this child. It was *he* who insisted she have the thing. She herself had intended to make another visit to the wise woman and have it cut out. Better done then than now, she had said. But he had left her no choice. He had insisted and now the deed was done. Well, Johann would simply have to find a wet nurse who could care for the thing. She wanted to be free of it. Free of them all. Nothing had turned out as she hoped – nothing. She was tired. She turned her head to the wall. She wanted only to sleep, to forget.

' "Take it away," she commanded with such vehemence that even the midwife, used to the basest forms of abuse, was taken aback.

' "I want no part of it. Find a woman to suckle it for I shall play no role in its future existence." Then, her head buried bitterly in the softness of a down pillow which Ludwig, Johann's father, had given her for her confinement, the dark-haired woman slept.

'The child *was* taken away. The midwife carried the infant, silent now after drinking the very life from its mother's breast, to the kitchen where sat the husband. He had returned to the house only minutes earlier in the company of a musician companion. Both were swimming in Rhenish.

' "You have a fine son," she told him, placing the child in his arms.

'He looked down at the shrivelled red face peeping out from beneath the soft cloth which had been prepared to swaddle the thing and smiled, his breast swelling so much from her words that he began to look like a cockerel ready to crow.

' "Healthy?" he asked, being careful to pronounce each syllable with the precision appropriate to a gentleman to whom an heir has just been delivered.

' "Aye, healthy enough," the midwife replied. "But thy wife is none too fine. She wants not the care of the infant."

'The man flushed – whether from anger or embarrassment, the midwife could not tell.

' "I know," he mumbled, raising his eyes in what he hoped would implore the help of the short woman who with her garlic breath at this moment stood altogether too close for his comfort.

' "Alas, what's to be done?" he whined.

' "There is a woman who lives in Kollerkerstrasse to whom I delivered twin infants only a week ago," said the midwife. "She is a lacemaker, without spouse and one of the infants has died. Should I take the baby to her and ask if, for a fee, she will suckle it?"

' "Yes . . . ah yes, an excellent plan, dear woman," said the husband. "Be so kind as to do so immediately. We must give the young fellow everything he needs without thought for pennies. Indeed. First things must come first. I am, that is, we are – my dear wife and I – greatly obliged for your aid."

' "He cleared his throat and sat down heavily at the table. Then, recognising that his posture did not reflect the dignity of his position, he quickly straightened his back and made a gesture of mock graciousness with his right hand.

'The midwife asked to see the servant, to whom she gave a few final instructions about clearing the wife's room of the rags she had accumulated and the various pots of water that needed emptying. Then she took the infant and departed, intending to return in the morning as was customary to claim her fee.

'The child went to the lacemaker, with whom he stayed for a month. The father, Johann, made only two journeys to see it, both during the first fortnight. Both took place late in the evening after returning from the wine cellar to pay the woman who suckled his second-born son. He gazed into its face wondering if, like his first son this one, whom he had also named Ludwig in the hope that his father from whom the name was borrowed would foot the bill for the creature's care, would die too and if the money he was spending would therefore be wasted. Meanwhile the mother slept – for two days. Or rather she pretended to be sleeping each time any person entered her room. She took no food, drank only boiled tea, and rose only to use the chamber-pot, which was dutifully emptied by Frau Hauser who lived in the apartment below, since the servant had flatly refused to do the job.

'Johann's, or rather the elder Ludwig's, money was not wasted. The child lived, thrived. He consumed more milk from the breast of the wet nurse than any three normal infants – so much that she was forced to refuse the offer of a further child to suckle even though she had been blessed with an abundance of milk and needed the money badly. After Christmas the demand for lace fell abysmally each year until Easter and that was yet many weeks away. None the less, after a month the wet nurse, whose coffee jug was now depleted of its last pennies, picked the child out of its makeshift cradle, nestled it into a musty piece of lambskin and trudged through the January streets of Bonn in snow so deep that when she finally arrived at the father's house she had to step over a two-foot mound before she could cross the threshold.

'The door to the flat was opened by a servant: a plump dark-haired girl, little more than a child. She coughed and had the habit of hanging her head so that when she spoke her eyes rarely met those of the lacemaker, whom she ushered into a small room at the rear of the house where stood a clavichord, two chairs and a small table on which rested a magnificent silver candlestick so out of place in these surroundings that it caught the woman's eye immediately. The room was cold and smelt of laundry left too long to sit before hanging out. The floor of rough oak slanted heavily from one side to the other. It was completely bare except for one rather worn dark red patterned rug beneath the table and the two chairs beside it. In one of them she was directed to sit, the infant in her arms, while the mother was called.

'Minutes passed in silence. The only noise the lacemaker heard was the sound of a mouse making its way along the wainscot. She glanced about her, pulling her shawl high up against her neck. The room was cold and of an unusual shape. Its only window was set in a narrow wall that overlooked a courtyard, cutting the space at a sharp angle which gave the room five sides rather than the usual four. The child began to stir. She groaned. His constant appetite had so depleted her of energy that despite her sturdy build and solid constitution she had been forced of late to sleep too much, even at odd hours of the day, whenever she gained respite from the demanding infant. He began to squirm and root towards her bosom. She sighed, pulled open the bodice of her dress and put him to suck, covering breast and child with her shawl to keep them warm.

'The mother entered the room. She was a small woman, lean and pale olive with skin so dry that even at her early age – she could not have been older than twenty-five – deep fine lines had already been etched into it: from the sides of her nose to her chin, between her thin brows, in the hollow just in front of the ear. Her eyes alone were free of lines as though infrequently if at all subjected to a smile. This was one of those times. For the smile came, measured, careful and ungenerous as the mother held out her hand to the wet nurse.

' "Good morning. I believe that you have been taking care of my little Ludwig. I am most grateful."

'The mother gathered her heavy skirts, the wet nurse remarking that they were of considerably better quality than anything she had yet seen in the house excepting the silver candlestick which sat upon the table, and lowered herself with brittle carefulness into the second chair.

'"How is he? I regret not having been to see you both but I have not been terribly well these past weeks."

'Then, without waiting for a reply she continued, "What can I do for you?"

' "Madam, I am come to rid myself of the care of your child. He has nearly drained me dry – eating twice as much as my own daughter and still he is never satisfied.'

'Then, as if in justification of her statement she added, "Here he is again at the breast although I fed him fully not an hour since. I cannot continue to support him." She lifted the shawl, revealing the back of a head covered with a very heavy crop of pitch-black hair.

'The mother leaned forward in her chair, cautiously peering over the bundle held in the woman's arm in an attempt to see the face of the child. She was hesitant, shy about her curiosity, afraid the woman might take the infant from her breast and put it in her own arms and for that she was not yet prepared.

' "I'm sorry. Is my husband not providing you with adequate payment for your care? I am sure I could speak to him about it. We are not, as you can see, rich folk but I should think more money could be found." Resuming her seat and holding her body erect she waited for a reply.

' "It has nothing to do with payment. I simply cannot keep up with the demands this child makes upon me. I have my own daughter to think of, only ten days his senior, and I must soon resume my work to be prepared for demand at Easter."

' "He is strong then?" the mother enquired.

' "Strong? He is as strong as a young bull. Just look at the flesh upon him."

'She pulled away his swaddling to reveal a tiny but well

rounded thigh. The child kicked out enjoying the freedom of the air, however cold. Then it raised a small hand to press against the naked breast. The mother cocked her head to one side, drew a quick breath then smoothed down the surface of her skirts with trembling fingers. She leaned over and placed the tip of her right index finger against the back of the infant's head. There was the pulse of its heart where the skull had not yet joined. She could hear small grunts from its throat as it swallowed. She could even smell a strange sweet odour which she had never smelt before. It seemed to emanate from the back of the infant's neck. In silence she sat for what seemed to the lacemaker an interminable period, staring at the child before her. Then she shuddered, cleared her throat and said; "Are you telling me you want to leave the child with us?" the mother asked.

'The lacemaker nodded, taking the infant from the breast where he had finished feeding and restoring her clothing to normal.

' "But you can't do that," said the mother. "You mustn't. I have no means of caring for him." She paused, tilting her head to one side.

'Seeing that her protest brought no response from the woman she resumed speaking.

' "I have been ill, you know. I am never very strong at the best of times, and my breasts have been tightly bound to dry the milk. So you see I am afraid I have no means of feeding the child. Neither am I fit enough to care for him," she added. Still no response.

' "My servant, you have met her, is a pleasant enough girl but not very bright and certainly not hard working. I don't know how she could manage the child either." Her voice rose in a last effort to make her words heard, "You simply must not desert us when we so badly need your help!"

'The lacemaker sighed, raised the baby on to her left

shoulder and stroked his back. A piece of fluff from the shawl had lodged itself in the crease at the back of his neck. This she carefully removed before answering.

' "Madam I cannot, I *will* not keep him, much as I have developed a certain fondness for him these past weeks. With all his greed and demand he is not a bad child. I myself wanted a boy. God chose instead to bring me a fine daughter. This child is yours by rights and so he will remain. I appreciate your position, the need you have for a wet nurse and I would not like to see him go a-wanting. But I shall not take him back with me. He is now yours to care for as you see fit and to worry over, for I will have no more of him."

'The lacemaker rose and gingerly placed the infant in the arms of the mother who, surprised by this sudden move, received the baby awkwardly and with a certain revulsion as though someone had placed in her lap a joint of meat she feared might soil her dress.

' "The best I can offer," continued the lacemaker, "is to nurse him for you, but no more than four times a day – provided of course that the servant girl brings him to my house with regularity at the times we agree. For this I ask two-thirds of the fee on which we had previously agreed. Perhaps you would like to consider my offer before deciding. That is the very best I can do."

'She rose, turned stiffly and started for the door.

' "No, don't go. Please don't go," cried the mother. "I. . . I. . . Of course we agree. The servant will bring him at the times you wish. But, what shall I do? What shall I do?" She received no answer to her plea for help. The lacemaker was gone before her words had finished. The mother called the servant girl, placed the child in her arms, directed her to make frequent visits to the house of the lacemaker, to prepare some kind of curd which the child could take in water in the mean time should it begin to scream, and told her to make sure the child was kept in the kitchen where it was warm. Then she left the room.

'When Johann returned, she informed him of the arrangements. An argument ensued during which he complained belligerently that the money earned by the "sweat of his brow" – not altogether accurate since Johann was in fact a singer in the Elector's choir – was not to be spent so freely. She reminded him that all monies paid the wet nurse had so far been a gift from Johann's father, Ludwig, who had also, she forced him to recall, provided the silver candlestick that graced his workroom – the only thing, she added, of real beauty in this "miserable" house. Glaring at her from beneath a heavy brow, he snorted, turned and stamped three times then crossed to the door, opened it, walked through it and slammed it behind him. Nothing more was said.'

BILE

> They make sacrifices of their own blood, some-
> times cutting the edges of their ears to shreds and
> thus leaving them as a sign of their devotion. At
> other times they pierced their cheeks, other times
> the lower lips; again they scarify parts of the body;
> or again they perforate their tongues in a slanting
> direction from side to side, passing pieces of straw
> through the holes with horrible suffering; and yet
> again they slit the foreskin of the virile member
> leaving it like their ears, which deceived the
> general historian of the Indies into saying that they
> practised circumcision. . . . Furthermore, with the
> blood of all things that they possess, whether birds
> of the sky, beasts of the earth, or fish of the sea, they
> were always anointing the face of the demon.
>
> Bishop Diego de Landa *Relación de las cosas de
> Yucatán*

So ended Storyteller's first tale, a tale which separated him
from all of Ludwig's other personae which appeared during
those last weeks by his ability to sustain a story and his
absolute insistence that I record every word he spoke. I did
not know what or who I was listening to and by this time,
after weeks of no sleep, I could do nothing but comply.
Besides, Storyteller by his very presence demanded almost
complete obedience – an obedience I found easy to give, so
dazzled had I become by this all-encompassing world into
which I had been drawn. In these last weeks before

Ludwig's death, during the daylight hours his intense dislike of me increased and he developed a great distrust of anything I said or did. He spoke again and again of calling in my colleague – an old confidant of his, Johann Malfatti, founder of our Vienna Society of Physicians, a fine doctor with a warm Mediterranean character. At last Malfatti was indeed called and although he was reluctant to come, after much urging on the part of Breuning and Holtz and much assurance on my part that to do so would breach no professional ethic, he arrived one morning, to Ludwig's delight.

Malfatti grasped at once the extent of degeneration which had taken place in his former patient's body and the depressive state of his mind. In an attempt to relieve Ludwig's suffering, he introduced cabbage baths. They were of no help. Then he swept away the drugs I had been giving and prescribed instead a frozen alcoholic punch which he knew would please Ludwig and which he hoped would relieve some of his sufferings. That night, when I arrived just after midnight as had become my habit, I found my patient sleeping peacefully. There were no strange alterations of consciousness, none of the changes in his physiognomy to which I had by then become accustomed. I spent the entire night sitting next to a fire which burnt ceaselessly yet gave off no heat, bundled in my overcoat and gloves, gazing across the room at this man to whom by now I found myself inextricably bound.

Ludwig's attacks occurred with increasing frequency as the weeks went on and as his body became weaker from the tappings which I was impelled to carry out to keep him alive. Each of the presences that shared his ailing body demonstrated a completely different level of vitality from the others. The gypsy child could hear well and appeared to be completely free of the heaviness which ordinarily plagued

Ludwig's body. The Left-Handed Scribbler had a similar facility in moving his body freely and maintaining a high level of concentration and energy while producing notes on the page without faltering. Yet he was completely deaf. I am aware as I write these words that if by some strange twist of fate this manuscript survives and at some time in the future is read, all of it will sound far too phantasmagoric to be believed. I am no stranger to such disbelief. I lived with it not only during those first long sleepless nights at Ludwig's bedside but all through the fifteen years since – years during which I have done my best to convince myself that all of it never happened.

None of us likes admitting into belief that which defies explanation, that which contradicts the precepts by which we live, that which challenges our assurance about where reality is bounded and what it contains. After Ludwig's death, and the death of Breuning which took place but a few months later, the reason I did not pursue my investigations into his medical condition, as Ludwig in his waking state had made me promise to do, and write the medical report I had intended on both his illness and the fugues, lay entirely within the realm of cowardice. For after he died, although I could in no way explain the strange alterations in psyche and physiology I had lived through with him, I was at last free of their constant disruptive effect on my own life – and free, or so I then believed, of the obsessive secret life I had been living with him. I could, or believed I could, leave both behind and forget them so everything would return to being as it was before. I had told myself that I would once again be able to continue to sit on the stone bench in our garden beneath the great lime tree reading as I had once done, that my wife and I could continue to enjoy our early mornings together with steaming coffee as we used to do, and that my work as a doctor would become as it had been before

Ludwig entered my life – clear and ordered, simple and humane. It is only now, years later, having lost everything – my home, my work and the woman I love most in the world that I know how deceived I was. Once the veil to other worlds has been lifted, once the boundaries of the known have been breached, there is no closing them again. If you try, as I did, the gods of fire, at whose mere existence I would once have scoffed, find ways to pursue you. But more of that later, if there still be time.

At first I delved deep into the medical literature, even examining the strange records of those scientists more intrigued in the workings of the human psyche than the human body, such as Anton Mesmer and the rest. I discovered that Herbart, Kant's successor at Königsberg, had put forward the notion that ideas could exist below the lumen of consciousness in a state of inhibition as 'tendencies' which, although a person was unaware of them, none the less carried energy that could alter behaviour, values and feelings. But I found little else in his work to satisfy my need for an explanation of what I was witnessing night after night at Ludwig's bedside.

Finally, against my inclination and with a great unwillingness in my heart to open up the wounds of my own disappointment which had occurred when I left the seminary, I began to sift through what literature I possessed of a mystic nature – reports which sought to elaborate the unusual experiences and behaviour of great saints, great sinners, and some of the early church fathers. There were many such books on my shelves. Most were covered with dust for they had remained untouched for more than thirty years. As I opened the first volume – a copy of Bishop Languet's biography of Marie Marguerite Alacoque bound in crimson leather – it was like entering into an age long past, another time – a life I believed I had left far behind for ever to be replaced with something far more rational and valuable – the morality of human kindness, duty and compassion.

Since my decision to leave the seminary I had left behind any concern for the Church and all it represents. Yet I remembered much from my seminary days of what we were taught of the nature of a so-called saint – a person who having lived an exceptional life was said to be in heaven, drinking the beatific vision and living in His Presence. The saint or mystic, we were told, is someone who possesses an exceptional ability to invoke the presence of and hold intercourse with powers and entities of the invisible worlds. I had found such teachings very difficult to swallow let alone digest into the body of what could be called true knowledge. For I reasoned that if these exceptional people did indeed establish affiliations with the Kingdom of Light as we had been taught, then by rights they must also be given entrance into the infernal realms of Darkness. For was it not an historical fact that occult manifestations of a demonic nature frequently appear in the lives of the saints and mystics in the Church? It was a question to which I received no adequate answer from my teaching – only rather limp assurances from the monks that the Son of God protected all who loved him as a good shepherd cares lovingly for his helpless flock.

As I began to read page after page of mystic writing from St John's *Dark Night of the Soul* to St Theresa's *The Interior Castle* I knew that it was the singular intensity of their practices and the lack of distracting influences which made such men and women sensitive to a degree quite beyond the experience of those of us who embrace the concerns of worldly life, and I saw certain parallels in the way in which Ludwig's illness and deafness had in their own way concentrated his energy through a prism largely free from distracting influences. I discovered in my reading that it had been vividly chronicled that Egypt's St Antony, the father of Christian monasticism, was a man tempted by legions of malicious entities. So, I discovered, had been St Benedict of Nursia and the holy St Gregory the Great who in his *Dialogues* records that he was much haunted by a demon in the form of a blackbird who beat its wings against his eyes, pecked doubts deep into his heart, willingly enticed him to leave behind his passion for God, and when it departed left echoes of evil temptations behind.

I remained troubled, for none of what I found seemed quite to fit with what I was witnessing with Ludwig and in any case he, after all, was no mystic, no saint. He was a musician: an artist who during his daylight hours behaved much as anyone else might, given his choleric nature and the fact that he was seriously – mortally – ill.

It was very late on the night of 3 March that Storyteller told his second tale – although Storyteller is most assuredly a misnomer for this persona who after that night appeared with ever increasing regularity until Ludwig's death. For Storyteller had none of the finesse of a good weaver of tales. When he spoke it was always in a cursory manner, giving but the barest skeleton of memories, raw sensation and ancient events . . . I am not altogether sure what they were. They were presented in a manner that was primitive, rough and lacked every refinement which educated society demands from its tellers of tales. It was as though Storyteller was a man from another time – not time past but rather from some future time when every grace and every embellishment is to be removed from a man's words. When Storyteller was present Ludwig always appeared to be furthest away from the present – living altogether in another place and time. His eyes would grow very wide and still. Then, slowly in his strange cursory language – a dialect which embellished nothing —he would speak with infinite darkness as though he were but the watcher of the group – a being which, like the eagle, gazes down with piercing eye to describe every detail of reality, every nuance of events with a deathly clarity. He recounted sensations and feelings as though they were unfolding before my very eyes at the moment of speaking. This was his second tale.

'The house was dark,' he said, 'as dark as the house he lived in before. And what seemed curious to the child was the way the room at the back had the same strange five-sided shape as the back room in the previous house. The window overlooking the courtyard was bigger in this house, though. And taller too. He too was bigger. So big that now the servant sometimes allowed him to leave the kitchen and to sit in this room. It was a funny place. The walls made echoes. He knew they were echoes because Grandfather had told him so that day in summer when they had walked to the mountain and played a game of shouting as hard as they could. Grandfather's voice had been so loud and deep, like the sound the dog made sometimes just before he went to sleep. His voice was tiny and thin. But in the mountains when you made a noise it came back to you again and again – like a friend agreeing with everything you said. That, Grandfather had told him, was an echo.

'Ludwig liked echoes. He liked to make a noise and hear it repeated over and over again. In this funny room you could hear lots of echoes. Echoes were magic. He knew that. And he was magic because he could make them happen. Of course he could only make little noises here. If they were too loud his mother might hear and send him out to play in the street. He didn't like the street. Too many people, so much noise you could not find echoes when they happened and also it was lonely there. But it was never lonely in this room because of all the sounds. That is why it was his favourite place. When he grew up he decided he would have such a room and he would allow no one into it. Then he would be able to stop them from shouting when he made the kind of noises they didn't like. He would live by himself or with Grandfather. Grandfather said they were alike and that is why they both had the same name. He knew it was true. Grandfather was such a tall man. His hands were warm and his neck smelt like white lilies and tobacco. He knew the reason why they had the same name – Ludwig. It was because they were so much alike. But Ludwig was a silly name. It sounded like the fat white sausage Herr Klaus sold in the market. He didn't dare say that to his grandfather. It might make him angry. He didn't like it when Grandfather was angry. He decided he would never tell anyone about the name. Maybe if he never mentioned to anyone that he knew his was a foolish-sounding name no one would never notice how funny a name it was. That was important. He did not intend to be laughed at.

'Sometimes people laughed at his father. He didn't like that. Once when his father walked through the market holding his hand, Ludwig heard someone say words which he did not understand and point to his father. The father did not seem to notice but Ludwig grew hot and turned red. He could feel his skin go all prickly. He hated the itchy feeling but he hated even more the way in which his father pretended not to know. Nobody laughed at Grandfather, though. His chest was big and when he looked at you over the top of his glasses and warned you not to spill a drop of your gruel his dark voice was warm as the belly of a cat and his eyes were little and bright. If his hand struck you for something you had done wrong it was never too hard. It never made you burn with fire the way the hand of his father did.

'Grandfather was coming today. The servant had said so when she dressed him in green breeches and fine white

stockings and warned him not to soil himself by sitting on
the floor. He had not seen his grandfather for what seemed
to him a very long time. That, the servant said, was because
Grandfather had been ill. He knew what ill was because he
had been ill himself once – hot and wet. Then cold and
shaky. Then the servant had left him in the five-cornered
room to wait while she tended the baby in the kitchen. At
one end of this room facing the window was a magical box –
a wooden thing so tall he could only just reach over the top of
it when he stretched up high. It made echoes. But unlike his
own voice or the voice of his grandfather, the echoes the box
made when you touched its special places were all different
in their sound. They could be made to pour over each other
so they all got mixed up together like the fountain he saw in
the market-place or like flames of the fire when you watched
it at night. You could sit for hours moving your hands over
the top of the box making echo after echo, each one special
and different. Some had a sweet sound like the way honey
tastes when you keep it on your tongue and don't swallow it.
Some were ugly and not interesting. Others were scratchy
like sand. He liked the scratchy ones. He liked to stand in
front of the box and tap his fingers over its surface to find
new noises. But he had to do it very quietly or *they* would
hear him.

'Sometimes, like this morning, when they were not in –
when his mother had gone to the market and he was with the
servant, who almost never came into the room anyway – he
would hit the special places at the top of the box harder
making echoes that were not just scratchy but even louder,
sounds that reminded him of the sheets of light that smear
the sky before the biggest echoes of all come. Thunder. His
grandfather had taught him the word thunder. It was that
same day they had gone into the mountains together to
make echoes. But he was not afraid of it. He was never going

to be afraid of anything. Ever. His grandfather told him that
he should not be. He knew that Grandfather was never
afraid and because they were so alike he would never be
afraid either.

'Yet sometimes it was difficult. Especially when it was
very dark. He did not like the dark. Particularly at night
when there were no echoes. Once he had awakened, sat up
in bed and looked out the window but there was nothing
there to see and nothing there to listen to. He moved his
head. The linen of the sheet scraped against his cheek
making a new sound, a sound he had never heard before. It
was a friendly sound. It told him he did not need to be
afraid. So he had rubbed his cheek again and again against
the pillow and gone back to sleep feeling proud of himself
that he had done what his grandfather asked of him.

'Now in the empty room at the back of the house once
again he rubbed his hands over the surface of the box and
the rubbing made jumbled noises, not soft, not scratchy, not
sweet. He turned to look behind him. The door was closed.
He turned back, climbed upon the chair in front of the box
and, very carefully, tapped one of the slim white keys
directly in front of him. A single sound. Pure and cool as the
smell of lemon. Then, reaching as far as he could stretch, he
hit another one. So tiny was its noise. Like the voice of a
mouse. Again he hit it, and again. Then he stretched the
other way as far as he could reach, further and further. He
pushed. The sound came – a barking dark and deep noise
like the grumble the dancing bear had made on the day of
the festival when his trainer had tossed him a fish. He liked
the bear sound best of all, he decided. When he made it by
tapping on the key he became the bear himself. Not small
but strong and tall like Grandfather – someone who could
do anything.

'Thus he remained standing on the chair leaning over the

clavichord tapping the keys one after another and listening to the voices that spoke from them for the better part of an hour. Then the door opened behind him and silently, like a big lion, a man entered and crossed the room to stand behind the child who was so absorbed in his sound-making that he did not know he was no longer alone. The man, whose hair was white and whose shoulders were very broad, reached out to touch the child before him. The child, lost in his noise games, like someone coming out of a deep dream, slowly turned his head to see the man's face.

'Like a snake darting forward to capture its prey, the small arms shot up begging to be picked up. The man lifted the small body into his arms and for a moment man and child were lost in a sea of tickling. Then, his eyes glistening, the man carried the squirming bundle to a chair and lowered himself into it.

' "Ludwig. Have you been playing with the echoes again?"

' "Yes, Grandfather. And this morning I heard a mouse behind the wainscot as well."

' "What sound did it make, Ludwig?"

' "Scritch, scritch, scritch."

'The child gathered his fingers into small claws and scrunched up his face, wrinkling his nose. The man laughed, throwing back his head. His laughter became a fit of coughing which compelled him to lift the child off his lap, place him on the floor and reach for a kerchief to cover his mouth. In silence the child stared at the man shaking in front of him. When the coughing ceased there was blood on the kerchief.

' "Grandfather? Are you sick?"

' "Yes, Ludwig, I am sick."

'The child reached up to touch the man's cheek. "You'll be better soon, won't you?"

' "Yes child . . . soon."

'Then clearing his throat he rose from the chair, took the boy by the hand and walked back to the clavichord.

' "Would you like to know how to make good echoes on the box, Ludwig?"

' "Yes grandfather." He forgot the worrying red kerchief as the man lifted him up to sit in front of the instrument.

' "Listen child."

'The man played *do* then *do* and *mi* together then *do mi* and *sol* all at once while his eyes watched the child's eyes which, each time a new note was added, shone with pleasure as though he were being initiated into some secret ritual that would make him even more like his grandfather. Then the child touched the keys himself – *do* – *mi* – *sol*, one after another. He found he could just reach the *do* and the *mi* with his left hand but he needed his right index finger to strike the third key at the same time. He laughed. He was pleased with himself for he was not afraid, just as Grandfather said he must never be.

'For more than an hour the two remained at the box hitting the keys – one after the other, then two or three together. Then, pretending that he was a mouse, Ludwig made his fingers walk from one key to the next. Sometimes he made animal sounds. Sometimes he laughed. Sometimes he put his head close to the board itself to listen to the way it trembled when a key was sounded. The man stood next to him silently except that every now and then he would name a key or play one or two together to make a new sound. This was a game they had played before – a secret game which only they knew. Ludwig loved the secret nature of it, loved the magic of the sounds, loved the sense of power in his fingers when they touched the keys. He saw himself big like his Grandfather. He remembered the visits to the cathedral, he had not been for many weeks now, where his grandfather presided over all of the men who made the sounds together, the way they stood silently waiting for Grandfather to begin, the way even the slightest movement of his grandfather's hand or head would call forth wonderful mixtures of sound. Grandfather was a master of sound, a magician who held dominion over a universe of sound, weaving it in and out in shapes and patterns so strong they poured through Ludwig's body like a rich waterfall filling it with the fat pleasure, making his head spin the way it did when the two of them had stood together at the top of the mountain that day when Grandfather had first explained about the echoes. The child decided that he, Ludwig, would become a sorcerer as well, a master of sound and he would live in a house like Grandfather's – a house where raindrops hung from great candled trees on the ceiling. And like Grandfather, when he fired his candles the raindrops would move ever so slightly, making patterns of light on his floor and on his walls. The child liked to sit on the floor of Grandfather's house and to watch the moving lights. They filled his belly with a lightness that fed his dreams.

'He found it hard to dream in Father's house. There were no raindrops in Father's workroom, no lights, no dreams. There was only a grumpy lamp with a smelly wick that burnt through greasy glass. It was all right, though. So long as they left him alone with the echoes. Then it was all right. When he was not alone bad things happened. He didn't know how or why and he could never remember them very well afterwards but he knew he must have done something very wrong and that he was the cause of them.

'In Grandfather's house everything was white and silver and shiny and cool to the touch. He heard his mother tell the neighbour woman one day that Grandfather's silver was very special. "Costly," she had said, wiping her hands on her apron. "And the linen is so fine I can draw it through my wedding ring." He stared hard at the hand she had raised to show the neighbour and decided she was pretending. The wedding ring was tight and her fingers, now covered with fat from the dumplings she was making, were puffed up like sausages. There was no way in which even the tiniest piece of linen could fit inside as well. He knew she was lying. But he did not say he knew. For she might not like his knowing.

'When he did or said things she did not like she would not shout at him as his father did. She would go very quiet, take a deep breath and let it all come out in one long puff. Then her body would go all crumpled like the marionette he watched one afternoon while the puppeteer was cleaning it. And her body would grow smaller and her head would hang. That was worse than his father. Worse than anything. Except the door to the cellar.

'The door to the cellar was hidden at the edge of the stairs. It was made of wood in such a way that it blended with the surrounding wall so well it was almost invisible. It was not very large. You could not even see it unless you made a special effort to look. But Ludwig knew it was there. And he knew what lay behind it. He did not want ever to go there again.

'Grandfather's house did not have a cellar. He lived up high in rooms with big windows – just the right kind of house for a sound magician. That was what Ludwig would be too. He would stand in the cathedral, his hands drawn high like Grandfather's, and make the universe dance to his will. He would wear a white cravat like Grandfather and a long coat and tall black boots so shiny they looked like mirrors and all men would bow when they passed him in the streets as they did to Grandfather. He would, he knew it.

'Tiring now of his play, he turned to gaze into the face of the man leaning over him. It was not pale as it had been when Grandfather arrived but red and the eyes glistened as the room grew dark with dusk. The child lifted his fat hand to touch the man's cheek. The man smiled. Years later, seated on a blue velvet bench as he pulled on boots which were shiny as a mirror, the same grown child remembered that smile. But then he could not separate the picture of those shining eyes from the growing darkness that surrounded him.'

BALSAMA

On the pavement
of my trampled soul
the soles of madmen
stamp the prints of rude, crude, words.

Vladimir Mayakovsky 'I'

Night after night, my visits to Ludwig's bedside continued. As the weeks went on, the separation between day and night events in my life became a chasm so deep and wide that I feared it could never again be bridged. At night I was the intimate confidant of Storyteller, Gypsy Child, Scribbler and others – a man who, although his presence was never acknowledged in a personal sense, had become witness to an unrecorded alchemical reaction which set into motion movements, dreams, voices and visions – some of them majestic and magnificent, others horrific and utterly terrifying. In the day I pretended to be the competent physician, a man of knowledge on whom an ailing patient can depend for healing, care and guidance. The awareness of the fraudulence of my daylight life soon became so intense that I was forever surprised that I had not been caught out by someone, that the mask of convention and flimsy rationality which I continued to wear had not suddenly slipped to reveal to all around me the face of a man unformed, as yet unborn – a monster of confusion as uncertain of his own identity as of that of his secret night-partner. Inexplicably this did not happen. I could not imagine why. Now, I know only too well that it was not because of any skill at concealment on my part but simply because the men who surrounded Ludwig, my wife, my colleagues at the hospital and at the university had no desire whatever to see beneath the veneer of conventionality. To do so might have threatened their own certainty. We, each of us, have learned to ignore that which we fear most to see. That is until, as with Ludwig's fugues, some person or presence or event beyond control breaks open the barriers to other worlds.

I continued to remain silent about what was occurring except once when I ventured close to the subject with Breuning. It was one morning when Ludwig was sleeping and Breuning and I had been unexpectedly left alone together. I asked if in his association with Ludwig he had ever noticed that his friend's voice and behaviour changed drastically without warning. Breuning turned to me and, with soft blue eyes gazing into mine, said, 'Dr Wawruch. Are you not perhaps over-exerting yourself? How very tired you look.'

There was only one of these night visitors who appeared in Ludwig's body that I greatly feared. He arrived early on one evening while I was busy clearing up unwashed dishes and linen which the servant had left behind. The same momentary fluttering in the eyes took place and then the metamorphosis began. Ludwig's body appeared to grow in size and take on the appearance of a lumbering beast. His voice grew darker and more powerful than any I had ever heard so that although he spoke softly the words seemed to reverberate through the very walls of the room. This persona came only once, yet I have never been able to erase the words he spoke from my mind – nor the manner in which they were spoken.

'I am Ahriman,' it said, 'the darkest of earthly powers. I

was created in man's likeness yet I am far greater than man. I come to tell you, Wawruch, of wonders still waiting for you on earth – treasures of which you have hardly dreamed.' I was stunned by his words and by the way in which they seemed to be spoken entirely to entrap me in something. The voice continued: 'Have you ever smelt the fragrance of a woman's breast then touched and caressed the satin smoothness of her skin until her body gives off deeper, richer, darker perfumes,' it said, 'perfumes to catch and bind you in their musky beauty – perfumes to weave patterns of necessity about your soul. That is my power – a power which calls you deeper and deeper into the realms of beauty and weaves spells about you in its diversity.'

'My God,' I uttered, then caught myself saying the words as if they had meaning for me. 'What are you?' I asked. He did not answer but the dark deep voice rolled on.

'Speak not of God, Wawruch. He is long dead. Let those who will speak of heaven and all its subtle beauties pursue their empty fantasies. Meanwhile come with me and listen to the song of earth that calls you to its riches and to its power. You can *know* such power. You can weave your own spell of magic and have all mankind bow down to you. I can arrange that for you – you have but to listen to my voice. What is it Wawruch, my friend, that you want? You have only to ask and I will provide it. I will bring it to you – we shall dance together – exult together in the beauty and the power and the rare gifts of human life.'

'I want nothing,' I said, 'except to return to a humane life.'

'Do you seek a woman's darkness?' he continued. 'Do you want to plunge yourself deep within the folds of her body – soft folds which will encompass you – folds with which you can do whatever you please? Women are here only for your use, Wawruch. Taste them all, succour yourself at their breasts and plunge your body deep within their darkness. Make them cry out in pleasure so they become a slave to your body, or in pain to let them know the force you wield over them. This is the power I can offer you.' I listened to Ahriman's voice in fascination, the way a rabbit stunned and silent gazes into the eyes of the serpent who enchants it.

'Yes, Wawruch,' he said, 'listen to my words. There are those on earth who are simple ordinary folk. They lack imagination and they muddle through life never tasting real bliss. You need not be one of them. There is yet time. You with your wit and your wisdom can bend all things to your will – you have only to listen to me.'

As suddenly as he first appeared Ahriman dissolved away. I watched a shudder pass over Ludwig's body and his eyes turned upwards and closed. Ahriman had vanished for ever.

One night in late February a very different persona emerged. Like Storyteller he appeared to have some knowledge – however rudimentary – of the existence of at least a few of the others. Unlike Ludwig he was lean-faced and seemed, even when I was standing above him, to be constantly gazing down his nose at me. I came to call him the Persecutor. Persecutor would often describe to me in a world-weary voice how the advice he gave 'the others' was, to their detriment, rarely heeded. When he was present Ludwig's body moved in a jerky way with great angularity and effort. Persecutor was prone to speaking in homilies like a pastor dutifully guiding the members of a parish for whom he had utter contempt.

'Spare even those closest to you your secrets,' Persecutor told me one night. 'Do you dare to ask fidelity of them when you deny it yourself?' On another he said: 'Never betray the contempt you feel for people in your heart. There may come a time when you need their help.'

His eyes, like Ludwig's own daylight self, were small and glassy. He frequently spoke of the 'others' with disdain and seemed to enjoy relating to me how he sometimes felt obliged to cause them trouble through his carping, criticism and jeering, then he added in a conspiratorial manner that this he did entirely for their own good and that they most certainly deserved everything they got.

And there were more. A feminine creature – I called her Sweet-Curled Woman. She was shy and lonely and had the saddest look in her eyes I have ever seen as well as a voice so small that when she was in attendance I had to lean my face close to Ludwig's face to hear her words. Another I called the Lecher. He spoke with such a brazen knowingness of women and their physiology that it could make even a physician blush. In his presence Ludwig's face took on a strange lopsided quality and the words issued forth from the corner of his mouth, often creating a hissing sound. Despite my attempts to remain calm and objective as I studied, or so I told myself, the phenomena before me, Lecher would send prickles up my spine and make me giddy. Yet most haunting of all was Storyteller who made his final appearance at around one o'clock on the morning of 15 March.

I remember that date not only because I made a note of the appearance in my diary – the diary which with all my books and other papers has now been destroyed in the fire – but because it was that morning that three black birds had made an extraordinary appearance at the window of Ludwig's room. One of them held a piece of carrion in its beak. Where they came from and what they were doing in Vienna's skies in the midst of such a raw winter none of us could imagine. I assume they were ravens or overgrown crows. I noticed that their wings were very large with pin feathers resembling large black hands. This I could see with great clarity since, because of the fight which ensued over the prize of flesh, the three had many times to flap them wildly in order to hold fast to the sill. After the carrion had been completely devoured, the birds sat facing each other just behind the murky glass – still as death. I remember thinking that they looked like the strange animal totems carved in wood or stone to be seen in drawings of Eastern temples.

Holtz, Breuning and Ludwig's brother Johann were present that morning. For the longest while all of us stood in stunned silence watching these beasts. It was Breuning who finally spoke.

'They must be half starved,' he said.

Then turning round he picked up a piece of bread and the remains of a hunk of cheese which looked as though it been sitting on the plate near Ludwig's bed for some time as it had gone hard and crumbly. Opening the window slowly and carefully so as not to startle the birds, he made the three an offering of the stale food with the unutterable gentleness that was characteristic of his nature.

That evening I sat quietly penning Ludwig's words in the margin of books, on the back of music sheaves or whatever was to hand when Storyteller emerged for the third time. He spoke for an hour or more but never once addressed me directly. Had I known that I would never see him again I would have asked many questions I had been storing up for him. Instead I remained the scribe trying to record as much of what he said as I could. Here is his final tale – as much as I remember of it, for all of what I wrote that night was consumed in the fire. It was spoken in the same stark future language – words uttered in the dark silence of ancient winter nights before death – words which look as though they had been scrawled by the hand of a man who by then had himself lost all sense of what was real and what fantasy.

'Ludwig hated words,' Storyteller said. 'They were

awkward things, pointed and one-sided. They limited him. Nothing must limit him. The sounds were different. They gave freedom. He could hold them in his hands and smooth them into shapes – slowly perhaps and with difficulty – but they did not bind him the way words did. Yet Neefe told him he must write words too. Neefe knew a lot. He had read books which Ludwig had never even heard of. Ludwig didn't mind books despite his hatred for words – that is, if they were big enough and if they were moral. He was not sure what this meant but he was sure he did not want to read a book that was not moral.

'Today for the first time he played the large organ. It was not difficult and they seemed to approve although he cared little whether or not his playing brought approval from such musicians. Neefe told him he must beware lest the jealousy of others cause him harm. He was not afraid of the jealousy of anybody. He was not afraid of anything. He knew he was great. God told him so . . . in his own way . . . every day. But sometimes he did not believe God's messages. Sometimes he feared that he himself was making it up. That is why it all had to be kept secret. He could not even speak of it to Neefe. He knew that one day he would bend to Neefe's will and play, that he would be a great man one day like his grandfather. Did not Neefe himself tell him so that day last spring when he explained the way the elect were separate from the rest of men who did not have the same vision and did not have the power? The elect were illuminated, Neefe had said. These illumined ones were the secret rulers of the earth. But they had to keep their light hidden because ordinary men would never understand. They had to know what was right for ordinary men and to guide them – Neefe even said "force" them when absolutely necessary – to do what was in their own best interest. Ludwig wondered if, since Neefe had told him all this, he meant to imply that he,

Ludwig, was also one of the illumined ones. He wanted to believe that. But he was afraid to ask. For what would he do if Neefe said no? Besides, asking meant he had to use words again and the only words Ludwig could bear were those that grabbed hold of you sweeping you up into great landscapes of feeling. Those of Schlegel for instance – it was Neefe who had given him a book by Schlegel to read – who said, "every concept of God is empty prattle, but the Idea of God is the Idea of all Ideas . . .". Was it not Schlegel after all who defined freedom and immortality as man's ability to "bring forth God and make him visible"? Or audible, Ludwig thought. "One lives only in so far as one follows one's own Idea. Individuality is the original and eternal in man." That was right. Ludwig knew it for in finding himself, the artist finds God. Schelling too, whom Neefe had insisted he read, said that the artist is only an instrument of revelation and the product of his creation is far greater than the mind of he who created it, for – How did it go? – Ludwig tried to remember: "the Self is conscious in its production, unconscious in its product".

'Later, he was to come upon the words of the great Goethe who teaches that the wise man – Ludwig was again quick to add "also the great artist", will "bring to full realisation the inherent forms of his being" only if he "hearkens to the involuntary promptings of his nature", letting them develop into a spiral which like a young seedling sprouting from the earth curves in its own direction in time flowering into a full-blown plant'. Later, too, Ludwig was to write to his friend Count Brunsvik of his composing, "The tones spiral like the wind, and often there is a spiral in my soul." He had known all of this long before ever reading of it anywhere from the promptings of his own heart. So that when he read the great landscape words of Schelling or Schlegel, or Schiller, they only echoed his knowing in the way the woodwind could echo a theme that had been introduced by the strings. Neefe seemed to know too. For it was Neefe who had given him all the books filled with landscape words. Did everybody know them, Ludwig wondered? He wondered too if he was not like everybody else. He feared he was. He was not part of some elite of illuminated ones of which Neefe spoke. He was completely ordinary. Except of course for the music. But then that was not his music, that came from somewhere else. He often worried what might happen if Neefe found out how ordinary he was. Perhaps Ludwig could go on fooling Neefe into thinking that he was special. But he feared that one day he would find out, and then what? And the worst was, he had no words to tell it all.

'Ludwig thought back to when he was a child – before soft hair had grown on his face and his voice had given way. It was no different then really. He had always needed to speak, always wanted to speak and yet never formed the right words. Then words had not mattered to him, only sounds mattered and he had learned the sounds well one by one in secret to escape his father's blows. Now Neefe said he needed to master words as well. He was not sure that he could ever do that. As a little boy how he would sit for hours listening to the scratching of mice in the wainscot. There was no confusion about that – no problem of understanding or not understanding. He would know immediately whether or not it was one or two small creatures, the exact direction of their movement and even whether or not they had eaten recently: the sounds of a mouse that has gorged itself on some sumptuous morsel is warmer, slower and less twitchy than that of its hungry brother. That was how it always was for him with sounds – all sounds.

'In the square dark room with the rough boards on the floor stood the clavichord with its hidden tones – scores of colours that could be mixed together, when his father had not been nearby to forbid it, to make the most amazing layers of sound. He still loved to layer noise, loved to mix the notes together. Sometimes they blended in a fine softness that filled him with dreams of peace, and at others they bit like a screech owl into the hollow silence of the room. Unlike words, sounds were always his to command. They had to do what he wanted no matter what. Without the weight of his fingers nothing came of the obedient instrument which he had always known was for his use alone. He knew that. The others did not know this of course – not the father with his foolish demands that scales be played over and over until perfect, although of recent he had left Ludwig alone, now that Ludwig was himself bringing home thalers to add to the family coffer, nor the mother, who understood nothing of the sounds. But he knew it to be true just as surely as he knew that no matter what happened in his life – no matter how alone he ever became – the one faculty that would never fail him was his hearing: the entrance and exit into his magic world of sound.

'Ludwig loved being left in the room alone better than anything else in the world. He loved the hollowness of it. It made him feel hollow himself as though a dark wind blew through his body – a wind that no one and nothing could interfere with. He would sit for an hour fingering the notes on his instrument, putting them together in patterns making chords that surprised him.

'Often when he played with sounds he would draw the curtains to darken the room, for you could hear better then. Even now, grown up as he was becoming, he still did this when he could get away with it – which meant when he was all on his own. Ludwig knew that the light interferes with the purity of tones, muddles the mixtures and makes you content with familiar chords alone. He had once tried to tell Neefe about this but he had fumbled with words, made a fool of himself and become angry: so furious that he thrust his fist through the panelling in Neefe's music room. Neefe responded with a lengthy diatribe about *control, balance* and the need for *illumination*. Ludwig never tried again in his life to tell anyone about his contempt for familiar chords. He knew they would never satisfy him as they had Neefe, Bach or his father. Never. About Neefe's fascination with light and with the illuminated ones who were secretly to rule the rest, Ludwig was not sure. He dared not ask too many questions about either lest Neefe see through him and know that he was not one of them.

'Some darkness Ludwig still hated. The darkness of the cellar. It was ugly . . . ugly. His father had put him there as a young child. He could never remember why. But it happened over and over again. To make him behave as he was supposed, presumably – to punish him for something inexcusable which he had done – like making up his own melodies when his father had told him to practise his scales, to play pieces with familiar chords. That had been a grave mistake on his father's part. His life belonged to himself. No matter what his father did to his body, no matter how hard he had tried to get Ludwig to play the songs that he wanted him to play, Ludwig would never give in. He would only hate. He knew that hating would keep him alive. It was the cellar that he hated most.

'The cellar was dark and cold and there was a smell of dust and damp rags. Ludwig never let himself be punished there as the father had intended. What his father didn't know was that there were always the noises there to keep him company. Even when he had been very small, even the very first time the father opened the square wooden door and shoved his tearful trembling body through it, Ludwig knew he could hear better than all the world. He had heard the sound of a cobweb moved by the air as the cellar door was shoved to, the rotting crumble of powder as the wood at the side of the stairway gave way under the pressure of his small boot, the trickle of water that slid down the stone wall beneath the only window – a window so encrusted with wood sap and sawdust that barely any light penetrated it.

'In the cellar Ludwig would listen hard for new noises. He knew so long as he could hear new noises he was safe from whatever silent monsters lurked there. Once he had been locked in for a long time, a very long time. He could not remember why. He seldom remembered why. But he remembered how his body felt – the burning in his flesh and the pain that rose up the spine from its base like white hot fire – so strong that he was forced to kneel on the stairs for it was more than he could bear to sit down. After many hours – maybe only two or three, maybe a hundred he did not know – his shoulders had grown stiff with cold but his ears had never grown tired of listening.

'It was then that he drifted into sleep and in his sleep sank deeper and deeper into the blackness, a blackness which changed from air to something far deeper – a great slick pool of dark water or something thicker than water. Out of the blackness rose a body – like the curved body of a great serpent, cold and smooth skinned. It had the face of a woman, or at least he knew somehow it was a woman. Ludwig was in the water, but it was an older Ludwig. And the bodies of other children were there as well. The dark serpent undulated through the wetness, part of her body appearing above the surface of the black pond then sliding silently beneath the surface to reveal another part of her. She was immense – as big around as the circle this dream-Ludwig could make with his growing body if he joined the very tips of his fingers in front of him and formed a great circle. She began to move faster and faster. No longer sinuous and rhythmical, her movements turned frenzied as she struck out with her huge mouth towards any living thing in her pool, killing, devouring everything that came into range of her great jaws. He, the dream-Ludwig, had taken a sword in his hand and struck out at the black twisting body of the serpent, hoping that in a single blow he would be able to cut her in two and arrest this rampant destruction. He succeeded. The sharp sword cut right through the powerful body exposing a severed spinal cord and releasing a copious flow of crimson blood, which was quickly swallowed up by the black water. Then Ludwig, this older Ludwig, stopped dead for a moment about to say a prayer to the only God he knew – the God of sound – for giving him the power to release these living children swimming in the water from destruction. But wait. No. It could not be. And yet it was. The horrendous slash through the serpent's body had disappeared, been mended. Again the dream-Ludwig struck out with his blade. Again he slashed through the monstrous dark flesh so that blood flowed free and she writhed in agony. That too was just as quickly mended. The monster remained untouched by his heroism and his strength. Ludwig the dreamer screamed from his bowels in fear and rage, yet no sound came. There was no sound left in the dark cellar. All was silent. Except for the soft whoosh of the serpent as she sank beneath the black water dragging with her the limbs of children she had devoured. Who could tell where in the black lake or when she would raise her head again. She was not finished. The dream-Ludwig knew that. Yet he himself had not been eaten. He could not imagine how.

'When the younger Ludwig awoke seconds later, it was into darkness and silence – a far better darkness than before despite his frozen limbs and the serpent-fear that stayed with him. For the white heat of pain that had risen from his bowels had gone softer now – soft enough for him to sit again and listen. And in this better darkness lay the familiar sounds on which he knew he could rely.'

CAULDRON

> . . . to learn to live and die, and in order to be a
> man, to refuse to be a god.
>
> Albert Camus *The Rebel*

As each night gave way to a cold and empty dawn the secret
worlds of Storyteller and the others became more important
to me than the ordinary world in which I pretended to be
living. I never knew from moment to moment who or what
would be present. So foreign was what I witnessed to
anything I had ever experienced that at times I believed I
was imagining it all – as though it were something taking
place in a dream and to someone else, not myself.

During the day, Ludwig's room continued to be peopled
with men who spoke of freedom, history and revolution in
strangely ominous tones while I tended Ludwig's wounds
and tried without success to alleviate his suffering as he
hurled verbal abuse at me and refused in every way to co-
operate even with simple requests. So completely immersed
in my tasks was I that I caught myself praying to a God in
whom I did not believe – that he silence these men. For
although they spoke in whispers, the words I heard, like the
night experiences with Ludwig, only served to dissolve
further every certainty I had of sanity.

Bending over my patient to change his dressings or clear
waste from his bed, I would overhear disconnected phrases
the meaning of which I could not decipher: '. . . illuminatus

rex . . . protocols . . . annuit coeptis . . . political polarisation of the goyim . . . novis ordo seculorum'.

So exhausted was I by weeks of sleepless nights spent trying both to save the life of Ludwig and to make sense of my researches into the nature of his physical and psychic illnesses that little now remains in my memory of their conversations. Yet they sent chills through my body. Schindler, Holtz, Breuning, Ludwig's brother Johann and the other men would come and go. Sali shuffled in and out bearing draughts I had ordered for her master who dutifully drained each one yet grew worse with each passing day. Breuning was the only one of the lot who seemed to take a real interest in Ludwig's state of being yet Breuning was himself seriously ill, so that several days would go by without his putting in an appearance. Holtz came infrequently now that Ludwig was becoming weaker and weaker. The rest often reminded me of birds of prey – present yet uninvolved in what was happening and waiting . . . waiting.

Karl and I arrived at the same time the morning of the 2nd of January. We met in the courtyard.

'Good morning, Karl,' I said.

'Good morning, sir.'

'You are looking very well this morning,' I said.

'I have come to say goodbye to my uncle,' said Karl. 'I leave Vienna this morning to take up my commission in the army.'

'Congratulations, Karl, you must be pleased,' I said.

'It was Breuning who arranged it for me,' said Karl, smiling. 'I have wanted it for a very long time.' He stamped his feet, shaking off the snow. The air was frozen and there was something very pleasant about standing in the courtyard watching our breath move about in the frozen mist.

'Does your uncle approve of your decision?' I asked.

Karl's body stiffened. 'Not altogether, I should say, but I am afraid things have gone so far that he no longer has a choice in the matter,' he replied.

'It must be hard for him to let you go,' I said. 'I sense he loves you a great deal.'

Karl shuffled his feet, then looked at me and said, 'Professor Wawruch, I too love him, but I cannot stay any longer. It would destroy me.' I put my arm around his shoulder. The stiffness in his body gave way as he leaned against me. Suddenly this determined young man became a boy again.

'Trust your heart and follow it, Karl. Your uncle will understand.'

He laughed, 'Yes sir,' he said, clicking his heels together, no doubt as he had seen military men do.

We climbed the steps together to the apartment and were ushered in by Sali. When we entered Ludwig's chamber he was propped up in bed. His small hands clasped in front of him, he was staring at the door.

'Good morning,' shouted Karl, leaning close to his uncle's ear.

'Good morning, my son,' said Ludwig.

'I have come to say goodbye, uncle.'

'I know,' said Ludwig. 'When shall you be leaving?'

'On the eleven o'clock coach, uncle.'

'A pity that the coach does not leave earlier,' said Ludwig. 'It is a long road you have to travel.'

'May I embrace you, uncle?' asked Karl. He put his arms about his uncle in a formal way. No emotion could be seen on Ludwig's face.

'Well, goodbye then, uncle,' shouted Karl.

'Goodbye my son, be well, and know you have my blessing.'

From the time Karl left the apartment not another word

336

was said about him. Yet the very next day Ludwig sent a letter to Dr Bach, his lawyer – a document laying out in black and white his wish that Karl van Beethoven, his beloved nephew, become universal heir to all the property which he possessed. Many weeks later, after Ludwig's death, I was to learn that this consisted in its entirety of seven bank shares hidden in a place of unknown origin, and very little else. Some time in the middle of January Ludwig received a short letter from Karl, to whom Schindler had written at Ludwig's request telling of the will. It was one paragraph long. Karl requested that in future communication his uncle include the date so he could estimate the speed of the post and said, evidently in response to what Ludwig had written to him, that he too felt some distrust of the physician – namely myself – but that he hoped his uncle would improve rapidly none the less. Finally he asked that money and also the flute part for a pianoforte concerto which one of his officers wanted to play be sent as soon as possible. After that, communications from Karl were few and very far between. This gave Schindler frequent opportunity to become the irresponsibility of youth both verbally to those of us who could hear as well as silently in Ludwig's conversation books. Ludwig's physical state deteriorated with each passing day.

Mine too deteriorated. Before that winter – the winter of 1827 – demons were to me nothing more than the inventions which fanciful authors used to people fairy tales. But after spending day and night by Ludwig's bed and watching as the life of this poor suffering creature ebbed away, I found that I too had entered the demon realm. It was like staring for too long at paintings in colours too vivid for the eye to bear and textures too rough to be comfortable.

Finally, three weeks before his life ended, Ludwig realised that the tappings were little more than a palliative, and resigned himself in stoic silence to the further accumulation of fluid. This was made worse by the appearance of cold rains in early spring which favoured a further increase in his dropsy and fuelled the fire of illness, which by then I was certain had its locus in a chronically inflamed liver and the organic deficiencies of his abdomen.

Each day his appetite diminished. As it waned I watched his strength ebb, so many vital juices had he lost. At first Dr Malfatti's iced punch worked admirably. It not only left Ludwig sleeping better at night but brought up a good sweat to relieve his body of some of the poisons that had accumulated. It also made him livelier in the day so that for several days he was able to spout witty ideas and dream of completing the oratorio he had begun, which he called *Saul and David*. But as I had foreseen, this improvement was short-lived. It was not long before he began to abuse Malfatti's prescription and to partake liberally of the beverage. What I could not understand was that each time he drank it it seemed to poison him, calling forth a powerful rush of blood to his head and causing great volumes of fluid to remain in the upper body, making him soporific and producing a rattle when he breathed like that of a man deeply intoxicated.

During the daylight hours Ludwig's speech would wander. To this was added an inflammation in the throat that produced hoarseness and even at times complete speechlessness. Yet each night when we were alone, provided he had not been made comatose by the alcohol, he spoke freely and clearly. Meanwhile his fugues became even more intense and the alternations from one persona to another more rapid. He grew more and more violent now – even during the daylight hours – for severe colic and diarrhoea had developed out of a chilling of his intestines. I knew the time had come to deprive him of his precious stimulant.

One morning as I entered Ludwig's room after completing my rounds at the hospital I found him sitting up in bed in a state of great agitation. He was alone except for Schindler, who sat in a chair pulled close to his bed and was busy writing in one of the conversation books. I was never to see what Schindler wrote but I saw enough of Ludwig's gestures and heard enough of his replies to be certain that the conversation had been taken too far and was exhausting him.

'Why do you call her a liar this time?' growled Ludwig, in a voice so hoarse that the sound of it scraping over the flesh of his vocal chords made it difficult to distinguish his words. Schindler quickly scribbled words in the book then held them close to Ludwig. On reading them his eyes grew wide.

' "A vile harlot," Schindler?' he said, ' ". . . Her very presence wracks your reason?" '

Schindler wrote in the conversation book. Again Ludwig read but shook his head.

'Perhaps you are right in what you say. She has misled me, it is true, but I know nothing of the nefarious events which you describe. Are you certain they are true?'

Schindler raised his eyes to the ceiling then scribbled once again. This time Ludwig did not read the words although Schindler attempted to make him do so.

'I had hoped,' said Ludwig, 'she had been chastened by the accident. Would not the threatened loss of an only son be expected to melt the heart of even the most wicked?' I thought I detected a playfulness in Ludwig, but if it was present Schindler gave no sign that he noticed. Again, perhaps intent at any cost on swaying Ludwig to his way of thinking, Schindler put pen to paper.

'Strange that *you* so hate her, Schindler,' said Ludwig, after reading the words that he had written. 'I thought you hardly knew her. "A witch from hell? A Lilith?" Surely you exaggerate. Of course, I thank you for your information, and your warning.'

Ludwig looked up then greeted me with uncharacteristic warmth, 'Ah, Wawruch,' he said, 'I feel somewhat stronger today.' I gazed at his wasted body, marvelling that anyone so ill and ravaged as he could show such spirit.

That afternoon I carried out the fourth tapping. From that moment forward, Ludwig in gloomy hours of presentiment foretold his approaching death. Unmistaken in his prophecy, he would receive no consolation offered to revive him. When of a morning I promised him that the warm spring weather which was rapidly approaching would alleviate his sufferings, he only answered with a smile, 'My day's work is done; if a physician still can be of use to me' and here he lapsed into English echoing Handel's *Messiah*: 'His name shall be called wonderful.'

So saddened was I by his words – so deeply did they move me – that I found myself obliged to confirm the truth of what he said. Ludwig's body grew weaker each day as the ill-fated moment of his departure approached. Night by night his fugues continued despite his wasted state. But with each night the words that passed his lips became more and more incoherent until at last they were little more than disconnected phrases. Soon the alterations in his face and body and voice began to come without discernible pattern giving the impression of impending chaos. The name 'Lilith', spat out with such distaste for the conversation with Schindler I had accidentally overheard, was uttered several times during those final nights: that name and another with whom Ludwig associated it – the name of Johanna, his much despised sister-in-law, the woman whom, I assumed with some justification, he was said to revile and hate most in the world. Yet as time went on, and her name came to be issued forth from his lips, it was uttered less and less as one would speak of an object of derision but more with awe or a strange kind of prophetic wonder. Other phrases too would pass his lips:

'I honour the entrance to the underworld that you offered me sweet Lilith – your narcotic lilies that set my brain ablaze . . . sweet wife before the coming of Eve . . . sweetest of all women, forgive my cowardice . . .'

Mid-March, at last I acknowledged my defeat and took upon myself the burdensome professional duty to acquaint my suffering friend with the necessity of complying with his civic and religious duties in preparation for the momentous day. I took up the much used conversation book and in the most gentle and respectful words I could manage wrote down a few admonitory lines and showed them to Ludwig. Slowly, as though in a state of deep contemplation, with incomparable self-control he read what I had written. His battered face became as one transfigured. He sat silent for a moment, then he reached out for my hand and in a manner both hearty and grave said, 'Ask them to send for His Reverence the pastor.' Afterwards he again grew quiet and reflective. Then nodding to me as he always did during daylight hours, that is when he deigned to speak to me at all, he said, 'Thank you, Wawruch. I shall soon see you again,' in the most friendly of voices.

Two hours later the pastor arrived. That was 23 March 1827, at eleven in the morning. Ludwig attended to his devotions with a pious resignation, evidently facing eternity with confidence. By dusk that afternoon he had lost consciousness, grown comatose and begun to breathe with a heavy rattle. When I arrived that night just after midnight no one lay in wait to greet me. Our secret meetings had finished. Only the laboured breath and the haggard face of a dying man remained. I did not sleep that night, nor the next, nor the one that followed. I sat before the pianoforte as candle wax gave off its greasy odour, staring at the face of this man, this conspirator, this strange being whom, like a lover abandoned, I had so completely failed – despite my will and his, despite my training, despite his dreams. I wished that it were I not he whom death was about to call. For I believed I had no further reason to live. This man who so hated and reviled me, this man who had shared with me the deepest, darkest and most hidden aspects of his being, this man who had become my destroyer had also become he whom I loved most greatly with a love that by necessity had remained unspoken. Together in silence Ludwig and I awaited the end.

The 26th of March began stormy and clouded. When dawn arrived I did not depart for home as had become my habit, for I knew beyond knowing that this was to be his last morning. I waited until the men arrived. Schindler and Breuning came first, as I recall. I gathered together the books and papers on which I had written nothing for three nights and I departed with a heart so heavy and dark I found myself surprised that it continued beating.

I never saw Ludwig alive again. Towards six in the evening a flurry of snow descended on Vienna as I was leaving the hospital to return to his side. With it came an extraordinary event – great crashing of thunder and sheets of lightning that shook the very sky above me. They came and went within the space of a quarter of an hour leaving no trace – only the gentle drifting of gigantic snowflakes as they settled to the ground.

SALVE

Decay is the beginning of all birth. It transforms
shape and essence, the forces and virtue of nature.
Decay is the midwife of very great things! It causes
many things to rot, that a noble fruit may be born;
for it is the reversal, the death and destruction of
the original essence of all natural things. It brings
about the birth and rebirth of forms a thousand
times improved. And this is the highest and
greatest mysterium of God, the deepest mystery
and miracle that He has revealed to mortal man.

Paracelsus

With Ludwig's death my own life seemed to pass away. My
ministrations and the night vigils had made me so much a
part of his body that the life within me died as it was lowered
into the earth. The chasm in which I had been living for
weeks between the humane world in which I had once lived
and this secret universe I had entered at Ludwig's bedside
grew wider when my partner in this strange yet infinitely
vibrant world disappeared. Within a fortnight of Ludwig's
funeral the split between these two worlds became complete, making it impossible for me to speak to anyone about
what had happened: neither my colleagues at the university
– whom in any case I had studiously avoided for some time –
nor even my dear wife. She had witnessed with a complete
lack of comprehension, yet with just as great a will to accept
what she did not understand, the disaffection of her once

343

attentive and loving husband. She waited in silence hoping for my return.

In an attempt to re-establish my sanity and to keep my promise to Ludwig, whom I had so completely failed to heal, I began a posthumous search for answers to the questions surrounding his illness – at Steffen von Breuning's bedside. Breuning was seriously, mortally ill. With each day that passed his life seemed further to evaporate. Lying immaculate in a sun-drenched room massed with spring flowers, such a contrast to the chamber in which Ludwig had spent his final weeks, Breuning told me childhood tales of his late friend. Some days his words would be clear and concise. Others they would seem vague and disconnected. Yet, despite his growing weakness, he was as pleased to speak of Ludwig as I was to listen – especially of their time together in Bonn. I found it strangely comforting to listen to his ramblings. I began to visit Breuning each day after dinner near the fifth hour, arriving on his doorstep, bag in hand, with some small token of kindness – a few apples perhaps, a bouquet of narcissus, some sweetmeats of which he was particularly fond.

His wife was one of the most modest and gentle women I have ever known. She never gave me the slightest inkling that she resented my intrusions. Each afternoon she would greet me with a warm handshake and the smile of an angel, then she would lead me into the airy room on the ground floor which had been rearranged to accommodate her husband's illness. Soon tea would arrive, served in the English manner for which there was such a vogue that year – a year during which our delicious Viennese coffee was not to be found in the houses of the well-to-do. Although Breuning did not belong to this class – his means were quite moderate – his home showed a rare sense of aesthetic awareness that transcends cost and class.

Some evenings I would remain for but an hour. As the spring moved towards summer and Breuning edged towards death I stayed so late that on leaving the house I would find the lamplighter making his rounds. Not a word of complaint did I hear from Breuning's family although I feel sure our meetings severely disrupted their lives, making it difficult for Breuning's son Gerhard to share as much of his father's final evenings as he should by right have been free to do. My enquiries about Ludwig's past intruded even more deeply into the sanctity of the Breuning household, for I would arrive to find that Breuning had spent the day painstakingly copying sheet after sheet of Ludwig's papers for my use. When I protested that such an occupation was far too demanding for a man in his condition, he would only wave aside my objections with his hand saying, 'Wawruch, my friend, if I do not copy them and God decides that it is time for me to quit this world they could fall into the hands of those who will distort truth.' During the second visit I made to the Breuning home he told me, 'While I am uncertain exactly how I may be of help to you, of one thing I am certain: my friend Ludwig was adamant that anything ever written about him after his death adhere strictly to the truth. You may not know this, Wawruch, but Ludwig was well acquainted with Plutarch. He had no fear of the whole truth being known. The notion that the flaws of a hero could tarnish his virtues never concerned him in the slightest. I recall one afternoon in the second month of his illness when Ludwig, Schindler and I were discussing Plutarch. I took the opportunity to ask him which of his contemporaries he should prefer as his biographer. He answered without the least hesitation: Rochlitz.'

I had heard the name but told Breuning that I knew nothing of this gentleman.

'Johann Friedrich Rochlitz,' he replied. 'The writer on

music whom Ludwig met two or three times and whose work he greatly admired.'

Breuning continued:

'That morning, raising his hand and looking directly into my eyes as if to preclude any of us speaking, Ludwig said, "You may be sure that after my death many officious pens will hasten to amuse themselves with tales and prattle about me – stories utterly destitute of truth. For such is the fate of any man who has influenced his times. Assure me of one thing: that whatever hereafter be said of me is in every respect consonant with truth, no matter how hard it might bear upon this or that person or indeed upon myself." '

Schindler, Breuning told me, had taken it upon himself to approach Rochlitz about the matter at the end of summer, when Ludwig's state would be fully settled.

'If Rochlitz agrees,' said Breuning, 'then all of Ludwig's papers will of necessity be passed on to him. In the meanwhile, Wawruch, you are welcome to any I have in my possession – his notes, a few letters, his conversation books. Perhaps they will be of service to you in your investigations. Do allow me the pleasure of copying whatever I believe might be of use to you. At the very least it will keep my hands occupied,' he added. 'As you see, there is little else I am fit for confined as I am to bed for what my physician assures me, even should all go well, will be at least a month. I am also more than happy to make you privy to my own recollections of our past together – Ludwig's and mine – if you think they may be of assistance in your better understanding the source and development of his illness.'

Then Breuning laughed, and leaning back against a massive pillow which his wife kept scented with rose and lavender in her attempt to make her husband's confinement less wearisome, he said, 'I am nothing but a government clerk, Wawruch. But by God, I will offer good service until the end.'

Thus it was that our talks began – evening after evening. They did not always directly concern Ludwig yet somehow we always seemed to talk *around* him, rather the way one does when someone to whom one is not directly speaking sits in the room in silence. Breuning, because of his love for Ludwig, had become my one remaining link with him, while my fascination with Ludwig seemed to give Breuning an opportunity to reaffirm the friendship which had meant most in his life. Ours was a fragile bond, however, for I knew that Breuning was dying and that this bond too would soon be severed.

I would come away from Breuning's home carrying many sheaves of paper written in his clear tight hand. On arriving home I would go immediately to my study and place them atop the cabinet near my desk. By the end of three months they formed a considerable stack. Yet to my shame, not once did I read them. For fifteen years they remained unread until within the space of an hour, fire turned them into ashes.

Several times at Breuning's bedside I attempted to speak of what had developed between us during those last nights. Each time something interfered with my doing so. Once Breuning began to cough uncontrollably. On another occasion his wife entered the room, or again he would misinterpret what I was trying to say and wander off at a tangent speaking slowly but at great lengths of times long distant – of parties on the banks of the Rhine as a boy which he and Ludwig had shared.

Because I could find no explanation for Ludwig's fugues it became more comfortable to dismiss them from my mind. Yet I pondered long on the rampant nature of the degeneration I had witnessed taking place in his body, on what could possibly have caused the reversal on that eighth day and on what possible connection either might have had to his deafness. And I made many notes about my musings.

I had long been aware that ears, liver and limbs work together and appear to form one organic system through which the human will is expressed. I had also long observed that the stream of energy which is designed to lead to decisive action in a man appears to begin in the liver then conducts its full force outwards towards the limbs, thereby activating his body. When a man moves his muscles they vibrate. Many times I have listened to this with a stethoscope and heard the sound of a man's will in clear audible form through the muscles of his limbs.

I had also observed over many years that in the ear itself the opposite applies. The eardrum stops the movement of this will-force by resisting it. It is out of this restriction of vibrations in the air that we are able to discern sounds. I continued to ponder on Ludwig's deafness and the appalling state of his liver, which had not only given him excruciating pain all the months I treated him but which Wagner, the pathologist, described as the worst liver he had ever dissected. I know that from the time of the great physician Paracelsus the liver has been associated with the production of gall. In a man of choleric temperament, of which Ludwig had been a supreme example, the liver is continually affected. In Ludwig I noted that the stream of energy which leads to movement was continually hampered in its action. It was as though the will to action would arise within his body, yet because of some internal inhibition could not be dissipated in external action.

Yet Ludwig's individual will *was* continually expressed through music. Indeed it appeared to have become the driving force behind most of the music he had written – but only *after* his hearing had begun to fade. The worse his hearing had become, the more ravaged his body – the richer did his compositions grow, reaching their apotheosis with his final quartets – written when to all intents and purposes

348

he had completely lost the faculty. Why? And there was another irony too. For as Ludwig's indomitable will became expressed more and more in his music as he grew older, in his daily life (and Breuning confirmed this in our conversations) his ability to carry out a simple task or make a mundane choice such as what he wanted to eat or where he wished to live dwindled so greatly that he had become a martyr to indecision.

I reasoned that Ludwig had suffered a supreme deficiency in this whole ears–liver–limb complex. His choleric temperament continued to struggle against this deficiency so that all the movement which should have been carried through his limbs into action, all the will which could have made it possible for him to make common decisions about his life, instead built up in Ludwig's body, creating a pressure that was almost unsupportable, and resulted in much of the intolerable physical suffering he had experienced. This inability for his will energy to be dissipated in action meant that the stream of energy had turned inwards, building to such a great extent that it destroyed his capacity for hearing, but like a voracious animal eating away at his liver, and resulting in the build-up of fluid in his body. All this in turn further hampered physical movement.

In effect, with his liver stunned and his ears contracted, was not the only way Ludwig could survive to quite literally lift up the force of his will to heroic proportions, expressing it through his music? In doing so, of course, his body had to be forsaken. Had he only been able to continue living so long as his body could withstand the onslaught of a will for which there was no outlet save his art?

I remembered the fugue-filled nights we had spent together during which one persona after another manifested through Ludwig's body. It seemed as though two things had been happening. Rather as in the new steam-driven engines, when heat and steam build up until they have to be released or it explodes, Ludwig's body, his psyche, his whole being would be temporarily broken open to dissipate excessive will pressure from the inside. Yet this 'opening' which released pressure also made him susceptible to titanic forces from without – forces which entered his body flooding it with foreign energies and entities. This only intensified further the demand that he raise his will into transcendent realms.

These thoughts I shared with Breuning, who never seemed to tire of listening to me speak of his friend. Often as not my words and questions would trigger off in him past memories.

'Strange,' Breuning said one day, 'how as one gains in age the memories of forty years previous are far clearer than those of today.' This was his response when yet again I had tried to broach the subject of Ludwig's fugues. He then began to speak at length describing memories of childhood.

'Mama adored him,' Breuning said, 'she always saw the best in everyone and Ludwig was no exception. He always tried to do the right thing and to be graceful but Mama used to say "Steffie, quick, put the porcelain away, here comes Ludwig." You know, Wawruch, she was the only person I ever knew who could tell Ludwig what to do and what not to do without causing offence.'

'How was that, Steffen?'

'I don't know,' he said. 'Mama seemed to understand his moods, she overlooked his awkward manner. She also ignored any signs of sullenness in Ludwig. They appeared often enough, you know, every time she spoke to him of some duty or obligation. She was gracious, and Ludwig would always comply with her wishes.'

'Really?' I said, surprised at the docile picture of Ludwig which Breuning was painting.

'Oh yes,' said Breuning, 'you see she always knew when to let him be. Whenever he got that faraway look in his eyes she would say, "leave him alone, Steffie, he has his *raptus* again." Then she would take Ludwig by the chin and say, "Good day, my young Prometheus, get along with you now."'

The words 'young Prometheus' echoed in my brain. Of course, why had I not seen the connection before? The titanic force I watched at work in Ludwig, which destroyed his body from inside out and also expressed itself in his music, was indeed Promethean – even Wagner who performed the autopsy on Ludwig's body had observed this.

I searched my brain in an attempt to recall the myth of the Greek god. Had not Prometheus been one of the Titans who helped Zeus conquer the others? Did not the name itself mean 'forethought' – someone who knew far in advance the results of every action that he took. Was this the case with Ludwig too? My mind raced on. To Breuning I said: 'Prometheus – was it not he who is said to have fashioned men?'

'Indeed it was,' said Breuning, then smiled the broadest smile. 'It is a wonderful tale,' he went on, his eyes sparkling. 'We used to read it over and over of a winter's evening in the drawing room. Ludwig was particularly fond of it. We had a big book in the library that had a drawing of Prometheus chained to a rock. Ludwig would sit sometimes for hours staring at the drawing without speaking a word. Mama loved to tell us the tale and Ludwig loved to listen.'

'Would you tell it to me now, Steffen?' I said, 'provided, of course, it does not tire you greatly to do so.'

'Ah no,' said Breuning, 'storytelling brings me the greatest joy – of course I can never tell it quite so well as Mama did.' Settling himself down in his feather bed and closing his eyes he said, 'Let me see . . . I think it goes something like this. When Zeus, king of the gods, battled the Titans for the rule of heaven and earth, he spared Prometheus. For Prometheus owned the gift of looking to the future which had helped Zeus claim his victory. You see, Prometheus had foreseen the outcome of Zeus' rebellion against the old god Chronus,' said Breuning, 'because he was the wisest of all the Titans, so wise that it was he who acted the midwife at Athena's birth as she sprang forth from Zeus' forehead.'

I leaned back in my chair and watched Breuning as he spoke, marvelling at the way his cheeks – pale as death until now – had taken on a glow of colour.

'In return, Athena taught Prometheus many arts,' he continued. 'Astronomy, for instance, and mathematics, architecture and medicine, metallurgy and navigation. She also taught him to fashion tools and weapons. Anyway, after his victory Zeus gave Prometheus an order to descend to earth, and by the banks of a great river to fashion man – creatures from the clay that he would find there. This the Titan did with much enjoyment using clay and water to create they who, alone of the beasts, raise their faces heavenwards to gaze at the sun, moon and stars with longing.'

The door to Breuning's room opened. His young son, Gerhard, approached his father's bed. 'Papa, would you like some tea?' he asked.

'No, Gerhard,' said Breuning, putting his hand upon the young lad's shoulder, 'but it is kind of you to ask me.'

'Papa, are you telling a story?'

Breuning laughed and ruffled his son's hair. 'That I am.'

'May I listen?'

'Yes of course you may,' he said, patting the edge of the bed. The boy sat down, and very seriously watching his father's face listened as Breuning told his tale.

ARS MAGNA

Religion may have been the peculiar means for enabling individual men to enjoy but once the entire self-satisfaction of a God and all his self-redeeming power. Indeed – one may ask –would man have learned at all to get on the tracks of hunger and thirst for *himself*, or to extract satiety and fullness out of *himself*, without that religious schooling and preliminary history? Had Prometheus first to *fancy* that he had stolen the light, and that he did penance for the theft – in order finally to discover that he had created the light, *in that he had longed for the light*, and that not only man, but God had been the work of his hands and the clay in *his* hands?

Nietzsche *The Joyful Wisdom*

'Zeus looked upon the men and women Prometheus had made as he did his cattle, his birds and all other creatures – as beings made only for his amusement,' continued Breuning. 'In time however the great god became irritated and wished to destroy the race of man as a punishment for his sky-gazing. For unlike the bulls and bears and oxen who roam content upon the earth's surface asking for nothing more than sustenance, man had grown greedy. He wanted to *know*, to reach upwards, to become himself *as a god*.' Gerhard smiled, grasping his knees and rocking gently back and forth as he listened to his father's story. He, too, had heard it many times before, it seemed.

'When Prometheus learned of Zeus' intention to obliterate his creation,' Breuning went on, 'he pondered long on what he might do to prevent this from happening. He had grown to love his man-creatures with a compassion that lay beyond reason, beyond right and wrong, beyond even concern for his own destiny. So he devised a scheme – a plan which in time he knew could help man not only to save himself but also make himself truly free – independent even of Zeus himself. Prometheus decided he would journey to heaven. Then from the forge of . . .' here Breuning stopped, perhaps unable to remember.

'From the forge of Vulcan, father,' his son whispered, leaning forward across the bed.

'Quite right, Gerhard,' said Breuning. 'From the forge of Vulcan he would steal some of the immortal fire. This he did –one dark night while Zeus was carousing with his latest nymph. Carrying the fire of the gods in the pith of a giant fennel, Prometheus returned with his treasure to earth and placed it in the hands of his clay-based creatures. That is how he became the inaugurator of individualised human culture,' said Breuning turning his head to look me in the eyes. 'He brought to man the gift of writing and of the other arts and provided him with a flame for the creation of war machinery and for magic. But with his gift for seeing into the future, Prometheus knew full well what the consequences of his action would be.'

Breuning's voice faltered. I picked up a glass of water by his bedside and held it to his lips. 'Thank you, Wawruch,' he said when he had drunk a sip. 'And as if to fulfil the very prophecy of his knowing,' he went on, 'Zeus chained Prometheus naked to a rock in the Caucasus mountains there to remain "for all eternity". For thirty years –'

'No, Papa,' said Gerhard, 'it was thirty thousand.'

'Well, thirty thousand then,' said Breuning, 'he was to

languish whilst each day a greedy vulture tore away at his liver and each night it grew whole again.' At this Gerhard wrinkled his nose.

'There was no end to the pain the Titan suffered,' said Breuning. 'His flesh was exposed to the cruel elements of frost and cold, yet his body was to be bound for ever in immortality.' Turning to me again, Breuning added, 'One does not challenge a god's power without infinite suffering. Yet Prometheus bore his punishment without rancour. He even sent a message to his tormentor to warn Zeus not to marry the nymph Thetis lest, as had been prophesied, the union of that marriage produce an offspring greater than the king of the gods himself.'

I listened in silence to Breuning's tale, feeling blessed to be in the presence of this father and his son. Yet my mind raced on knowing beyond reason that the tale he told – this ancient story of Prometheus – was also in some strange way the tale of Ludwig himself. Had not Ludwig, defying the gods, laid hold of heavenly fire and through his music brought it down to man on earth? And in so doing he himself seemed to have become bound to the rock of interminable suffering while battles initiated by jealous gods – but who or what were these jealous gods? – waged in his body. What the ancient Prometheus had accomplished in spatial form, Ludwig had somehow repeated in the world of music. Of course the *Eroica* would have to be lived before it could be written. Ludwig had transported the fire of Spirit from heaven – bringing it to each man who heard his music, enabling him to build a bridge between heaven and earth which, if only he were strong enough and wild enough to have a taste for freedom, he could use to walk his own way. Then to Breuning I said: 'But how did Prometheus break free?'

'Ah that was . . .' he paused, searching for a name.

'Hercules, Papa,' said Gerhard, moving closer once again and taking his father's hand in his own.

'Hercules,' echoed Breuning. 'After completing his twelve labours, Hercules was greatly moved by the suffering of Prometheus. He went to Zeus to plead his cause. Zeus was grateful of course for Prometheus' warning about Thetis but, after all, he was a god and bound by his own words condemning Prometheus to everlasting punishment. He had his dignity as king of all the gods to consider. He agreed to grant a pardon but decreed that Prometheus' sufferings should continue until some immortal voluntarily offered up his immortality to free him. He also said that if Prometheus were freed he would have to wear for ever the brand of a prisoner – a ring forged from the metal of his chains set with a stone from the very mountain on which he had been bound, and to carry a wreath of willow, worn for ever as a crown,' said Breuning.

'That is the tree of tears,' Gerhard said, turning to look at me.

'In the end it was the wounded centaur Chiron, father of medicine – you should know him well, Wawruch – and of the martial arts who roamed the world healing all illness yet was unable to heal himself who came to Prometheus' rescue. Weary of his immortality and in a state of endless suffering himself, the half-beast, half-man Chiron delivered up his immortal body to free the Titan.'

'And by Zeus' decree Prometheus was released,' said Gerhard, smiling.

'Once he had become mortal, Chiron's wound did heal and in due time of course he died,' said Breuning, sighing deeply and closing his eyes. Gerhard let go his father's hand and rose to make his pillows more comfortable.

Breuning's tale had evidently finished. I rose. 'It is a wonderful story,' I said. 'I can see why your mother called Ludwig by Prometheus' name.' The two of them smiled.

'I must go,' I said, reaching out a hand to touch Breuning's forehead. I saw with a detached curiosity that the hand was trembling. I bade them both goodnight, then Gerhard showed me to the door.

IRON

Terrified, I sent out the
greatest shriek, saying: 'O
mother where are you? I would
suffer pain more lightly if I
had not felt the deep pleasure
of your presence earlier . . . Where
is your help now?

Hildegaard von Bingen

The air was cold for summer and I was grateful for its
coolness. I arrived home to find my wife had gone to bed. I
entered my study and lowered myself into my familiar chair.
I could smell tobacco and leather. My hands and arms
continued to tremble and my brain began to whirl. It was as
though some wild energy, a cold wind, a whirlpool had
descended through my skull. I closed my eyes only to find
the swirling in my head had produced ever-changing
coloured lights that moved in and out of each other like
ribbons in a wind or like writhing snakes. Before me stood
Zeus, omnipotent ruler of cosmic wisdom, decked in all his
raiment. With his left hand he held a magnificent mask to
his face – a mask that was the colour of flesh complete with
ruby lips and cheeks the colour of a fine sunset, yet which
glimmered in the inner light of my mind as though fashioned
of beaten gold. He bowed with great flourish. As he did so,
he removed the mask. Only on unbending his body to

restore himself to full height could I discern the face that had been hidden beneath. Angular and pointed, it bore no resemblance to the countenance of a great Greek god. Its eyes were the colour of lead. Zeus' right hand had been transformed into the beak of a great bird poised to strike at its prey – any prey so long as it was infinitely smaller than himself. I could see quite clearly that Zeus, the jovial god, was in truth a cold master of the world who bore little love for the fruits of his creation.

A revulsion came upon me. I opened my eyes. My mouth filled with saliva. The muscles of my solar plexus began to contract violently. Was this not the same revulsion that thirty years before had drawn me away from the seminary and thrust me through the doors of medicine? Disembarrassed of his mask, was not Zeus the same god of indifference who allowed the arms of a child to be torn from its starving body by carriage wheels? The same god who had allowed inhuman forces to do battle within the body of my now dead patient, tearing Ludwig's liver to shreds each day –and the same god who in his greed for cruel amusement allowed the very tissue that had been torn asunder in the daylight hours to be reconstituted in the night so that he could upon the morrow indulge himself in the same heartless pleasure yet again?

I rose from my desk and staggered across the room to the window where my wife had placed a vase overflowing with white lilies. I leaned over, breathing in their dark fragrance. Again I closed my eyes. This time there were no moving colours, no masks, no ancient gods. The scent of the flowers had calmed my body yet my mind raced on.

I saw clearly that this ancient god was no figment of imagination, but a real power – a power cold and ruthless which ruled the psyche and perhaps the world. A power to whom men bowed their backs, made sacrifice, prayed, seeking but a peaceful life, believing in their delusion that the great Father in His love and wisdom would grant such favours.

If within the psyche such powers do exist, do they not also have their counterparts in the body's physiology? How then, I asked myself, is this Zeus power focused within the cells and organs? Where had this force been seated within the body of Ludwig while he breathed and walked the earth?

I had to ask the question but once. It is the plastic force of thought which from the head downwards builds the human form. The answer came as though spoken from within yet with absolute clarity. And if that is so then what within the body does oppose it? What, in the words of the great Hegel, is the *antithesis* of this Zeus energy? I saw immediately, clearly and with a sureless I could not then, nor can I now, explain that the power opposing the Zeus force within the human form is nothing less than the *individualised will* which, originating in the liver, is carried through the limbs to action, and that the fire of this Promethean will in Ludwig's body had done constant battle against Zeus' formative power of the mind – each attempting to take possession of his organism.

My nausea returned. I sat down again in an attempt to quell it and put pen to paper, scribbling furiously to record my thoughts. All the while I was aware that in the context of the medicine in which I had been trained they made no sense whatever. Yet I knew that for a brief moment some veil forever covering my eyes and obstructing my *knowing* had been lifted, allowing me to see what lay beyond – this realm *behind* the world of tables and papers and promises in which we live out our lives day to day like blind creatures fashioned from clay. Thoughts came to my mind so quickly and with such shifting force that I could barely set them down.

Why had I not taken Wagner literally when he described a battle of Promethean proportions having been waged in the body he dissected? That was precisely what *had* occurred. No wonder Ludwig's skull had been so heavy. It had to be to support the agonising force of conflict it would sustain. I recalled from my anatomy that within the inner ear is to be found one of the hardest bones in the body – so hard that we in Germany call it *Felsenbein* (rock-bone). It is its hardness that gives sound resonance. Ludwig, choosing to forsake the hypocrisy of being a 'good son' to anyone, had himself been chained to the rock. That was in his twenty-eighth year. Only then did his hearing start to fade. Then too his liver waned, devoured by the vulture of a ruthless god – a god jealous of this raucous upstart who dared to steal the fire of immortality and travel with it to earth, irretrievably blending it as music with the blood and tears of human passion.

What of Mozart then, and the great Emanuel Bach? Had not they too touched heaven's fire? I asked myself. Yes, of certainty they had, yet they remained protected from Zeus' wrath for they created music still transcendent – untouched by human passion – a music which belonged not to the world of men but to that of the Olympian, to which it pays endless homage. Only Ludwig had the arrogance, the foolishness and the courage – perhaps because of some indescribable human need, regardless of what it cost him – to feast on heavenly fire, to take it deep within his body and then to transform it – not only figuratively through the humanity of his craft but through the labyrinth of his own physiology – within the mineral-based substance from which his own flesh and blood and bones had been made. The music he created for all who dared to hear was but an effluent of his union with that fire – a product of waste like that which a man himself produces on consuming food to fuel his body processes. I smiled at the obscenity of such a notion, knowing full well were I to voice it amongst my medical colleagues or my musician friends I would either be branded a fool or accused of sacrilege.

Now I knew why I had always taken so little interest in those books and paintings which are much prized by fashion. Craftsmen who but play with art, those who believe in all their cleverness that they know what they are doing: all of these are liars – men who deal in fraudulent ways with the powers of the living gods, pretending to create yet bringing forth naught but moribund form. They are the *safe* men who have not the right to be called artists. They are the men who pretend to boldness yet challenge not the powers of the gods nor the ways of society. They change not. Yet so long as they can sustain the falsehood by which they live and work, neither do they suffer. They continue to congratulate themselves on their cleverness in belonging to an elite so gifted with Zeus' cold wisdom that they can gaze down perfect noses at the messiness of such as Ludwig. They can laugh at his peasant ways yet use him when it so suits them in the mimicry they call their art. These men would eat of Ludwig's flesh for power yet they have not the stomach to digest their meal. So they choose instead to stand about his bed while he is forced with every breath he takes to *live* the power of Zeus' fire within his wasted body. For Ludwig to have written the Symphony in E Flat Major, he had to have lived it. And in the living of it, whatever certainty he had about himself, about those he called his friends, about anything whatsoever that would give any ordinary man a sense of safety and sureness about his life, had been burnt away by the fire that possessed him.

I remembered the long discussions which had taken place at Ludwig's bedside amongst those whom he called friends – a thousand thousand words spoken about art, about politics, about the necessity of guiding the common man who in his blindness and stupidity had not the wherewithal to guide himself. The sickness in my gut grew worse. The pneuma of the room had become thick and heavy. I noticed that a faint smell of sewage permeated the air.

My thoughts were interrupted by a church bell chiming the hour. I rose from my chair, leaving open books upon the desk before me. I pulled the watch from my waistcoat. I was surprised to find it was three o'clock. How could it have grown so late? The tightness in my solar plexus had subsided yet my head had grown hot and the flesh all over my body was wet with perspiration. Snuffing the candles, I went to the window intending to open the sash for air. I found that it was jammed. Unable to budge it, I decided to leave the house in the hope that the chill of early morning would calm the fire that burnt within my body. The faint rotting odour seemed to accompany me wherever I went, like a dog that trots at your heels without reason. I walked most of the night. Of where I walked or how long I was gone, I have no memory. I passed a coach gate which opened on to a splendid courtyard some time near dawn. In the middle of the courtyard was a fountain built in the Italian style of marble so white that the first rays of the sun touching its surface flooded it in blood. Later I watched a fight take place between two cats. Although I have no recollection of how they looked, their cries cruelly hurled into space still echo in my mind when I think of that morning. Somehow I arrived at the Allgemeine Krankenhaus. Once there I collapsed while on my way to the consumptive ward to do my rounds. The attendants carried me no more than thirty feet to a bed. I there remained for more than a fortnight while the fire kindled that long and lonely night burnt through every layer of my flesh.

Of these days and nights when Wawruch the physician

became Wawruch the victim I recall little – only visits from my wife, bandages tied around my arm as I had done so often for others, swollen veins cut open to spill red fluid that was collected in a basin held beneath my arm – and the delicate sweetness of an exhaustion so profound that every smell or sound, the touch of linen on naked flesh, each isolated breath entering one's body, all this becomes unspeakably precious. Then came the leeches and the promises. That I would leave behind my life with Ludwig. My wife was adamant. And I? I had no will to fight. I smelt her hair, felt the whiteness of her hand upon my forehead, and yielded freely to her pleas.

The path that for a time Ludwig and I had walked together had led me into a dismal forest. It now dwindled to nothing. Crouching alone in the darkness, I had but one wish: to return to the life I had lived before the winter of 1826–27.

MIASM

O dreadful is the check – intense the agony
When the ear begins to hear and the eye begins to
see;
When the pulse begins to throb, and the brain to
think again,
The soul to feel the flesh, and the flesh to feel the
chain!

Yet I would lose no sting, would wish no torture
less;
The more that anguish racks, the earlier will it
bless;
And robed in fires of Hell, or bright with Heavenly
shine,
If it but herald Death, the vision is divine!

Emily Brontë 'The Prisoner'

It was as I lay in bed recovering that I learnt of Breuning's
death. That was early summer. Rochlitz had been approached about writing Ludwig's biography, but declined.
During the months preceding the autumn of the year 1827, I
heard from Steffen's wife that every one of the papers which
he had copied for me had been given to Schindler on the
understanding that he would pass them on to Rochlitz, or
had vanished without a trace from her home – as had most of
Ludwig's personal effects from his own apartment.

I heard this with a strange detachment. For with the
giving of the promise to my wife I vowed to myself that I

would leave behind the strange night visions shared with Ludwig to return to the world I had known before that fateful winter. In my naivety I believed such a thing was possible. Each morning I would wake and give thanks for the light that poured through the windows of the familiar house in which I lived. I knew my body had been ravaged by illness and fatigue yet I rejoiced in the vividness of the summer flowers which adorned the table in the mornings as I descended to take my coffee. I would look deep into my wife's eyes – eyes that had been troubled for almost a year by the rash behaviour of a neglectful husband. There, despite the numbness in my body and my soul, I discovered that once again I could be charmed by her gentleness, by the grace with which she moved, by the rustle of silk each time she entered the room. Thus did I manage to convince myself that a return to normal life was possible. For that too I gave thanks, promising that I would never again let myself become enthralled by anything. Neither would I take for granted the commonplace nature of everyday existence with its dedication to a work that is simple yet in its own way honourable – the task of caring for the sick and celebrating reason.

The diaries and letters which Breuning had so painstakingly copied for me in his measured hand, I locked carefully in a drawer of the desk in my study. As I turned the key, I shut away the chaos, the memories, the passions of those months with Ludwig. I believed for ever. For fifteen years the drawer remained locked. For fifteen years I lived with the illusion that our strange union had been but a wrinkle in time – that it, like the papers, could be shut away with the turn of a key. For fifteen years this was true. I lived free of Ludwig's demons and from the chaos which destroys all structure and dissolves all reason – free from the winter of 1826–'27 – until three months ago. Then the hauntings started.

They began with dreams, or I would hear Ludwig's words in spaces of my mind echoing darkness. They would come to me, they *do* come to me – always when I am least aware – obliquely when my mind is focused elsewhere – the way at dusk in a darkening sky one can only just make out the form of objects directly in front when one's eyes look sideways. What do they say? Strange things – half-sentences and phrases – like words repeated again and again without meaning. When they began I started to get mild fevers and dizziness. At first when I awakened I would go immediately to my desk and record the incident. I found I had to do this otherwise the echoes would fade to nothing so that by ten o'clock the next morning I would convince myself that no words had been spoken, nothing had been heard and all things were still as I wished them to be. Yet these visitations troubled me greatly. They seemed profoundly threatening to the fabric of my life. As I know now, this portent of threat was no figment of my imagination. I started a diary hoping this would clear my mind and enable me to maintain a hold on my life. Fragments of it remain:

4 July 1842

Still little sleep and what comes is troubled. Last night was cold. During the hours of darkness we sustained a heavy rain. I awoke to the sound of a dog whining. At three I rose from my bed and descended in search of its source. I raised a light and passed from the house into the courtyard only to discover a wet and mangy animal whimpering and trembling with cold. I don't know what possessed me to bring the ugly beast into the house. Taking hold of the long matted hair on his neck, I guided it down the steps making a place for it to sleep in a pile of rags next to the fire in the scullery. Then, feeling embarrassed at the absurdity of this act, which neither the housekeeper nor my dear wife would condone, I settled myself next to the fire and sat for several hours waiting until its trembling ceased. Then I went to the larder, pilfered some roast meat and I fed the creature by hand. I felt ashamed, like someone engaged in a surreptitious act he wishes no one to discover. At dawn, its stomach full, the beast skulked towards the door. I ushered it into the courtyard and released it through the iron gate into the street. It looked towards me with what I perceived to be grateful eyes. As I shut the gate I knew that it was I, not the dog, who should be grateful. For it was not out of caring that my ministrations arose. It was out of a need to involve myself in any way possible in the world of the living – to tend the needs of any living creature, even a dog – lest once again I be sucked into the chaos of the dead. Still I cannot stop thinking of Ludwig. Vienna was never a joyous place for him. Too dark, too formal, too uncomfortable for the beastly body he carried.

No sign of them for three nights, no 'hauntings', no need to open up the past nor to dwell on the dead.

7 July 1842

The respite has been short. Last night they returned – disconnected words whose meaning I could not catch. With them, memories flood my brain: bitter nights in Ludwig's chamber – a smouldering fire drew air from one's body to yield a bleak deathly fog in which all colours were distorted and reason made not its presence known.

Yesterday at the hospital Herr Professor Skendling drew me aside. My eyes, he observed, have grown dark about the rims and my mouth, he said, is now pursed and firm in an uncharacteristic way. He insisted that during a surgery while I was removing a growth from the throat of an ageing man, my hand shook. I refuse to believe that his observation was accurate. Skendling says I should request time away from my duties. I have no such desire. Perhaps, however, it would be wise for me to rest each afternoon before dinner. Perhaps too I should take the waters early this year. No doubt a fortnight of walking and warm baths would do me good. My wife I believe would not object to our going early. Above all I must and will retain balance and conceal these unwelcome night events. There is much to be said for silence.

8 July

The hauntings have returned after another almost sleepless night. I left my wife just after midnight sleeping soundly, ignorant of her husband's wanderings, and descended to light a fire in the study. Then I poured myself a brandy. Not even that could calm my racing heart. I sat close to the fire for my hands and feet were icy although the back of my head was burning with pain. The room lit only by flames and the warmth of the wood fire overcame my resistance to sleep. I found myself plunged into darkness. It was not the darkness of oblivion but of an eerie inner chamber. A dream? No not a dream, for my body was altogether with me. I had been transported to the door of St Stephen's cathedral that very night. The streets were empty save for an old woman huddled near a wall in rags. A dark-coloured chariot drawn by six white horses drew nigh and stopped before me. It was followed by a dozen or more dark liveries mounted upon black steeds. Within the chariot perched a lean man of dark majestic mien with long black hair that floated in the wind – yet there was not a breeze to be felt anywhere. His eyes were black and sunken. His complexion was darker than that of any man I have ever seen. From his eyes flashed a wild phosphorescence. His lips bore the traces of ineffable scorn. So sublime was the look of this black stranger that my body trembled icy cold just to gaze upon him. It was a cold made the more hideous by the knowledge that the atmosphere in which he sat was of itself hot and suffocating. Ignoring my trepidation, the stranger requested that I mount beside him in a voice of such quietude that it brought with it the utmost in commanding power. Unable to refuse, even before I realised that I had moved I found myself seated beside him. The chariot took off at the speed of the wind. For some time we travelled through the deserted streets of Vienna while the horses' hooves made not a sound against the cobbles. He spoke no word. After half an hour or more we drew up in a square before a great building which I had never seen before. In the square stood perhaps a hundred people as though waiting for some event. They took no notice of us. From this I judged that we were not visible to human eyes. As we descended from the chariot my companion's garment like the train of a bridal gown but heavier and utterly black, a blackness that drew one into its folds – touched my hand. The heavy silken finish burnt my flesh with icy fire. I drew back my arm. He smiled.

Beyond the heavy door at the top of wide steps lay a great stone anteroom on the walls of which hung sconces held in human hands. As we passed first one and then another the arms of flesh supporting them opened outwards, beckoning us further in. The passage ended in the great hall of what appeared to be a vast yet ruined castle. Everywhere stood strange contraptions made of wood or ice or the dried skins of animals all covered with ropes and pulleys. I followed my mysterious guide for I had not the slightest will to resist his whim. We went from room to room, each large and dimly lit. In one stood a circle of marble pillars, huge and half ruined like something taken from a Greek temple. There a legion of men, or what once had been men, were assembled moving slowly in and out amongst the columns debating the progress of some plague or other – a pestilence so wide, to judge by the words they uttered, that it would cover not just a city or a land but the world over.

We left them and walked on through other rooms equally grand yet enveloped in the thickest darkness except for flashes of lightning which at unexpected intervals illumined their contents: ghost-like not-quite-human creatures with hideously lean bodies spoke in gibberish and ran about pursuing each other as though participating in some insane game – leaping over each other's backs, hanging from the rafters, rolling up and down the walls. We passed by them and moved through an archway then descended perhaps two hundred steps to where a sluggish river ran far beneath the earth – its black poisonous waters insinuating themselves into the very walls of the building and making them crumble. The stranger spoke not a word. Yet he was able to communicate to me in some unknown fashion that these poisonous waters had been made to quench man's thirst at some distant time, bringing upon him a plague of such power to distort his reason that not even the most holy would be able to touch his affliction.

As silently as we had arrived we now withdrew from this dark underground world. We now entered a vast treasure house filled with gold and precious stones illumined by a light so bright I thought it to be the daylight of a cold grey winter's day. Yet nowhere was a window to be seen. On the walls were paintings of which I had only heard. The final supper of Jesus hung on one. On another was placed a magnificent woman's head and torso in the style of Rembrandt. The room itself was of opulent proportions and of such splendour as I had never before encountered. Yet its proportions were distorted – not grossly so but just enough for one to feel wild and uneasy at beholding them, as if one were witnessing something which should be right and yet was not quite as it should be. A ceiling rose far too high. The point of an arch to my left was not centred, as by rights it should have been, so that at first encounter I thought myself the victim of an optical illusion which unceasingly teased the mind even after the deception had been unmasked.

The black stranger again in silent voice told me with unmistakable clarity that all I saw before me was to be mine if I but knelt and worshipped him. I could feel my knees begin to bend. He held out a chalice in which an ointment festered as though a thousand maggots crawled within its golden bowl. Speaking to me in the same deathly silent voice, he declared I was to smear the door of every house with this pestiferous salve.

Then did I hear music. It was of Ludwig's making and glorious, yet, like the arch and all the room's proportions, subtly twisted in rhythm as though it had been altered to serve a strange eccentric whim. I listened and in the listening nausea arose within my belly. I could feel the power of his magnificence. Every particle of my being was pulled downward to seek the protection of his being. Yet my eyes were once again drawn to the paintings that hung all round me. I noticed that they too bore certain oddities which at first I had not remarked. Rats with gleaming eyes had been painted beneath the table of the last supper. The feet of figures gathered in a soft pastoral frolic were wildly twisted. From the breasts of the voluptuous golden-haired women grew masses of hideous dark hairs which I had at first taken to be shadow playing on the flesh. Still the subtly distorted music wound round my body, louder now, drawing me down, down towards the stone floor. Then, suddenly, there before me in the air hovered the mask of Ludwig's death – a hand raised to one cheek, its eyes shut, its face wasted with suffering. My own eyes flooded with tears. So heavy was the flow for several moments that I could not even make out the outlines of my dark companion. The spell was broken. I recoiled in horror and stood up. My lips began to move against my will repeating ancient words with meaning long before forgotten: *Sta. In nomine Patris et Filii et Spiritus Sancti, dic mihi qui sis et quam ob causam veneris.*

The stranger scowled. A clap of thunder crashed above my head as blinding light burnt through my eyes. The next moment I found myself again before my study fire as Ludwig's voice spoke softly in my ear. It said: 'Speak of this to no one, record all that you know, do not procrastinate, there is little time.'

I sat bold upright and in a carping voice spat out: 'What truth can I tell?' No answer was to greet me. All that remained was the knowledge that the life I thought belonged to me to do with as I chose, to live in reason and in peace – this life was not my own. Some ancient ritual carried out thousands of nights before had bound me to a pledge which was now called, no matter what was lost in the honouring of it – be it peace of mind or reason or the comfort of a woman's love. That was but chaff carried on the wind as flour is extracted.

11 July 1842

I have taken respite from my duties at the hospital. What use can a physician be who cannot even heal himself? Last night I rose and walked about the streets of the city in search of the castle which I know in certainty was no dream. I found nothing. My wife has begun to question me about these night wanderings. I do not know what to relate to her since I can speak neither of the man in black nor of Ludwig's whisperings. I cannot let her know it has been resurrected –

this bond with Ludwig which fifteen years ago made her life utterly miserable. I try to see these circumstances with the distant eyes of the physician yet I am blind. I have no idea what is causing these aberrations. Can it be that my nervous system is overtaxed? Has my digestion become so poorly of late that some food or herb to which my body takes exception fills my blood with a chemical that poisons my brain? Yet I know it is not so. Is it my conscience that troubles me? For having made a vow to record these facts of Ludwig's case of which I have true knowledge yet desisted from the fulfilment of that vow, it is not beyond possibility that these intentions made and unmade could so confound my mind that it is sending me obscure messages of guilt. Each of these hypotheses is not beyond possibility.

So ended my attempt to reason with myself. So ended too my daily scribblings. From that day forward events followed one another in quick succession. I spent two more sleepless nights during which I rose and walked about the streets in search of the castle which, although my reason told me otherwise, I knew was no dream. I did not find it. However, I did find the same old woman I had seen in rags huddled against the doorway of St Stephen's. Past midnight on the last night it was. I approached her and kneeling down spoke softly in her ear:

'Old woman, do you at least remember a chariot drawn by white horses?'

Her face was ugly beyond description like a piece of meat in the process of decay.

'Speak not of abominations,' she said, 'lest they consume you. The man in black waits for you beneath the veil of illusion. Life is over – do you know it not?'

The third morning I went for the last time to the hospital

where with the support of Skendling I formally took extended leave on grounds of overwork. I resolved to return home and begin work on the papers which had lain in the drawer untouched for so long. On arrival my wife greeted me at the door filled with endless questions about what I was doing and why. I had no words to offer her. I did not know myself. So I lied. I told her I was unwell – a nervous disorder, I said – developed as a result of overwork – that I needed time alone to recover. She was, I could see, beside herself with worry and frustration. She wanted only to be of help to me yet I could not make her privy to what was in truth happening. A row ensued. Her eyes flooded with fear and tears of frustration. I longed to reach out and comfort her yet could do nothing. I entered my study and closed the door. At dinner she informed me she had written to her brother near Nydharding and would be travelling on the morrow to pass a fortnight with him. I knew she wanted more than anything in the world for me to plead with her not to go – to tell her how much I needed her care and her love. But I could speak no words. It was as though I had passed through a gate into a realm from which there was no return. Even my heart had grown cold.

The next morning I rose at four, set a fire in the study and started to sift through Ludwig's papers. My eyes burnt, so exhausted had I become from weeks without sleep. She rose at five and departed on the dawn coach. As I helped her into the carriage she reached out to me, laying her perfect hand to my cheek. She held it there for almost a minute while gazing into my haggard face – a face once plump and ruddy but now grown cadaverously lean. I was not to see her again.

On returning home I could feel how weak my body had become. There was excruciating pain in my right heel – so much that I could hardly walk. My hands were trembling. I went immediately to my study and resumed my activities. An hour later the housekeeper announced that a gentleman had arrived at the door asking to speak with me. She said she had shown him into the morning room and asked him to wait while she enquired if it was convenient for me to receive him. She handed me his card: it read:

'Anton Schindler . . . ami de Beethoven.'

LACGESIS

> And oftentimes, to win us to our harm,
> The instruments of darkness tell us truths,
> Win us with honest trifles, to betray's
> In deepest consequence.

> Banquo in *Macbeth*, I.iii

I had not met Schindler since the first week following
Ludwig's death. I had heard reports of him since then of
course. I knew for instance that when Rochlitz refused to
write Ludwig's biography, Schindler had collected material
for a biography of his own. This was to take him many years
to accomplish for he moved to Budapest soon after the
'Master's' death where his sister, a singer, lived. There he
evidently worked as municipal director for several years
before moving on to Aachen as conductor of the cathedral.
The biography took him more than a dozen years to
complete. It was published two years ago here in Vienna –
1840.

This calling card which identified him as 'ami de
Beethoven' was not altogether a surprise. I had heard
rumours that Schindler had spent some time in Paris where
he had been handing out cards on which had been engraved
this message. It brought back memories of the self-imposed
proprietorial role Schindler had taken towards Ludwig, his
possessions and his public persona – and of the intense envy
that Schindler had displayed towards anyone for whom

Ludwig had shown the slightest affection. As part of my intention to leave behind completely the part of my life which involved me with Ludwig I had studiously avoided reading Schindler's biography; however, two colleagues at the hospital had informed me that it did not reflect favourably on my handling of Ludwig's final illness. Because Schindler was not a man whom I held in high esteem, I had made no attempt to maintain connections with him. Except for once when we passed in the street some eight or ten years previously and greeted each other silently yet most formally, I had not laid eyes on him since Ludwig's funeral.

I asked the housekeeper to show him into the study and rose from my desk to greet him. My limbs were shaky, due to my physical state. He wasted no time in taking my hand. This he shook weakly, at the same time bowing respectfully in the excessively formal manner of a gentleman at the turn of the century. I had remembered him as a cool, rather pompous man with a pock-marked face. As he raised his head to look into my eyes I was shocked by the alterations that had taken place in his appearance. His eyes were rimmed with purple shadows. They had sunk deep within his skull. His face had a strange formless quality to it. There seemed to be a curious discrepancy between the upper and the lower part of it as though each belonged to a separate person. He had the same deathly pale flesh.

He smiled broadly yet in his eyes I could not detect the least sign of warmth. They registered instead a wild terror like those of a cornered animal – fearful, tortured, uncertain of its own fate yet unable to take any action to alter the course of events. My revulsion for him quickly turned to pity. I admonished myself for my coldness of heart in the face of a creature who had obviously suffered some torture – I suspected of the mind – since we had last encountered one another. I recovered my composure and spoke.

'Schindler, how good it is to see you. Do sit down,' I said, pulling up a chair.

'Good-day, Wawruch.'

'Would you care for coffee?'

'Thank you no, that is, I have only just breakfasted.'

He sat stiffly on the edge of the chair, brushed his legs as though banishing imaginary wrinkles from immaculately pressed trousers and then stuck the fingers of his left hand beneath the lapel of his coat in a gesture I had seen him carry out a hundred times those many years before.

'You are perhaps wondering why I have called, Dr Wawruch. I know that we have not always been, shall we say, on the very best of terms.' He raised his hollow eyes to look into mine.

I said nothing.

'It is concerning the Master,' he continued. 'You may not approve altogether of what I have done, Dr Wawruch, and what I have written, but there are those who would deface the Master's good name and it is I believe essential that we who knew him, regardless of whatever personal differences we may have had from time to time, band together to protect it.'

'I do not know of what you speak, Schindler. I have myself left far behind my involvement with Herr Beethoven. Those days,' I lied, 'are part of my past, not of my future.'

His face brightened. 'That is good, Dr Wawruch. I have of course read the brief report you wrote about the Master's final illness. It was, if I may say so, wisely written. Not on any account would it be prudent to say more than the absolute minimum about the intimate details of the Master's life. Would you not agree, sir?'

'Herr Schindler, it has always been my belief that one should tell the truth as clearly and simply as possible whether that truth be sparse or full. That is all I attempted

379

to do. At the time the medical record to which you refer was written I told as much as I knew to be true. How could I have spoken of that which even I myself did not comprehend?'

He looked at me strangely, searching my face for a meaning that might have been concealed. What he did not realise is that I had no desire to conceal a thing. Yet there were a thousand unanswered questions in my mind – questions upon which, without the answers, I could write nothing of any sense to anyone.

'Then,' he continued, 'am I to assume you can give me your assurance that you do not intend finally to publish further in the area of the Master's illness or other events of which you yourself may have knowledge regarding his life, the causes of his death . . . and regarding his music? For music after all was his life. Was it not, Dr Wawruch?'

I did not reply. I found Schindler's tone so objectionable that I could not find the words to reply.

He continued. 'Music is a useful tool. Would you not agree? The Master's music was, as I am sure you know, not his own but of far greater origins. He was, one might say, little more than a pawn in the hands of the great ones.'

Much taken aback by Schindler's words, I was about to counter them when he continued. 'By saying so, I do not by any means intend to challenge the Master's talents – only to bring them into clear perspective. The sadness, my dear Wawruch, lies in the way the Master's life, and your most considerable medical skills, were wasted by a refusal to acknowledge *their* supremacy. Had he done so he would surely have lived to write far greater works – works which in the mathematics of their musical form would have been able to, shall we say, enthral the men who heard them for their highest good. The Master's tragedy was in his wilfulness, one could say arrogance, and commitment to a lower value.

He chose to fight them and in so doing poisoned his own body. Would you, yourself, not call it that?'

I could hardly believe the words I heard him speak. Again I remained silent.

'Pity,' Schindler said. 'The Master still might have been alive today. Tell me, my good doctor, just how much of this did he impart to you in those final weeks? How much did you commit to paper? There are those of us, you understand, who needs must know.'

Despite the weakness in my body and the sympathy I felt for this gaunt and wasted man obsessed with protecting his long-dead companion from some ill-imagined misfortune, I could feel my face redden. Anger leapt into my voice.

'Damn it Schindler, what are you talking about? I do not have time to waste construing your riddles. I cannot, I will not, give assurances of such a nature to you or any man. So long as I live and breathe I will continue to do what I believe is right. I owe you nothing. If any debt is to be paid, be it only to Ludwig himself who looked to me for salvation of his body and whom I failed to heal. My skills were not adequate for the task; neither, sir, was I enough of a man to meet my patient – my friend – fully in the worlds which he himself inhabited. Is it not time that you left well enough alone? Is it not time for you to forsake this futile attempt to create a public face for a man far greater than any pastiche such as you could manufacture?'

Foolishly, I picked up a stack of papers as yet untouched by my morning's attempt at order and shook them, spreading dust everywhere.

Schindler's eyes flashed with an energy that had until then been completely missing from his countenance. It was as though my words or actions had set off a chemical reaction that transformed not only his look but his whole demeanour. His eyes gave off a cold radiance which was directed towards the pile of papers, now dust-free, all but one of which I still held in my right hand. He dusted off what had until that moment been immaculate trousers then slowly and with great concentration bent over to retrieve one sheet of paper that had fallen on the floor. Studying it carefully without, I perceived, appearing to do so, he returned it to my hand. I remained trembling with shock at the unexpected nature of my reaction. 'Ah no, Herr Doctor,' said Schindler. 'There are secrets which need to be kept for they are dangerous to the common man. It is necessary to suit what is said to the character, temperament and prejudices of the greater number; what one reveals to some will revolt others and alienate for ever spirits less bold and consciences more easily alarmed. I have, Dr Wawruch, only withheld that which by necessity demanded concealing – and for the good of all people. I stand by my right and by my conscience.'

He paused, searching my face for some response. I listened in shocked silence. He continued.

'From the Jesuits I have learned a great deal, Dr Wawruch, about men and how to alter their minds. Weishaupt, our great visionary, admired above all else the Jesuit practice of dispersing men all over the globe under one head – each and every one seeking the same goal. Although our goals – that is the goals of the illumined men, of which Ludwig as you may have guessed was one – although he did his best at times to deny it – our goals are diametrically opposed to theirs. Nevertheless, of their methods we have made good use. They, like we, insist on the total abandonment of individual will and judgement in service of the cause. We are careful to enlist our members by subtle methods for, you see, not every man is able to grasp the meaning of the cause. We must, I am sure you understand, then practise a certain subtle yet completely harmless deception and for some time at least lead them to a goal which to them remains unknown.'

Schindler's words recalled the endless discussions that had taken place in Ludwig's chamber fifteen years ago. He spoke with the same imperious tone I had often detected in the voices of the men who took part in them, as though he had to be particularly patient in explaining something of importance to those whose capacity for understanding was so limited that it was irritating to have to do so. I did not respond. He scraped the heel of his left foot against the carpet twice, brushed his trouser leg once again and stood up, drawing himself up to his full height. I felt suddenly exhausted and somewhat dizzy. I reached back to support myself on the desk behind me.

'Forgive me Dr Wawruch,' he said with an equanimity so perfect it made my own behaviour appear intolerable, 'I see that I have spoken out of turn. You are of course a man of science and as such must be allowed the freedom of whatever investigations you wish to carry out either now or in the future. I am, I assure you, entirely sympathetic to your cause.' He paused, glanced around the room as though recording indelibly everything that he could see. Then he continued, 'May I say however that I fear there are men at large not so understanding as myself – men who would ensure through whatever means fell to their disposal that you do not meddle in affairs which should by all that is reasonable be of no concern to you.' He turned as if to leave, and then turned back.

'Quite right, Dr Wawruch. Quite right. I trust your wife is well? Such a fine woman. It is a pity that the Master was never fortunate enough to experience the bonds of matrimony with a woman of noble character. You do recall the sister-in-law, don't you?'

He looked searchingly into my eyes as though expecting some reply. I said nothing.

'Of course you do not know, how could you since as you say

you have had nothing to do with the Master's affairs for near a score of years. She lives still. What was it the Master called her . . . Ah yes, "Queen of the Night" was it not? Herr Professor Wawruch, how true it is that the wicked live on to exact their pound of flesh while good men like yourself do so very often die in their prime. Curious, would you not say? Do give my best regards to Frau Wawruch . . . a fine woman, yes indeed.'

He turned and was gone so quickly that it was as though he had never been there at all. I walked to the window to assure myself that he, unlike the black stranger, was of this world and not some other. I found to my surprise that he had paused at the bottom of the steps to speak to the housekeeper. I could not make out his words but it did seem for a moment as though he had passed her a small package of sorts – crossing her palm with silver, I supposed, to show his appreciation for having been admitted on a morning when I had left strict instructions not to be disturbed. Then he disappeared.

As I turned to take up my work again, I recalled the whispered words about Johanna – the wicked Johanna. Of her too I had heard little since Ludwig's death – only that she had continued to take many lovers, that her son Karl, now himself middle-aged, had returned to Vienna after resigning his commission and had lived for a time with his wife and the unholy mother in a section of the city which was not altogether salubrious. The last I heard, the mother now lived alone with her bastard daughter. Even her son had chosen to divorce himself from her wayward life.

Brushing aside Schindler's visit and my musings about the infamous Queen of the Night, I sat down to resume my work on the papers. At half-past three the housekeeper entered the room and asked if I would prefer to take dinner at my desk so as not to disturb too much the course of my studies. I thanked her for her consideration. A few minutes later it was served – a thick beef soup, some freshly baked bread and sweetmeats. Then she left the house. I had no desire for food of any kind. So distorted had my appetite become that even what should have been a delicious soup seem tainted as it touched my lips. I forced myself to eat half of what lay in front of me since I knew I had much work ahead of me and needed strength. I found I had difficulty concentrating, not because my mind was unclear but because my vision had by a twist of fate become blurred, rendering me unable to follow words upon the page. By dusk I had begun to feel very ill indeed. The symptoms however were nothing like those I had experienced since the hauntings had begun – headache, fever, sleeplessness and all the rest. There was a twitching in the muscles on my right side, my stomach felt decidedly upset – I reasoned that this was due to my having eaten more than I had been accustomed to in recent days – and there was a strange metallic taste in my mouth. I wiped my brow which by now was dripping wet, rose from my desk and took to my bed without so much as tidying the papers. There I slept with a deathly weight on my body. My mind was plagued with dreams – dreams which as swiftly as they appeared gave way to other dreams, where faces floated before my eyes: that of my wife and of the hideous Johanna dissolving into one another.

I did not rise from my bed until past dawn. My limbs were trembling a little but my vision had been restored. I descended and entered my study once again to find the desk exactly as I had left it – covered with Ludwig's papers and the half-eaten meal. I smiled as I remembered how many half-eaten meals I had cleared from Ludwig's chambers before his death when there was no one else to do it for him.

At half-past ten the housekeeper knocked at the door

requesting the tray. She returned half an hour later with coffee and bread, smoked fish and a little cheese. I could not bring myself to partake of the food despite my arguing with myself that I should do so. But I drank heartily of the strong black coffee. I was troubled by the strange metallic taste it left in my mouth – the same taste I had experienced in the night. My work did not continue until dinner as it had the day before, for the curious aberrations in my vision had again begun making it impossible for me to read properly. I rose, aware of my actions in a strangely detached way, and gathered all the papers save a small handful. I locked them in the desk before picking up the rest and staggering upstairs to the bedroom. The housekeeper, not finding me at my desk, knocked on the bedroom door at about five enquiring if I was ready for my meal. I had been lying in bed trying against all hope to keep the right side of my body from twitching. Through the door I told her that I was feeling rather poorly and asked if she would be kind enough only to make me some strong tea before she left.

I drank the tea that she prepared. It did not alleviate the cramping in my stomach as I had hoped. Nor did it clear the metallic taste. Near dawn I began to be afraid. I had retained enough of my reason to know that I was becoming very ill and needed treatment. Yet there was no wife to turn to, no one I could trust to seek it out for me. I rose with great difficulty as pain now permeated the entire right side of my body and then I dressed. Slowly, with the same pain-stakingly accurate movements I had often witnessed in patients who are very old, I picked up the papers I had taken up to bed with me and, carrying them with me, descended the stairs to the street. With great difficulty I raised my hand to hail a passing cab. I knew it was early, yet reasoned I could reach the hospital in time to catch Skendling before he began his rounds and request him at the very least to make some rudimentary diagnosis. However, my calculations were more than an hour and a half awry.

I sat myself with as much decorum as I could manage in the anteroom just outside the office of the registrar, since I knew that no one would be using it until past nine, and I waited. My eyes continued to trouble me. It was as though blurred vertical lines had been drawn across my field of vision, although the twitching and pain had subsided considerably. I dozed briefly, then was awakened by the sound of two men talking in the registrar's office. Their voices seemed familiar yet I could not be sure if I was really hearing them or only imagining their words:

'. . . I am appealing to you for help . . . he should not be left at large . . . deeply concerned . . . dangerously imaginative . . . supervision . . . yes we knew each other before the Master's death . . . it was two days ago I saw him last. . . .'

I pulled up sharply, shaking the fuzziness from my head. The voice was Schindler's, I was sure of it. And the other? That was too low to tell until:

'. . .very good, Professor Skendling . . . I knew you would want to be made aware of the gravity. . . '

I stood up and, knowing what the hunted animal must feel, stumbled into the hall. I had to get away from the sound of those voices. As I staggered down the steps from the hospital the registrar himself was coming up. His face revealed the shock he felt at being confronted with a man in my state.

'Professor Wawruch, are you not well?' He reached out his hand to take mine.

Still clutching Ludwig's papers to my chest, I darted past him like a weasel. With a strength that belied my poisoned state, for by now I was sure this was what it was that had so affected my body and my vision, I shouted for a passing cab and gave the driver my address.

My house was no more than twelve minutes from the hospital by carriage – or close enough that on a good day in times past I used to walk there. We left the hospital without delay – yet as we were passing through Graben the carriage was brought to a standstill. In the air I detected the scent of smoke. Fear leapt within my breast. I got down from the carriage and, supported by some strength beyond my own, made my way through the crowd. I knew in my heart already what I would find. As I turned the final corner and entered the square in which my house stood, the air had grown hot. It took no more than a few moments to confirm my wildest fears. The house ablaze across the square was my own. Before it stood a hundred people, some of them engaged in passing tubs of water from hand to hand in an attempt to quench flames already leaping from every window. Others stood aimlessly as people often do when fascinated by the destruction they witness before them. I stopped, and leaned against the railing of the building next to me to gather my strength. It was then I saw him, only from behind of course, yet I was certain it was he. How can one mistake a body of such height – this man of darkness whom I had seen but once before? He turned as though sensing my eyes upon him. I could just make out the same twisted smile pass over lips still infinitely thin.

Stuffing the papers I carried in my hand beneath the coat I wore I turned and ran down a passageway into a courtyard. It in turn gave way to a garden beyond which I could see a field. I had to escape. But to where? And how? How now could I commit to paper any of the little I did know about Ludwig and our nights together? How was it possible for me to fulfil a promise I hardly understood when even the information I needed to begin the task had now been almost completely destroyed? Within the garden where I found myself stood a strange round fountain with a great twisted figure of a goat in its centre, from whose horns poured forth great volumes of water. I could not tell if the stone animal was indeed itself twisted or if my sight of it made it so. But the animal was most certainly huge and such an unexpected thing for anyone to set in the midst of a well-tended garden.

As I looked upon it I saw myself – Azazel the scapegoat dedicated to a god that he may pardon mankind – killed as a sin-offering so that his blood will wash clean the sanctuary and make sacred the tabernacle – Azazel whose gore placates the angry god, atoning for the uncleanliness of men – for their transgressions and their sins – Azazel whose very remains are so unclean they must be burnt outside the camp – Azazel, he who bears away all their faults unto a desert place.

I clutched the papers which remained in my possession to my chest. Above all else they must not be lost lest the blood of the sacrificed goat lose all meaning. I had to find a haven, a sanctuary, any small refuge wherein I could, in whatever time is left to me, commit to paper what little I knew – a place in which I could fulfil even the smallest part of my promise to Ludwig. But where? I knelt beneath the goat and drank the waters of its fountain, splashing them over my burning cheeks. Again, I looked up at the strange animal figure. If he is I and I am he, where would Azazel go to escape being thrown over the cliff to his death? Where indeed but into the darkest recesses of the night. There and only there might he hide away from such as Schindler – by the grace of the earth to which his body belongs, from such as Schindler and his likes? One place I knew where even Schindler would not dare to seek for me. I had to find Johanna.

After endless hours of search through twisted streets, I did. Here in her small stone house I have rested – here in the shadow of Ludwig's Queen of the Night. I mused on Schindler's cloying words and on the poison, wondering if I was not the first whom Schindler had singled out for such a fate. I remembered another housekeeper fifteen years before whose palm he had crossed with silver. Was this the secret Schindler feared I would expose? For which the *dark one* pursued me? And why had he set my life ablaze? Such waste. It was a secret I did not know.

This room is filled with the scent of summer basil. Here beneath Johanna's snow-white linen I lie while the slow poison extracts its toll. I have committed to paper all I yet have strength to tell. Just now my hand is trembling so I fear I can write no more today. There is a small window at my side. When I can draw myself high enough upon the pillows and when this blurring of my vision clears somewhat, I will, they tell me, be able to look upon a willow of magnificent stature. But this morning the sun tosses a light upon the counterpane so fierce that I shall have to wait a while.

Third Movement

GRACE
arioso dolente

KYRIE

> That while it may be that some operators of UFO
> are normally the paraphysical denizens of a planet
> other than Earth, there is no logical need for this to
> be so. For, if the materiality of UFO is para-
> physical (and consequently normally invisible),
> UFOs could more plausibly be creations of an
> invisible world coincident with the space of our
> physical Earth planet than creations in the para-
> physical realms of any other physical planet in the
> solar system. . . .

> Air Marshal Sir Victor Goddard
> Anthony Roberts *The Dark Gods*

When I finished reading Wawruch's manuscript I felt still
inside – something I had not been for a long time.
Wawruch's tale had absorbed me completely – drawn me
into it the way a haunting melody gets hold of you and won't
let go. It was as though I had lived it myself. I was not alone
in having been haunted by Ludwig, then. I was not the only
one whose life had been ripped to pieces, whose cover had
been blown by coming in contact with – how was it
Wawruch put it – 'Ludwig the living and Ludwig the dead'.

Reading the manuscript had inexorably bound me to
Wawruch. Yet there could not be two men more different: in
time, in place, in personality. Of that I was sure. I
understood his cowardice, of course – his wanting to forget –
to lead some kind of ordinary life. It was *my* cowardice. No

wonder I had joined SF, doesn't every coward have to prove he is brave? I knew Wawruch's anger too – at a God in which he professed not to believe. Yet the contrasts between us seemed immense. Wawruch was a man who had tried to be true to himself and was aware of his own failings. I was a man who for ten years had run from mine. He had lived by the rules he knew – rules of compassion and honour. Being touched by his words made me all too conscious of how little I was living my own.

After Ludwig's death Wawruch had been forced to wrestle with the same kind of issues I had been wrestling with ever since Mirabehn slipped the faded red package into my hands. Yet he had done it with a courage I had never mustered despite my decorations. When I left SF I arrogantly believed I could put some kind of a bandage over the wound of betrayal I felt and ignore the festering anger. Such are the tales that tough guys tell themselves. Wawruch had the guts to stick around when things got rough. As for me, when things get hot Michael splits – from SF, from America, from Paris, from Fiona. I had always told myself I was being clever – that whatever happened I had an ace in the hole. Now I saw that my only ace in the hole had been to quit.

I got up from my chair. My body had gone stiff the way it does when, after burning yourself out for days on end, you are finally allowed to rest. It was one of those summer evenings in London when the sky stays light until after ten o'clock. I thought about going out – about walking in Regent's Park to get away from this flat, this room, this evening alone. I rejected the idea and lay down on the lumpy sofa with my hands beneath my head. I was just about as sick of running as you can get. I guess I had Wawruch to thank for that, too.

When I quit the SF and went to Paris to work as a foreign correspondent I had dumped my warrior's dreams of

MICHAEL

banishing tyranny and fighting for freedom. It was too
damned risky when you are one small flea pitted against an
army of hairy dogs. But it was more than the risk that made
me run. I also had an awful sense of impotence – that
nothing I could do could make a damned bit of difference.
My pride had gone and so had my hope and the fun. Life
was no longer a game of defying the odds and getting
through. Even the pranks were finished. Remembering the
pranks made me smile. I was always in trouble with the
brass hats. Like the time I printed up the alligator warning.

It was during an ORE – Operational Readiness Exercise
– two weeks previous that I got the idea. Realism lay at the
core of SF training. Unlike the conventional army the
training scenarios which were set up for you – and which I
then set up myself for my men – often involved live fire –
.50-calibre heavy machine guns, hand grenades, C-4 plastic
explosives and 60mm mortar – on carefully primed targets
like old missiles, tents, helicopters and anything else we
could scrape together; or secret mock missions involving the
planting of SADM – Special Atomic Demolitions
Munitions, tactical nuclear weapons with low yield useful
for taking out a hydroelectric plant or causing one little
Chernobyl –kind of mini-atomic bombs that fit neatly into a
briefcase. The realism of our exercises invariably offended
nit-picking generals in the regular army, who were not all
that happy about our blowing up army property although
there was not a lot they could do about it. That was back
when I had a fun game to play and still loved playing games.
That was in the Canal zone while I was 'in between'
commands. Such a funny phrase – in between. In the SF
when you are not out there leading A Teams they keep you
busy running training programmes or they send you to
school. That is how I collected two Master's degrees – all to
keep you out of trouble. Occasionally we would get involved

in large-scale exercises which involved the regular army. Then live ammunition was not on. As a result they were never so interesting or fun. That was why I introduced the alligators.

I had been asked to lead a large-scale training operation which involved parachuting into a low-lying swampy basin in Central America. There a few of my SF detachments were to confront a full brigade of regular soldiers. I knew the operation was a pushover so I decided to add a bit of spice to the exercise. I had several hundred flyers printed up. The afternoon before the exercise began I got them dropped from the air into the soldiers' camps. They said: 'Warning all personnel: the area in which you will be carrying out manoeuvres is believed to be infested with 6,000 of a rare breed of Guatemalan alligator. These animals have migrated south due to climatic alterations. All are man-eaters and known to attack without warning. These animals have no natural predators. Their only fear is of fire. It is therefore recommended that fires be lit immediately upon landing throughout the area. Under no circumstances should any personnel sleep on the ground. . . .' I finished off the handbill with the words, 'signed CINCSOUTH' – Commander-in-Chief Southern Command. By the time they were in the hands of the soldiers anything said to contradict the notice by officers with enough grey matter to figure out it was a hoax just didn't get through. Next day it was a beautiful sight to see – the whole countryside sparkled with hundreds of boy scout fires to keep the beasts at bay.

When I left the *New York Post* for Paris I tried to pick up the pieces of my life by playing a new game – the game of the investigative reporter going in where angels fear to tread to bring truth to a world which I sure was eager to hear it. I had been appointed 'energy correspondent' for a chain of American newspapers. I thought that sounded OK at first –

writing about oil and nuclear power. But every story they asked me to investigate had two things wrong with it – one, it was all about economics, and two, it was dull as hell.

The work was easy. And since I had time on my hands, I decided to dig deeper into some of the stuff I was researching. Before long I was quite clear that economics was not the dull subject I had thought. I found it far closer to being the power that ruled the world, and almost always in a highly deceptive way so the stories that came through the media written by people like me in magazines and newspapers seldom told a straight tale. Take the oil industry. The more I learned about it, the more I realised how far away the truth was from the official line. The so-called oil crisis following the Yom Kippur war I discovered had not been caused by a problem with the Arabs as the media reported but by the fact that sharp international bankers who controlled transport ships bought up Middle East oil for \$15 billion and then held on to it. So by 1974 oil – with a well-head cost of a mere 25 cents for a 42-gallon barrel – had gone up to \$62 billion, and by 1975 to \$90 billion. This meant that by 1980 the world was paying \$300 billion for the same quantity of oil bought at the same well-head cost. Great story, I figured it needed to be told at home. I could see the headlines: 'Oil Crisis – What Oil Crisis? Were We Conned?' I went to the bureau chief. He didn't want to know. I even telephoned New York, over his head. Nobody wanted to know.

So I turned my attention to the past. I started to read American history – but from an economic point of view. I became fascinated by how superb a tool war is for making money – provided of course you are not one of the poor bastards who has to fight it. The men who bankrolled the American Civil War for instance were untroubled by any *inconvenient* allegiances towards either side. They dealt themselves the perfect hand for inaugurating the new covert game of global economics that is still being played in the Middle East, in Africa, in Eastern Europe, and they ended up taking the pot. It was in the process of my digging into America's past that I learned about the Federal Reserve.

All of this led to my 'Politics of Greed' piece – another story nobody wanted to print. So what did I do? I did a runner just like I always do – picked up one of those aluminium ladders lying on a floor, threw it out the window and escaped into the night. Only this time, instead of only turning my back on SF, I turned my back on the whole of life. I guess the game I had chosen of trying to put things into words had got too tough. So instead of persevering, I slapped another bandage over the festering wound and walked away mumbling, 'If the world doesn't want to know, to hell with the world. I'll just try to keep my nose clean.'

I went to Britain and started writing about health. Maybe here I could forget, maybe here I could keep out of trouble. And so I did – for five years – during which time I drank too much, worked too hard and avoided thinking about the past. That is, until I met Mirabehn and everything changed. Now here I sat mixed up in the life of Ludwig – a man who died a hundred and fifty years ago and it would seem had also found himself in the midst of a cover-up involving the secret agendas of absurdly arrogant men whose only principle was that the end – *their* end – justified the means. For some crazy reason Mirabehn, Ludwig, Wawruch, the manuscript – whatever was going on – had ripped the protective bandage from my wound. The abscess had begun to drain, and it may have smelt bad but for the first time since I gazed out over those endless fields of golden wheat as a kid I felt still inside.

Here in this chaotic room full of dust and papers I was stuck –stuck with Ludwig, with the demands of a sick old woman, with men in black, hallucinations in the bathroom, strange physical symptoms – in some kind of weird obsession I couldn't shake. I laughed out loud at the thought that this time maybe Michael had got himself into something he couldn't get out of – something that had to be lived. After all, the haunting and sickness seemed to follow me wherever I went. It was a cruel laugh – the kind of laugh you laugh when you're watching a movie in which the self-important hot-shot slips on a banana peel.

I sat up, stretched my arms and swung my legs over the side of the sofa. My head felt heavy. I looked around me. There were three plants in the room – gifts from Fiona. All three were dying. They had been given no water for weeks. I got up, went to the kitchen and filled a milk bottle then returned to water them. I wondered if they would live. I drew back the curtain and peered into the yard. There was nothing to see except the wrought-iron stairs leading up to the street and a patch of sky above, still light. I wondered if I should go out and walk in the air, out of this cluttered flat, away from the papers and the past. The thought made me smile – Michael on the run again. If you make a mess just say 'to hell with it' and leave. If you get angry or frightened, walk out. Everything is bound to be OK so long as you just keep moving.

I didn't want to do it any more. I was just too tired. I turned round. Mirabehn's postcard lay on the desk. I picked it up. On the front was a pair of hands clasped together – a painting of some sort, probably the detail from a painting. The hands were small. The nails were long but they looked as though they had just been manicured. I turned it over and read, 'BEETHOVEN'S HANDS – Oil sketch by J. Danhauser, Beethoven-Haus, Bonn – *This sketch dates from 28 March 1827, two days after Beethoven's death. Between his hands he holds a cross.*' I read her words again, '. . . two men in black. They know about the manuscripts. Be careful, Michael.

There are more papers but they are not in my possession. . . . I think there was a child. Does the name Bourdelle mean anything to you? . . . your life may be in danger. . . .'

I laid the postcard down again. I knew I could not go out. This dusty room filled with papers and chaos was of my own making. I had no idea what had happened to me since I met Mirabehn but I knew that I was up to my neck in something which, whatever else happened *this* time, I was going to stick out. This time I would use everything in my power to see things through to the end and to get to the bottom of all this – for *my* sake – for the sake of Wawruch, a dead man I never knew – most of all for the sake of Ludwig. Somewhere, some time, I guess I had known all along, I would have to stop running. Now was as good a time as any.

Suddenly I was overcome by deep fatigue. I went into the bathroom to wash my face and looked in the mirror. The man staring back at me had grown thin. His skin was a yellowish grey, his eyes rimmed in brown. I looked away. I could not deal with him now. I had to get back to Vienna – to Mirabehn. I had to know if she was all right and to find out where Ludwig planned to lead me next. I picked up the telephone, called the airport and made a reservation on the eight o'clock plane next morning. Then I rummaged through a pile of stuff under the window. I knew what I was looking for. I was looking for him – for Ludwig – at least his music, for that was all I had of his that I could be sure was *real*. I found a copy of the String Quartet 132 in A minor.

I slipped it into the Walkman and put the earphones on. The A Minor Quartet. I smiled. What else could it have been? The most pessimistic of all Ludwig's works – the quartet he wrote in the voluptuous tritone-infested Lydian mode – almost without the leading notes that might give any sense of resolution. Stone deaf and utterly alone, exhausted and defeated, he had written it at the time of a serious illness. I lay down on the sofa to listen. I wanted something from it. I *needed* something – courage perhaps or the promise that one day all this would come to an end. Maybe I only wanted to know I didn't have to run any more.

The first movement began – a voluptuous record of yearning and pain which I found I could hardly bear: his yearning, my yearning, the yearning of man and woman alone in a world where they feel utterly powerless. Stark, cold, crystalline notes spoke of the empty spaces between the atoms we believe make up our universe, of a purity beyond time and space, of that zero point out of which all form is created. Then it ended as only Ludwig could have made it end with a startling call like a trumpet's to an unearthly realm. The second movement begins telling of a weariness that is indescribable: a weariness not of the body but of the soul – a soul wandering for ever in a universe without meaning. Then a violin soars high, pouring forth a shower of arbitrary joy so pure it has no connection with anything that has come before or anything that can come after. This abstract joy is repeated again and again until gradually it swells into a slow movement whose generosity of spirit and thanksgiving, whose celebration only for the sake of itself become the most beautiful prayer I have ever heard – to be followed by a movement that tells of a strange wistful bravery where the very courage of which it speaks gives vent to the insufferable anguish it was created to conceal. The forsaken and bleak little processional march which follows strides forth towards no victory. It is a brave yet forlorn gesture. Then a terrifying moment of truth and once again surrender to dark conflict before touching hope again, continually changing, destroying and creating universes in ways that no man can bear and still maintain his sanity. An echo from the previous prayer returns, its theme grows faster and stronger until, with the last presto, victory is gained, a child is born: yet out of such weariness and such anguish there is no triumph – only a momentary feeling of relief and a stunned uncertainty that anything can ever be won.

As the notes entered my ears they were carried to every cell of my body, creating an ocean of sound which moved through me dissolving every boundary – my flesh, my bones, my blood, my thoughts, my feelings. I knew that my body no longer existed – at least not in any form I had known before. It had been subsumed in the energy that is Ludwig – the power that is life – broken open, scattered and being formed and reformed into different contours and textures the way a caterpillar inside a chrysalis turns into a mass of white jelly then begins to reshape itself, or the way the sea breaking against sand changes the shore – yet deeper, wilder, darker. For I *was* the sea of sound. I did not ride it, it rode me. Waves of fear, then joy, then bleakness broke over me, washed through me, carried me with them in my formless state wherever they wished. Me. What me? There was no me. I opened my eyes to look at the room in a desperate bid to find something to hold on to only to find that the room too had become part of the sea's movement. Books on the table no longer looked solid. They had become skeletons of reality. It was as though now I could see only the spaces between atoms – as though I were living in an empty world of horror where there are no structures, no rules, nothing to fight against or for, nothing to hold on to because there is no separation between you and what lies beyond you. For you too are made of nothing but spaces between atoms. Fear gripped me – a fear such as I had never dreamed of – a fear way beyond the fear of having a gun to your head or the threat of being wiped out because you know too much. It was a fear that nothingness is all that there is – that I was it or it was me or we were one. I could not bear such emptiness.

My heart was pounding. I wanted to make a joke of it all. I started to laugh. The room was undulating all round me. But the music continued. Its oceanic power echoed in my body, in the room, even though I could no longer hear it. I started to panic then got hold of myself. I wanted to cry out for help – to run anywhere – but there was nowhere to run, nothing to hold on to. Everything around me had become part of the motion. I staggered to the window. The sky had grown dark. The yard was a mass of shadows. Like the books and the table, the sofa and the dying plants, they too were only skeletons – empty spaces in constant motion. I crouched down on my knees pulling my head tight into my animal body like a hedgehog rolled up in a ball on the earth to protect itself from a dog drawn to its lair by the smell of fresh meat. But there was no protection because the threat was not coming from *outside* so it did no good to hunch my back against it. There *was* no outside – the outer and inner had become one.

It was not as though I were afraid of death. I would have welcomed death. It was dissolution I was fighting – the knowing that I was to be taken – taken far away to be made part of something infinite, something in which every vestige of my personal existence would be dissolved away. I got up and stood leaning against the desk. My body felt as though I were drunk or drugged yet my mind had no fuzziness in it – only an awful, cold clarity. This infinite space, this great ocean in which I floated, seemed neither good nor evil. Yet it was something so vast, so dangerous, so uncontrollable that human beings were not meant to look upon it, to touch it and to live. Yet despite the horror it held a strange and infinitely seductive power over me, like the voice of a siren luring me into the vastness of her womb, offering me everything and nothing. Should I go? Just enough of my mind remained to ask the question. Should I go? In a world where there is nothing, in which I had no existence, in which every belief I had chosen to honour had turned out to be empty, was there any reason to resist? Maybe I was being offered salvation – that final resolution – an end to struggle, a finish to battling with powers too great for man ever to defeat? Or was the lure of this ocean nothing more than a delicious yet terrifying drug designed to carry me yet further down the path of self-deception?

Waves of energy crashed over me, washed through me. The room continued to swell and move until it seemed as though the very walls would entangle me within the molecules of their own substance, within the flow of their own movement. I stood perfectly still in the hope that my stillness would calm the energy flowing through my body – through the room – through the universe. But there was nothing to hold on to. I turned my head slightly to one side in an attempt to look at what was taking place around me from a distance – to keep from being part of it. This only made things worse. I closed my eyes but so much dizziness broke over me that I feared I could no longer stand. I opened them again. The room continued to move, the books and papers, the dying plants – they seemed to be crying out in anguish for one last possibility to live, but why? Maybe for the same reason I wanted to go on living: not because life had any purpose, not because there was anything for me to believe in or anything for me to do but because to live, it seemed, had been embedded in my nature – etched within my genes at time's beginning. A question arose within me: 'Is it possible to live for nothing?' For nothing, for no reason, no reason whatsoever, no end, no purpose, with no expectation and no promises, with nothing to run from or to – to live like the plants do who might or might not survive the drought imposed by neglect.

All this went through my mind but there were no words.

The words are only made up later – facsimiles which arrogantly pretend to describe what can never be described. Yet in the midst of a wordless arbitrary world it was words that saved me – words as completely uncharacteristic of me as any words I have ever heard, words arbitrarily chosen from all possibilities – *let there be love in my heart*. They came from nowhere yet I knew that I and I alone had chosen them from every possible choice – *let there be love in my heart, let there be love in my heart*, I repeated the phrase over and over again out loud, clinging to this arbitrary, self-created mantra. The words became a log afloat in the great ocean in which I was being tossed. I clung to them in the hopes that some day, somehow I would be washed ashore – *let there be love in my heart . . . let there be love in my heart . . . let there be . . .*

Slowly, almost imperceptibly the room began to grow quiet the way the sea does after a violent storm. The waves break then hesitate then break again until slowly, slowly they withdraw. . . . *let there be love in my heart . . . let there be love in my heart.* . . .

The doorbell rang. I heard it the way you hear an echo from a far-off mountain – so distorted you are not even sure it is a sound, for it could have been something that came from your own imagination. It rang again. I moved slowly, with great difficulty, across the room, through the entrance hall to the door. Again it rang. This time the sound was unbearably loud. I realised I was standing just beneath the bell. I switched on the light and opened the door. The halogen bulb outside was so strong that it lit up the face of the man who stood before me with an intensity that at that moment seemed unbearable. It was the face of Charles – yet different, or at least I saw him differently – a Charles I might find in a dream or nightmare – a Charles whose face had been made transparent so that every part of his being, all that is ordinarily concealed beneath the veil of pretension and the shell of personality, had been stripped away. I felt ashamed, as though I had intruded into someone's secret world. I did not want to intrude. I did not want to harm any living thing. Not any more – not the plants, not Charles, not even myself.

'Good evening,' he said in a proper English voice. 'I am sorry to intrude. I hope it is not too late but I thought you might like –'

I broke in. 'Come in. . . Charles, here, give me your coat.' I noticed that my own voice sounded strange – like someone pretending to be human.

I led him into the room in which the heavy breakers no longer crashed although softer waves continued still to lap over the papers, the sofa, the walls. I wondered if he would notice. He didn't seem to. I turned on the light.

'Have a seat,' I said, more thankful to see Charles at that moment than I had ever been to see another living person – to make contact with anything human with which I could align myself.

'Can I get you a drink?' I said. 'Some whisky?'

'I won't say no,' he said.

He looked at me and smiled, surprised by my uncharacteristic cordiality. I wondered just how much of me was visible – was he too able to see behind the veil?

I went to the kitchen, only to find there were no clean glasses. I returned to the room in which he stood and collected two dirty ones. I was surprised to see that Charles had sat down in the midst of this room in total chaos as though it were perfectly normal. I went back to the kitchen, turned on the faucet and went to work on the glasses. The hot water felt good on my hands. I took my time polishing them – two big cut-crystal glasses I had purchased on a whim on my way back from a trip to Dublin a couple of years before. At the time I had wondered if drinking good malt out of such glasses would make it taste even better. I had been delighted to find that it did.

I filled one glass half full – that was to be his. Into mine I poured just enough so it looked like a drink. I had no intention of taking anything. I checked the walls again. Even here in the kitchen they were still swelling gently. The words, what were the words . . . oh yes . . . *let there be love* . . . I returned to the room and handed Charles the glass filled with what I hoped was enough of the finest whisky to keep him with me for several hours. I had no idea what time it was. But I had a plane to catch in the morning and I knew that whatever happened I didn't want to be alone. I hoped he would become the driftwood to which I could cling until I floated back to a shore I could stand on.

'I came to see you,' he began, 'about that manuscript. Well, not so much about the manuscript as some of what's in it,' he said, taking a sip of his whisky. 'My God, that's good stuff,' he added.

I held mine in my hand without touching it. I wanted no drug, no whisky, nothing that would make me forget. This time I wanted to remember, to remember anything that would keep me in the human world with which Charles in all his innocence was to be my link.

'The manuscript?' I asked.

'Mmm,' he said, taking another sip of the whisky, 'It's this men-in-black thing,' he replied. 'How much do you know about it?'

'Not much,' I told him. 'Only what was in the manuscript. Tell me,' I said, pulling my chair closer.

Charles smiled and took another sip. 'I don't want to keep you up,' he said, 'we could talk tomorrow if you prefer.'

'Listen Charles,' I said, 'I am not at all sleepy. It would be great to hear what you know, I don't give a damn how late it gets.' He could not hide his pleasure at being asked to expound on something about which he considered himself an expert. And so he began his wild tales while I refilled his glass again and again and gave thanks for his presence – for anybody's presence.

Charles told me that the men-in-black phenomenon (which he called the MIB) had been reported over and over again in UFO literature although, he said, there is evidence that it may be much older. They are supposed to be agents of terror – part of an ultraterrestrial secret police who carry out the bidding of their extraterrestrial masters. These guys, he said, who are not really men at all – or at least Charles did not believe so – but facsimiles of men who are able to appear and disappear out of another dimension, come in two types: short, dark-skinned Orientals or tall pale Nordics. They are known to pursue, harass and threaten those who come too close to finding out the truth about UFOs. They always (or almost always) dress in black – in suits which are either so completely dishevelled they look as though they have been slept in for a week or clothes so immaculate they do not look real. 'Often the soles of their shoes,' he said, 'are not even worn. MIBs frequently drive around in cars – usually black – pretending to be members of some official group – the army, the police, something like that. They threaten, ask inane questions, lie, and on departing often say, "We shall see each other again."'

I couldn't believe I was sitting here listening to all of this. It was so far-fetched, so absurd. 'Really?' I said to Charles, 'that's fascinating, go on.'

Charles took another sip of his drink, obviously relieved to find that he had a sympathetic audience. Then he went on. 'Their behaviour is unpredictable. Sometimes they are able to pass right through the wall of a room while at others they cannot get in at all if one door is locked. MIBs are always making a nuisance of themselves one way or another

– ringing their victims at all hours of the day and night, disrupting the post, making threatening gestures and promises they usually don't carry out.'

'But that sounds ridiculous,' I said.

'It is,' he replied. 'Their behaviour often doesn't make sense. They will return again and again for a particular report which they believe you have in your possession and then once they have it in their possession they will walk away and leave it behind. Often, too, they disappear into thin air or darkness. You know, of course,' Charles continued, lowering his voice as though he was about to impart information that must be kept secret, 'most of the serious researchers – I mean people of the calibre of Jacques Vallée, John Keel and James McDonald, senior physicist at the Institute of Atmospheric Physics – even John Keel himself –have not only had MIB encounters but have been plagued by mysterious accidents and misfortunes as they carried out their studies.'

Charles paused, glanced about the room as though noticing for the first time the disarray, then looked back at me in a questioning way.

'I've been researching the background to that manuscript,' I said. 'Sorry about the mess, I guess it has kind of taken over my life.'

He nodded and took another sip of his drink. My explanation evidently satisfied him. Only once was I in Charles's own flat. The floor was covered with piles of what appeared to be old newspapers and journals. It was like the room of an old Armenian tailor I had known on Second Avenue in New York. Neither of them ever seemed to throw anything away. I wondered if I too would now be granted entrance into the club to which they belonged.

'Charles,' I said, 'where did you get all this stuff?'

'From books, there are books,' he said, rather defensively, 'although they are often hard to come by.'

'I see,' I said. 'And these people disappear?'

'Well, take Arnold Bender,' Charles said. 'He was continually plagued by odd accidents and troubles that took on more psychic proportions. His research had taken him closer and closer to what he believed was a real understanding of the flying saucer phenomenon. He had even written to a friend to say that all the missing pieces of the puzzle had come together and that he believed at last he had an explanation for them. No sooner had he posted the letter than he received a terrifying phone call from a MIB. Not long after one arrived on his doorstep, as he said himself, "slant eyed, dark skinned and with an aura of indescribable menace".'

Charles looked up as if to see whether he was pushing his luck. For the first time since his monologue began I found myself caught up in what he was saying. I recalled with a shudder the face of the man who had stood behind me in the line at Heathrow and whom I had seen again from Fiona's parents' window.

'That was in 1953. Later on Bender was visited by three of these emissaries, who told him that he had indeed cracked the code of the UFO phenomenon but that there were certain essential details he had left out – details so nasty that when they filled him in on them it was enough to make Bender very ill and to keep him that way for a long time. From that time on,' Charles said, 'Bender was subject to strange physical ailments – symptoms of mind-interference and psychic onslaughts as well as very bad headaches. So long as he stayed away from his researches they would abate. Every time he tried to go back to them they would return in force. That is why it was another ten years before he wrote his next book.' Charles paused, then lowering his voice continued, 'That book is totally different from the previous ones, Mike, full of vague stories of a psychic abduction to Antarctica. It did more to discredit the value of his previous research than any smear campaign could possibly have done.' Charles's words gripped me. I remembered another author who, although he had nothing to do with UFOs and their like (at least so far as I knew) was himself for fifteen years plagued by insufferable headaches every time he tried to finish the research on a particular project, although he was free enough of them to write two or three other books during the same period – Alexander Wheelock Thayer, Ludwig's biographer.

The room was silent. Again I wondered about the time. By now the walls were only walls. The books comforted me in their solidity. My body had returned to some semblance of normality. Yet the drink in my hand still remained untouched. I felt so grateful for Charles – weird old Charles – sitting in this room with me this night. His voice droned on. Whenever he paused I either added some more whisky to his glass or asked a question: 'But if the MIB are not men, then what are they?'

'No one knows for sure. They seem to come from somewhere beyond the third dimension – to be able to enter our world at certain times and in certain places when there is an interface in time and space established between their world and ours – maybe, most likely, where ley lines cross on the earth. Maybe they are nothing more than thought forms manufactured by alien intelligences or even the space age versions of fairies and trolls – who knows.' Charles looked up at me as though asking for my approval.

'Fascinating,' I said. All I could think of was 'gimme a break'. Yet in some funny way the wilder Charles's reports got the more reassured I was about myself – the more ordinary I began to feel. I wondered what time it was but didn't dare to look at my watch. It might make him think he was staying too late and leave me on my own again.

Charles rattled on and on. He could have been telling me about the price of carrots or reading the telephone book from beginning to end so long as he stayed there, so long as somebody stayed there and just kept speaking words – words which, because I could hear and make sense of them, made me feel I still belonged in the world of humanity.

During the hours that followed Charles must have told me a thousand things – building an outrageous version of the world based on the assumption (he *assured* me it was well proven fact) that he spoke the solemn truth – every word of it. He told me about Markabians – beings from our own galaxy he said who lived on gold and diamonds and who were the bureaucrats behind computer programs designed to control men's lives primarily through economic suppression. The Markabians he said could take on humanoid form. They tended to be tall and blond. They had come to the earth in search of yet more gold and more control. Their leader Xenu throughout the past two or three hundred years had chosen periodically to take over the body of various men – all of them leaders in the world. Each one had some kind of physical disability that made him crippled or at the very least caused him to limp badly.

(*Xenu – the name rang in my head – I had seen it or heard it before, but where?*) For the past fifty years, 200,000 of what one might call 'junior executives' from Markab had immigrated secretly to Earth (without, Charles added, 'Grand Council Approval') to help Xenu and his conspirators take over our planet. This, he said, they do by usurping the bodies of key 'insiders' in the world of industry, banking, high finance, politics and certain secret societies. Of course, Charles informed me, leaning forward again and speaking like a conspirator, these men don't know they have been taken over – they delude themselves into thinking they are in control of what they are doing.

'Markabians are easy to spot,' Charles said, 'by their lust for status and control and their insistence on enforcing conformity – all typical Markabian characteristics.'

'Right,' I said, not altogether without humour. 'I think I've known quite a few.'

'We all have. And they are superb record-keepers. It is they who have developed the control mechanisms of identity cards, secret files, computer data and paperwork to a fine art, using them to suppress the economy in an attempt to regulate and control human beings. Their overall purpose and goal, according to my informant, is supposed to be one-world domination and control. To this end they have infiltrated government, industry, churches, and organisations of numerous kinds – anything they think will serve their ends – always surreptitiously hiding their motives. They always work behind the scenes, keeping out of sight – enforcing conformity, controlling thought, suppressing the spiritual nature of man, inhibiting survival, reducing people's space and freedom, taking over free groups which they think might be a threat to their ends. They have nothing in common with humans in their thinking – no idea of loyalty or honesty or justice. In fact they will fight viciously between themselves (always in hidden ways, of course) for status and control. Most important of all,' Charles said finishing off his description of the Markabian mentality, 'for them, the end always justifies the means.'

His words made me laugh in a way that was not very pleasant. What he was saying I was sure was absurd but his description was pretty damned accurate of some of the men at the highest levels of government and industry that I had known.

Charles went on. Next he talked about another race of aliens whom he called the 'Greys'. They were supposed to be altogether different from the Markabians. ET-like characters, they came, he said, not from our galaxy but far beyond it. They had to travel light years to come to the earth.

'Of course you know all about the animal mutilations don't you? That is the work of the Greys,' he said.

I had to admit that I did not. Charles looked genuinely surprised but remained undaunted.

'Oh they happen all the time, cows killed, goats, horses, geese – as though they have been cut open with the skills of a master surgeon although only one or two parts, say half a kidney or a heart, has been taken. In each case all of the blood is drained from the body. UFO crews have killed a lot of animals – whole flocks of sheep in Bolivia, for instance. In America there is even a case (well documented, Mike, I assure you) where a UFO chased an ambulance because it was full of bottle on bottle of human blood.'

'What happened?' I asked.

'It didn't take it,' Charles replied, 'because a lot of other cars arrived on the scene.'

I began to laugh, I guess at the fact that I was sitting there finding comfort in something as horrific as tales of animal mutilation. Assuming that I was laughing at the way the UFO had been foiled Charles joined in. I poured some more whisky.

'You know, Mike, all government agencies and media organisations have been given orders to suppress every mention of UFOs,' he said. I was silent.

'There is also a lot of disinformation put out by governments themselves like Dr Edward Condon's report paid for by US government funds. It was designed entirely to discredit the reality of UFOs. You know the kind of thing: mix the truth with a lot of information which can later be proven false and you are able to discredit everything so no one knows what is going on.' I knew it only too well from my SF days.

Lowering his voice and leaning forward, Charles's manner became suddenly conspiratorial. 'Of course, there are aliens and aliens,' he said as though so much intimacy had now developed between us that I would understand what he was saying without his having to explain further. 'Really?' I replied, drawing my chair closer.

'Really,' he assured me. 'The Galactic Federation is not going to let the earth go without a fight, you know. They say the earth is a planet which has been decreed free of outside interference – for self-determination, that is.'

'Self-determination?'

'Absolutely,' Charles replied. I noticed that he slurred the word. I noticed too that dawn was beginning to filter through the untouched glass of whisky in my hand, turning it a rich, deep bronze. 'Besides,' Charles continued, 'not all UFOs are threatening.'

'No?'

'Absolutely not,' he continued. 'I have every reason to believe that out there in the greatness of space there are beings with wisdom far beyond ours just waiting for a chance for us to invite them in to help us solve our problems. (We are damn well never going to be able to solve them without their help.) What we need is real *leadership*. Only highly developed extraterrestrials are going to be able to provide it.'

I sat quietly listening to his words and wondering why men are always looking for their leader, somebody who will tell them what to do so like good little sheep they can follow. I could not get out of my mind the vision of a great silver spaceship landing on the Serpentine in Hyde Park or on the lake in front of the Washington Monument. I watched as it opened its doors. A lean majestic man all dressed in white stepped out and walked across the waters, his hands upraised, his body illuminated. 'I am He-Whom-You-Have-Been-Waiting-For,' he says. 'My children, you have but to follow me and my people. We come from afar to help you – from beyond the stars. We bring you safety, security and freedom from the plagues of debt and drugs and dissolution that are destroying your planet. I will be your shepherd, you have only to follow me.' Why the hell did everyone want to get someone else to do it for them? What is it in men that makes us need to follow some religion, some party political broadcast, even to the point where we are willing to get killed for it. What the hell, the guy didn't need to arrive in the spaceship did he? Hitler offered such promises and for a time even delivered them. We all need somebody or something to fight for. It's just that somebody or something can so easily become distorted, a hook for control. Was it ever going to end? Would man ever really be free? Maybe not. Maybe freedom was too dangerous. Maybe it was better just to keep smiling and following some guy dressed in a white robe, or burrowing your nose in UFO books and reassuring yourself that if the earth hadn't been invaded everything would be all right.

I shook myself from my daydream and got up. I walked over to Charles who was looking decidedly sleepy, and put my hand on his shoulder. He looked up at me and smiled as though we had become real friends. He looked tired, pathetic. No more pathetic than I, however, who had spent most of the night just getting a man to talk so that I wouldn't be left alone. I figured it is pretty rough to be human, no matter who you are. Who knows, maybe he was right, we had become friends.

'Charles, thank you for all the things you've told me. Some of them are kind of hard to take in all at once. You could well be right. I have learned recently that a lot of things I didn't know existed happened to be real. We must talk some more. Look, I'm sorry but I've got to go now, I have a plane to catch.'

He rose, looking at me with the eyes of a child who seeks reassurance about the picture it has just painted or the song it has just sung. 'I really can't tell you how grateful I am for the time we've spent together tonight,' I said. He smiled, satisfied that I was telling the truth. He was never to know just how deep a truth I told.

GLORIA

This life is not a joke.
You must take it seriously,
Seriously enough to find yourself
Up against the wall, maybe, with your wrists bound.

Nazim Hikmet *'Of Life'*

I showered, shaved, threw a few things into a bag –
including both manuscripts and Mirabehn's card – and
called a cab. I took one last look at the chaos of books and
papers I was leaving behind and decided I didn't like what I
saw. I made mental promises to clear it all up on my return.
As I closed the door to the flat, I could not help but feel a
sense of excitement. I had made it through the night, I had
decided to stop running no matter what it cost me, and I was
on my way to see the one person in the world who I hoped
could clear up all the confusion – Mirabehn. It is a weird
thing. Once you make a decision like that all the considera-
tions – all the worries – all the possibilities fall away leaving
a straight road ahead of you. It felt good the way it used to
feel when I travelled behind enemy lines with a mission to
accomplish. They call it bravery when you crawl on your
belly through guerrilla-infested jungles or break through a
security net to assassinate some warlord. That is not
bravery. That's easy. Right, you feel scared – that's normal
– but you are sure of yourself. You've got a job to do, a place
to go. All you have to worry about is how to get there and

back as quick and easy as possible without getting yourself or your men killed.

Mirabehn would tell me what I needed to know, or provide me with leads to find out. Had she not said in her postcard that there were other papers?

I thought back to the absurdity of my plan. Research Beethoven's life a bit and dash off a cute little money-spinner in my spare time. The arrogance of it all made me smile. So did the irony. I had never made any money in my life. It was very unlikely that this was going to change now. But I no longer cared. Ludwig had pursued me. Now it was my turn to pursue him. I didn't know where the journey would take me. I didn't know if I would end up in Bedlam Hospital diagnosed a paranoid schizophrenic, dead at the hands of some guys in black who didn't exist anyway, or on my own in a foreign city with no idea what I was doing there or where to go next. But what the hell, when you have hit bottom there is nowhere to go but up. I noticed my head hurt but that for the moment the other physical symptoms I had been experiencing – nausea, visual disturbances, ringing in my ears, pain in my body – were being held at bay. I wondered if I would ever again get a good night's sleep. Then I decided that didn't matter a damn.

At the airport in Vienna I rented a car and headed out of the city. The fields which had been green and carpeted with wild flowers on my first visit had now turned gold. I had the curious feeling that I was on my way home, a sense made particularly absurd by my general dislike for Vienna. Yet I couldn't get rid of it. I was concerned about Mirabehn – that I had not been able to get to her immediately after I received her card. Yet I had a gut feeling that no harm had come to her and I looked forward to seeing her again the way a kid looks forward to school after summer vacation, knowing he will see a teacher of whom he is particularly fond. I turned off the main road and headed towards her cottage. Everything around me seemed to grow silent – the same silence I had experienced on my first visit. It was as though the day itself were poised perfectly between past and future in gentle expectation of each coming moment.

I did not directly approach the cottage. Perhaps it was the silence. I parked the car off the road, 200 yards away, in a copse of trees heavy with foliage, and walked the rest of the way. A hot sun poured over me melting the aches and pains in my body. As the cottage came into view I smiled, knowing I was coming to the end of a long journey. I remembered the delicious sweet tea the servant had brought and looked forward in anticipation to more. By the time I got to the door, I could already smell its spicy fragrance. I knocked twice. There was no answer. I knocked again. Silence. Even the birds had stopped singing.

Panic seized me. Where was she? Why was she not here? I turned round scanning the drive, the meadow, the little woods at the side of the house. All of it had the look of a place uninhabited for days, even weeks. I paced the outer walls of the house searching everywhere for some sign of life. Nothing. I looked through the kitchen window. The counter was completely bare except for one water glass tilted at an angle above a pink sponge cloth now dried out completely and gone stiff. Curtains covered the other windows. I went back to the front of the house. The air was still. The sun which had seemed so friendly a few minutes before now beat down relentlessly. I had to get into the house. My training served me well. It took me no more than two minutes to jemmy both locks and let myself into the hall.

Inside the air was cool and slightly damp. On the floor lay several unopened letters. I picked them up – one from England, an official-looking envelope from India, three cards and a copy of *New Internationalist* magazine. I put them down on the narrow table in the hall and walked into the living room. The furniture had been covered with white sheets. It gave the room an air of mystery women must have possessed in an era when even their ankles were kept covered for the sake of propriety. The light in the room, filtered as it was through unbleached muslin curtains, had turned everything a pale gold – a room frozen in time and so beautiful it made me weak. I walked across it to a simple table on which sat some writing paper, envelopes and a pen. There lay a white card with a black border on which, in a hand unfamiliar to me, had been written in English 'Our dearest friend Mirabehn is no longer of this world. She passed away peacefully by the grace of God on 20 July 1989. May she rest in peace.'

That was it – the end to a story which it now seemed would have no end. Mirabehn was gone. This last journey, begun in the hope of resolving my obsession with Ludwig had come to a dead end. I held the thick card in my hand and rubbed my thumb over the slanting black script as though trying to erase what had been written. A wind rushed through some hollow space in my guts. Tears came to my eyes. Where do I go from here?

I turned to face a bookshelf on my left on which stood a great pile of books of all shapes and sizes, many of them Indian editions of Western works printed in Calcutta or Delhi which sell for a pittance and always have unlikely spelling errors: *Complete Poems of Rainer Maria Rilke*, *Life of Sri Ramakrishna* compiled, the title page told me, 'from various authentic sources', Ouspensky's *In Search of the Miraculous*, *The Revolutionary Road* by Ho Chi Minh, *The Affluent Society* by John Kenneth Galbraith, *Kali, the Feminine Force* by Ajit Mookerjee.

At the very end of the bookshelf next to which I stood sat a pile of big coffee-table books. I went over to them. One was on Beethoven – some kind of bicentennial edition published by the Beethoven-Archiv in Bonn – a two-volume set of the complete works of Michelangelo in colour and a splendid edition of *Tibetan Sacred Art . . . The Heritage of Tantra* full of colour plates of Buddhist thankas and artefacts. I opened the Beethoven book and began to thumb through it. There was a sketch of his birthplace in Bonn. It did not appear to have the strange cut-off shape in the courtyard which Wegeler described in his letter to Wawruch. Then I remembered that the family, shortly after Ludwig's birth, had moved. On the same page was a photograph of the entry of Ludwig's baptism in the baptismal register of St Regmigius church. It was followed by an engraving of the market-place in Bonn that Wegeler had described in his letter to Wawruch. I also found a painting of Ludwig's grandfather – the elder Ludwig – a portrait which Ludwig kept with him all through his life. The caption beside it informed me, 'passed to his nephew Karl and to the latter's descendants'. Then there was an engraving of Neefe in profile dressed in a powdered wig and ruffles. He looked a strange bird-like man with a haughty air. I also came upon a portrait of Ludwig's brother Johann – a man with coal black hair, thin-rimmed steel glasses and a squint. He had a bearing so pompous it made me smile. Ludwig's death mask was there too – his hollow cheeks and wasted face lay in repose before me. It seemed appropriate that I should be staring at it in this room with its shrouded furniture, its soft golden light and its exquisite silence.

This room, I thought – was this room to be the end of it all? A final resting place for some relentless wild energy which took hold not only of Ludwig himself, splitting apart his body and mind, but of Wawruch, Wegeler, Rolland, Mirabehn and myself? How many others had there been who were also caught up in this ruthless dance of fire that tears you apart and, at least in Wawruch's case, leads to death.

Conspicuously absent from the book was a portrait of Schindler – a curious omission from a book filled with hundreds of illustrations, published in Germany and issued in several different languages. Germans are generally accurate to the point of tedium in their researches. I wondered where the great Schindler was and who else since Ludwig's death had become trapped by the obsessional power he carried. Rolland? Bourdelle?

As I said the name I remembered Mirabehn's card: 'Does the name Bourdelle mean anything to you. . . .' Then my eye fell on a book right next to Michelangelo: *Bourdelle et la critique de son temps* by Michel Dufet and Carol Marc Lavrillier. I opened the heavy volume with new hope. I found photographs in black and white of colossal statues – warriors on great horses, a majestic woman holding a staff or spear wound round with fabulous serpents, a dying centaur, Hercules naked drawing a bow as tall as he was. There was the naked Adam, with sensuous male body that almost smelt of lust, a head that was bowed in shame. I had never seen anything quite like them. The quality of the craftsmanship combined with passion in the sculpture captured my attention at every page: heads and torsos twisted in wildness yet gripped in a vice of powerful architectural control. I got the sense that Bourdelle, like Ludwig, had also been wrestling with opposing forces – one a will towards uncontrolled self-expression which moved outwards, the other some kind of rigid classical containment that prevented its full release. All of this resulted in works which vibrated off the very page, almost as though Bourdelle had been able to capture the wild forces of creation and to hold them within some self-imposed struc-ture for a split second before either force could destroy the other – just long enough to crystallise in bronze or stone.

On one page was the torso of a naked warrior, his massive sword raised to strike, his opposite arm stuck out at right angles to his body, its blunt fingers splayed in a gesture of aggression and power. The face was contorted with fury, the mouth opened violently to utter the wordless cry of battle. I continued through the book. There were women too – a full-length statue of a wonderfully buxom Penelope, her head on one side waiting for Ulysses to come home.

It was then that I came upon it. On page 162 there was a head of Ludwig – not the Ludwig of the bicentennial edition published by the Beethoven-Archiv, nor the chocolate-box portrait that Steiler made of Ludwig where he looks like a cross between Jimmy Stewart and a nineteenth century Robert de Niro, nor the Ludwig of Thayer's tidy biography. Here before me in perfect form was the Ludwig of Wawruch's nights in all his terrifying power. The photograph was of a bronze head – 'Beethoven dit Metropolitan 1902' the caption read. Its face exploded with life energy – a force which had no concern for the comfort or well-being of the vessel it inhabited. The hair was thrown back, the thin lips set in defiance, head bowed just slightly, eyes closed. On its facing page was another Beethoven head, equally powerful yet completely different. I turned over the page. There were two more: 'Beethoven à la Cravatte 1890', 'Beethoven aux Grands Cheveux 1889'. Again I turned the page, again I came face to face with Ludwig or what Wawruch called the 'personae' of Ludwig –each of which had spoken through and lived through the face and body of the man. It seemed incredible that anyone, long after Ludwig's death, long after Wawruch's own, could have captured so accurately in bronze again and again the fugues of Ludwig about which only Wawruch himself appeared to have known.

424

Next to the book was another, also in French, entitled simply *Bourdelle*. It too was co-authored by Dufet but this time with someone named Ionel Jainou. On its cover was the bronze Hercules. I opened it to find a photograph of Antoine Bourdelle himself, who looked remarkably like Ludwig in some way. On the page that followed there was a quote from the sculptor. It said simply, 'To *be* is wonderful but how moving it is to feel oneself *becoming*.'

I began to read. Antoine Bourdelle, I learned, was born on 30 October 1861 in Montauban, France. He died on 1 October 1929 in Paris. He had studied at the Beaux-Arts in Toulouse and then gone on to Paris in 1885 where he worked with Jean-Baptiste Carpeaux and Jules Dalou before entering the studio of Rodin. The book went on about his life, about his theories, yet there were virtually no references to Beethoven. This seemed strange. Bourdelle like Brancusi, the introduction informed me, was always aware of the presence of occult forces within things, which he considered to be far beyond human understanding. In a letter to André Suares, the sculptor described time as the *fourth dimension* in art and wrote of the existence of yet a fifth dimension, *the least known and surely the most imperiously indispensable of all*. According to Bourdelle this fifth dimension is a mysterious force which inhabits human beings, a second invisible reality which divulges to those willing to look for it *the diapason of the divine*. I stopped reading and went back to looking at the sculptures. As well as all the photographs, the book contained a list of what purported to be all of Bourdelle's sculptures, the date when they had been made, the number of castings done in bronze and their where-abouts. Among them I counted thirty-two works on Beethoven. The first was cast in 1887 when Bourdelle was close to the age at which Ludwig's deafness had begun to take its toll. The last was only finished in the year when

Bourdelle died. At the back of the book were more photographs of the sculptor's works, some copies of those in the larger book, others new yet equally marvellous. I wondered how a talent such as that of Bourdelle could be so little known. I came to the Beethoven section of the book. There were two of the bronzes I had seen before. I turned over the page. Staring at me in all its horror and all its splendour under the title 'The Tragic Mask' was Storyteller's face – the cold, clear, rawness of his presence – a man who, in twentieth-century language, tells it like it is.

I was on to something. On the frontispiece of one of the books I read that there is in Paris a Musée Antoine Bourdelle. I had to get there. I replaced the books on the shelves, fearing that in rummaging through Mirabehn's library I might have disrupted the sanctity of this golden room – her room – the room which, the moment I entered many weeks ago – or was it centuries? – had altered my life for ever. I wondered if she knew that I would come, that I would touch her belongings, enter her private world, be drawn further and further into the web of Ludwig – a web which she in all her beauty and with all her will had woven to entrap me. I could feel her presence in the room. It was playful, like a nature spirit who peeks at you, doing its best not to break into peals of laughter. This woman – she whom Gandhi had called 'Sister Mira': *it is my name. When you call me any other I don't know who you are talking to.*

Mirabehn had also loved Ludwig, been haunted by Ludwig. She too needed to gain freedom from the hold which the manuscript had exerted on her. I wondered if that freedom had come with death. Then I decided that the godpower, the serpentpower, the power of creation is probably not hindered by death. I thought back to the afternoon I had spent in Mirabehn's presence, when she had insisted that I take the manuscript. Me –the most unworthy and unsuitable of knights to carry out this fine lady's bidding. It all seemed ridiculously funny. I began to laugh. The sound of my voice resonating off the walls of this golden room made the air sparkle as though it had caught the resonance of Mirabehn's own joy – a joy which had stayed in the house even though the woman who created it no longer lived here.

The golden light had begun to grow dim as evening settled in on the small cottage at the edge of the woods. I realised I was hungry. I could not remember when I had last eaten. I did not want to leave the cottage to go down into a village in search of food, yet to take any of the food still remaining on the shelves of Mirabehn's kitchen seemed a sort of sacrilege. Hunger would wait. I crossed over to the day bed on which Mirabehn had lain. Being careful not to disturb the white shroud that covered it, I lay down then slept with a soundness I had not known for years while minute flecks of golden light danced in my brain. In sleep I felt the gentle touch of long tapering fingers against my cheek and heard distant laughter.

I did not awaken until half-past nine. I got up, walked down the hall through the kitchen and noiselessly let myself through the kitchen door out into the small orchard behind the house. Instead of following the drive as I had done the day before, I walked along a tiny path cut through the trees from the house to the copse where I had parked the car. I wondered if the path had been made by Mirabehn on her walks. Had Ludwig ever walked here, maybe one day when he had been able to escape the ugliness of the city world in which he had lived?

I found the car, got in and started it. Slowly, as though I now had all the time in the world, I drove back towards the main road. The sun's light danced through trees over-burdened with vibrant leaves. I turned the corner. There, parked just beyond the junction to the road, was a long black car. In it sat two men dressed in black.

CREDO

Are you willing to be sponged out, erased,
cancelled, made nothing?
Are you willing to be made nothing?
dipped into oblivion?
If not, you will never really change.

D. H. Lawrence 'The Phoenix'

Coming upon them was like coming out of a meadow filled
with flowers to discover a group of madmen performing
obscenities in the street. I felt less fear than revulsion. It
quickly turned to anger. I passed the car, looking straight
ahead. Its engine started. It began to follow me down the hill. I
accelerated. So did it. I slowed down. It made no attempt to
overtake me. Flesh and blood or aberration which had
developed out of my distorted mind – whatever they were, I
wanted no part of these creatures. I wanted rid of them the
way a dog wants free when its fur is entangled in brambles.

On my way to the cottage the day before I had noticed
that a mile or two further on, just beyond two hairpin bends
in the middle of a wooded area, the road branched in three
directions. Two of these three roads were hidden by a thick
growth of trees so that anyone following me, unless they
were immediately behind, would not know which road I had
taken. One road turned back on itself. When I got there I
spun the wheel and turned into it, almost reversing the
direction in which I was travelling, and I killed the engine.

The black car sped on. My heart was pounding in my chest; a sudden rush of energy had turned my face a lobster red. I wanted more than anything else I could think of to grab one of these bastards by the throat and rip him in two. But I could do nothing but wait . . . wait . . . the hardest thing in the world for me. The seconds ticked by, each one seemed an eternity. After three or four minutes I started my engine and got back on the road.

I cursed my vision, which had gone blurred again. I had hoped all that was finished, though I was seeing everything through ripples – like the ripples you get along a hot road in the summer except that these were vertical rather than horizontal. I blinked, hoping to dispel the distortion. Maybe I could pretend it didn't exist. I felt my heart racing. I figured it was anger but there was something else too – something happening in my body – pulsating waves that seemed to have a life of their own. I started talking to myself out loud, hoping to calm what I sensed was mounting paranoia or a lot of weird physical symptoms that felt very much like it. *There is a perfectly good explanation for all this. All you have to do is stay alive long enough to find it* . . . stay alive . . . forty-eight hours ago I didn't give a damn whether I stayed alive or not. Now things had changed.

I arrived at the airport expecting a sinister black limousine to be waiting for me. I found nothing but a handful of officious porters. I had to wait four hours for a seat on a plane to Paris as the visual distortions continued. So did the paranoia despite my best efforts to talk myself out of it. Every person I saw had begun to look suspiciously like a bird of prey out to get me. I went into the restaurant and ordered the biggest breakfast I could think of. Then I left it sitting there uneaten. A good-looking German waitress came over to ask in her broken English if everything was all right. Even she looked threatening.

When I got to Charles de Gaulle airport it was late afternoon. I took a taxi into the city. The journey was short since it was August and the French had all departed *pour les vacances*. I went directly to a small hotel I knew on the Left Bank with a view of Notre Dame. It was cheap, out of the way and I figured would not, like most, be jam packed with German and American tourists since the couple who owned it always pretended they spoke nothing but French. They had one room left. It was on the top floor and had a shower. This meant a minute *salle d'eau* with water running not only from the faucet but freely and continuously down the insides of the walls as well.

The disturbances in my vision continued. I took a shower, changed my clothes and went down to the lobby to find out about the Bourdelle Museum. I could hear men's voices speaking Portuguese in the next room. I caught two or three phrases. I wondered what they were doing there. I wondered if they were dressed in black. I wondered if I had been followed. Maybe these creepy guys had been trying to put me off the scent by letting me get away in Austria. Maybe they didn't *have* to follow me. Maybe they had ways of *knowing* where I was. Maybe there was nothing I could do to get away from them. Maybe. . . . What the hell was I talking about? I must not let all this get to me. I had to hold my centre. I took a deep breath and moved back to lean against the wall. This way I could make out more of what they were saying while I waited for the concierge.

One voice told a joke: 'President Bush asked God, "Will there ever be communism in the United States?" "Yes," replied God, "but not in your lifetime." Gorbachev asks God, "Will there ever be capitalism in the Soviet Union?" "Yes," replied God, "but not in your lifetime." Finally Sarney asks God, "Will Brazil ever be able to pay back her debt?" "Yes," replies God, "but not in *my* lifetime." '

I wanted to put my head around the corner and get a look at these men but I was afraid that would put an end to their conversation. Eventually the concierge wandered out from behind a glass door wearing a smudged flowered pinafore and carrying a broom. She looked at me in surprise as though she had no idea I had been standing there for five minutes and had rung the bell three times.

I asked her about the opening times of museums. She presented me with a tourist brochure in French which looked as though the last user had spilled most of his lunch on it. I opened it and read: 'Musée Bourdelle, 16 rue Antoine Bourdelle [Métro Falguière]. 45.48.67.27. Tlj sf lun et jours fériés de 10h a 17h40. Ent: 18F TR:12F. [Musée accessible aux handicapés physiques]. The last line made me smile. I wondered if I fell into that category.

So my visit would have to wait until morning. I thanked her with the excessive formality that endears you for ever to ageing Frenchwomen and went back to my room. I took the manuscripts from my bag and wrapped them in some brown paper I found lining the plastic waste basket. Then I tucked the packet under my arm and went down to the lobby and out into the rue St Julien le Pauvre.

The distortions in my vision kept coming and going as I walked along the quay. I turned and crossed the river, passing Notre Dame. As I looked up I noticed that its gargoyles were following me with their eyes. I shuddered. Waves of heat began to flow over my body making me sweat profusely for five or six minutes. Then they would be replaced by chills even though the evening was warm. I entered the Marais and walked on, gazing into windows beautifully dressed with hams and sausages or flowers or books or shoes. At the Centre Beaubourg a group of jugglers was performing. Their balls, batons, clubs and bean bags had been laid out in tidy rows on white sheets on the ground, their ghetto blaster was booming with the nickelodeon music you hear on carousels at about 150 decibels. They were surrounded by a crowd of maybe fifty people.

When they finished their act a man of about sixty arrived on the scene. He was dressed in a shabby dinner suit. He carried a long narrow suitcase in one hand and a cardboard box containing two puppies in the other. Setting the box down with loving care, he opened the suitcase. Out came swords of all sizes, batons wound with rags soaked in methylated spirits, a tin of what looked like lighter fuel. He started to slide swords of progressively larger sizes down his throat. Then, lighting the batons, he proceeded to carry out the same actions with flaming sticks. As a finale he squirted the fluid itself into his mouth and lit it, spitting flames like a human blowtorch. The crowd cheered.

I was standing next to a tall lean woman with long black hair, curiously dressed in a luminous green sequined T-shirt, jeans and motorcycle boots. There was something strangely familiar about her. I watched her – watched it all in fascination as though there were no reality but the present all-encompassing moment. I held tightly to the package beneath my arm. The weird changes in temperature in my body continued. As the fire-eater finished a small man dressed in a raincoat with his hair slicked back like a 1939 ad for Brylcreem replaced him. He proceeded to take pigeons for a walk on an imaginary leash with skill that would have put the great Charlot to shame. His act ended. Applause, the collection of money. The sky had grown dark.

At one corner of the great expanse of pavement I could still make out an organ grinder who played while his monkey, tied to the box on a long red cord, collected coins – leaping on to men and women in the crowd and stuffing its tiny fist into their pockets and purses. At the opposite corner a dwarf stood upon a stack of three big blue boxes waving his hands about and shouting to get people's attention, 'My friends, we are coming to the end. Nation rises against nation. There are earthquakes and pestilence. A man will kill his father and a husband his wife. These are dark dark times,' he said, pausing to wipe slather from his huge mouth. 'It is not I who speak,' he shouted, 'but the holy book: . . . *the locusts were like horses arrayed for battle; on their heads were what looked like crowns of gold; their faces were like human faces, their hair like women's hair, and their teeth like lions' teeth; they had scales like iron breastplates, and the noise of their wings was like the noise of many chariots with horses rushing into battle. They have tails like scorpions, and stings, and their power of hurting men for five months lies in their tails. They have as king over them the angel of the bottomless pit.* . . . I am nothing,' he screeched. 'I have never been anything. You can see from this twisted body. But I, my friends, know my place, I know that Jesus Christ is my saviour.'

He raved on and on shouting about the Holy Spirit, redemption, sin and the end of the world which was, he insisted, upon us. No one paid the slightest attention. I felt sorry for him. How strangely out of place he seemed here, where his hell fire and damnation drew so small an audience. Who worries much in a Catholic country, where you can be forgiven for your sins on Friday evening then start afresh to sin again on Saturday – such a *practical* religion, Catholicism. Yet the size of his mouth bothered me and the way it opened and moved with the greed of a starving animal. Behind me a great rectangular fountain rose out of the pavement. It was filled with brightly coloured metal sculptures including a huge pouting red mouth. The dwarf's mouth? It had begun to look as though it would open and swallow me. The waves of heat were getting closer and closer together. I went over to the fountain, dipped my hands into the water and splashed my face.

A gypsy child with eyes like chunks of coal came up to me begging for money. Her hair was long and red, her cheeks white. From her ears hung heavy dangling earrings. She was dressed in a filthy scarlet skirt that reached the ground and had curious ornaments hung around her neck on top of a gold lamé T-shirt. She couldn't have been more than nine or ten yet she looked like a child who knew all there is to know about everything. Her eyes burned as they looked upon me. 'Est-ce-que vous pourriez me donner un franc ou deux pour me dépanner, Monsieur? Mon Papa il est parti. Ma Maman, elle est morte. J'ai trois frères et soeurs. Elles sonts malades. Je suis toute seule . . . toute seule. . . . S'il vous plaît, vous auriez une petite pièce pour me dépanner?'

Horrified by the child's appearance and by my own lack of compassion, I reached into my pocket, grabbed the first bill I touched and thrust it at her – anything so long as she would go away. But my unintended generosity had the opposite effect. The hideous creature reached out her hand to rub the inside of my right thigh and gazed up at me with the eyes of a whore. 'Vous êtes très gentil Monsieur, si grand, si fort.' I saw that her face was covered in theatrical make-up. Had it been there before – unnoticed in the dark which by now covered the square – or was what I now saw a projection of my own mind? Strange words began to filter through my brain like an unholy ancient liturgy . . . *in the great abyss lived a fiery spirit called Lilith . . . in the beginning she cohabited with man . . . now her face derives from opposition and suppression . . . she shall be called impure . . . seductive witch . . . death-dealing succubus . . . Lilith has no feet for copulation . . . yet the adornments she wears do make it seem so . . . the feet of the serpent were cut away by God when He discovered it had seduced Eve.*

The child who would not leave me alone now pushed her head against my belly. I could smell a dark musty pit opening up before me. I drew back. . . . *and so did Lilith, sired*

434

by demons, leave Samael, the husband of her childhood . . . the harlot
descended into the darkness of the underworld . . . now, on earth, she
flies like a screech owl to fornicate with men who sleep alone in the
desert . . . spreading her demonic blood, alienating the living God.

I stood there, clutching the brown package to my chest
like a condemned man waiting to take the cattle train to the
gas chamber. The child still pursued me trying to fondle my
legs, bending in obscene postures to kiss my feet. I leapt on
to the edge of the fountain and cried out. My voice drew the
attention of people standing nearby. They began to laugh. A
group of black musicians was beating dark provocative
rhythms on African drums. Like an animal facing death at
the jaws of a predator only inches away, I began to search
frantically for any way out. The crowd was dancing in time
to the drumbeats. I looked to my right, intending to jump
from the edge of the fountain. There on the ground not ten
feet away from me I could just make out the shapes of three
huge black birds fighting over a piece of raw meat. Their
wings beat the air as they tore first at the flesh and then at
one another. Flashbacks: the windowsill of Ludwig's room,
the square near Lincoln's Inn Fields. My body started to
sway. I knew I was going to vomit. I reached out a hand but
there was nothing to hold on to. I looked down to steady
myself then raised my eyes searching for something
ordinary, anything on which I could rely. There behind the
birds who continued to devour their prey, against the
window of a building not twenty yards away stood two men
in black.

I could feel myself falling slowly, spinning round and
round as I was sucked down into a black hot space. The
mouth. It had taken me. Down I fell, down like Alice in the
rabbit hole, down endlessly. At last I hit bottom smashing
my left knee against the pavement with a crack that sounded
like a chunk of ice hurled across a frozen pond. Red-hot pain

shot through my body. I could not move. I figured I would never move again. I could only just make out the shape of human figures gathered around me. No one came to help me for at least a century. No one. Then I felt a woman's hands take hold of me beneath the arms – a strong woman. The hands pulled me up. My eyes began to clear. It was the woman in the green sequins whom I had stood next to an hour before. She grabbed me by the hand and dragged me from the square, running across the street, away from the building, away from the men in black.

She was laughing. The pain from my knee shot through the whole of my body. I did not think I could move. Yet somehow I followed her or was dragged, stumbling and falling to the pavement each time the leg gave way beneath me. She led me to a large bike and motioned for me to get on behind her. I went to swing my leg over the cycle but could not lift the damaged knee high enough. With a jerk of pain I dropped the brown package. She started the engine, pulling at my jacket. I leaned down to retrieve the manuscript. With what felt almost an inhuman effort I swung my left leg over the bike and put my arms around her body.

We took off. The sequins covering her body felt like fine armour beneath my fingers or like the scales of a fish or snake – a snake whose body is all of a piece, whose flesh and muscles move together in absolute union, who knows no reason, who lives by pure instinct. Their roughness comforted me. We sped down a narrow alley and turned a couple of corners into the rue de Rivoli. Her long black hair blown by a warm wind caressed my face the way giant leaves of seaweed sway against your body beneath the sea. No she was not a snake, she was a mermaid, and I was her captive, being drawn deeper and deeper into the welcoming sea. The sound of the engine, the movement of the bike, the clean smell of this woman's flesh, all were inexorably bound together with the summer night in a living sanctity which, like the snake's body, was all of a piece. I held on, hoping the ride would last for ever.

I lost track of the route we took. I know at one point we passed the Pont Alexandre III. Its magnificent lions stood patiently to be garlanded by naked children so perfect their flesh seemed to breathe. We went by a hospital somewhere and then a cemetery. We rode for what must have been half an hour. Finally we stopped at the edge of a ravine where trains come out from underground near the Parc de Montsouris. My companion parked and locked her bike under a bridge, presumably so it would not be seen by passing cars or people. Still without a word, she took my hand and led me down into a ravine at the side of the tracks. I followed gladly. I didn't know where we were headed but I knew there was no way I was going back to my hotel tonight and I was grateful to have a companion. I also knew that tomorrow morning no matter what happened I was going to be standing outside the Bourdelle Museum at 10 a.m.

The sound of a train. She grabbed me by the arm and pulled me back behind a pillar. It sped past, its windows making strobe effects on the tunnel walls. When it had gone she led me down some steps into an underground tunnel. The walls were damp, the air was cool yet surprisingly fresh. Still we had not spoken a word to each other. At the bottom, the stairway opened out into a small space with a ceiling so low I could not stand. It must have been 25 feet beneath the ground. There a small group of people – five men and two women – were squatting around a butane camp stove which gave off the only light available. Most were dressed in outdoor clothing and walking boots although one girl wore high heels and a skimpy summer dress. She looked very out of place and seemed very anxious. They appeared to have been waiting for us. The men looked like men who had lived alone in the wilderness for a very long time. They had none of the airs and graces of the middle class. One of them appeared to be the leader. They called him Gérard.

Someone handed me an old coat. I put it on, stuffed my package beneath it and tied the cord around the waist to hold it tight. It was damp and smelt like it had been beneath the earth for a long time. For some reason the smell, the fact that it was old and shabby and the way it had been given to me by a complete stranger brought tears to my eyes. My companion had moved away from me to crouch beside a short man with a light beard. Gérard spoke softly in French: 'Trois cent quatre-vingt-dix kilomètres de carrières, de galeries, d'égoûts et de voies ferrées nous attendent. Dépêchons-nous.'

Gérard wore a miners' light strapped to his head. He reached up and turned it on, then ducking his head, crawled into a tunnel to his left – so narrow and so low that I had not noticed it before. The others followed. I was fourth in line. The earth beneath my hands was wet and muddy. Spikes of stone stuck out here and there from the ceiling of the tunnel and from its sides. It was hard to avoid hitting your head or shoulder against them for the only light was carried by Gérard and he was far ahead.

I had no idea what I was doing in this place. It was as though I were being drawn down deep into the earth, as though I were being taken back to something I had known before, yet that was absurd. I followed with the obedience of a domestic animal. Everything had become simple. There were no more thoughts about Charles and his UFOs, or Mirabehn and her shimmering room, not even about Ludwig, or Wawruch or Bourdelle. There was simply the earth and the will to follow.

After five or six minutes the tunnel opened out again into a large room the floor of which was completely covered in bones. There must have been thousands of them – skulls, thigh bones, pelvic bones – some whole, some in fragments that were scores, maybe even hundreds, of years old. Crunching beneath our feet as we moved, they made a reassuring sound. The room which was high enough for me to stand appeared to have three arched exits. From one of them you could hear a faint sound of water flowing. We went through an archway into the passage on the right. It led into a tunnel high enough in places for me to stand, which descended deeper into the earth. We went down, down, in short shuffling steps to keep from sliding, so wet was the ground. The tunnel opened out at the bottom into a place where a small river flowed and where the slippery muddy earth turned into pure sand – the banks of an underground river. The walls of this room had been carved out of stone. Gérard lay down on the damp sand, put his hands behind his head and pretended to be a sunbather at the edge of the sea. Two of the men laughed and joined him. The girl in the green sequins took a small flask from her handbag and offered it round. I took a sip. It was like firewater – smooth and hot and pure. It tasted like a combination of aniseed and some kind of green grasses.

I sat down next to Gérard here on this strange under-world beach which must have been 75 feet beneath the streets of Paris –a place where nothing lived, no insects, no animals, where there is nothing to eat, nothing to do. I had lived in Paris for two years yet had no idea that such a place existed. A place of no light yet a place in which I felt completely safe. No man in black, I told myself, would enter this chthonic realm.

We remained on the 'beach' for perhaps ten minutes. Then Gérard got up, looked at his watch and announced that it was time to go if we were to arrive at 'Salle Z' on time. In time for what?

We followed Gérard across the river. The water came up to my thighs. It was surprisingly warm for water flowing so far beneath the surface. On the opposite side we entered another tunnel at the edge of which the rock protruded in the shape of an animal's head. At first I thought my eyes were playing tricks on me in the dim light, but as I crawled past the opening I realised that the rock had actually been hewn into the rough shape of the head of a dog.

The tunnel which we crawled down narrowed. I found it difficult to squeeze my shoulders through in some places. My body began to feel uncomfortable, quite unbearably heavy as though pressure from all sides were squeezing me into too small a space. I was unsure how much these sensations were the result of the tunnel and how much were coming from my mind. All I knew was that I did not want to be there. The sense of comfort that had been growing in me ever since we entered this subterranean world was rapidly disappearing. Everything seemed to be going haywire.

When we had left the beach I had been last in line. This meant that the light strapped to Gérard's head was so far ahead of me that the tunnel was almost completely black. Yet I had begun to see colours and geometrical patterns in front of my eyes. I closed them but the patterns continued. They resembled the patterns you see in mosques but were in constant motion and sprinkled with light. In my left ear the familiar buzzing or ringing which had been silent during the past forty-eight hours began again. My limbs started to itch uncomfortably. I wanted, I needed, I was becoming desperate, to stretch out my arms, to unbend my back. How much longer would this go on? Then I realised that I no longer heard the sounds of my companions moving. The tunnel had branched two or three times. I must have taken the wrong branch.

I noticed with curious detachment that my body had

begun to shake again. I was alone. I had never felt more alone in my life – a man without a country, without a purpose, without value. The tunnel, which before had been low and curved, now became high and narrow. Its walls ran at right angles to one another. I turned a corner to my left. Another opening presented itself. I took it. Suddenly the ceiling grew lower. I ducked and ran on. I ran head on into a wall of what felt like old narrow bricks. The wall appeared to have an open space where the bricks had crumbled away. Then I realised to my horror that there was no pathway. I was lost in a maze of extraordinary complexity – a maze which operated not only on two dimensions but on *three*. Not only did the height of the ceiling change, the pathways led upwards and down in a pattern which was completely indecipherable.

For what seemed hours, I scrambled in the dark hunting for a corner that would lead into a new passageway and bring me out. The story of the Minotaur flashed through my brain. I could not remember what Theseus had done to find his way out of the maze – ah yes, thread. I remembered Hansel and Gretel with their trail of pebbles. I had nothing. My pulse was racing, the air had grown stale. I had to crouch down to go forward, then to crawl on my belly. I feared that where I was crawling would lead to a dead end so narrow I would never be able to get out. By now the passage was so low that the package I had tucked under my jacket was the only buffer between me and the ground. It pressed hard against my chest.

I decided to stay still for the time being to gather my wits and make some kind of a rational decision about how to get out of this place. It was then that the terror began. My body started to move of its own accord – to twist, to contort. I felt sick, intoxicated, poisoned. I told myself I must not vomit. I must not. It was suffocating. There was a horrible taste in my mouth – the taste of death, of rotting, decay, decomposition. This had to be the end. Wawruch, Charles, all of them were right. I had become possessed by dark metaphysical beings, I was sure of it – beings I couldn't see or touch but who were controlling everything that was happening to me – trapped in some diabolical machine. I could hear its grinding noises. A hideous monster had taken me in its jaws and was crushing me to a pulp: a leviathan – a dragon – a python – a whale. No, it was the giant red mouth hovering over the fountain at Beaubourg. Only now it had opened completely to reveal cold hard blunt teeth which were about to crush me. At least it would be over in a moment, I told myself. Then I would lie dead in the wet earth 100 feet beneath the most beautiful city in Europe. I welcomed death. But it did not come. Instead I stayed stuck, encaged, entrapped within the nightmare while my body moved in strange contortions. I remembered Wawruch's visit to the castle. Where was the great being who would promise *me* everything if only I would serve him? I did not even rate that, I'd been cheated.

I heard voices. There was hope. They knew, they were coming for me – whoever *they* were. Thank God. But no. It was not they. Instead, contorted bodies, some wrapped in strait-jackets, and disembodied heads swirled in the rocks around me – inmates from an insane asylum, sinners from hell. They were laughing and speaking in French yet not the French I knew. Some seemed to be masquerading as figures from history – the Flying Dutchman, Sisyphus, the crippled Hephaestus and his infinitely vain wife, and Prometheus, his liver oozing black putrescence. They were there, all of them. Then just as suddenly as they had appeared they vanished leaving a hideous deathly silence. I was alone again in a cold empty pit of the world – like the spaces between molecules, like the skeletons of my books two nights ago – or was it two centuries ago? – such emptiness. I was nothing, less than nothing, disgusting in my pretensions to be human, an absurd cardboard cut-out of a man, a mindless robot in a cruel circus sideshow. My entire body was being mechanically compressed like a tube of toothpaste in a meaningless world while some mechanical voice sang a jingle over and over again.

By now my sense of suffocation had become so great that I felt my fingers and toes, then my limbs, grow numb as the breath of life withdrew from them. But I could smell, and the smells in this dead inhuman place were all of the human body – blood and mucus, urine, faeces. I was involved in some titanic life and death struggle and I was dimly aware that although all of this was happening in a very real sense to my body it was happening from inside out, as though I were reliving some ancient memory, some primordial ritual that was my ritual and yet all rituals. The pressure on my body grew to such a degree that I felt I could no longer bear it. I knew I was going to die. It felt like the end of the world, an impending catastrophe of enormous proportion. I was losing everything, I was passing through, I was being annihilated. Everything I had been and known and felt and done was gone. Everything that had ever had meaning in my life was destroyed in this inevitable, crushing, titanic movement. I was separated from death by only a hair's breadth, and still I held on in terror. Then all at once it seemed that the ground beneath me was heaving, raging, as though I had been caught in the midst of it, had become part of it. And I knew I had a choice – to fight or to let go. Yet I had no choice whatsoever, not now. It was too late. I let go. Total annihilation overcame me. I could feel my body being destroyed. Every thought, feeling, idea I had ever known was washed away. I had experienced the ultimate in failure. Damned throughout eternity. The pain had gone, the scenes of mutilation had given way to fantastic visions of light and radiance and beauty. Now rainbows, colourful images of rape, obscene burlesque and aboriginal ritual orgies, passed before my eyes. And the energies that had been crushing the life from me only moments before became the most intense sexual arousal that I had ever known, not only in my genitals but throughout my whole body. It drew me higher and higher, promising release, becoming more and more ecstatic. I had passed through, I had gone beyond. I had died, I had been born, a strange transformation had taken place in me. Like a caterpillar I had been spun into this cocoon of rock only to be dissolved into a white gel. And the dissolution I had so feared was more blissful than anything I had known in my life. This sexual energy drew me higher and higher until the world exploded around me in a fountain of light. Mirabehn's words echoed in my brain, 'Don't worry, the next time such beauty comes, you *will* be able to bear it.' Light swirled round me, all through me. Light dissolved me, destroyed me, but there was no longer any pain, there was only pure joy. All the aloneness had ended, I knew I was part of something, part of a process of birth and death that would go on for ever. The power that destroyed me recreated me, I was part of that power. Yet I was nothing.

I took a breath, my first breath, then again I was nothing but a drop of water in an ocean of light. Yet no, not that, for there was no drop to be measured. I was the stars, I was the universe – the earth – the sea – the freedom of air – the power that made green shoots push upward from dark soil. They were me and I was them, we were one. I opened my eyes. There before me, just above my head, a face looked down on me. It was Ludwig's face. The wild hair and the heavy brow were unmistakable. Only this time the tiny eyes glistened and the fine, thin mouth was drawn into a bow. I closed my

eyes again and I heard laughter. I knew the laughter was his
and that somehow in this strange dark tunnel far beneath
the surface of the earth I had been blessed, with a joy I
neither earned nor deserved, the joy of birth, the joy of new
life. I opened my eyes again but he was gone. In his place
were words that echoed in my brain. . . . *and all things shall be
well . . . and all things shall be well . . . and all manner of things
shall be well.*

AGNUS DEI

Brother! I have not become downhearted or low
spirited. Life is everywhere life, life in ourselves,
not in what is outside us. There will be people near
me, and to be a man among people and remain a
man for ever, not to be downhearted nor to fall in
whatever misfortunes may befall me – this is life;
this is the task of life. I have realised this. This idea
has entered into my flesh and into my blood.

Fyodor Dostoevsky *Selected Letters of Fyodor Dostoevsky*

How long I lay alone in the wet darkness I do not know. It
could have been hours or days, I lost all sense of time. All
fear had gone. I found myself enveloped in a sense of peace
such as I have never known. The physical symptoms I'd
been living with for weeks had vanished. My body had been
renewed, regenerated as though every molecule of it had
been changed. It felt light and easy despite the cramped
position in which I lay. The mud beneath me, the rough wall
against which I was huddled, the silence – all brought me a
sense of comfort. It was as though I had been cradled in the
arms of a goddess of infinite warmth, patience and forgiveness. I could see the absurdity of it all: I was lost in a maze a
hundred feet beneath the surface of the city, wedged into a
tiny space, without food, without water, yet there I lay like a
fat toad in the mud, as content as the village idiot – smiling.

After what seemed like aeons, I reached out. I could feel
the walls on either side of me close up against my body. But

446

they held no fear. My mind was clear and razor sharp. For the first time in months I could think straight. I discovered that the narrow passage had grown narrower. I could choose between sliding forward in the hopes that it would open out a few feet further on or scooting backwards. I decided to move ahead. I slithered on my belly for no more than a couple of yards before I came out through a hole into a passageway at right angles to the tunnel. It was high enough to stand in. I got up, steadied myself, and turned left. I had no idea where I was going, how big the maze was or if I would ever find my way out of it. There was not even the faint hint of light to act as a guide, and the only sounds were of my own breathing and the slosh of feet in the wet earth.

I walked on – perfectly at peace. When I came to a corner and had a choice of direction to make, I would take the route which allowed me to stand up or had the highest ceiling. I walked for what must have been twenty minutes. I had no further anxieties about finding my way. If I got out then I would get out. If not, then what better place to spend the rest of my life? I laughed out loud at the idea. I had developed a fantasy that, like a homing pigeon, I was being guided by some atavistic energy which I felt had always been part of my body but which I had never tapped into before.

At the end of the narrow corridor down which I had been walking I was surprised to find no outlets, no pathway at right angles. I was about to turn around to retrace my steps when I noticed that the lower part of my body was illuminated by a faint light. Kneeling down, I found a square opening on the left side of the passage through which the light was coming. I crawled through it. The light grew brighter. I turned left and found that I had entered a huge room in which were seated small groups of people in a great circle lit only by many small butane stoves.

447

I walked between the groups looking for those I had come in with. No one paid the slightest attention to me. I spotted Gérard together with the others. He was eating something. I sat down next to him. He handed me a bottle of beer and a sandwich on a crushed baguette. I took a bite. It was the best food I had ever tasted.

'I wondered where you'd got to,' he said to me in peasant's French, 'you were a long time coming. I figured you knew what you were doing and would find your own way.'

I took a long drink of cheap watery French beer. It too tasted wonderful.

'Thanks,' I said. 'Where are we?'

'Salle Z.'

'What?'

'It is the biggest room in *les carrières* – 100 metres long with only one entrance. It is part of the quarries, the underground tunnels from which the stone was taken in the eighteenth century to build the city of Paris. You have just passed through the labyrinth. There is only one entrance into the hall itself. Unless you know your way, it can be as hard to get out of Salle Z as it is to get into it.'

'Are there more passages into the quarries other than the one we came through?'

'Yes. Several. There is a tiny winding staircase that descends from l'Hôpital St Anne, there is an entrance in front of l'Observatoire near the statue, and a few others. But the police keep a close eye on them these days. That is why we prefer to come in through the 14ème near Montsouris.'

'Gérard, what is l'Hôpital St Anne?'

'A mental hospital. In the eighteenth and nineteenth centuries they used to wrap difficult inmates in strait-jackets and send them down the stone stairwell beneath the ground near the far side of the labyrinth.' I remembered the visions of bound madmen I had seen only an hour ago – maybe a century ago.

'How deep are we here?'

'About 35 metres.'

'Who are all of these people?'

'They are nobody – like me – like you.'

'Nobody?' I said. The idea of being 35 metres beneath the ground in the presence of a hundred nobodies made me laugh. Gérard laughed with me.

'What is your name?' he asked.

'Michael,' I replied.

'Michael, that sounds like a good name. They really *are* nobody, Michael, just people like you and me – some are farmers, some are bankers, some of them are artists. Some work for the secret services, some are scientists, some doctors, some mothers. They don't belong to any organisation. Just about the only thing they have in common is a belief that life matters and a willingness to do what they can to protect human freedom and look after the earth.'

'Sounds good to me,' I said as though all of this were a common occurrence. 'Why are we here?'

'We meet one weekend each month. We know the information that comes through the media is selected, distorted, by those who wield power for their own ends. So partly we meet to find out what is really going on – politically, economically, ecologically. We also meet to learn everything we can about what action can be taken to protect ourselves from environmental threats as well as about how scientific discoveries or depth psychology or new techniques of one kind or another may be useful in expanding consciousness or increasing personal power for change. Tonight, as always, we are meeting to discuss things.'

I didn't know what 'things' were but in my new unusually

449

calm and comfortable condition all he said seemed to make perfect sense. A circle of people on my right were laughing. Twenty feet away a man got up and addressed everyone in French. The moment he began to speak there was silence. The hall had remarkable acoustics. He had hardly to raise his voice to be heard. There must have been seventy-five to a hundred people in Salle Z, maybe more. It was difficult – near impossible – to see any of their faces clearly as the only light came from these butane stoves. He said, 'My friends, I am pleased to welcome you. Some of you will have been with us before. To the others – especially those of you who have travelled hundreds, in a few cases thousands, of miles to be here – may I say how grateful we all are that you have made the journey. I gather several friends have reports to make tonight about survival issues, and other matters.

'We ask each of our friends to speak frankly,' the man went on. 'We also guarantee each of them – as we guarantee you all – the protection of complete anonymity and freedom from any possible religious, political or economic constraints. We believe that it is only through such freedom – a freedom which as you are all aware is becoming less and less possible on the surface – that we can ever hope to come to a workable understanding of how we can help each other.'

Damned right, I thought. Freedom is what it is all about. Yet we live in such a crazy world that only here, encased in some massive chamber hollowed out of rich, dark earth, did anybody dare to speak freely. There had to be some ironic justice in all this.

When he had finished speaking, a tall, lean man got up on the other side of the hall. He too began to speak in French, about the irradiation of food. 'Irradiation,' he said, 'as many of you know, is permitted here in France for onions and garlic. In the United States it is used for sprouting wheat. In Holland it has been widely used for some time. I am sorry to report that it is soon to be used in many other European countries. Food manufacturers and transporters irradiate foods both to destroy the micro-organisms that rot food and to inhibit the ripening of grains, fruits and vegetables. We who have been investigating irradiation believe it must be prevented from spreading. Our research shows that it is of no benefit to human life. It only benefits the nuclear industry, for which it has created a good market for spent cobalt and caesium fuel rods, and the food industry, which likes the idea that it can reduce its spoilage losses and extend shelf-life.'

'What is the problem with food irradiation?' asked a woman sitting by the side of the man speaking. 'Does it make food radioactive?'

'Yes, but all food is radioactive to some extent and the proponents of radiation claim that any free radicals which form in the foods will long since have disappeared from them by the time you put them into your mouth. The major problem is twofold: gamma ray bombardment not only wipes out vitamins and other nutrients from food, leaving it depleted in nourishment, it also destroys any indication that a food may have gone off. This means you can be eating foods that are spoiled or contain the poisonous waste products of killed bacteria without realising it. There are also some early studies showing that irradiated food fed to animals causes genetic distortions and possibly malformed foetuses. We believe you are going to see a lot of promotion and publicity for food irradiation in the near future. It will be linked to the idea of producing pure food and enhancing health. It is important that we do all we can to prevent irradiation from becoming more widespread, that we lobby for the marking of all irradiated foods so buyers can identify them and that we get as much information as possible to the public about irradiation hazards. If anyone would like

further information or would like to work with me on the
project of disseminating information, let me know when the
meeting is finished. Thank you.'

I remembered the press releases on irradiation that had
come through to me in recent months as medical writer for
the newspaper, all from those quasi-official bodies with
highly official names like 'The Pure Food Foundation'
funded by the multinational food industry. They were full of
propaganda about 'purity' and 'protection for the consumer'. At the time I had ignored them. I had been too busy
with other things or too full of my own self-importance to
bother. I regretted not having the chance to investigate the
issue properly and write about it. I would not make the same
mistake next time – if there was a next time.

Next, a woman spoke about a sewage project that she was
involved in and asked for information about certain
chemical processes. Someone offered to give her this and
they agreed to meet after the meeting. Then a man reported
on new arms sales deals currently in the pipeline in various
places throughout the world while I wondered what could
possibly be coming next.

'There has recently been an increased foreign demand for
US Patriot missiles from Middle Eastern countries,' he said.
'Syria is currently negotiating a $2 billion deal to buy
military equipment from the USSR. I also received some
last-minute information just before I came down this
evening that Malaysia has plans to buy 300 British Hawk
fighters worth US $400 million. Meanwhile, in Africa we are
concerned that the cost of buying conventional weapons by
both centralising military governments and rebel groups in
the Horn is bankrupting the area. Sudan, Ethiopia, Eritrea
and Tigre are currently being supplied with weapons by
both the United States and the USSR. This continues to
disrupt significantly their food production. We are hearing a

lot currently about famine in the Horn. It is important that you understand that the famine is not the result of drought as the media have led us to believe. Periodic drought has always been a part of the Horn's climate and always will be. Famine results from two factors. First, fertile Horn land has been taken from people who need it to grow food, and used instead to grow cash crops for the European and American markets. Secondly, continuing arms deals where all factions are being supplied with weaponry and incited to violence through planned political activism is wreaking havoc with social and political stability in the countries. The issues are complex. For any of you who would like to know more about what is happening there is a conference being held in Toulouse on the 24th of next month. I am happy to supply details after the meeting. Thank you.'

He sat down. I knew exactly what he was talking about. I didn't know much about the Horn of Africa but I knew a hell of a lot about insurgency warfare, indoctrination, and how to pit pseudo-gangs and counter-guerrillas against one another for your own ends – like selling more guns for instance and wiping out most of the population so you could exploit natural resources. Our military industrial complex had been doing this all over the third world under the guise of helping our neighbours. Then we branded them 'savages' for their insurrections and made pompous speeches about 'peace keeping'. War is such a racket.

The next person to speak was an Englishman with one of those perfect public school accents. I wondered where he came from and what he did. 'Good evening,' he said. 'I want to report the latest information on what is being done in the way of economic and political control and constriction of individual freedom. Singapore has issued a new ID card with a bar code. It is a debit and credit card which is used instead of money by direct debiting from an account any money spent on goods, food, rent, mortgage and so forth. These new bar-coded cards are part of the expanding electronic grid system which is now being set up in Japan, in the United States and in Western Europe to compile and control information about individuals. Bar codes, as you know, are the markings you find on most goods these days. They give information about price and can be read by electronic scan. At the headquarters of the EC there is a three-storey computer set up ostensibly to regulate the personal tax affairs of all EC citizens, as well as to store information about the nature of products encoded in their bar codes. According to our information this computer – which has been nicknamed the 'Beast' by those who run it – is intended within the next ten to fifteen years to hold detailed information on every individual who lives in Europe and eventually on every individual on the planet. We believe it is the intention to mark every person on earth with a bar code. This is by no means certain, yet following the Singapore example it is quite likely that that is the intention.

'I would like to tell you how it works,' he went on. 'It is a simple matter to explain to any man or woman how convenient the Singapore-type ID card can be in the so-called cashless society. It replaces money, it makes paying for goods and services simple and almost instantaneous. It acts as an identification card since it carries personal bar code marking which makes the electronic scanning of the card quick and easy. Sounds good – the ultimate in convenience shopping. However, let me give you an example of how it works in practice. Say you have gone into a supermarket in Singapore to buy food. You go to pay for it with your bar-coded ID. The machine reads the bar code and instantaneously connects with the central computer. This indicates whether or not your mortgage, maintenance payments, taxes and so forth have been paid up to date. If not, then it does not give a sanction for you to proceed through the checkout line. You are delayed, ostensibly while the sanction is being granted. Then, as is already happening in Singapore, you become the target for an 'electronic arrest'. It is only a matter of a few minutes before a police officer arrives to take you away. I realise this may sound far-fetched or shocking to some of you; however, may I assure you that this is exactly what is happening in Singapore now. Highly detailed inside information and projections indicate that this is being carefully prepared for all of Western Europe as well as the United States, Japan and South America.'

I did not like what I was hearing yet somehow it made sense too. I knew a little about bar codes. Not long before I had written to the Department of Defense in the United States for some information I needed to fill out an American tax form. They returned twenty sheets to me on which was a bar code which presumably represented myself. At the bottom of the first page it said, 'Please check the enclosed information, if you find it to be all true and in order simply tear off and return the bottom of the final page. If not please make any corrections necessary and return them to this office by 6–1–88.'

The man went on, 'There are also indications of a plan to take bar coding even further. It is now used as a way of marking animals. This can be done electronically so that the mark is permanent but does not show on the skin. We have reason to believe that in the next twenty years a public concerned about the possible loss of their bar-coded ID cards will be easy to convince that it is much more convenient to have the bar code marked on their hand where it can be read instantaneously and electronically. This, they will be told, will give protection against the possibility of loss

455

or misuse of their card as well as acting as a driver's licence, passport and tax identification. It will probably be promoted under the guise of the mark representing citizenship in the planned new world order about which we have begun to hear glorious phrases from politicians lately. The power that such tactics wields over people is dependent upon keeping secret from them the real intentions and implications behind such actions. We want to do everything possible to expose them.'

I remembered Henry Kissinger's comment that 'in order for history to succeed it must be negotiated in total secrecy' and then recalled the conversation Wegeler reported in the tavern between men so arrogant they would rule the world. Things haven't changed much. His voice went on.

'I would be grateful if any of you who have inside information about how or where any of the things I have just mentioned are taking place, either in Europe or elsewhere, would speak to me after the meeting. I am also glad to answer any of your questions. Thank you.'

The 'organiser' stood up again. 'Thank you for these reports. I would ask you once again to respect the anonymity of each of our speakers as they have agreed to respect your own. Should you recognise or be able to identify any of these friends later on at the surface we request that you do not speak of it to anyone. It is sad that we live in a world where such a request has to be made but we feel it is necessary. We need – how shall I put it – all of us, to become conspirators, moving in silent ways to protect human freedom and the future of the planet. Perhaps we should be called *white conspirators*: people concerned with nurturing rather than destroying life – people who value autonomy and celebrate the power of the human spirit. That is why we have asked those friends who will be speaking next to acquaint us with what each in his or her own field is doing and with their discoveries. We hope that in very practical ways some of what they share with us may help us understand more about the nature of life and the potentials of human consciousness. The first person who will be speaking is a physicist,' he went on. 'She, I hope, will help us understand more about how the seen and the unseen worlds interface and react with each other. The second is a psychologist whose work in mapping the nature of human consciousness I personally believe to be unequalled in the English-speaking world. I would like to welcome them both.' There was polite applause, then a young woman seated near him stood up and began to speak in French. She had a beautifully modulated voice.

'Welcome to all of you. I am a scientist. My colleagues and I have been playing with the laws that govern physics,' she said. 'And we believe that we have come upon a rational explanation of how the many dimensions in our universe interact.' She then began to describe in laymen's terms some of the more esoteric theories of physics and to talk about tornadoes, whirlpools and Einstein's notion that matter is 'frozen energy', most of which I didn't understand a word of. Yet as I listened to her beautiful voice deep beneath the streets of Paris, I had the sense that I had become part of a new kind of congregation in a strangely primitive cathedral – as though we, all of us, who sat on in the dark on the soft earth beneath Paris, were taking part in a new kind of Mass. Her words and the words of those who had spoken before her were part of a liturgy that carried some unseen power to invoke not the gods of war or money or power but the gods of life. I looked around. There was an ordinariness about everything, despite the secrecy and the place. It made me feel for the first time since I left the SF – maybe for the first time in my life – that I belonged. I smiled at how ridiculous such a thought was, remembering that I had been brought here by a chance meeting with a girl in a green sequined T-shirt. Yet was it chance? After everything I had been through since meeting Mirabehn, I had begun to wonder if anything is ever by chance or if in some weird way each one of us is inextricably entangled in a living web and if only we – what was the phrase, *had eyes to see and ears to hear* – we could grasp the connections, both seen and unseen. I stretched my legs out. It felt good to move my body. I felt alive. I noticed how lean I had become. Every trace of the thick waist that had worried me when all those weeks ago I had stood in front of the mirror in that Vienna hotel was gone. That too made me smile.

After what seemed like a detailed explanation of how energy works according to modern physics, the woman with the lovely voice said: 'We have been exploring the nature of a totally different energy. Let us call it *rare-energy*. Let me explain. The speed of light remains the limiting factor to energy in *our* world and to the appearance of material reality as we know it, upon which it is dependent. The nature of rare-energy is quite different. It moves at a much faster rate. Of course rare-energy and the energy we know have certain things in common: spinning vortices which masquerade as matter in our world have parallels in the rare-energy world – a world completely different in *substance* from ours yet constructed out of the same *form* – namely, the spinning vortex. And although under ordinary conditions, our world of matter would not 'associate' with the *rare* world, this rare-energy whose spinning movement is beyond the speed of light does exist simultaneously with our own yet is both invisible and intangible to us. In effect it exists all around us – it can even move right through us without our ever knowing it.

'This can explain a great deal about much going on in the world today which is labelled supernatural – from the appearance and disappearance of UFOs to altered states of consciousness, as well as many of the magical, religious and quasi-religious apparitions and so on which in any other context seem so mysterious. For some quite amazing things happen when anything approaches the speed of light,' she went on. 'Certain changes take place in space and time. Space becomes compacted while time intervals get longer – so much so that eventually time vanishes altogether into eternity and space totally collapses in on itself. Of course movement faster than the speed of light, as I have said, is impossible in our reality. But consider this: if you take a ship, or a man for that matter, whose body is made up of atoms – that is vortices of energy spinning at less than the speed of light – and then suddenly increase the movement in the vortices, the *energy* will be transformed into *rare-energy*. And what happens in the process? The man or the ship will disappear. It becomes – *transubstantiated* – part of the rare-energy world which no longer interacts with the light or matter in ours. Therefore it becomes both invisible and intangible to us even though it remains very much present.'

How weird, I thought, to be sitting here taking in information of how many guns are being bought in the Middle East one moment only to be plunged into the machinations of quantum physics and told about how things disappear the next. I wondered what she was getting at.

'It can also work the other way round,' she continued. 'If you slow down the vortices of rare-energy of something from the invisible world then it will manifest in physical form in our world, appearing within our time-space reality as if from nowhere. And although in fact it was there all along, we were unable to see it before. My colleagues and I now believe that this is the manner in which things materialise and dematerialise: energy produces our space-time reality –

the one we live in day to day. Rare-energy creates another. The realms in which each exists are totally distinct from one another yet they are *coincident*: they exist simultaneously in the here and now. One is visible and tangible while the other is invisible to ordinary human senses. Of course it is probably a little more complicated than that since it is likely that there are not just two realities but many – perhaps an infinite number based on rare-energy I, II, III and so on – each encompassing all realms below it. All of the faster speeds of vortex movement contain the slower ones within them, like a Russian doll: a otiose doll has nested inside it a smaller doll inside which is a yet smaller doll and so on. And nothing is lost or gained in the process. For the *form* remains the same – namely spinning vortices of energy – only the *substance* has been altered by passing through the light barrier so that something either appears to vanish or to come into being in the process.'

'An infinite number of realities' she had said. All locked up inside each other. All were presumably accessible provided you could tap into the – what did she call it – rare energy of that reality. But maybe these realities tapped into *you* instead, maybe what she was talking about had to do with strange faces staring back at you in the bathroom mirror and scorch marks on bedroom carpets.

'OK. Thanks for bearing with me through all the complicated explanations. Now let's look at what all of this means in practical terms. Throughout history there have been records of what are called supernatural events. They could be better described as *rare*-events since they are probably a perfectly natural result of this alteration in the speed at which movement in the energy vortices is taking place. In every world culture and primitive society there are thousands of records of people being able to materialise and dematerialise: Jesus for instance, the Buddha, holy men in our own time such as the being known as Baba-ji who appears and disappears at will and who seems able to move forwards or back in time. Probably, quite simply, because they were able to alter the speed of movement within the energy vortices that constituted their physical bodies. There are also numerous records of people who have made objects appear or disappear at will: the loaves and fishes of the Bible, the 'creations' of Sai Baba – the Indian whose ability to materialise diamonds has been well recorded on film. These too appear to be the result of altering the rate of movement of rare-energy vortices from higher-energy realms to lower ones so that something materialises in our space and time, so we can touch it and see it.'

Her words brought memories of the dark figure that had stood behind me in the Heathrow immigration line, of the men Mirabehn's postcard described and of those men or whatever they were that sat waiting for me when I turned out of her drive. It seemed impossible that was only yesterday – that the world could change so much in so little time. But maybe the world hadn't changed at all. I wondered if these ugly men – these beings, these shadows of reality, whatever they were – had themselves been Mirabehn's vortices of rare-energy masquerading as matter? I could think of a lot more pleasant things to transmit from one universe to another: 'Scotty, beam me down a beautiful woman. Forget the MIBs.' Her voice went on.

'There is also a third category of *transubstantiation* – the category of so-called spiritual manifestations – the appearance of the Virgin Mary in such places as Medjugorje or Fatima for instance, apparitions of the goddess Kali such as those the Indian saint Ramakrishna experienced, the manifestation of devas or nature spirits, angels, trolls or demons throughout history. It would seem that when a human consciousness is able to attune itself in some way with a particular quality of thought or feeling it can call forth from the *rare*-realms a manifestation of that energy in our own realm – a manifestation which has all of the appearances of material substance, and which will seem to appear from nowhere and then to disappear again as readily. It would seem too that other people who are able either consciously or unconsciously to align themselves with the same thought, feeling or belief will also perceive the apparition – sometimes scores or even thousands of people.

'We believe that our findings are important in two ways. First it is our hope that the more we come to understand about the way that energy and rare energy interact to materialise and dematerialise form, the more we will be free of the unnecessary fear that comes from hauntings, extra-terrestrial contacts and so on. Also, it is our belief that the more we learn, the more we understand about the interfaces of dimensions, the more we may be able to use the powers of our imagination, our dreams and our intentions, to call upon those energies both seen and unseen to aid us in our work of rehabilitating the planet and helping ourselves and others make full use of our human freedom.'

As I listened to her speak I realised she was introducing me to a whole new world. It was a world not bounded by three dimensions like the one I had been living in until I met Mirabehn. It was virtually open-ended – a world in which almost infinite possibilities for creation and destruction exist. In recent weeks I had been dragged kicking and screaming into that world. I had been too blinkered and block-headed to even consider its existence. Ludwig knew, of course, but knowing it I was sure had been hell-on-earth for him. Mirabehn moved in and out of it with the ease of a hand slipping into water. That must be how she knew so much about dreams, prophecy. Maybe each of us who would survive, each of us who would participate in the creation of a life that isn't bar coded that doesn't live by exploitation will have to learn more about rare-energy and these rare-realities – to learn not theoretically from a physicist using long and complicated explanations but by experiencing them. I couldn't help but wish there was an easier way. She continued. . . .

'I hope some of what I have said may be useful to you or at the very least thought-provoking. I would also welcome the opportunity of discussing these things further after the meeting with anyone who would like to come and speak to me about them. Thank you.'

For a moment or more there was silence. A man got up and walked along one wall of the room until he was outside the range of the dim light. I could hear him urinating. Another man lit a cigarette. Then another got up from the same group, cleared his throat and began to speak – this time in English but with a thick accent that could have been Polish or Czechoslovakian – in any case East European.

'Good evening,' he said. 'I am a medical doctor by training and a psychiatrist by profession, working in the United States. My wife and I . . .' Here his voice was drowned out by two or three others who spoke in French, complaining that they did not understand. There followed a rapid discussion which lasted a couple of minutes after which the young woman in the green-sequined T-shirt got up and walked over to the doctor's side. Her face was for a moment reflected in the light from one of the stoves. I noticed for the second time how familiar it looked but still I could not identify where I'd seen her before. She began to translate into French each sentence he spoke. This made communication slow and laborious.

'Many years ago,' he continued, 'I became fascinated to explore not only the realm of the diseased mind but also

463

so-called normal human consciousness. I work together with my wife who is a physiotherapist, and who has herself from a very early time had to deal with many spontaneous psychic events in her own life. My wife knows what she knows from having experienced it herself first hand. I, I am afraid, have never been privy to such deep knowing. Instead, I act as the observer – rather like an eagle who from some tall pinnacle surveys the landscape. We have worked together for almost forty years. I must say before I begin to describe to you some of the things I have come to believe about the nature and powers of human consciousness, that everything I tell you comes from a combination of my wife's inner knowing and my own objective observation. Without her I would have learned nothing.

'In our work we explore the nature of the human psyche, using a number of methods: hypnosis, consciousness-altering drugs such as LSD, Ketamine, MDMA and the natural psychedelics, breathing techniques, yoga and meditation. After hundreds of thousands of hours working with patients and colleagues we have concluded that the human mind is a great deal bigger than any of us realised and that we need to make use of far more of it than we do if we are to nurture life and care for the planet. The human mind encompasses not only conscious awareness but the unconscious, which was described in quite different ways by Freud and Jung, as well as what we call the *"superconscious"*. After hearing what our friend the physicist has said it would be more accurate to call it the "rare-conscious". In any case this superconscious or transcendent mind can give a human being access to information about the microcosm and the macrocosm which is quite simply unavailable through normal channels.

'Unusual events occur when the superconscious realm is entered, whether as a result of intense physical exertion, by mind-altering techniques or drugs. Entering this realm can give access to verifiable information about the present world and also about the past or future. In fact there are many parallels with the way our friend the physicist has described interactions between the energy that constitutes our every-day world and what she calls "rare-energy". When transcendent awareness is triggered a person is able to receive information from other realms while still remaining in a physical body. In such circumstances someone can *experience* for himself, not just imagine or dream, say life as a single-celled plant, as a galaxy or as another person altogether –occasionally even all three at once by a simple shift of focus. Sometimes too a person will relive an event from the past as though it is occurring in the present moment complete with the entire gamut of bodily sensations that come with it – or even an event in the life of another. Infrequently a person in the superconscious state can even experience more than one event simultaneously, especially when all of them carry the same kind of emotional charge.

'People who have experienced these things experience other curious happenings: they can find that the dichotomy which normally exists between form and emptiness becomes transcended, for example. They sometimes simultaneously or alternately experience a unity with another person living or dead as well,' he said. 'Or even with a group of people or an entire nation while at the same time maintaining a sense of their own personal existence. Sometimes too they experience a unity with certain "gods" – or with what Jung called archetypes – the Wise Woman, the Great Father, the Fool. Finally, they can and often do experience themselves either as manifestations of the microcosm in terms of subatomic particles whirling in space, earlier life forms, plants or minerals, or of the macrocosm – stars, asteroids, great suns whirling in space.'

I wondered if what the doctor was saying had anything to do with what had happened to my own body when I was lost in the labyrinth – with the visions and the physical contortions and finally with the light and the peace.

'Thirty years ago,' he went on, 'I, like most doctors, would have been inclined to treat the reports of such phenomena as figments of imagination. Now, having worked for many years both with what are called normal subjects as well as those with obvious pathology – from manic depressives and schizoid personalities to severe multiple personality disorders I can no longer uphold such a belief. I am quite certain that what we witness happening to people in these intense transpersonal states – abreactions of experiences of trauma for instance, or the dissolving of ego boundaries, or fluctuations in perceptions of time and space – not only reflect the subjective perception of a person but also carry information about external reality.

'Let me give you an example. We have worked a lot with the multiple personality disorder, an extraordinary syndrome in which two or more integrated selves coexist simultaneously in the same body. The history of MPD is traceable back to the eclipse of the concepts of possession and exorcism. It was first noted late in the eighteenth century when the notion of possession was replaced by the idea of a psychological disorder. In 1791 the German physician Ebhardt Gmelin reported a case of 'exchanged personality' but only in the past twenty years here in Europe and in the United States has MPD been systematically studied. Let me tell you a bit about what we have found.

'There is a rapidly developing body of data that demonstrates quite conclusively not only that posture, voice, physiognomy and right- or left-handedness alter when a person with MPD switches from one personality to another but that remarkable changes in their physiological, neurological and immune system variables take place as well. Even brainwave patterns and electrical skin responses alter. One woman I worked with recently demonstrated a severe allergy to dust which completely disappeared less than a minute after the switch to another personality took place. Another MPD had chronic high blood pressure. This also normalised within two minutes of a switch.'

This man's words were like a high-tech version of those Wawruch had used to describe what he called Ludwig's 'fugues': *this man who only two minutes before had been oblivious to my presence, racked by pain and so swollen with fluid that he was hardly able to move unaided from one side of his small bed to the other, had physically metamorphosed in front of my very eyes . . . the voice was new . . . even the rate of his heartbeat and the quality of his pulse would change beyond all recognition. . . .* Had Ludwig been a multiple personality? Did this explain the appearance and disappearance of what Wawruch had called his personae?

The doctor continued: 'The reason why I speak of the multiple personality disorder is because it is probably the most extreme form of psychic aberration. It is also in many ways the most interesting in relation to the superconscious realm. For MPD victims demonstrate the most widespread alterations in physiology, psychology and brain functions. They can go from the intelligence level of a two-year-old child to that of a genius quite literally at the flick of some internal switch which we don't as yet understand. The average number of personalities present in a multiple is generally between eight and thirteen, although what we call super-multiples may display more than a hundred. Patients with MPD often appear to tap into, or perhaps it would be more accurate to say they themselves are tapped into by, exceptional levels of consciousness – sometimes levels of artistic genius, sometimes of great wisdom, or intense demonic power, or high intellect – which are in no way accessible either to most of us or even to themselves in their more common personality states. They also demonstrate psychic gifts – pre-cognition for example or psychokinesis or telepathy – which are not manifested in their usual consciousness. How or why the switches that underlie MPD take place from one personality, or even from one physiology, to another we do not know. But we do know that something is going on which is far beyond anything we can explain through the rational mind.'

I listened to this man's words, astonished by what he was describing and wishing that Wawruch could be present to hear them. So inexorably had my life been bound together with his and so much did I owe to his compassion, his patience and his persistence on his own deathbed in writing a narrative which had changed my life that it would have been a wonderful gift to give Wawruch in return – just to let him know he was not alone in living with Ludwig's fugues. I felt a terrible sadness that it could never happen.

'Ninety-seven per cent of patients with MPD,' the doctor said, 'have experienced severe sexual or psychic abuse in childhood. These memories of abuse are frequently re-pressed so they are completely unknown to the "everyday" personalities that inhabit the body. When in the course of therapy a personality does appear which was present when the abuse took place it will describe a scene in which someone, most often the parent, is carrying out an act of aggression or abuse against the young child. The child in quite a "real" way dissociates – appears to leave its body, to stand aside from the scene that is taking place as though it is happening not to it personally but in an abstract way to "somebody else". This way it is able to protect its image of the parent as a loving person, a belief necessary for the child's security and well-being, and even to avoid feeling much of the pain implicit in the attack. He or she quite literally, "lets someone else do it". Meanwhile any memory that remains, remains only with one of the personalities or is expressed only obliquely in dreams or mythic visions of devouring monsters or all-consuming blackness – dreams which are frequently triggered by a particular sound or smell or place, of which the MPD demonstrates extreme terror.'

The doctor's words brought back to me Storyteller's tale of the serpent in the cellar. I wondered what had happened to Ludwig there. I decided I would go back to Wawruch's manuscript and Storyteller's words. Had this event been the crux of Ludwig's fragmented consciousness?

'Having myself worked with almost thirty MPDs,' he continued, 'and having examined the work of my colleagues, I have come to the conclusion that a human being – particularly a child in whom the ego structure is weak – who experiences extremes of trauma quite literally opens itself up to what in former times was called "possession" by energy, entities, or realities from other dimensions – perhaps what my physicist friend whom we heard earlier calls the "rare-energy" worlds.

'Trauma, when it is severe enough and prolonged enough, appears to cause a break in the energy field or fields which maintain biochemical balance and which order life processes. When such a break is made a subtle form of transubstantiation takes place. It is as though intense emotional trauma creates some new energy field around the person giving him access to unseen levels of reality or indeed making it possible for him to be possessed by these levels. In the case of the person with MPD this happens *to* him – he is a "victim" of powers, energies, entities, which enter his force field and for a time take over his being – in effect *using* him rather than *serving* him. Of course MPD is an extreme case, far removed from the experience of so-called normal people.

Yet we have found that virtually all people, given exceptionally stressful circumstances – say the death of a loved one, or the loss of security are similarly capable of tapping into other levels of being.

'We have discovered, however, that through the controlled use of meditation, breathing, certain drugs, sensory isolation and other methods – and we have come to favour simple breathing techniques over the use of chemical substances and drugs – normal people can gradually learn to tap into "rare" worlds of knowledge at will and also gain access to wisdom and power that may, if it is wisely directed, help us solve the world's problems and our own problems as well as enhancing our autonomy and the control we have over our own lives. An expansion of consciousness is central to the development of an awareness of the preciousness of life in each of us. Once it occurs it can help us prevent the further waste of human and planetary resources. It also gives us access to levels of creativity which transcend the powers of the intellect, allowing us to find solutions to problems not discoverable by other methods.

'Although on one level we human beings are insignificant – almost infinitesimal biological systems when we measure ourselves against the cosmos – on another we are infinite. We have come to believe – no, not to believe but to know that human consciousness contains within it not only all information and creativity needed to enable us to solve the problems facing mankind today but access to any level of reality we need to call upon for help. It is there within. We need only learn how to use it better. That is why we have come here tonight, not only to share our work with you but to make available to all of you who are interested some very simple techniques for tapping into the superconscious mind. Please speak to either of us at the end of the night if you would like to explore this.'

I liked the words he spoke. I wanted to know more. I wondered if the anger, the hatred and the sense of power-lessness which had plagued me for ten years were the results of trying to live too big a life in too small a space. I figured I had learned to kill, I had learned to survive, what the hell, maybe it was not all that far-fetched to think some newfangled breathing techniques could, what had he said, *expand* my consciousness. Since it had been the size of a pea until now anyway it probably wasn't going to be all that difficult. Besides, it might be fun to try.

The doctor thanked the girl in the green sequins for translating his words, and sat down. She returned to our group. The silence was broken by many voices speaking in low tones. Gérard turned to me.

'How are you feeling now?'

I was puzzled by his question. I smiled and nodded my head, 'Good.'

He handed me another beer, which I opened and drank thankfully. I had been very thirsty.

A few moments later Gérard stood up. Hardly raising his voice he began to speak. The hall fell silent.

'Friends, I was hoping tonight to bring with me a man who I believe has much of importance to tell you. His name is Salvador Freixedo. He is, or was, before they excommuni-cated him for his writings, a Jesuit priest. Señor Freixedo lives in Madrid but I am sorry to say he could not be here in person. His books which are well known in the Spanish-speaking world have not yet been translated into French or English. It is my belief that what Señor Freixedo has written about may be of importance not only to the protection of personal freedom from control that can come about through the misuse of religious and political power.

'Since Señor Freixedo could not be with us tonight, I have asked another friend who reads Spanish and speaks fluent

French – although with a rather heavy American accent – to read us a few passages I have marked from two of Señor Freixedo's books: *La Religión entre la Parapsychologica y los Ovinis* and *Israel Pueblo Contacto*. I hope you will find this both interesting and relevant. Michael, would you mind . . .'

I was in no way prepared for Gérard's words. He could not possibly have known I spoke both Spanish and French. He did not even know my name until an hour ago or where I came from. Yet he did know. These curiously connected 'ordinary' people sitting around their little stoves in their underground hall seemed to know all sorts of things which by rights they should have had no way of knowing. Perhaps it was the same way in which I had known how to find my way through the maze into this strange room, or the way I had ended up at Mirabehn's door many weeks ago. I wondered if in the same way I might come to know where I was going from here. Then I noticed with surprise how little the question concerned me at that moment. Just now I didn't know much – only that the experience of the labyrinth had in some way dissolved my boundaries, turned me into something, or someone, new – the same yet different. I knew it had also altered for ever my future.

The future. What was in the future? I asked the question with detached curiosity. The name Bourdelle came into my mind as though from some far distant place. Of course: '*Musée Bourdelle, 16 rue Antoine Bourdelle [Métro Falguière]. Musée accessible aux handicapés physiques.*' That was the next step. Remembering this filled me with a sense of supreme certainty which made me laugh: who needed to know anything beyond where to take the next step?

I took the books from Gérard's hand. He picked up the light which had previously been strapped to his head but which was now lying in his lap, turned it on and held it over my shoulder so that I could see the text. He had marked a number of passages in green pen. I began to read first, from *Israel Pueblo Contacto*. It was a brilliant and disturbing exploration of the thesis that the Jewish religion had developed as a result of extraterrestrial contacts. I have tried without success to buy Freixedo's books since that night. The gist of what he wrote was both intriguing and highly incendiary – little wonder, I thought, that he was excommunicated for his writings. Were his works more widely known in the English-speaking world he would surely be the *bête noire* of organised religion. As I read the words I could almost feel the hackles rising on the backs of a few of the necks around the room.

When aliens arrive on earth from other dimensions, says Freixedo, they are so much more highly developed in their intellects and powers than men that they appear to be divine, something to be feared and worshipped. In effect, he says, they 'do deals' with men they contact, much as Yahweh did with Moses, bestowing upon them certain powers or abilities in return for which, unbeknown to the contactees, they also extract a toll. The toll is a pricey one: they feed off of some kind of subtle energy which men possess, says Freixedo. In the process they often drain from these people their very life-blood, giving them a deathly pallor. Freixedo's words recalled the description of Schindler – pale and bloodless – repeated again and again by everyone who knew him.

According to Freixedo, the contactee – although completely unaware that it is happening – becomes a source of 'meat' for his mentor. When an alien takes over the body of an earth man, he irradiates him in some way which not only gives the contactee supernatural gifts but makes it possible for the alien to extract the force, energy or subtle substance from the contactee's body which the alien needs for its own life.

473

The passages I read from Freixedo's books were beautifully written in highly educated Spanish. I am quite certain that my ad lib translations did justice neither to his vast intelligence and scholarship nor to the ideas he was putting across. What seemed to concern him most in both books were two things: first his observation that the Elohim in the Bible, which literally translated means 'great beings' who promise man freedom, keep their promises only so long as it suits them. These unearthly forces or energies or entities, insists Freixedo, are playing with us. They enjoy our confusion and our suffering. In some mysterious way he believes they use our emotions and our pain as fodder for their own life. The idea made me shudder – so hideous did it seem. I tried to tell myself it could not possibly be true.

The last passage Gérard had marked was a paragraph in which Freixedo's passion so impressed me that I remember it still almost word for word:

> Ordinary man, exiled and lost as he is on our earth,
> uncertain of his origins and of what happens after
> death, is always searching for leaders or supermen
> who will take him by the hand and give him some
> security in his mysterious journey across the life
> threshold towards an unknown future. For this reason,
> when someone does seem to be in contact with the
> unknown beyond (be it mystical or spatial), ordinary
> man, feeling himself to be the orphan of the universe,
> blindly follows him even though all reason may dictate
> against his doing so.

He could have been speaking to me alone. I knew well the need for a leader. I knew it from both sides of the fence. As a child I had looked for someone or something I could serve. That turned out to be my mistress – SF. From the other side as a commander I could sometimes tangibly feel the power of my men's faith in me – the way they looked up to me and honoured me – so much I often felt they gave away their own power to empower me. They all needed to believe in somebody who knew what was right, whose skill or luck or strength would pull them through. I wondered if maybe there was another way – a way of trusting yourself and honouring that trust instead of bargaining it away for some sense of security – the security of a political party, a religion, an elite group, money, a marriage, whatever. Why, I wondered does man so loathe himself that he grovels in the earth before false gods, and why is he afraid?

When I finished my reading, the man who had introduced the evening got up again. 'Thank you,' he said. 'Friends, it is growing late. It is almost time for us to return with our groups to the surface. It is my understanding that the return has been organised by the various leaders so that each group leaves by a different exit in order to attract a minimum of attention. We will be meeting again here tomorrow if you would like to join us. After that our next meeting will be on 21 September and the day following – that is, the full moon. We will begin at the same time tomorrow. I do hope all of you will join us. There will be the same restrictions on information as always. Before we say goodnight I would like to ask that we join in a silent wish that, together with men and women from all over our earth, we can not only find a way to live in harmony and respect for the planet but, using all the resources at our disposal as human beings, also find ways to ensure that each man, woman and child on the earth is given what seems the absolute minimum as a birthright – self-respect, enough food and shelter, and the right to live simply with those of like mind.'

For five minutes silence reigned in this underground chamber – a silence one could never know on the surface of the earth.

SANCTUS

> One shall not kill 'the evil impulse', the passion, in
> oneself, but one shall serve God with it; it is the
> power which is destined to receive its direction
> from man.

Martin Buber *Hasidism and the Modern Man*

It took us no more than half an hour to reach the surface
from Salle Z. We left *les carrières* through an exit at the side of
a statue near l'Observatoire, emerging into a still and misty
dawn. I undid the rope which had held my package inside
the borrowed coat all through the night, took off the coat
and hoped that whoever it belonged to would notice and
claim it. A young man with a gold front tooth reached out to
take it from me. I thanked him. He smiled. The package
looked battered. It was wet on one corner and the ink from
some of the papers had run. I tucked it under my arm.

No words were said as we dispersed into the foggy
morning. I would probably never see any of these people
again, yet I felt I had found those with whom I belonged. I
didn't need to know their names. It didn't matter what
language they spoke or what kind of sex life they had. It only
mattered that they were straight —that they tried to be true
to themselves and that they were willing to go to bat for what
they believed in. Oh yeah, and one more thing – that they
had the guts to stand on their own two feet instead of
handing over responsibility for their lives to the banker,

476

doctor, president, talk show host, – fill in the blanks. I knew there were others like them in every country of the world. I knew that something simpler yet far more powerful than a religion or political system binds us together – not rigidly with rules and regulations or under the banner of some high-falutin cause, but loosely, organically, the way living things are organised. I wasn't sure what to call it – maybe common humanity.

I walked around the Observatory then up l'Avenue Observatoire to Boulevard Montparnasse. At Port-Royal I turned into back streets making my way east towards the Jardin des Plantes. The sun had risen and the mist was clearing. The gentle morning air, the strength in my thighs as I moved, the clarity of my vision had made the world wondrous. There was new energy in my body – a body made leaner now than it had been for years. Nor was it hard and big as it had been during my military days. It had changed radically. I liked what I felt. My knee, still very swollen from last night's crack was something towards which I felt kindly – the way a father feels when he sees his son bruised from a football match in which, despite his size and limitations, he has given everything he had.

It was still too early for the museum. I walked along the quay to Boulevard St Germain then followed it west past Odéon. I turned south on rue du Bac and wandered on through twisting back streets which I hoped were taking me towards Falguière. I considered returning to my hotel, then dismissed the idea. The morning was too wonderful not to stay in it. I walked slowly, taking in the world around me with a simple pleasure I had never known before.

Shutters were creaking open, people and animals were waking up. Women with besoms in their hands washed and brushed the pavement in front of houses and shops, cats were coming home with bellies heavy from a good night's hunting. Men in uniforms were busy with machines cleaning the streets. A group of tourists gathered together next to a huge coach in front of a run-down hotel while the driver put their bags into the hold. I heard a woman arguing with her husband above me. She banged the shutters to the window when she opened them. An old man who had been sleeping in a doorway slowly and with difficulty shed the cardboard cover and a holey blanket which had been his bed. He look up at me as I passed wondering, I suspect, if I were some official who had been sent to move him on. All of it, beautiful and ugly alike, seemed to be exactly as it should be – even a broken bottle still lying in the gutter which this morning had been missed by Paris's immaculate street cleaners – it could happen only once in a hundred chances – and the tearstained face of a heavily made-up girl dressed in shorts and fishnet tights searching her bag. I thought she was looking for a handkerchief. Instead she took out a blood-red lipstick and smeared it over her already badly smudged mouth.

Around half-past nine I ended up at Bienvenue with all its silly modern buildings. I crossed over and turned right up l'Avenue du Mainc. On the left I saw the street sign, it read *rue Antoine Bourdelle*. I turned into it. Thirty paces further on, on the right-hand side, was the Musée Bourdelle. It consisted of more than one building – both old and modern – grouped around a small courtyard of earth in which stood statues I had seen in Mirabehn's books. The tall wrought-iron gates were still locked. I waited. At two minutes to ten a middle-aged woman came out carrying a set of keys. She stood at the gate until the exact moment, opened it and returned immediately to one of the houses.

I did not go in. It felt right somehow that I should wait a little. This was, I knew, my last chance to fit the pieces of the puzzle together – Ludwig's fugues, Wawruch's haunting,

Mirabehn's manuscripts, secret societies and men in black, my own bizarre behaviour, Salle Z and all the rest. I didn't want to blow it. Not this time.

I remembered reading somewhere, years ago when such words held no meaning for me, that there are two principles of evil which man encounters in his struggle for freedom. These two, the article had said, could be likened to two spirit-beings – Ahriman and Lucifer. Lucifer is the light-bearer – he who would deceive man into believing he has no earthly task and that his body is of no value. Lucifer seduces us into believing we are 'pure spirit' and as such superior to the other animals on the earth. He suffuses us with vanity, pride, fanaticism and false, idealistic dreams. Ahriman is purveyor of quite a different set of illusions. He is lord of bestiality, of every form of materialism, and of the world of the senses. Denying the existence of all that is spiritual, Ahriman trades in addictive sexuality, junk bonds and BMWs. The article had described Jesus' connection with an esoteric Jewish order – I think they were called Essenes – whose members led an ascetic life of meditation strictly governed by the laws of their order which isolated them from the Israelites. The article described the dismay of Jesus at the spiritual posture of these Essenes. They were people who in their self-centred striving for the perfection of their own souls avoided confrontation with both Ahriman and Lucifer. And in doing this they placed a far greater burden of evil on the shoulders of the rest of humanity. Lucifer and Ahriman, the article argued, are not to be avoided as the Essenes had done. They are to be wrestled with. Each man must fight his own battle with evil in his own way. For evil is bound to the evolution of man. It is out of doing battle with it that human creativity is born.

I thought back to the CIA's drug dealing and to all the ways that those who would control the earth wield their secret powers – turning white against black, son against father, man against man. Having sold us the tools for human destruction, this illuminated elite wash their hands of any connection with what is going on, and sit back to watch us destroy one another while filling their coffers with gold. I thought about all their bullshit talk and misuse of language – of the illusory world they create where having 'spirit' means drinking Smirnoff. I thought, too, about all the lies told by purveyors of the 'new world order' – false-hoods woven to imprison man under a cloak of phoney 'brotherhood' and then convince him he cannot do without a new washing machine, which they are happy to loan him the money to buy in return for his poverty, leaving him powerless as a laboratory rat in an electric maze.

I remembered my own anger at the secret government in which I myself had been a pawn, and Ludwig's struggles with the Illuminati which I still only partly understood. Were the Illuminati to be destroyed like the bad guys in a Rambo movie? Or were they part of the workings of Ahriman and Lucifer: not an evil to be excised in an attempt to create the perfect, sterile, pure life but forces to be wrestled with despite despair and fury and meaninglessness in the process of becoming.

Maybe it did all fit together. Maybe there was an interconnectedness to all life, just like the woman with the beautiful voice said. Who knows. Maybe too Freixedo's theories were more than the product of a brilliant mind. In the context of everything else that had happened to me, to Wegeler and the others, the way he explains things made at least as much sense as anything else.

It was time to go in. But if the answers were here in the museum, I sure as hell had no idea how to find them. I mean what do you do: go in, buy a ticket, give the little moustachioed man behind the counter an American smile and say, 'By the way, do you know if Bourdelle ever had any problems with men in black?'

I walked through the gate. The courtyard was on my left. Behind it an arched loggia connected three buildings. I walked straight on and entered the oldest one ahead of me, over the door of which was written *Caisse*. The room was simple. No money had been spent to create that modern yet noble look the French so love imparting to their official buildings. There stood a wood and glass case in front of me behind which sat a woman who took your money, gave you a ticket and sold postcards and books. It was early of course but I had the sense that no matter what time of day you arrived you were not likely to find this little museum jammed with tourists. I noticed only five people there that morning besides myself. Two were Japanese, the others elderly and French.

The room led back on to another room equally simple and austere in which were placed small heads and figures on what looked to be wooden blocks. The woman at the counter motioned to me to go back through the door I had entered and said something half in French, half in English about the exhibition beginning somewhere else. I went out again, ticket in hand and turned right, walking along the loggia towards what looked like a large hall with glass doors through which I could see massive statues in bronze and stone.

Bourdelle's work turned out to be even better than I could possibly have imagined from looking at photographs of it. Wandering from room to room, house to house, I looked at small heads, strange bronze twisted figures, paintings, pastels and busts of mythological figures. Everything he did, from the tiniest study in clay to the monumental figure of La France with a strangely innocent serpent twisted round her spear, seemed to have been built as an arrangement in space

which took into account the emptiness as much as the mass.
This gave a remarkable wholeness to his sculptures as
though matter and spirit had become one essence poised in
momentary stillness between earth and sky. There was no
bric-à-brac – no clever or fashionable additions – to mar the
artist's honesty in this museum which, I learned from one of
the guards, had been Bourdelle's home for most of his life.
As I continued through the rooms, around the statues, up
and down the stairs, I looked for Ludwig everywhere. There
was not a sign of him – not one of the Beethoven busts which
I had marvelled at in the book – no Storyteller, none of
Ludwig's fugues, nothing. Had they been figments of my
imagination? And this peace that had come upon me in the
night – this certainty that I, like one of Bourdelle's dazzling
statues, was living in poised equanimity for the first time in
my life. Was it some final ironic delusion of a tired and
thwarted mind?

I had been through all the buildings in which the artist's
works were displayed – all that is except one: the one in which
the *caisse* sat. At the bottom of the stairs I turned right and
entered the door to it again. The woman behind the counter
looked up to see how many tickets she needed to tear off,
recognised me as somebody who had been her way before, and
dropped her head back into the magazine she was reading. I
closed the door behind me and walked across the room and
through a doorway into the next one. The old wooden floor
creaked under my feet. There was no one in this part of the
museum. I passed through the second room, past the small
figures displayed all round and on into a third. Still nothing.
Here the *sens de visite* forced you to turn left again and go
through a doorway into another old and not very well-lit room.
It was as I entered it that I came face to face with him – with
Ludwig – a dozen massive heads or more each sitting on its
pedestal displayed for all who cared to see.

A sense of wild elation overcame me. I no longer cared about explaining anything. No goal, no end, no purpose mattered – neither Schindler's lies nor Wawruch's truth. Not past nor future. Only my being here now in this old room with him – the Ludwig whom I had never sought to know yet whom I had come to know far better than myself. Not Ludwig the great composer polished and pummelled into whatever shape would serve commercial interest but Ludwig the man in all his shapes and forms. Mirabehn's question buzzed inside my head, 'Do you *know* Beethoven?' – a question I had laughed at, had not understood. Now I could answer her, 'Yes, Mirabehn, I know him,' were she alive to hear my words. Bourdelle too had *known* Beethoven – I was sure of it – possessed by his energy, by all his majesty and all his horror. Ludwig whose face had terrified me gazing out at me from the mirror I smashed with my fist, Ludwig – Wawruch's patient and Steffen's friend, Ludwig the dreamer, Ludwig the destroyer, Ludwig the victim, Ludwig the living and Ludwig the dead. He was here. This small room and the one beyond it were filled with him – in bronze, in paint, in pastel, clay and plaster. I wondered if there had been others who had also *known* Ludwig, besides Wawruch and Wegeler, besides Mirabehn and poor Rolland. I had come upon a head of Rolland by the sculptor in another room of the museum. Like his friend Bourdelle, Rolland had spent years of his life obsessed by Ludwig. On the block beneath one of Bourdelle's many masks of Ludwig – a head in stone – there was carved *moi je suis Bacchus qui pressure pour les hommes le nectar delicieux*. The words made me laugh. How many of those I wondered, how many of us who had *known* Ludwig would describe the nectar he pressed out as 'delicious'.

Against the edge of the opening which led to the next room a folding chair stood. I walked over to it and sat down.

From there, only by turning my body I could see every one of Bourdelle's Ludwigs – from the first he had made in 1887 – its powerful spirit only beginning to stir in this sculpture of a head, its eyes closed, leaning against the fist which has emerged unfinished from the stone. It had been made – I knew it – when Bourdelle had just begun to taste the nectar. He had been a young man of twenty-five, innocent of the nature of this fiery fluid which had just begun its pathway through him.

Each piece of sculpture was labelled with the date at which it had been created. As you passed in chronological order from one to another you could see the way liquid fire – the godpower – had flowed through Bourdelle's body and how Bourdelle – strong enough and brave enough to let it pour through him – had forced it out again with his hands, himself changed by it in the process. Everything was reflected in the statues: the awakening of the spirit fire, the way it danced its dance, now slowly, now wildly as the artist worked in clay, on paper, stone and bronze over forty years with Ludwig's image. They were here in this little room – all of them – Storyteller in the rawness of his truth, Persecutor, Gypsy Child, Sweet-Curled Woman, all burning forth from the denseness of matter. Even Ahriman with his promise of animal pleasures, Lecher in his coldness and Gentle One were here. I wondered how Bourdelle had known them – if he too had smashed mirrors; if he had read Wawruch's manuscript, Wegeler's letter. I wondered if he had met the young Miss Slade and if she had seen these heads during the years she spent in Paris learning French before her meeting with Rolland. My heart was still but my mind raced on asking endless unanswered questions – questions which would never be answered. For the long and tortuous trail I had followed now came to an end in this small room. There were no further papers, or if they had existed, any chance of my finding them seemed to have died with Mirabehn.

I sat there, the package on my lap, with Ludwig – among Bourdelle's bronzes of him whom I had come to know better than any being I had ever known on earth. Strange how deeply one can know a dead man.

Only two people entered the small room of the museum while I was there. They came in separately, catalogue in hand, glanced quickly at one or two of the busts and then left. I think they sensed – how was it Wawruch put it – beneath *the lumen of consciousness* – that they were intruding on an intimate meeting and thought it best to leave us alone. Finally I got up. I wanted to touch one of the masks of Ludwig before I left. I went over to it. The head was huge, the hair wild and flared out from a brooding forehead. The eyes were closed, the mouth set hard in determination, the thin lips turned down at the corners. I walked around the head. Its back had been hollowed out leaving a great black pit. I put my hand into the hollow. It was rough and cold. I continued round to the other side then stopped for one last moment in front of the bronze before leaving the room, the masks and all they stood for. I only wanted to gaze into his pitted face.

I felt a hand reach out and touch my shoulder. I had heard no one enter the room. I turned round to find the woman in the green sequins standing beside me. Now dressed in a superbly tailored man's pinstriped suit and a silk shirt, her hair had been pulled up and tied at the back of her head. In her hand she carried a soft briefcase in black and brown leather. She was smiling. I realized that she was extraordinarily beautiful and wondered why I had not noticed before. Then I remembered where I had seen that face before. It was not exactly the same, yet hauntingly familiar – the face of Johanna in my dream.

'Bonjour,' she said.

'Bonjour.'

'Tu vas bien?'

'Oui . . . vraiment bien.'

They were the first words we had spoken to each other.

'Nous sommes contents que tu sois enfin venu. On t'attend depuis longtemps.'

She unzipped her briefcase and took out a pile of yellowed papers which had been tied with a thin black ribbon.

'Je crois que celles-ci t'appartiennent,' she said, placing them in my hand.

'Je les garderai bien, je te promets.'

'Oui, tu les a meritées, tu sais.'

'Je sais.'

'Et moi, je sais que tu feras ce qu'il faut.'

She leaned forward and kissed me on the cheek. Then she turned and walked away.

I no longer needed to ask how she knew I would be here, where she got the letters and why she gave them to me, or for that matter why she ever bothered to rescue me from the pavement at Centre Beaubourg in the first place. I knew now that these were not questions for which there could be the usual two-dimensional answers. What answers there were would depend upon an understanding of the way in which seen and unseen worlds interface – worlds of which I had not even dreamed, until Mirabehn. If I ever had enough understanding to answer them, the questions would have become irrelevant anyway.

I tucked my scruffy brown package beneath my arm and holding the letters in my hand left the museum. The sun had risen high in the sky, which was clear and of the palest blue. I did not know what the letters contained. But I was pretty sure who they came from. Johanna had to be the missing link – the key to a puzzle which otherwise wouldn't fit together.

I didn't know if the Illuminati and their modern-day

equivalents – men who behave like adolescent boys mastur-
bating in secret hovels – were only arrogant and greedy
bastards caught in the web of their own intellectual
machinations. Or if, as Freixedo says, they have actually
sold those souls and are, unbeknownst to them, being eaten
alive by some bloodthirsty forces who bargain with power so
they can exploit human life and steal the planet's resources.
. Maybe the papers would tell me. Maybe I would never
know what to believe. Since meeting Mirabehn I had
learned that it doesn't make much difference which you
believe – that beliefs are only attempts to explain life –
something no more explainable than the excitement of the
SF or the way Ludwig's string quartets bring tears to your
eyes and make you want to laugh at the same time.

It was not Ludwig's *beliefs* that entered my life the day I
met Mirabehn. It was his being, his presence, the godpower
that was he – that is each of us, but in a unique form. His was
like a phoenix fire consuming itself so he could rise again
from flames in yet a different form. Ludwig's music carries
such a fire – the fire of his spirit. Once ignited in the heart of
man it burns away the dross of pain and all that is illusion.
There is no *belief* in that. There is only a *process* – a painful
and dangerous and fascinating and bloody process which
brings you face to face with who you are – warts, darkness
and everything – and then insists you eat it all.

Way back when I used to gaze over wheat fields moving in
the wind like an ocean of gold I knew my life had got to be
about fighting for freedom. The trouble was I mistook the
map for the terrain. I believed the ads that tell you freedom
is owning a pair of Levi 501s. Now, thanks to Wawruch,
Mirabehn, Ludwig and to my new friends beneath the
earth, I know freedom will never be found in philosophies or
governments or high-sounding phrases or even rum com-
mercials shot on white sandy beaches peopled with bronzed,

beautiful bodies. You find it in living the truth of what you are. That Ludwig demanded of all of us. Because he himself had had the courage to fight for ever if necessary against the tyranny of illusion, because he was willing to eat his own darkness no matter how bad it tasted – Ludwig's fire burns so very bright it still fans the flame of spirit in the hearts of all who dare to let it in.

I knew my next step. I had a dusty room in London to clean, some stolen books to restore to their rightful owners and a country waiting for me that I left behind because I had lacked the courage to live my love for it. What my future was to be I wasn't sure. I would know when it was time for me to know. Now all I needed to know was that I love life and this battered earth with more passion than ever before and that I will do everything I can to care for them. Now it was time for me to go home.

I walked up the rue de Rennes then along Vaugirard to the top of the Jardin du Luxembourg. I entered the garden hunting for a bench where I could sit to read the letters. I found one in the Petit Luxembourg. It was surrounded by children playing ball and laughing. I sat down and began to untie the letters. I opened the first one and was just beginning to read when the ball they had been playing with knocked against my ankle. I picked it up and threw it to a lanky kid with flame-red hair and more freckles than skin. Something behind him caught my eye. Here in this perfectly ordered French garden in the middle of a glorious summer day stood one of Bourdelle's busts of Ludwig warmed by the summer sun.

GOLD

All the pilgrim centres exist in a woman's body.

Purascharanollasa Tantra

Baden – 15 July 1889

Dear Monsieur Bourdelle,

The bronze head arrived not three days hence – the wooden
box in which you contained it badly damaged. Three sides
remained, of those only one intact. I am happy to tell you
that the head, wrapped so carefully as it was in chippings
and swathed in wool, was unharmed. It would seem that
some gentleman in the custom-house had hopes of finding
something valuable – gold perhaps, or malachite. A corner
of the wrappings had been torn away to reveal darkened
bronze which to any prying eyes must have looked frus-
tratingly worthless.

I cannot convey to you – within the limitations of writing
in your language, not my own – how magnificent I find it. I
understand now why Etienne so praises your work. Truly it
is more Ludwig than Ludwig himself – that dark, brooding
silence which at any moment threatens to explode into
violence or laughter, the sadness in the eyes, the way in
which the features all turn inward, away from what has
wounded him. That *is* Ludwig, exactly as I remember him,
though I was but six or seven when last I saw him, and the

way Johanna spoke of him throughout endless days and nights when she could speak of nothing else.

You have wisdom, M. Bourdelle, not to sentimentalise or embellish as so many artists have done since Ludwig's death – even while he lived. The others have had an axe to grind – something they are trying to sell the way fishmongers in Vienna paint fishes' gills with red to deceive their customers. Your bronze shows none of that.

Etienne's gift – your sculpture – is most precious to me. Etienne is one of the few who know about Ludwig and Johanna. He tells me when he visited your atelier and saw this head he wanted, at whatever cost, to purchase it for me, that I might see it before I die. I am grateful to him for his kindness and for yours in taking all the trouble you have done to send it.

The head now stands on a table in front of a small window in the room in which I live. I had Etienne place it there. The window faces south west. As the light alters, the expression of Ludwig's face is forever metamorphosed. I sit for long hours each day watching him. I leave my room seldom these days. The thinness of my body and the steepness of the stairs restrict my movements. Etienne visits once a fortnight to bring me news of the city. You may rest assured that although your work of art is seen by few, it has, in myself, at least a constant companion, nor could it be cared for more lovingly.

Etienne tells me this is not the first head of Ludwig you have sculpted. He says it was no easy task for him to persuade you to part with it. Little wonder, for it is so beautiful. Neither will it be your last, M. Bourdelle. Ludwig has something to say to you which can only be received through the medium of your hands. Etienne tells me you have a certain fascination with our Ludwig. He called it a 'haunted quality' in your eyes when you speak of him. You

are not the first, M. Bourdelle. Ludwig's presence has had
something to say to each of us who really knew him. So
many who thought as much merely mistook the surface for
the man. Your bronze tells me with absolute certainty that
you *know* him. Whether that *knowing* will be a blessing or a
curse I cannot say. Often in my own life I have been
surprised to find that those events I once believed to be
blessings at length brought me infinitely less joy and
meaning than did the so-called curses.

I have lived a very long time, M. Bourdelle – longer than I
ever dreamed I would. But then I have always had a will to
live. Johanna too had a will to live, as Ludwig had a will to
music and you a will to art. Some are born with such a will.
It is, of course, no sign of virtue. If such as we had been born
animals, driven by our greed for life, we would in all
innocence crush the smaller and weaker in the litter in our
lust for survival. My will at times has created for myself
great difficulty. Always when something appeared before
me that I wanted or needed – I took it. Money . . . pleasure
. . . freedom. . . . Like Johanna, with whom I have much in
common. When we did not get our way at first, we waited. I
don't mean patiently or with any great virtue – simply
because a woman has to wait. She has no choice. The
weakness of her body and the ways of the world – a world
owned by men – would have it so.

May I send you my heartiest congratulations on your
work, and also my encouragement. At my age a woman
must be allowed to sound patronising if only by virtue of her
longevity. Do persist with it no matter how difficult it may
become and no matter how little acclaim you may at times
receive for it. Age has taught me that persistence in a task
counts far more than it is ever given credit for. You have so
very much talent to share with those of us who have so little.

Yours with admiration,
Susanna Reiss

Baden, 10 September 1889

Dear M. Bourdelle,

Your letter arrived yesterday. It took more than three weeks
to make the journey. I am uncertain how to reply. Many of
the questions which you have asked of me I am unwilling to
answer. This is not, I assure you, out of any concern for
Johanna's reputation or my own. These useless trinkets
were long ago tarnished beyond redemption. In part this
was the result of our own actions. In part it arose from the
actions of others – men who sought a hook to hang their fears
upon.

There are, M. Bourdelle, those who destroy far beyond a
woman's reputation – men who kill and steal without
remorse believing that what they do is given purpose by
their desires alone. Without compunction would these men
destroy a child within its mother's arms – destroy a nation or
a continent – to meet their ends. It was Ludwig's misfortune
to have known such men. Johanna herself did know one.
Out of such knowing is my silence fashioned.

You say that you sense Ludwig's presence – 'feel his
breath upon me', you have written. Having gazed long upon
the lively sketch you sent me, for which I must thank you
from my heart, and living as I do with this wonderful
bronze, I am not surprised by what you say. Of course you
feel his presence. How could it be otherwise? You feel as
Ludwig did, you think as he thinks, and have been touched
by the same flame. You know the loneliness and the passion
which was his. Does not nature seek its likeness? So it is with

men and with we women who do love them, be they dead or alive.

You have asked me about Ludwig's state of health when he walked the earth. It was, Johanna told me, never very good. He suffered great pain within his stomach. He was virtually deaf at the end of his life – and unbearably lonely, made more so I am afraid by the separation which took place in spirit between himself and Karl –Johanna's son to whom he was the guardian for many years.

Ludwig's nature was not easy. He loved deeply yet not well. His love for Karl – for love it was despite the anguish it created – was desperate in its nature. For though he greatly longed to give Johanna's son all that he should have, Ludwig's every effort served only to entrap Karl in a web of guilt and fear which made him the more distant. He loved Karl in the way a barren mother loves her adopted baby, fearful that any moment it will be taken from her. Karl's putting a bullet to his own head heralded the end of Ludwig's life. For he had given Karl everything he had to give of love. And if the fruits of such a love are naught but suicide, such was for Ludwig the measure of his own worth.

I presume you know how Ludwig hated Johanna – with a hatred as intense as was his love of Karl. Everyone in Vienna knew. For years he forbade Johanna to see her son and summoned her to court. There he slandered her, doing everything within his power to destroy the love she bore her child, and Karl for her. Karl was Ludwig's final hope – of making for himself a family: something he longed for all his life, yet was denied by virtue of his character.

The questions which you ask are hard and with a power of persistence which echoes Ludwig's own. How dare I answer them? Never did I dream I would commit to pen Johanna's secret words. Only to Karl and to myself did she impart the knowledge of what took place between them. In truth this secret was one which I believe she on no account intended to impart. But Karl blamed himself so deeply for the anger of his uncle – an anger which Johanna said belonged to her. She had no other recourse than to release him from a guilt she feared would scar his life for ever, by sharing with him the sketchy details. To me in later years she spoke more freely – as two women do when they have such a common bond. The secrets I will share with you were offered me because, although she was thirty years my senior, we were of a kind, Johanna and I. They call such women witches. They know not what to say. We are no witches – only set apart, and thus the recipients of a freedom others only dream of.

I hear your need, Bourdelle. Although I cannot answer all your questions, I will at least impart to you the more personal details of their relationship – information I have shared with none. I ask only that you remain silent about what has been said.

Yes, she knew Ludwig – how well she knew him! How little did he know himself when they first met. It was the spring of 1805, after she had been acquainted with Caspar, Ludwig's brother, but a few months. She described it so often in the years we lived together that I came to know it well:

He arrived unannounced one afternoon at our little house in a dreadful hurry, my Susanna, banging on the front door, distracted – as so often he was – by his own concerns. Caspar was sitting at the table finishing the coffee I had made. He rose and went to answer the door, somewhat annoyed that anyone should demand entry in such a brutal, noisy way. He was surprised to find his older brother standing at the portal. They had quarrelled some weeks before and were, as was often the case, not on speaking terms. Ludwig's clothes were

well fitting and clean but his hair was wild, and his
boots caked in April mud. Caspar hesitated, glancing
back at me, then taking hold of Ludwig's shoulders
drew him to his chest embracing him heartily and
said: 'Come in, Ludo'.

Ludwig entered, his body moving in a careless way
as if darting from one place to another even when his
destination was but three feet away. Ludwig seldom
saw anything except that which was straight ahead of
him – until, that is, he altered his course and followed
another straight line with the same stiletto-like thrust,
all of which brought an atmosphere of chaos to the
small room in which we stood. When he walked,
Ludwig's head was always a good few inches in
advance of the rest of his body. He flung his coat on a
chair and tossed the papers which he was carrying on
to the half-cleared table.

'It is these damned publishers, Carl,' he said.
'Swindlers every one of them. I need your help. Let me
show you what they have done now.'

This short-legged stocky man with his dark complexion leaned over to unscramble the mess of documents in front of him. As he did so his eyes, until then
self-absorbed, lifted to find me standing by the dresser
beside the door to the kitchen. In my hands I carried
dishes which I had been in the midst of clearing away.
His body stiffened, he reached up and removed the hat
which still sat on the back of his head. Then he made a
curt bow in my direction.

'Ludo, I would like you to meet Johanna Reiss, a
dear companion and friend,' said Caspar.

'Good-day,' he said, his small eyes narrowing as
through I were a servant who could not be trusted with
the silver.

'I am most pleased to meet you,' I said. 'Caspar has told me many wonderful things about you.'

'Indeed,' was his response.

His eyes stared with the same stiletto straightness. Silence. The air, until that moment troubled by the darting of his body, slipping through a gate in time, turned viscous. I knew that Ludwig no longer saw me. I felt the piercing black eyes swell then soften and flow over my body as water does. They landed on my cheeks, my shoulder, my breast – then, splashing over the curve of my belly, spread out over the floor at the edge of my skirt. Now the room grew still as the sunlight which lay silent as a sleeping cat upon the wooden floor beneath the window.

How long we stood there in that manner I will never know, perhaps no more than a few seconds although it could have been an hour. A saucer I was carrying slipped from my hand and shattered against the edge of the dresser. I made some excuse, rushed to collect the pieces into my fingers and left the room. When I returned a few minutes later to gather the remainder of the dishes from the table, the two of them sat together, Caspar poring over the documents which his brother had brought, Ludwig expostulating on the un-chivalrous nature of businessmen in general and publishers in particular. He did not look up. I was left wondering if what had happened only a few minutes before had indeed happened at all and what possible meaning it could have.

I did not see Ludwig often. Caspar kept the two of us apart. When Ludwig came to the house he usually did so when I was out or elsewhere engaged. Ludwig received the news of our marriage badly: it took place some three months later when I was already heavy with child. He called me a whore – said I had seduced his brother and got myself with child so as to force Caspar to keep me.

His accusation may well have been true. I am unsure what my motives were in those days. I know, however, that more than anything in the world I wanted a child. If seducing Caspar was what it took to get one then I was surely guilty. Yet I loved him too. Caspar was not handsome – short and stocky with flame-red hair and a temper to match. But when we married he was sweet to me and kind and when we lay in bed his body – warm and gentle in its manner – made mine respond with sureness and with joy. During the early years of our marriage I saw Ludwig no more than a dozen times. We never had the least thing to do with each other although he and Caspar, whom he called Carl, were very close – the most intimate of companions. He was Ludwig's confidant, collaborator, protégé and manager of affairs. Sometimes Caspar seemed verily to grow in size beneath the admiring gaze and flattering words of his elder brother.

'*We*,' Caspar used to say when speaking of a new quartet by Ludwig which he was attempting to sell – '*We* must insist that our publisher act in accordance with our stature and pay in accordance with *our* merit.'

In truth, Caspar I believe little recognised the greatness of his brother's work, yet he knew well the lavish affection that Ludwig bestowed on him and he did his best in his rather childish way to get as much money as possible for his brother's works. At other times the two of them would fight like children.

When Caspar became ill, the years of his brother's having turned his back on us gave way to days of passionate concern. Ludwig would arrive each morning bearing what he considered appropriate medicaments – a new herbal mixture from some doctor whom he respected. The respect did not last long, for with each failure the doctor who supplied it would be relegated to the status of failure in the bargain. Sometimes he would bring a fine bottle of Rhenish wine, some flowers, a book from which he would read to his much-loved brother Carl in that strange croaking voice of his which one moment would go soft and smooth as butter and the next turn shrill as a screech owl's. Every day Ludwig was in the house, leaning over the bed, making suggestions – criticising the doctor's care, the way I had made the bed, the number of pillows beneath his brother's head. The care he lavished on Caspar was greater than a mother gives her newborn.

'What would you like to drink, my Carl,' he would ask. 'Name anything and it shall be my pleasure to obtain it. Go ahead, make it difficult, I like a challenge.'

Poor Caspar, so weak and pale towards the end, found even eating more effort than it was worth yet he would try to think of some request which would make his brother feel he was contributing something to the sickroom.

Mostly Ludwig ignored me when he came, casting a cold eye over my face and body. Near the end, when he often stayed the night slumped in the chair beside his brother's bed, I noticed he would strangely alter. For an hour or so, he would look at me as though I were someone he knew and trusted. He would talk of his childhood with Caspar and Johann, of his grandfather whose portrait he treasured all of his life, of the tenderness he felt for his mother. Later on, as night followed night, the silence would be broken only by Caspar's thin dry cough and Ludwig's muttering. One evening, however, Ludwig was exceptionally talkative. He told me of a woman whom he had loved – more dearly he said than anything else in the world. The loss of this woman – she was the married sister-in-law of Bettina Brentano – seemed to represent for Ludwig a loss of hope.

'I knew then that God had not provided for me a marriage,' he would say. 'I knew then that my life belongs not to myself but to my music – wishes are as ashes to my destiny. It has always been so: each woman I have loved is lost to me – always at that moment when I am most conscious of the loving.'

Moved by his warmth and his loneliness, I knelt before him and took his head in my hands, gently drawing it towards my bosom in the wish to comfort him. I, as exhausted as he with our nightly vigils, was easily overcome with compassion for this childlike figure which knelt at the bedside of the sleeping Caspar. With no word further he buried his head in my breasts, grabbing me by the shoulders with great violence as a man might do who, being without hope, clings to whatever appears beside him.

He spoke of his anguish. No longer could he hear, he said. No longer could he conduct his written works. He told me he planned greater works than he had ever made before – of his agonising loneliness – that he did not trust the servants – that they were always stealing from him – that no one could be trusted – that he had tortured chickens as a child at the back of his family's house, watching them die with satisfaction, knowing that he had power which could be inflicted upon

others as the power of life had been inflicted on him.
He spoke also of the future, of his dreams, of his wish to
move men in their hearts, to awaken them. And still he
clung to my body. He clung with such a need it took
my breath away. I could feel a surge of heat rise up
within my womb. I could see the man, my husband,
lying on the bed asleep before me and still the fire
mounted. I began to stroke Ludwig's hair, to smooth
over the heavily pitted skin on his cheeks as though by
doing so I would make all well again for him – for
Caspar – for me – for my dearest son who slept on in
the adjacent room. I watched it all. I saw the lamp
burn low. It needed attention as did the fire, which by
now barely burned at all. The heat still rose within. I
don't think Ludwig knew. I don't think he knew
anything except his need for closeness, the sense of
freedom for a few brief hours which fatigue and trust
had brought him. I don't think he even knew who I
was. I was only life, woman, the place where he could
lean his head. He reached for me, unconscious of the
movement.

'I need to lie with you,' he said, groping beneath my
skirt to slide his hand gently against my thigh. 'I will
not touch you. I will not violate you. I need to be near
you. Let me come near you.'

There was drunkenness in the room. I thought that
nothing would take place. I knew that he could lie
within my arms upon the carpet and that Caspar
would never awaken – no one would ever know. By
now the fire of tenderness consumed my womb – went
licking at my womanhood. I could do nothing but
agree.

And so he came to me – like a man in a dream, not
knowing what he did. The first time it was like nothing

I had ever known before. Without his knowing it, without even I myself being aware of what was happening, he spread open my legs and entered me, taking my left breast in his hand with such violence that I should have cried in pain. But I did not cry – for all was silent like some secret pact only two can share, and then only within the hours of darkness.

Thus did I become his, Susanna. Ludwig moved me more than any man I have ever known. It was his pain I could not bear. I prayed that it be given me, that it be taken from him, that he need no longer bear it all alone. Then it was over. He had drunk wine that evening, the wine he brought as an offering to the brother whom I and he that night betrayed. I say 'betrayed', Susanna, because that is what convention would have me say – yet no guilt did I feel.

You see I am no stranger to men, Susanna, I have known many. They are like a salve to me. I crave their maleness, I drink it in as Ludwig drank his wine, as some men drink their politics and women their possessions. They say I am a whore. And they speak truly. *Whore* – do you know the word, Susanna? It means *woman made naked*, woman as she is in all her softness and her need. Every woman is a whore at heart. Few perhaps discover it. With Ludwig I came to live it with an intensity I can think of no way to describe.

During those last days before Caspar's death we met, Ludwig and I, body to body, soul to soul. I believe it was the horror of Caspar's impending death, the hollowness within me longing to be filled with love, and the pain which Ludwig carried so close to the surface all the days of his life, that opened the door for us to another world. We lived, the two of us, in that

universe which lies beyond time and space, beyond
right and wrong, beyond reason or justice. Desire
which flowed between us formed a cauldron into
which God's fire descended. I speak these words
without hesitation, knowing I would be accused of
blaspheming. For they are so. The fire that burned out
of our union, although we lived it through our bodies,
through our voices, through our eyes, was not of this
world. Nor had it anything whatever to do with him or
me – as man and woman, friend, or enemy, or lover.

It was as though the two of us in meeting as we did
had called another universe into being – a world in
which everything was consumed by the fire of the love.
It was not just I who knew it, he as well. I could read
that in his eyes. When he came through the door, the
mere touch of his hand on mine melted my body to
helplessness. Concerned for Caspar's welfare and
terrified he would awaken and discover what was
taking place night after night, in the house where he
lay dying, I would promise myself that when Ludwig
appeared there would be no touching, no fire, no
penetration. Yet the mere act of his entering the house
drew out every fraction of will left in me. I was his, I
would love him no matter what, no matter if we were
both damned in hell for it, no matter, and I speak these
words with fear even now years later, if the loving
meant Caspar's death.

Such was the tale she told those distant nights ago. I heard it
every time anew. It had a sound of truth from which one
could not turn away. That was Johanna's truth – she whom
they called whore. It is a name to make a woman proud.

I see your work, Bourdelle. It tells me that you are no
stranger to passion, that as you mould the clay that made his

face your hands do move with such a passion. You know the horror it can carry with it – the way it tears away the veil of honour, every trace of sureness – how it demands of you everything you have to give – burns all away until but the fire remains.

Ludwig was not a pretty man. His head was heavy, his shoulders curved in the posture of a bear, his flesh was thick and oily. Yet every time she looked into his eyes Johanna said it drew her very womb out of her body. Have you such a passion for your clay, Bourdelle? It is a question worthy of an answer. Here is more of what she told me:

In every pore of his skin lay fascination for me, my Susanna. It was as though through each I could penetrate his inner world. Hungry for his touch, I could not get enough. His body became wonderful to me, like some totem through which my very life was fed. When the touching started, it would go on for hours. Neither of us could break away, so strong was this bond that tied us heart to heart, body to body.

There was nothing pretty about the way in which we loved. I was not his servant nor was he mine. Neither of us gave a thought to what we did or to the words of fire we spilt into the air. He would whisper to me of love, of how he loved my thighs, my breast, my secret places. His dark liturgy of unspeakable words would be repeated over and over again – the fire of the love making them holy.

'I own you. You are mine,' he would say. 'You belong to me. I can do what I want with you.'

'Yes,' I would reply, 'yes, my love, you own me. You can do what you want with me. I am yours.'

Then he would take hold of my flanks, my neck, my breasts and he would ride me as though I were a part of himself. If I moved either out of pleasure or discomfort he would order me to keep still. And I would do as he said.

'This time it is mine.' he would say. 'You will have your time. But this is mine.'

Sometimes – often – from my throat would issue the soft animal moans of a woman lost in love. 'Oh God, Oh God, Oh. . . .'

'Be still,' he would order, 'be still. I don't care what you feel. This one is mine.'

Then he would tell me I could move, that now the loving belonged to me, that I could do whatever I desired. And I would move. I would love him with my mouth, my fingers, and my eyes. I would spread myself open above him and draw his darkness deeper and deeper into my body, moving or not moving as the drunkenness of love possessed me. Sometimes he would rise up from his back, grasp my hips in powerful hands and move them to suit his pleasure. Others he would lie suspended between this world and some other like a child in wonder of the beauty which he felt – helpless before the power of love in which we were both trapped.

Once, not long after my husband's death, for the love continued despite our grief, or perhaps the grief itself fuelled the cauldron in which we lived, when we had loved all night and dawn was slipping through the window, Ludwig rose to relieve himself. I caught sight of his body standing before me next to the bed. I took hold of his hips with my hands and told him not to move. I was transfixed by the power of it. His body had become a deep well from which I had only to drink to live. The drinking could be done with my eyes and through every pore of my body. I worshipped its every flaw. It had become God's voice to me. What it said in every movement – that I heard.

Our loving was stark, bleak, cold and naked. I bowed down before the godpower in Ludwig, mated with it in all its rawness, all its truth and then poured forth the ecstasy and the horror of that mating. The sacred space in which we loved was numinous – a cathedral beneath the sea into which one enters naked after having left all one's possessions, all one's masks, all one's hope at the door.

How does one mate with God? As an animal, Susanna – only through the body, for we are human beings and that alone is our medium of knowing. It is done in all innocence and all knowingness like a creature who dives into a sea of fire and knows the fire will consume her, yet knows too that it holds nothing of value which should not be consumed. That is how we loved, Ludwig and I. When in the presence of the godpower there is no shame, no fear, no hope to dilute the power of that union.

He, Ludwig, asked that of me the first moment he reached out towards my body at the bedside of my dying husband. For whatever reason – yet there *are* no reasons – I could do nothing but surrender to his demand. His touch, his need for my body, the anguish he concealed within his breast – they drew from my heart all that was contained within: my tears, my longings, my lust, my terror. We lived them together in our embraces. Our embraces tore away the veil of lies which so control man, limiting his life. And for a time we could dance the dance of ecstasy together – no, not together – there was no *together*. Who is to say where my body ended and his began?

Sometimes the force of what had taken hold of us

would frighten me. 'What am I doing here?' I would ask myself. 'Is this me or not me?' This union was too terrifying – this bond with God. I wanted to cry out that a mistake had been made and to run backwards through the door of time. Yet I could not. The mere smell of his flesh drew me deeper into a sea of love so deep that finally even fear itself drowned in the waters. I was lost, truly lost in that sea – beyond control or judgement. I would find myself praying to God with words unfamiliar to any priest:

'Beloved. I surrender to You and You alone. Lead me ever closer to our union. Don't let me go astray. Keep hold of me. I cannot hold myself. I no longer know what is so and what illusion. Only You can show me. Come closer, enter my body through my darkest places, penetrate my being, or I am lost for ever.'

The words would echo too over and over in my head: 'Love me, only love me.' I would not know if they were words from God or words from Ludwig.

The fathers of the Church would have you believe that God is your friend, Susanna. I can assure you it is not so. God exists not to comfort but to destroy you. Such destruction comes in many forms – for Ludwig it was music, for me His body, for you it will be something different. That is the secret of the godpower – a secret you can never understand yet which each one of us is asked to honour every moment of our lives. Honour it and live. Turn away from it and all of life thereafter is but a living death. It was I who turned away. That is what I did to Ludwig. That is why he so despised me and how our union ended.

I found my body had grown tired, as though I could not bear the violence of his loving any more. It was the tiredness of deception – the tiredness of a creeping death with which I had made a bargain, although I did not know it then, Susanna. Ludwig would come to my body and I would sigh to take him in. But I no longer gave myself. I could not. It was too much, too much. With Caspar dead, I had a son to care for. My heart was filled with guilt when I was not with my child. It would wash away the moment he came near only to return when next we parted. He sensed I was no longer there for him. Ludwig knew it not with his mind but at the deepest levels of his humanity – he knew that the bond which, through my body, had been forged between him with the earth had gone. Like a wounded beast he writhed in pain, striking out at anything and everything around him.

It was then the legal battles started – the fight for Karl. Ludwig looked upon me as the darkest of evils. He soon convinced himself I had drawn him down into a vortex of lust and destruction away from the purpose of his life – his art. I did not blame him when the love he bore me turned to hatred. Does not the beast destroy that which it wants most in the world when it can no longer fill its belly? I loved my son more than anything on earth – so much I would gladly have given him to Ludwig if I had believed it best. And so the fight began – a fight which lasted for a decade, tore apart my life, and ended in my son attempting to take his own. It also, dear Susanna, made clear the way for Ludwig's own destruction.

Such was Johanna's truth, my dear Bourdelle. Ask yourself if you can live such truth. Such too is the way of passion, when one whom it has chosen is unable or unwilling to meet its challenge. Such is the nature of the godpower: meet it, honour it, embrace it or it will destroy you. Well you know it. Do you not? Again I thank you for the sketch. I shall treasure it. So must you treasure your own gift.

Yours in truth and silence,
Susanna

Baden – January 1890

Dear Bourdelle,

Forgive the delay in answering your last letter, which I am ashamed to say arrived six weeks ago. My silence is this time on no account intentional. Every hour I have sat and dreamed the words that I would write you. But it has taken time to put them down. For I am frail in recent weeks – at times it has been hard for me to leave the house even for half an hour's walk. Happily the pension which has been provided for me is adequate to pay my rent and I have a little left over for tea and meals. I can no longer take coffee – it taxes my nervous system too greatly – that has been hardest of all to give up.

I also have thought of you. I am conscious of the bond you say has grown between us. How could it be otherwise when I spend every waking hour with your bronze Ludwig in this room alone and you each day with Ludwig's breath upon you? Yes, dear Bourdelle, there have been others who have known that breath. A doctor – a fine man whom I met when I was twenty-two, many years after Ludwig's death and near his own. His name was Wawruch. It was he who tended Ludwig through the long and painful months before the end and he who did his best to tell a truth which all others, save Johanna, would conceal.

Wawruch came to us in the summer of 1842, arriving on

our doorstep at the edge of death. He looked like an animal who, having lost its paw to a snare, has little strength to fight. He arrived believing, as Ludwig said, that Johanna was the *evil principle* personified, yet in such a state of need he had no other place to turn. She took him in and made a bed for him. Here he remained until he died, writing like a man possessed by a remorse so deep he could not share it, while she and I did what we could to ease the suffering of his body, applying milky mixtures and gentle touch, yet another gift that comes to women who live outside the world, Bourdelle.

We spoke little. Yet the three of us came to know one another well, the way one can in circumstances when all marks of falseness have by necessity been erased.

Wawruch had a passion of his own, it was a simple one: to stay alive just long enough to tell his tale. This he scribbled, in a wild hand, on endless reams of paper. When he died, Johanna kept the papers knowing that if others were to find them they, like all that which was of value to Ludwig's life, would be altered or destroyed. Karl himself knew nothing of them. She never showed them to a living soul. Only on her deathbed did she give them into my hands wrapped in the same red silk as you receive them now. In truth I had decided to commit them to the fire when at last death knocks at my own door. For surely I shall know the hour.

So here, Bourdelle, I place within your hands what Wawruch wrote before he died. In no way will it offer final answers. Each and every man must find his own. At least it will confirm that you are not alone in what you witness.

So long as you honour the fire which burns within you, choosing to fashion from it the architecture of your forms, it will not harm you – no matter how hot it grows. Is that not how Prometheus shaped his figures? The question is simple:

are you willing to live in emptiness and let the flames burn through you?

The words are meant for you and you alone. For with them comes a power beyond words. It is the *silence* in between that wounds those who, unwilling or unable to embrace the fire, would play with it instead. Should you ever in the future decide to share this *silence* with another – choose wisely, dear Bourdelle. The way of love, say the Sufi saints, is but a bridge of hair across a chasm of fire.

Bless you,
Susanna

Baden, 24 June 1890

Dear Bourdelle,

Twice you have written and yet received no answer. I have thought long and hard about what answer I should send. I hoped Wawruch's papers would suffice to quench your thirst – to silence all your questions. You are most persistent, my Bourdelle. That too you share with Ludwig and Johanna. And I? I am still kind enough, or foolish enough, to be seduced by your entreaties.

You ask me how they knew – the illumined men – that Wawruch had begun his task of compiling all he knew of Ludwig's illness. Your question, my Bourdelle, makes me smile. I had forgotten how young a man you are. It is easy to forget your years when faced with the size of your talent. In time, as you walk your own passages, you will come to know this answer and will need no such explanations. For now, let me say but this: all the worlds in which we as humans are immersed are coincident. Those beings have intelligence greater than ours so it is no labour for them to know the hearts and the intentions of men even if they cannot always capture them. I know that this can be a frightening thought. But rest assured their knowing is of no consequence in itself. For it is our choice whether we give them the power to act upon it or no. The moment Wawruch made his commitment, the *great ones* knew and alerted Schindler, a bodily link between the worlds.

Johanna knew many men. I told you once before – she did so need them. Many called her *whore*. Ludwig preferred 'Queen of the Night'; the irony of his phrase – the one he chose to damn her – always made me smile. Johanna felt no shame for any union she had made – bar one. That was he about whom you now so persistently question me.

I yield to your entreaty, dear Bourdelle. I shall describe it to you since now you have agreed that you impart these words to no one. I wish I could be brief, Bourdelle, for my body grows weak and every pen stroke costs me more than you at so young an age could know. Yet this is a lengthy process in the telling. I fear there is no other way.

It was a dispute with Ludwig which brought Schindler into Johanna's life. It centred on the final of his symphonies – the D Minor, which they call the Ninth. This work in its choral ending elicits tears from our new breed of German romantic, men poisoned with moralic acid who have a passion for universal brotherly love. Have you not a similar group in France, my dear Bourdelle? Yet this same symphony was a source of shame and self-betrayal to Ludwig himself.

He had composed all which precedes the *Ode to Joy* in search of safety from engulfing terror and as an end to a yearning in his breast to make himself a part of human life. Throughout these first three movements, Ludwig's spirit climbs the tortuous mountains as Moses did on Sinai crying out for a vision of God himself.

Schindler and those illuminated men with whom he consorted knew this. They knew too the dark power of the music Ludwig had composed thus far – the lofty power of that great adagio of the third movement – the unearthly heights to which the composition had now come and how such a power could be put to any ends if one could but direct it.

Ludwig, no matter how he wrestled with his melodies, could not find the movement which in its culmination would give answer to the questions he had posed. He was engaged in greatest difficulty to discover a plausible bridge passage to the final movement – one which would answer the primeval darkness that precedes all creation of the previous three – that godforce which, although it conditions our human world, yet plays no active part in it. This power, Ludwig knew too well, has no benevolence despite the necessity of its presence in the moulding of a human soul.

Ludwig worked unceasingly yet nothing came to him. He had to find an answer – some culmination that would complete the work. All the while Schindler had played the helpmate, sharing in Ludwig's search and giving re-assurance that he might gain his deepest trust. Then, having gained Ludwig's full confidence, Schindler presented him with an answer – a fog of portentous epithets in the rearrangement of Schiller's 'Ode to Joy': 'all creation drinks joy from the breasts of nature' . . . 'all men shall be brothers there where thy gentle wings tarry' . . . 'brothers, above the starry vault, there surely dwells a dear Father'. In Ludwig's need to complete the work and his frustration at being unable to do so, he gave in to Schindler's promptings unaware that in so doing he was committing this work to the will of those illumined ones who, often unbeknown to men, control their very lives. So Ludwig surrendered his true ideals, choosing instead to answer his theme of fate as universal destiny with little more than a form of comforting cliché, a magnificent final movement which although it sates the palates of those who hear it, begs the question of man's quest for individual freedom and union with his God within. Thus he completed the work and in all innocence committed it into their hands to do with as they would.

It took no more than two months after this symphony was first played for Ludwig to realise he had been hoodwinked – that in the name of *brotherhood* the energies of creation had been bent by those who would imprison man instead of set him free. Confronting Schindler with full knowledge of the trick that had been played, Ludwig threw him bodily from the apartment. That was when this man whose flesh was white as any maggot came slouching towards Johanna, bringing tales of woe and pleas for comfort. She was, I think, too gentle of spirit to turn him away. But perhaps it is best to tell you what passed between them in Johanna's words: how many times she told me I cannot now remember. They are so much simpler than my own.

It was the year before my Karl took the pistol to his head – you were but a tiny child then, my Susanna. It was that year that Schindler came to me. Although Karl had reached the age of manhood then, Ludwig still took every action to prevent our meeting. I watched dear Karl – my son – be tortured by an uncle whom he loved yet in whose love crushing sadness was his reward.

He, Schindler, had written the day before asking permission to call. He said that he had every reason to believe that Ludwig could be softened. He told me he would see if he could be of aid. After years of torture, I was prey to any empty hope that might alleviate the anguish I witnessed mounting hard upon my son. Anguished in myself to change things, I did receive him.

That morning Schindler came to the house and stood before me with eyes such as I have never seen. He was ugly – a man of pocked face perhaps a year or two younger than myself. From his eyes helplessness shone forth while his flesh looked like an animal drained of all its blood – the way some butchers kill their cows. Each time I saw those eyes I tasted horror. It was like looking on the face of one who feels himself cast out from God. Moved by his suffering and by the twisted form into which it shaped his body and his being, I could not bear his pain. Too closely did it touch my very own. He entered the house and then we spoke. In truth, he came not to give my Karl the aid with Ludwig that might secure his freedom, but because he himself was despondent over a breach that had come about between Ludwig and himself two weeks before.

He came to me for help. I did not want to give it. I wanted to remain alone. I wanted to withdraw into the safety of the world I knew – a world I had built myself – a world of duty to my child. Schindler stayed with me three hours. He spoke of strange and horrid things which ate away his heart. I listened – too willing to pass time with anyone who for an hour or two did not attempt to cast me out. He came again to call, and once again, and then once more. Then did he ask me for my love. I did not want to give it. I wanted but to lend him kindness and then to send him far away. I prayed and asked the God within my heart, 'Must I love this man?' The answer returned without hesitation. I sighed.

Then autumn came, my dear Susanna. You went to my mother's house – that was the year I had been ill, you may remember. We two were left alone: Schindler with his loneliness, and I with my need – a need so great that we soon became lovers of a sort. I say a sort. He was the only man I never wanted yet to whom I gave myself despite this truth. Even now I am not sure how it came about. It was his pain I think and my own tears of sorrow.

Our union was a strange one – without passion. Between us lay a powerful bond. Yet of a sort as I had never known. Often he spoke of unspeakable things – of beings whom he said did drain one's blood and in so doing brought a living death – of men who were to take the world within their grasp and of the *great ones* whom they serve, although they knew it not. And I? I did listen for at some dark place within me slept a longing. I had been alone so very long. He had a lust for blood, did Schindler, a sense somehow that they, the *great ones*, required it of him – covenants, he called them. Strangely did it torture and yet lure him. Sometimes we loved both day and night – so foreign for me was this strange cool power that drew me to him while I surrendered to it again and again.

One night within a month of our first meeting the moon was full. Thus did my body pour forth its full measure. He begged me that I share with him this red mark of my womanhood. The flow was heavy. This seemed to excite him in ways unfamiliar – in his face were written not shapes of pleasure but those of pain. When in our bed I questioned him, he could hardly speak of that which held him. He did, however, utter certain sounds – the name of Mordecai I do remember. And then again of covenants of blood. I lay beneath his body rendered silent by the anguish of his face. Then I spoke to him of something which I hoped could give him ease:

'Schindler, you and I shall make a new covenant,' I said, 'a blood covenant of our own – fashioned from the only blood which nature freely offers – the only blood that flows without a killing: that from a woman's body. This blood and this alone will wash away your anguish – dissolve these ancient bonds and set you free.'

He drew himself upon his knees to kneel upon the bed. I knelt to face him. Cupping a hand beneath my body I did collect fair measure of the flow. Then did we pray together that all covenants of torture be forsaken – not just for him but all men so entrapped. Into the red fluid did I dip my finger. With it I fashioned the sign of a cross upon his forehead. It coloured crimson for the liquid was abundant. Then did I touch the same wet hand to his lips and to his chest.

Tears came into his eyes. He was like a man sentenced to death who has at the very final moment been reprieved. We closed our eyes together, giving thanks that peace at last had visited. Silently I uttered words of supplication for his freedom. For Schindler was a man in chains. He trusted no one, Schindler – nothing. I came to know that he relied on magic practices learned here and there to shape-shift energies to his own advantage. I said a simple prayer that this be ended.

A minute later I opened my eyes. There he sat upon the bed before me – yet no trace of blood remained upon his body. All of it – each drop, each tiny speck had been somehow absorbed into his skin. It was not possible. This I knew. Yet this erasure had most certainly occurred. I gave to Schindler a mirror to show him what had happened. He was as shocked as I and just as gratified. He smiled, then surrendered to fatigue.

With this new covenant of peace the terror in his eyes melted. His face lost its wild and tortured look, becoming that of a simple man. I gave thanks for the miracle while he that night lay in my arms like someone whose life has been redeemed. I did not know it then, but Schindler, with whom I shared a bed, had been himself possessed by forces that would barter human life.

For a fortnight he remained at peace. The wildness in his eyes would flash, the fear surface for a time. Yet he was better. I myself began to feel strange feelings – energies of which I had no previous knowledge. I feared that I would leave my body. I was forced to repeat words of prayer over and over – *please God help me . . . please God help me . . . please God help me . . .* to keep me sane. I was not able to catch my breath. My head would spin.

The dark miracle of the blood was but the first of many strange events in which a thing appeared or disappeared. So entangled had I become with Schindler that my body soon reacted as if it were his. He drank wine. I would taste the colour of it. Once when he was far away I found myself surrounded by a cloud of smoke and smelt the fragrance of tobacco. On seeing him again he told me he had smoked a cigar – this was not his usual habit – at the exact time at which I did perceive this.

The blessing of the blood which I had prayed would set him free brought little more than respite from his tortures. They soon began again. At times he sought to take his own life. The love I bore him – for love it was, if of a kind so strange and cold it makes me shudder even now to speak of it – this love entangled me as Persephone was entrapped by Pluto, and sucked me down into an underworld. It forced me to descend into the darkness of my soul and live horrors of my being which had until then remained beneath the surface.

Then I knew for certain what was happening: Schindler was possessed by energies inimical to life. Periodically something overwhelmed him, wanting only to destroy him. When this came upon him it would create for him, and often for myself, so closely was I bound to him in sympathy, insufferable physical symptoms or fill him with self-hatred so hideous he would then see himself as poisonous to everything around him. This energy or entity was peculiar. It seemed, as far as I could see, to be in substance the illusory energy of the intellect – mind taken to its absolute extremes. Now that I am older – now I know such energy holds a mirror to the evil in our times.

It is that which chooses to believe that through some system, be it religious or political, man can gain control of Nature – that ends do justify the means – that man is but a worm beneath the stars. This energy did draw the very life from Schindler: it drew his blood then, using him as messenger, it fed upon each person with whom Schindler made a bond – so each himself became as fodder. It had, like every evil thing, no life to call its own. I did everything I could to help him break the bond – so much did it tear upon my heart to see this man suffer. But greatly did this cold love which I bore him drain the very life out of my body. I took him to a priest to no avail. I prayed for him. At first he honoured my perceptions. When for a time he was free of their power – this was always when he was in my body, for only then it seemed that they could not possess him – he told me all the truth of what he knew. He told too the secrets of power and possession:

'You trap people into believing you,' he said. 'By giving them a treasure – some gift or thing which makes them feel the better – this draws them to you,' Schindler said, 'then you can feed upon them, making chains of energy between you which you can feed on.'

'What do they want?' I asked him, 'these beings who would drain you of your life?'

'Blood,' was his reply. 'Blood – not of the body but of the ether which surrounds it. It is so much the richer in its potency,' he said. 'They cannot bear that you might escape. Love is most dangerous of all to these sky beings. To love is to break the bonds of the power which binds you to them. Then do they attack in earnest, to drive you wild with grief and fear until either you destroy yourself or you surrender.'

Such moments of clarity grew less frequent when the autumn came. Schindler's love for me became more fevered and I – I wrestled with the powers that would steal my life away. Then came the day when I could go no further. For he even denied the truth of that which he imparted to me. He grew insanely jealous and would accuse me of disloyalty. All the while I fought with those energies within my breast that caused me fear of death and made me tremble so that at times I could not walk. Then one day he requested of me something, I do not now remember what it was, that in its purport did go against my loyalty to my children. I therefore refused him. He threatened to destroy himself, aware that he or *it* was loosening its grip on me. Then he began to threaten. He told me he would crush me – 'bring me to my knees' he said – so I would know the power of my love for him and would be 'healed'. He threatened to expose me to the world. I could not help but wonder what further damage to my reputation he could do in consideration of all that Ludwig had himself accomplished.

My sympathy for Schindler and his suffering was overridden by a power more primitive than any I had known. It lay within me – the power of survival. I was no longer willing to yield my woman's body to the rule of any man who so little valued its sanctity. I told him clearly: though I blessed him I would have nothing more of him. His rage was endless. The threats went on for weeks, through letters and mysterious 'presents'. I would find them lying on the doorstep. Sometimes his face would appear at the window. All the while I lived in fear. Not so much of Schindler, for I knew that he was impotent – made so by the very 'gods' who gave him power. From moment to moment my spirit pulled against my body. I took long walks beside the river praying that the earth would keep me. And I grieved for him. For despite all the horror and the threats, I loved this man as one might love a tortured animal – a child who mirrors one's own wounds.

Then all began to heal. I was set free from the illusion into which I had ventured – the mythic realm of the dead, the charnel ground in which he and I had walked together. The trembling ceased as did the strangeness in my breath. I lost all sense that I should lose my body. Each night before I slept I said a prayer for this poor tortured being. I slept peacefully at last.

Such was Johanna's tale of Schindler. But there is more, of

course – more than even Schindler himself knew. These *great ones* sought to usurp the godpower that flowed through Ludwig at great cost to his body and his life and then to use it for their own ends – that of enslaving the world. Given modern man's willingness to accept facsimile of change, if in doing so it is able to protect him from his own metamorphosis, *they* knew his music in its passion and its power could be used to deceive man. Coupled with uplifting rhetoric, it could lead him down illusory paths. They knew that even the scribbled words of such as Ludwig, who despite his great confusion and his chaos had the courage to wrestle with the godpower, carried danger to any man on the border of self-deception. They could in time cause him to forsake pastiche and seek instead his truth. So they sought to destroy all that they could – the conversation books, the letters and the dreams which Ludwig in his search for truth committed to paper.

It was Schindler who carried out their multifarious deeds. He burnt the books, destroyed the letters, stole every piece of clothing Ludwig wore so that none of the power might be leaked away. Then he poisoned Ludwig – an action carried out in strict obedience to the will of the illumined ones. The poisoning was, Johanna said, an agony for Schindler to execute. Yet despite all this he did so with the aid of an old housekeeper whom he paid to do the relentless work slowly day by day that none might know. He did it for *their* sake and for the vision of brotherhood and the new world order which they would fashion in time and of which he knew himself to be a part.

Make no mistake, my Bourdelle. Schindler was no evil man despite his deeds. He was in truth a man of weakness – a man who did not dare define his being, so seduced was he by the power of the *great ones*. He was a man of tiny heart and small imagination who yet had one small passion – the obsessive love a mother bears her offspring, protecting it from anything she thinks will threaten life and reputation. His 'child' of course was Ludwig. And every mother loves her child to the limit of her ability, believing that what she does to it even to the point of killing is done for its highest good. So distorted was his reason that he would stop at nothing to hide every sign of life and passion within the man he valued most. Men such as Schindler know a very special kind of love – the love of a commodity – a love that can be bought and sold – the way some collect paintings or others gold. Schindler could not bear the fire of truth. It dazzled him. He worshipped it. He witnessed it in Ludwig and thought that by association he could absorb it – the way his sky gods absorbed his blood.

Far worse, Bourdelle, were those whom he called brothers. The Illuminati – *men of light* – they called themselves, although the name is of no matter since such men exist in every aeon and call themselves by any name they choose. Beneath the cloak of reason and of righteousness they destroy – wielding power based on fear and lies – telling themselves fine tales of their nobility.

In truth these men are nothing more than foxes licking the cream produced by herds of men grazing sleepily on rich green pastures. They take the blood, the money and the power from those who will allow it, all the while insisting we are free. Alas, most do allow it, dear Bourdelle. Most men would rather dream of peace than take up sword to challenge the deception. Men, you know, were never fashioned to be servants of the gods. It is life they are designed to serve – and yet they are afraid. So Schindler and his parasites feed upon them: they feed on human herds – all the while unaware that they themselves are meat for subtler predators, with whom in secret ceremonies they strike their bargains.

Enough is said Bourdelle – enough – for either you will know the truth or it is not a truth worth knowing. My hand is weary as my heart. It brings me no joy to speak of such waste in a world needful of life.

I trust your work is well.
S

Baden, 21 September 1890

Dear Bourdelle,

This letter, my Bourdelle, will be the last. I shall not live much longer I can tell. Do not grieve. I feel no pain, neither am I ill. Like an old cat which used to share this room with me, I have no further interest in food. So I grow thin and fine. I feel inside the way the sunshine looks when in the early days of spring it blesses every sleeping blade of grass with gentleness.

It should not surprise me that you return with yet more questions. Young men have so many questions and every one so urgent. I cannot answer them – not all – not because I hesitate but because time grows short and I am weak.

Yes Bourdelle, there was a reconciliation between them, despite the lies that Schindler told the world. She saw Ludwig twice before he died. The first meeting took place two weeks before the end. The servant, whom she bribed with coins for information, arrived at Johanna's house before dawn with news that Wawruch had departed early leaving a space in time for her to come unnoticed.

Ludwig greeted her with love, she said.

His face had grown transparent, my Susanna. It was such joy to see him. How I did love him. How I do love him still. We spent an hour in that tiny room. It was the hour before dawn, the darkest hour of the night. I held his hand and stroked his brow. He smiled and in that smile I understood what does happen as passion passes through the gates of death. It does not die, Susanna, it is transfigured to a finer substance which in its very lightness grows the stronger.

He told me what they offered him, these *great ones* who visited on the night his fever broke. They promised to fulfil his dreams and to restore his life – that he would write another symphony and then some more – provided he would write them as they asked – provided he would forge their chains of power through his notes. They told him that his body would grow strong – they offered him a name that spanned the globe. They made but one mistake, he told me, these *great ones*. Amongst the treasures that they offered there was one which they forgot – *the truth*. So he could not stomach all the rest. Thus he cast them out in rage – a rage that broke apart his very life, although it took a dozen weeks before his body yielded.

'Beware the dealers of death, Johanna,' he told me, 'the eaters of the soul – the bright darkness. They suck you into their dark vortex consuming all.'

No words of grief or of forgiveness passed between us. There was no need. 'Stay silent and outside the world,' he said. 'You yourself will be protected – by all that men in their stupidity hold false. They do fear you, Johanna – as once did I.' He laughed, then made me leave within the hour.

I shed no tear, Susanna. I said my prayers that I could be beside him at the end. I knew they would be answered. No one would deny me that. So I came home and waited.

Johanna did not have long to wait, Bourdelle. Ludwig went into coma – two days I think it was – before he died. Her prayers were answered. All prayers of life's worshippers are heard. The day arrived. She knew the time had come. He slept, the servant said, the men had gone. Johanna of course had known they would. She made her way across Vienna to his bedside – no one save a distant acquaintance was present, a man who knew her not.

'I am Frau Beethoven,' she told him. He reported to the men on their return that the sister-in-law had visited. They, of course, assumed it was Therese.

It was magnificent, my Susanna. He slept so heavily – the rattle of death in his throat – as he had rested for two nights and a day. Then came a clap of thunder, and another. His eyes opened. He looked at me and smiled. When yet another shock of thunder sounded, even louder than before, he raised his fist in triumph and he cursed them – these *sky gods*. Then his hand fell back upon the bed for ever. The *great ones* could not take him – even now.

I felt no grief. For all was as it should be. I knew it in my womb, Susanna – where all real things are known.

So ends my tale, my dear Bourdelle. Schindler, Weishaupt and the rest – these men who weave their secret plans to rule the world believe they can transcend the dance. For power alone they sell their souls not realising the value of what they have exchanged. Then, knowing not that they have done it, they live within abstraction. Such soulless creatures issue progeny round the world – dead men driven by false religions, prey to the *great ones'* powers by a ruse so subtle it would dazzle their fine minds if they but perceived it. They extract gold from ordinary men – men too stupid to know that they themselves are godly. No man needs permission just to live.

Sometimes when I sit before my window gazing upon the shifting light of day I see things no woman's eyes should see – things worse than death. Bloodless men and women treading the streets with angry hearts and empty eyes. Women and their men who have forgotten the scent of morning. Yet their boots are clean and they speak with a facsimile of wisdom. The earth itself is but a prison for their souls. Far better is it for streets to run with blood from children slain by cruel hands than that man's living spirit be so damned with deathly cold. All this too I see within my dreams.

In such a world as this – in such a world as we have made – only one man lives: not the worker, not the ruler, but the artist. Only he will dare to dream his dream. Only he is not afraid to wrestle with his soul. Only he defies mob rule. Only he is bored by the dazzling darkness. When a hurricane destroys his home, if fire should burn his flesh, when every thought and every place of safety is destroyed, he yet gives thanks to be alive. And in that space of emptiness where he stands he dares to dream *his* fiery dream and then to follow it. Such was Ludwig, my Bourdelle – and yes, since you have asked, I was christened in the name of 'Ludovica'. Ludwig was my father.

And now the tale is yours, Bourdelle. What will it be?

Susanna

CODA

morendo

It was a year and a half ago that I met Michael and fell in love with him. That was something I certainly never meant to do. I had told myself that life was about other things – returning to South Africa for instance where I had initiated a system of close-cropping of vegetables that I hoped would supply a native family of four to grow 70 per cent of what it needs for sustenance in an area of poor soil no bigger than three square metres.

Michael had been in Britain for a week taking part in a forum on restructuring world economics. He was spending a few free days afterwards in Wales before returning to his native America. From the moment I saw him I knew he was special – different from every other man I had ever known. Partly it was his eyes – dark and penetrating, yet innocent like the eyes of an animal. They looked straight at me when he spoke yet they never made me uncomfortable.

We spent a long weekend together walking the twisting coast paths in Pembrokeshire National Park, making love on the cliffs and swimming in an unusually warm Irish Sea. After that I never saw or heard from him again. Nor did I learn anything more about his life. I know only that he was passionately concerned about the state of the planet and spent all of his time initiating and carrying out plans to improve it.

529

JOHANNA

We parted on a Tuesday morning in May after having breakfast in the sunlight outside a stone cottage-cum-restaurant in St David's run by a young couple who produced surprisingly good coffee and home-baked bread. This we spread with local honey and ate greedily.

That morning Michael handed me the manuscript about which he had previously told me nothing. He said, 'I wanted to give you a gift but I've nothing to offer . . . except this. Some of it I wrote myself. The rest . . . well you will see. I've kept it for four years because I didn't know what to do with it and because there was no one I could give it to . . . until now.'

I took the package from him. Then we parted – he by car and I by train to Heathrow to catch my plane for Johannesburg. My lengthy journey gave me the opportunity to read the manuscript in its entirety although it was not until my return to London six months ago that I was able to verify the historical existence of Wawruch, Mirabehn, Rolland, Bourdelle, Johanna and the rest.

Events – both internal and external – that have occurred in my own life since the manuscript came into my hands have left me certain that the words it contains and the haunting it carries have that purpose. Perhaps this is to clear away the poison and illusion which bind each one of us to a belief that we are impotent. Or perhaps the words are nothing more than catalysts for change like those chemicals which prompt the caterpillar to spin a cocoon and then dissolve it to a white gel before reforming it into another creature.

Such dissolution is without question what has happened in my life since reading the manuscript. Whether or not that is a result of my closeness to Michael – for I love him still and fear I always shall – or carried in the words themselves I cannot say. One thing is clear, however: metamorphosis is never a comfortable process. What creature would choose to have every structure of its life dissolved away? Of course the discomfort that it brings may have value if in the end it produces a butterfly. Does such discomfort, does any kind of suffering, have a meaning? That remains to be seen.

A month ago I decided to publish the manuscript. It is only right that I should do so. For, as in the case of Michael himself, it never really belonged to me. It was, one could say, only on loan for a time. What effect it may have on others who read it I cannot say. Nor do I know if hauntings will continue. Of its effects on me I could speak at length, but that would be another tale. . . .

Acknowledgements

Dannie Abse Poem adapted from the Hebrew of Amir
  Gilboa, *Way Out in the Centre*. London: Hutchinson
  Publishing Group, Ltd, 1982. Copyright © Dannie
  Abse, 1982. Reproduced with permission of Sheil Land
  Associates, London.

Martin Buber *The Ten Rungs of Hasidic Lore* and *Hasidism
  and the Modern Man*. Used by permission of the Estate of
  Martin Buber.

Joseph Campbell *The Hero With A Thousand Faces*.
  Bollingen Foundation Inc., New York. Used by
  permission of Princeton University Press.

Albert Camus *The Rebel*. Translated by Anthony Bower,
  (Hamish Hamilton, 1953), translation copyright ©
  Hamish Hamilton, 1953.

Bishop Diego de Landa *Relación de las cosas de Yucatán*
  (Mórida, 1938), as quoted by Sylvanus G. Morley, *The
  Ancient Maya* (Second Edition).

Fyodor Dostoevsky *The Brothers Karamazov*. Translated by
  David Magarshack (Penguin Classics, 1958), copyright
  © David Magarshack, 1958.

Selected Letters of Fyodor Dostoevsky by Joseph Frank and
  David I. Goldstein, editors. Andrew MacAndrew,
  translator. Copyright © 1987 by Rutgers, The State
  University. Reprinted by permission of Rutgers
  University Press.

Nazim Hikmet 'Of Life'. *Turkey: Peace on Trial* edited by Jean Furtado. London: Merlin Press Ltd, 1983.

Pär Lagerkvist *The Sibyl*. First published by Albert Bonniers Forlag AB, Stockholm 1956.

D. H. Lawrence *The Phoenix*. Used by permission of Laurence Pollinger Ltd and the Estate of Frieda Lawrence Ravagli.

C. S. Lewis *That Hideous Strength*. Used by permission of The Bodley Head, publishers, and the Estate of C.S. Lewis.

Vladimir Mayakovsky 'I', *Mayakovsky and His Poetry*. Translated by George Reavey. Bombay: Current Book House, 1955.

Paracelsus *Selected Writings*. Jolande Jacobi, translated by N. Gutterman. Used by permission of Routledge & Kegan Paul.

John Dos Passos *The Big Money*. Houghton Mifflin; Harmondsworth: Penguin Books Ltd., 1966.

Jean Rhys *Good Morning Midnight*. Published by HarperCollins Ltd. Used by permission of Sheil Land Associates, London.

Anthony Roberts & Geoff Gilbertson *The Dark Gods*. London: Rider/Hutchinson & Co (Publishers) Ltd, 1980.

Theodore Roethke 'In A Dark Time', *The Collected Poems of Theodore Roethke*. London: Faber & Faber Ltd, 1966. Copyright © 1960 by Beatrice Roethke as Administratrix of the Estate of Theodore Roethke.

Irena Tweedie *The Chasm of Fire*. Used by permission of Element Books, Longmead, Shaftesbury, Dorset.

W.B. Yeats 'The Second Coming' *The Collected Poems of W.B. Yeats*. Macmillan Ltd. London, 1933.

Diligent efforts were made in every case to obtain rights from copyright holders. In a few instances, the efforts were

unsuccessful. The author is grateful for the use of this
excerpted material.

I would like to thank Beth Humphries for the skilfulness of
her red pen, Caroline Upcher for her passion and her skill
and Yvette Brown for being the best friend anybody could
ever have when wrestling with Ludwig.

A Selected List of Fiction Available from Mandarin

While every effort is made to keep prices low, it is sometimes necessary to increase prices at short notice. Mandarin Paperbacks reserves the right to show new retail prices on covers which may differ from those previously advertised in the text or elsewhere.

The prices shown below were correct at the time of going to press.

☐ 7493 1352 8	**The Queen and I**	Sue Townsend	£4.99
☐ 7493 0540 1	**The Liar**	Stephen Fry	£4.99
☐ 7493 1132 0	**Arrivals and Departures**	Lesley Thomas	£4.99
☐ 7493 0381 6	**Loves and Journeys of Revolving Jones**	Leslie Thomas	£4.99
☐ 7493 0942 3	**Silence of the Lambs**	Thomas Harris	£4.99
☐ 7493 0946 6	**The Godfather**	Mario Puzo	£4.99
☐ 7493 1561 X	**Fear of Flying**	Erica Jong	£4.99
☐ 7493 1221 1	**The Power of One**	Bryce Courtney	£4.99
☐ 7493 0576 2	**Tandia**	Bryce Courtney	£5.99
☐ 7493 0563 0	**Kill the Lights**	Simon Williams	£4.99
☐ 7493 1319 6	**Air and Angels**	Susan Hill	£4.99
☐ 7493 1477 X	**The Name of the Rose**	Umberto Eco	£4.99
☐ 7493 0896 6	**The Stand-in**	Deborah Moggach	£4.99
☐ 7493 0581 9	**Daddy's Girls**	Zoe Fairbairns	£4.99

All these books are available at your bookshop or newsagent, or can be ordered direct from the address below. Just tick the titles you want and fill in the form below.

Cash Sales Department, PO Box 5, Rushden, Northants NN10 6YX.
Fax: 0933 410321 : Phone 0933 410511.

Please send cheque, payable to 'Reed Book Services Ltd.', or postal order for purchase price quoted and allow the following for postage and packing:

£1.00 for the first book, 50p for the second; **FREE POSTAGE AND PACKING FOR THREE BOOKS OR MORE PER ORDER.**

NAME (Block letters) ....

ADDRESS ....

....

☐ I enclose my remittance for ....

☐ I wish to pay by Access/Visa Card Number ☐☐☐☐☐☐☐☐☐☐☐☐☐☐☐☐

Expiry Date ☐☐☐☐

Signature ....

Please quote our reference: MAND